Readers love the Lions & Tigers & Bears series by K.C. WELLS

A Growl, a Roar, and a Purr

"The romance was definitely the key to this story. It leaped off the pages and heated up the sheets."

—The TBR Pile

"In this paranormal romance, Wells explores the shifter and fated mates tropes in this fun action-adventure romp that includes an epic heist and a sweet romantic through-line."

—J.L. Gribble's Book Reviews

A Snarl, a Splash, and a Shock

"This novel contains a super range of characters, from the despicably evil, the super good, the conflicted, and more. I found inter-relationship dynamics most amusing. The journeys of Vic, Saul, and Crank made for splendid reading."

—Love Bytes

Visions, Paws, and Claws

"... once everything was slotted into place, I thoroughly enjoyed the adventure and eagerly looked forward to book four."

—Love Bytes

By K.C. Wells

BFF
Bromantically Yours
First
Love Lessons Learned
Step by Step
Waiting For You

DREAMSPUN DESIRES
The Senator's Secret
Out of the Shadows
My Fair Brady
Under the Covers

LEARNING TO LOVE
Michael & Sean
Evan & Daniel
Josh & Chris
Final Exam

LIONS & TIGERS & BEARS
A Growl, a Roar, and a Purr
A Snarl, a Splash, and a Shock
Visions, Paws, and Claws
Mysteries, Menace, and Mates

LOVE, UNEXPECTED
Debt
Burden

MERRYCHURCH MYSTERIES
Truth Will Out
Roots of Evil
A Novel Murder

SENSUAL BONDS
A Bond of Three
A Bond of Truth

With Parker Williams

COLLARS & CUFFS
An Unlocked Heart
Trusting Thomas
Someone to Keep Me
A Dance with Domination
Damian's Discipline
Make Me Soar
Dom of Ages
Endings and Beginnings

SECRETS
Before You Break
An Unlocked Mind
Threepeat
On the Same Page

Published by DSP Publications
SECOND SIGHT
In His Sights
In Plain Sight
Out of Sight
Line of Sight

Published by DREAMSPINNER PRESS
www.dreamspinnerpress.com

MYSTERIES, MENACE, AND MATES

K.C. WELLS

Published by
Dreamspinner Press

8219 Woodville Hwy #1245
Woodville, FL 32362 USA
www.dreamspinnerpress.com

This is a work of fiction. Names, characters, places, and incidents either are the product of author imagination or are used fictitiously, and any resemblance to actual persons, living or dead, business establishments, events, or locales is entirely coincidental.

Mysteries, Menace, and Mates
© 2025 K.C. Wells

Cover Art
© 2025 L.C. Chase
http://www.lcchase.com
Cover content is for illustrative purposes only and any person depicted on the cover is a model.

All rights reserved. This book is licensed to the original purchaser only. Duplication or distribution via any means is illegal and a violation of international copyright law, subject to criminal prosecution and upon conviction, fines, and/or imprisonment. Any eBook format cannot be legally loaned or given to others. No part of this book may be reproduced or transmitted in any form or by any means, electronic or mechanical, including photocopying, recording, or by any information storage and retrieval system, without the written permission of the Publisher, except where permitted by law. To request permission and all other inquiries, contact Dreamspinner Press, 8219 Woodville Hwy #1245, Woodville FL 32362 USA, or www.dreamspinnerpress.com.

Any unauthorized use of this publication to train generative artificial intelligence (AI) is expressly prohibited.

Trade Paperback ISBN: 978-1-64108-756-8
Digital ISBN: 978-1-64108-755-1
Trade Paperback published June 2025
v. 1.0

For Parker Williams, who's been with me ever since I saw a photo of a lion, tiger, and bear who'd grown up together and were the best of friends. Thank you for all the videos of Horvan, Rael, and Dellan. And thank you for all the precious time you gave reading and commenting. Love you.

Author's Note

CASTEL SANT'ANGELO, Gawthorpe Hall, and Thurland Castle are real places that I "borrowed" for this story.

Chapter One

Aric was fast coming to the conclusion that hearing his mates' thoughts was both a blessing and a curse. Sure, he loved knowing they were safe, that they were thinking about him. *Who wouldn't love that?* And while it made keeping secrets more awkward, he could get around that with the mental lock boxes Horvan had told them about.

The last half hour, however, had been nothing less than torture.

Okay, so they were safe. The mission to liberate the Maine camp was over, and the inmates had all made it out alive. Better than that—they were all on their way to someplace where they could be safe, and it wouldn't be long before whoever was left got shipped out, heading back to Illinois or wherever Aelryn's base was located.

What tortured Aric was one man.

Well, one monster.

Aric had sat in the sunshine, and despite its warmth, his blood had run cold every time Fielding opened his mouth, every time Jake revealed some new atrocity.

How could Seth stomach it?

In the camp, Aric had lost count of how many times he'd seen Seth all weak and wobbly after coming back from their goddamn tests, but still doing his best to care for Aric. *And how did they treat him once they'd separated us?* Once Seth was too far away for Aric to feel his distress, his exhaustion. Even when he'd seen Seth in his dreams, Seth had hidden his fatigue.

And then there was Brick. He would have heard Fielding's interrogation too. Aric had known countless nights when he'd lain beside Brick, conscious of the inner turmoil Brick couldn't hide.

He's already suffered so much. This is making it worse.

All Aric wanted was to hear Fielding's fate. Execution by firing squad sounded like a good solution, and Aric wouldn't draw the line at aiming a rifle at the son of a bitch. He was a crack shot—he'd grown up around guns on his dad's farm—and having that bastard in his crosshairs might go some way to healing the pain.

Yeah, right. As if they'd let me.

And that right there was the problem. Aric felt useless as fuck.

I want to help my mates, to help them *heal.* Except what could he do? *I'm not a polar bear. I'm not a big cat. I'm a freakin' house cat, and that means I can't overpower anyone, I can't run fast, I can't take down bigger animals....* All Aric had going for him was his brains, and his recent attack on Fielding should have proved to everyone that underestimating him was a big mistake.

The base felt empty. Aelryn's people were all but gone. The medics had done their job and checked how all the prisoners were faring, so now they were heading out too. Doc hadn't left, though, not that Aric was surprised. Right then he was with Jake, and Aric thought nothing short of an atom bomb would drive him from Jake's side.

Jake seemed a little older than the last time Aric had seen him, before they'd sent him to Maine. Gods knew what the Gerans had subjected him and Seth to.

Fielding was part of that. Yet another reason to plant a bullet in his brain.

Aelryn, Horvan, and Saul were deep into planning… whatever they were planning. There'd been whispers, something about artifacts, a tomb; it all sounded a little surreal. Aric's chest had swelled with pride to learn Seth had been a part of whatever it was they'd discovered.

Eve, Roadkill, and Hashtag had taken off in the C-17, along with the rest of Horvan's team, and were on their way back to Illinois. Aric longed to go there too but was torn between yearning to start his new life with Brick and Seth and needing closure. He'd walked around the base's perimeter three or four times, trying to calm the muddle of thoughts and fears that fogged his mind.

So far he'd had little success.

"Ready to get out of here?"

He jumped at the sound of Brick's voice and turned. Brick and Seth strolled toward him, and he ran to them. Brick's strong arms enfolded him, and Aric breathed him in. Seth's hand was on Aric's back, a welcome connection.

"Can we go now?" Aric asked.

"Soon," Brick murmured. "We're almost done here. We're waiting on H and Saul. They've let Jake sleep a little longer. He was wrecked."

Aric kept his cheek pressed to Brick's chest. "So what happens to Fielding?" He managed to keep his tone nonchalant, except he knew that wouldn't work around his mates.

Sure enough, Seth stroked Aric's hair. "That hasn't been decided yet."

Aric stiffened. "They can't just forget about him."

He wouldn't let them.

"Hey, no one's said that will happen," Brick said in a low voice. "But right now Aelryn and Horvan have a mission to plan, and they might need him."

Aric pulled away from Brick. "I don't think so. I think Jake and Seth got all they're going to get out of him."

Seth huffed. "You may be right."

"And if we're at war," Aric continued, his heartbeat quickening, "that makes Fielding a war criminal."

There was only one way to deal with those.

Brick sighed, gazing at him with compassion. "We're trying to stop this war before it even starts."

"Brick? H wants you," Crank hollered across the tarmac, beckoning him. "And Jake's asking for Seth."

Seth chuckled. "No rest for the wicked." He kissed Aric's forehead; then he and Brick strode to where Crank stood.

"Hey, Seth!" Aric shouted after him. When he turned, Aric smiled. "You don't have a wicked bone in your body."

Seth grinned. "Maybe, maybe not, but I get a wicked *boner* when I think about a certain kitty cat. And if we're lucky, we'll *both* have a wicked bone in our body when we're alone with Brick."

Aric could feel Brick getting hot at the thoughts Seth was sending out, not to mention the delicious thrill they sent through Aric, but he shoved his desire somewhere deep.

Right then he had to think clearly, and the last thing he needed were images of Brick's dick taking up space in his head.

How big does that dick get?

He watched Brick and Seth until they were out of sight, then hurried over to the hangar where Brick had stowed his combat gear while they waited for whatever transport was going to take them out of there.

His heart pounded, and his mouth was dry as a bone at the thought of what was about to happen.

What he was about to do.

Aric made sure no one was around as he snuck into the hangar. Brick's combat harness lay next to his duffel bag, and Aric saw the M17 handgun in its holster. His hands shook as he picked it up. The manual safety was on. Aric removed the magazine and checked the bullets.

Don't think about it. Just do it.

He stuffed the weapon into the waistband of his combat pants, hidden below the baggy shirt they'd found for him to wear. Then he scanned his surroundings for the prop he needed.

There it is.

Aric grabbed the first aid box and headed out into the sunshine. He leaned against the hangar wall and assessed the situation. The guard hadn't moved from his position in front of the building where Fielding was being kept, and there was no one else in sight.

Now all Aric had to do was make his move.

The sun was at its highest point when another soldier came out of the hangar, a tray in both hands, and walked toward the makeshift jail.

Perfect.

Aric ran across to him. "Hey."

The soldier came to a halt midway between the hangar and Fielding's temporary prison. "You need something?"

Aric pointed to the tray, which contained a plastic bowl covered in foil, a plastic spoon, tortillas, a snack-size packet of peanut butter, a bag of mixed fruit, and a bottle of water. "Is that for Fielding?"

"Yup." The soldier grinned. "And no, you can't spit in his cheese tortellini."

Aric grimaced. "Oh my God, is this one of those ready-to-eat meals I've heard the guys talking about?"

He chuckled. "Sure is. Fielding should count himself lucky he isn't getting the curry chicken I asked them to give him. It was cruel and unusual punishment, they said, because he'd end up shitting through the eye of a needle." He gave Aric an inquiring glance. "Well? Did you want something, or are you delaying me so his food gets cold?" His eyes twinkled. "Because gee, that would be tragic."

It appeared as if Aric wasn't the only one who held Fielding in pretty low esteem.

Aric held up the first aid kit. "I was going to change his dressings. I might as well take him his food and save you the trip." His heart hammered.

Say yes. Say yes.

The soldier chuckled once more. "Wait a sec. Weren't you the one who gave him the wounds in the first place?"

He bowed his head, trying to look suitably ashamed. "Yeah, but I'm feeling bad about it now. The medics have all gone, Doc's busy with Jake, so I said I'd do it. I do have a little first aid training." That wasn't a lie, but then again, he had no intention of delivering any aid.

The opposite, in fact.

"Well, okay, then. Knock yourself out." The soldier handed him the tray. "I'm not about to argue with you, especially as you'll save me from having to get too close to him again." He shuddered. "That guy gives me the fucking creeps with the way he stares, like he's seeing right into your head."

Aric thanked him and waited for him to head back to the hangar before approaching the building.

The guard glanced at the tray, then Aric. "You been conscripted?" he said with a smirk.

"Just helping out—delivering his food and changing his dressings," Aric replied, holding up the first aid kit again.

The guard nodded. "Okay. Knock when you're ready to leave and I'll untie him so he can eat." His eyes gleamed. "But no shifting this time, okay? I thought you were murdering him last time. All that screaming…. How much damage can kitty claws inflict anyhow?"

Aric snorted. "He's still alive, isn't he? So not enough, obviously. And I won't shift. You've got my promise."

What Aric had in mind wouldn't require shifting.

The guard didn't open the door right away, however, but regarded Aric for a moment. Aric tried to keep his cool. His heart was beating so fast, he was sure the guard could hear it. Finally, the guard nodded. "I guess you'll be safe enough. He can't shift, and while he might give some pretty impressive glares, *they* won't harm you." He opened the door, and Aric went inside.

Fielding sat in the same office chair, his ankles and wrists secured with rope. He glanced at Aric with disdain, his lips curled into a sneer. "Well, if it isn't the kitty cat again. Come to inflict more damage?" There were four Steri-Strips on his forehead and cheeks, and his hands were all scratched up. Fielding peered at the tray and shuddered. "What muck are they giving me now? It should come with a health warning."

"You don't need to worry about that." Aric's voice shook. "Food's going to be the least of your worries." He put down the kit and the tray, then approached Fielding's chair. His fingers trembled as he unfastened the rope around Fielding's ankles, then his wrists. Aric stepped back quickly and pulled the handgun from its hiding place, pointing it at Fielding with as steady a grip as he could manage.

"Why have you cut me loose? And what are you doing with that?" Fielding seemed almost amused.

Aric raised the gun a bit higher. "Taking back my fucking dignity. Taking it back for all of us who you hurt, tortured, and killed. You can't be allowed to live."

Fielding sneered again. "You? You don't have the guts. You're a weak, pathetic little thing. The only reason we kept you was because we wanted Seth to comply." His smile was cruel. "If it wasn't for him, you would have been one of the first to be culled."

"Well, this weak, pathetic little thing is going to end you." Aric spoke clearly, not bothering to mask his thoughts.

Come on, Brick. I need you.

Aric pulled the trigger and the gun clicked. He did it again with the same result.

Fielding smirked. "See? Pathetic." And before Aric could take a breath, Fielding lurched out of the chair and grabbed the gun, knocking Aric to the floor. "Are you so stupid you didn't realize the safety was on?" He moved his thumb and smiled. "But it's off now, not that I need it to finish you. I can do that with one hand, but I'm not going to waste time killing you. Especially since you might have some use after all—as a shield." He grabbed Aric around the throat and squeezed. "How many guards outside?" He released his grip a little, and Aric coughed.

"One," he croaked. "Everyone else is inside."

Now would be a good time, Brick.

Fielding nodded. "Armed, of course." He dragged Aric to the door and opened it a crack, the gun raised. Then he shoved Aric through the doorway, aiming at the guard, pulling the trigger—

And nothing happened. Fielding's shocked expression was almost comical.

Then a ferocious roar shattered the silence, and Aric scrambled to his feet, his heart thumping. Somewhere, Seth cried out, "Don't shoot him!"

A solid mass of white fur crossed Aric's field of vision, barreled into Fielding, and shoved him out of sight, accompanied by Fielding's shriek. Thunderous noises filled the air as heavy paws slammed the ground, and Aric winced at the sound of Brick's deafening roar as he hurtled after Fielding.

I have to see.

He turned in time to watch Brick slam a hefty paw into the side of Fielding's face with enough force to snap his neck. Fielding dropped like a stone, but Brick wasn't done. The air was filled with noises that curdled Aric's blood: The scream that was cut off, the gurgle of blood, and the crunch as Brick bit through bone and cartilage. He closed his jaws around Fielding's throat, and by the time he was through, Fielding's head was hanging by its tendons.

Aric jumped when arms encircled him.

Easy, baby. Only me.

Aric turned away from the sight of blood staining Brick's maw and buried his face in Seth's chest. Seth held on to Aric, his hand on Aric's nape. *Trust me, you don't need to see any more.*

"Hey!" Brick yelled. "Can I get some help here? Got some trash that needs scraping off the tarmac."

Then there was the sound of boots thudding on concrete and raised voices.

"What the fuck?" That was Crank.

"Here." That was Horvan. "Wipe yourself off with this." A pause. "Good thing we found out everything we needed, huh?"

"He was going to kill Aric!" Brick retorted. "And the world's a better place without that fucker. What's going to happen to him? What's left of him, at any rate."

"Aelryn will find a deep, dark hole to bury the POS in, where no one will ever find him. That's one grave that won't get a marker."

Aric. Turn around.

There was no way Aric could ignore Brick.

He turned to be greeted by the sight of a naked Brick, a bloodied towel in his hand.

Brick was glaring.

"Why would you go after him with my gun? And I *know* it was loaded."

"Yeah, it was." Aric reached into his pocket and withdrew the bullets. "Now you can put them back."

Seth gasped. "You set him up. You knew Fielding would go for the gun, and you made sure we knew what you were doing."

"Of course." Aric glanced at the tarp-covered lump on the ground. "Fielding haunted Brick's dreams. I wanted to give Brick the chance to kill him, to rid us of him forever." What surprised him was how the memory of what he'd seen only moments ago, what he'd heard, was fading with every second, as if his mind didn't want to hold on to it a moment longer and was already into the process of expelling it.

Aric was fine with that.

Brick pulled Aric to him. "I've already talked to you about putting yourself in danger. What the hell do I have to do? Put you over my knee and swat your ass as a reminder?"

Seth coughed. "Uh, Brick?"

Brick's head snapped toward him. "What?"

"Okay, so this isn't the time, but ixnay ethay unishmentpay alktay. Aric likes a little pain with his pleasure, so you're not exactly helping."

Brick narrowed his eyes. "What the hell does that mean?" he demanded, his deep voice reverberating through Aric.

Seth sighed. "I swear, *no one* remembers classic pig Latin anymore. I had to teach Aric so we could talk in the camp when I was too tired to show him my thoughts." He met Brick's gaze. "It *means* exactly what it sounded like. Aric likes a little pain with his pleasure, so threatening to spank him? That isn't a deterrent."

Brick's mouth fell open. "He... what?" Then he frowned. "Wait. I thought you two haven't—"

"That's right, we haven't. That doesn't mean I didn't get to see something in Aric's head once when we were jerking off. And we did share fantasies."

"Hey, will you quit giving away all my secrets?" Aric growled. He had to admit, the conversation helped ease his tremors, even if it was the most surreal thing ever with Fielding's remains only feet away from them.

He'd been Aric's definition of a bad guy while he lived, and dead, he was fast becoming nothing but a bad dream.

Right on cue, a couple of guys appeared, and Aric didn't break eye contact with Brick, because that was way better than watching them clear away what was left of Fielding.

Brick bit his lip. "Fantasies? Okay, that's hot. Still...." He ran a thumb over Aric's face. "You're going to look so beautiful in our bed, all spread out, needy for me. For us." His voice cracked.

Aric smiled. "We can't wait to be there with you. Although...."

Brick stilled. "Although? There's an *although*?"

Aric glanced at Seth, who nodded.

Time to tell it like it is. And talking about what lay in their future was way better than thinking about what had happened minutes earlier.

"Well, you see.... Seth and I? Zero interest in topping, which means basically we're going to work you to death in bed, because it'll be up to you to satisfy us both." Aric smiled again. "Don't worry, though. I've been stocking up on multivitamins to give you energy." When Brick arched his eyebrows, Aric nodded. "Seriously. I gave Crank my shopping list. He thought it was hilarious."

Brick laughed, something Aric hadn't heard much of, but what he sensed in Brick was even better. He'd seen it all: the fear, the crippling loneliness, the pain at the loss of his parents. It was as if that bright laughter had broken the chains holding Brick's heart hostage.

What flowed from Brick was love.

Then Brick's arms closed around him. "Don't worry. I'll fuck you both into a coma every day, and that's a promise."

Seth snickered. "He doesn't know a lot about cats, does he?"

"Apparently not, but now we're together again? There's plenty of time for us to learn."

Brick raised Aric's chin with his fingers. "But if I can be serious for a minute? This is the last time you pull a stunt like this, kitty. Got me?"

Aric knew what that meant.

He craned his neck to look Brick in the eye. "If it helped you to move on? I'd do it again in a heartbeat."

Brick chuckled. "What do I always say? Never underestimate the kitty. And I'm deadly serious."

"You're deadly, I won't argue with that," Seth murmured.

Brick towered over Aric. "You *will* be doing therapy."

It wasn't a request.

9

Aric stuck his chin out. "I don't need it. I'm fine." *See me? You just ripped Fielding apart and I'm still here. I'm not cowering under my blanket.*

He was made of strong stuff.

Brick scowled. "That's bullshit, and you know it. And it's no use you arguing. This is nonnegotiable."

"Listen to him." Seth's voice was gentle. "You'll need someone to talk to."

Brick stared at him. "Excuse me? This involves you too. Both of you will be seeing someone."

"But we don't *need* to talk to anyone," Aric protested. "We can talk to you."

"What he said," Seth added.

Brick pulled him closer. "Sweetheart, you're more than welcome to talk to me. Anytime. But I'm not a professional. I'm more of a kill first, ask questions later kinda guy. You need someone who can empathize with you. And I'm not big on empathy."

"This is such bullshit," Aric muttered. "I won't need therapy."

"And yet you're gonna do it, and you'll go into it with an open mind."

"Why?" he demanded.

Brick slid a finger over Aric's cheek. "Honestly? Because I think the real you is hidden beneath all this stuff you've been dealing with." He kissed the tip of Aric's nose. "I love you, and I'll love you even more once the rest of you shines through."

Aric knew when to give up a fight. Then he realized he could play this game as well as Brick could. "Then you're going with us." He folded his arms. "And like you said, this is nonnegotiable."

Brick smirked. "Or what?"

Aric gave him what he hoped was a suitably smug smile. "Or we won't put out."

"Considering we have yet to do anything, that sounds like cutting off your nose to spite your face." Brick drew himself up to his full—and very impressive—height. "Don't forget who's in charge here."

Aric could fight dirty too.

"And don't *you* forget you're not alone. We need you, just like you need us. It's ridiculous for you to think you can get through this alone." He batted his eyes. "Please, Brick? Do it for us?"

"Please, Brick," Seth added.

Aric could sense the battle of emotions taking place inside his mate. Finally Brick sighed. "Fine. But if I agree to this, what's in it for me?"

Aric arched his eyebrows. "Two very happy mates. What more do you need?"

He could see the moment Brick relented. Brick pulled them both close. "Okay, but I want sex. Lots of it."

Aric grinned. "Whenever, wherever. Just say the word."

Brick gave a satisfied smile. "Then we'll go together. How does that sound?"

Seth chuckled. "Like I want to be home to collect on a blowjob reward. When do we leave this place?"

Aric closed his eyes and breathed in the heavenly scent of his mate. Then he caught the tail end of a thought.

"Wait a minute. You said Horvan and Aelryn had a mission to plan. *What* mission?"

Chapter Two

Two months in that god-awful camp had been more than enough for Jamie. He'd taken dozens of showers and still didn't feel clean. How Jake had put up with it for more than thirty years, he would never know. Jamie was thankful the Gerans had sent him to the same camp.

And now we have time to get to know each other.

Except that might have to wait a while.

He'd been watching Jake ever since Fielding's interrogation, and he wasn't happy. Nor was he fooled. Outwardly, Jake tried to maintain an air of strength and quiet dignity, but Jamie couldn't help but notice how he shrank back whenever loud noises filled the air. The least little thing seemed to startle him. His eyes were forever darting around, and it didn't take a genius to work out Jake was keeping a lookout for—and being ready for—trouble.

The shoe hasn't dropped yet. He still doesn't feel safe.

Jamie guessed he might feel the same way if he'd been through half the shit Jake had. It wasn't until he noticed how Jake kept his head down most of the time that Jamie finally understood.

They all but broke him, but he still refuses to give in.

Jake's mask had to slip sometime. What he really needed was to talk to someone—a professional—who could help him heal.

Doc didn't count. Doc was too involved.

Maybe I could use a little therapy too.

In less than three months, Jamie's world had changed beyond recognition. He'd been a Geran who'd been brought up to believe they were superior to both humans *and* Fridans, and what they were doing was the right thing, preparing shifter kids for the world they would inherit.

Then he'd discovered the truth.

Bombshell number one—his parents had lied to him his whole life. And they *weren't* his parents.

Bombshell number two—Dellan was his half brother.

Bombshell number three—Jamie was probably the result of the Gerans breeding Dellan's dad, Jake, with other shifters before he was adopted. As for who his mother was, unless someone found it in the records they'd taken from the camp, he might never know.

Was I taken from her? Did she simply give me up?

At least he had Jake, Dellan, and Seth.

Bombshell number four—any kids *not* accepted at the school for shifters where Jamie worked, suddenly "disappeared," their parents seemingly unconcerned as to their whereabouts. The consensus of opinion was that they'd been sent somewhere to be trained—as foot soldiers.

Cannon fodder was probably a better description.

All of which added to a swift one-eighty, and Jamie changed lanes. He'd gone back to the school in Boston to learn whatever he could—undercover—that might help Horvan and his team, only to be taken the moment he crossed the school's threshold.

Almost as if they'd known everything.

Jamie had never figured out how that could have come about. Once he'd gotten over the shock of finding himself a prisoner, they'd whisked him off to someplace in the middle of nowhere and kept him isolated. As soon as they'd let him out, he'd found Jake and Seth.

Every cloud, right?

Of all the Fridans to sweep in and liberate the camp, it had been Horvan and his guys. So here Jamie was again, about to head back to Dellan's home in Homer Glen, with no idea of what lay in his future beyond working with the Fridans to rescue more prisoners and close down more shifter schools.

He should have been happy, right? He was free, wasn't he? Then what the fuck was wrong?

It took him a day to work that out.

One of Horvan's team was avoiding him like the plague. The polar bear, Brick—the one who'd torn Fielding into itty-bitty bad-guy pieces—wouldn't meet his gaze. He kept a constant distance of at least twenty feet from him. Sometimes if Jamie walked into the hangar, Brick walked out.

Is my BO that bad?

Joking aside, whatever the problem was, letting the situation continue without trying to fix it somehow was *not* an option. And seeing as Brick wasn't about to do anything, it was up to Jamie.

Like, now. Before Brick got sent off on another mission. Horvan had already said they were packing up.

Jamie had nothing to pack anyway. All he had were the clothes on his back. Dellan had promised to do something about that when they returned to Illinois, and in the meantime Jamie was making do with fatigues loaned to him by Hashtag, who was a similar size.

The thought made him smile.

Those three are something else. Anyone seeing how Eve, Hashtag, and Roadkill interacted would be forgiven for thinking they'd spent years together, not weeks. Watching them made him yearn to find his own mates.

And that was something else that had changed—his belief in mates. How could he do otherwise when he was surrounded by people who'd found theirs? Jamie wasn't sure how he'd feel if one or both his mates turned out to be human, it would be hard to overcome his years of programming, but who was he to argue with whatever higher power saw fit to join them? Saul and Crank clearly adored the ground Vic walked upon—not to mention the water he swam in—and as for Eve, she was a tough little cookie, but it was plain to see she was smitten with her two human mates.

I want that too.

Judging by the speed with which the others had found their mates, he had to believe it wouldn't be too long before someone strolled into his life and turned it upside down, the same way Rael and Horvan had done to Dellan's.

That still left him with his present predicament.

Jamie strolled into the hangar where Brick was cleaning his weapon. There was no sign of either of his mates.

Perfect timing.

He walked toward Brick, his heart pounding. Brick turned his head, his eyes widened, and he rose.

Aw fuck.

"Please, don't leave," Jamie blurted. "Not again."

Brick froze. "I… I can't talk to you."

"Fine. You clearly don't like me, although I'm not certain why. I'm a decent guy, I have a great sense of humor, and I'm kind to animals. So I guess it's just my personality you can't stomach."

Brick paled. "What? No, you're a great guy."

"Then why do you avoid me? And don't tell me I'm imagining it, because we both know that's bullshit."

"I...." Brick swallowed. "You *really* don't want to talk to me, okay? I'm not the guy you think I am."

"Well, I'm never gonna get to know who you are if you keep walking off every time I get within a few feet of you."

Brick's Adam's apple bobbed. "I'm the reason the Gerans threw you into that camp."

Wait—what?

Of all the possible answers Jamie had anticipated, this wasn't one of them. He blinked. "You?"

Brick nodded. "I told them all about you. And Saul. That's why they knew he was coming."

Jamie couldn't see through the tide of red that rose up and blocked his vision. He was *this* close to shifting and tearing every scrap of white fur from this bastard's back—until his brain kicked in.

Now wait a minute. Horvan trusts him. Why would Horvan trust a traitor? Why would he even keep Brick on his team, knowing what he'd done?

Unless he didn't. There was always that possibility, even if it seemed unlikely. Horvan was one smart bear.

Seth obviously trusts Brick too. And Seth was no slouch in the brains department either.

That left one avenue to be explored.

"There's more to this story, isn't there?"

Brick hesitated for a moment, and then the words tumbled out of him. Jamie listened in growing horror as Brick revealed how the Gerans had taken his parents, threatened them if Brick didn't supply the information they needed—and how it had emerged that the Gerans had killed them anyway, never intending to release them.

Jamie was ashamed to have been a Geran... and thankful he'd learned the truth at last.

Brick regarded him with glistening eyes. "I'm so sorry. As soon as I heard Dellan had lost contact with you, I knew they must have taken you, and that it was all my fault."

Jamie's rage had subsided. What was two months in a camp compared to what Brick had suffered?

"You did what you had to do to save your parents. And because you did, I was reunited with my *real* dad and a new half brother. I might never have found them but for you." Jamie threw his arms around Brick's large frame and hugged him.

Brick stiffened for a second, then relaxed, a sob escaping him. "Thank God."

Jamie turned his head toward the voice. Seth was smiling.

"I was about to arrange an intervention. I kept telling Brick it would all work out fine, but he wouldn't believe me." He gave Brick a pointed stare. "See?"

Brick chuckled. "Okay, okay, you told me." He wiped his eyes.

Seth came over to them and put his arms around them. The three stood in silence, and for the first time in a long while, Jamie was at peace.

I have my real family at last.

And it didn't matter that only a few of them were his flesh and blood.

MILO PACED up and down the hallway of the wing where the Maine inmates were staying. He'd been on edge ever since the plane had landed in Boston and he'd lost sight of Jana.

Except that was a lie. He knew she was okay—he could hear her in his head, and she sounded cheerful. She was in good hands. Aelryn's people had been kindness itself. Okay, so the accommodation was not unlike the camp in that they slept in dormitories—understandable when their present location was a school—but that was where the similarities ended. Comfortable beds, showers, and *oh my God* so much food. The clothes had arrived only hours after they did, and judging by Jana's squeals, she was more than happy to be out of her previous clothing.

More likely she's happy to be out of anything that reminds her of the camp.

No, Jana wasn't what concerned Milo—it was his future, and how he'd be treated by the Fridans. The latter had been on his mind ever since they'd liberated the camp.

It doesn't matter that I helped the Fridans. I was still the enemy.

Milo hoped Aelryn would pave the way to Fridan acceptance. He also hoped Aelryn would agree to his proposal, the one that had brought him to the door where he now stood, waiting for someone to respond to his knock.

He has to agree. He will, won't he?

Milo was about to find that out.

The door opened, and a young man stood there, smiling. "Come in, Milo." He stood aside. "Aelryn can't be here—he's still in Maine—but he asked me to speak with you." He held out his hand. "I'm Scott, Aelryn's mate. I work here as part of the medical team."

Milo went into the small room that clearly served as an office, and sat in the chair Scott indicated. Scott picked up a folder on the desk and opened it.

"I'm sure you want news of your mate. Jana is fine. She's—"

"I know that, and while I want to see her, that's not why I'm here." His heart went into overdrive. "I want to join you."

Scott blinked. "Join us?"

"I met some of Horvan's team. Do you know him?"

He smiled. "Yes, and I've met some of the team too. Three mates—Vic, Saul, and Crank."

"Well, I'm sure Aelryn has teams too, and that's who I want to join. I can be useful. I've worked in many of the Geran camps, I know their systems, their routines, their—"

Scott held up his hand. "Whoa there. I know how you helped us infiltrate the Maine camp. We couldn't have done it without you. But I'm not the one you'd have to convince. You'd be fighting alongside shifters who've been battling the Gerans for a long time. Some of them might be hard to win over."

"But that's why I'm here." Milo swallowed. "I hoped Aelryn would speak for me. Surely whatever he says will carry weight."

Scott stroked his chin. "Yes, it would. And you're right. With his backing, more of our fighters would be willing to accept you. I'll call him right away and we can get to work." His smile was warm. "Call it a PR campaign. But in the meantime, he's instructed me to find you two a place to live."

"Jana doesn't have to stay here?"

Scott's eyes twinkled. "There isn't a lot of privacy in the school. I don't want to leave her in the dormitories. But until things become more permanent, there are rooms in the teachers' wing. I'll have one of them made up for you. And now"—he grinned—"let's go find your mate."

Milo followed him out of the office, his head in a whirl.

I'm a step closer to my future.

Aelryn would make it work. Somehow.

Scott led him into the library, and Milo picked up Jana's scent in a heartbeat. Then he spotted her at a long table, her nose in a book.

He didn't have to say a word.

She jerked her head up, closed the book, pushed back her chair, its feet scraping on the wooden floor, and ran to him, her arms wide.

Milo gathered her up, holding her against him. "I've missed you."

I've been waiting for my next kiss.

He didn't make her wait a second longer, losing himself in the smell of her, the taste of her lips, the tiny sounds that spoke of happiness.

You're really here, in my arms.

Jana tilted her head to gaze at him. *And if I get my way, I'll never leave them again.*

Milo kissed the top of her bronze head. *From your lips to the gods' ears.*

Then he realized that might not be possible, not if he got his way and joined forces with Aelryn. "Jana, there's something you need to know. I—"

She placed a finger on his lips. "Do you think Aelryn will have room in his ranks for an otter who wants to fight for the Fridans?"

Milo's heart skipped a beat. "You want to fight?"

She blinked. "Well, *you* do, so why shouldn't I? And I can be useful too, especially with some training."

He said nothing, but squeezed her tight. Milo closed his eyes and sent up a prayer to whoever had placed Jana in his path.

Thank you.

"What are you doing here?"

The strident voice cut through him. Milo turned, and came face-to-face with a man he recognized from the camp. The guy glared at him. "Why aren't you in chains? Why aren't you facing a firing squad? You're one of *them*."

Jana whirled around and glared at him. "Don't you *dare* speak to my mate like that again. And have some respect. You'd still be in that godforsaken place if it wasn't for him. Who do you think gave the Fridans all their information? Hm? I'll tell you. You're looking at him." She clenched her fists, her face red.

The former inmate stared at her. "He's your mate?" He gazed at Milo. "Really?"

Milo nodded, his arms around Jana once more, feeling her relax against him. "What she told you is true. And if you don't believe her, it won't be long before you hear the same thing from Aelryn's lips. You'd believe *him*, wouldn't you?"

The man nodded, openmouthed.

Milo took a deep breath. *This is going to happen a lot, isn't it?*

Yes. And I'll have your back every single time. Jana craned her neck to peer at him, her eyes gleaming. *Now can we go see our new room? Seeing as I have you all to myself for the first time.*

There were better places to be, and sweeter things to be shared.

Especially if—when—they found their third mate.

Chapter Three

"I'll be in Boston tomorrow," Aelryn confirmed.

Scott smiled. "Best news I've heard all day. I miss you. Especially since it seems Maine is too far to hear you in my head." He'd missed that too.

"What *you* miss is the ability to talk to me when your mouth is full."

He laughed. "What can I say? I like multitasking. And I certainly don't hear *you* complaining about it."

Aelryn chuckled. "What right-thinking man would do that?" He paused. "Thanks for seeing Milo. He's right. I can smooth things for him. Has there been any trouble so far?"

Scott frowned. "A little. Some of our new guests have objected to having him around, but his mate is one fierce woman. I don't think they'll do that again in a hurry."

"We'll have to discover what the best role for them would be. But we can discuss this when I get there." Another pause. "Is it strange that I don't want to hang up?"

Scott knew that feeling. "The sooner you do, the sooner you'll get back here. And then you're mine—until someone else comes along and you go back to being the Fridan leader again."

Aelryn sighed. "Can I share something with you? What *I* want to go back to is how things were before I found myself embroiled in a war that was never declared. When if someone wanted to see me, it wasn't to report atrocities or casualty lists or—"

"You want to be the professor again," Scott interjected. "To teach about ancient history."

He laughed. "If Jake Carson is right—and Rudy Myers and Valmer Cooper—ancient history is about to come knocking on our door. And then I think everyone is in for one hell of a shock."

"You're putting a lot of hope into whatever it is Jake is hoping to discover, aren't you?"

"You didn't see Fielding when Jake reached into his mind. That...." Aelryn's voice quavered. "I hesitate to use the word man when *monster* is far more applicable. He was afraid, Scott. First of Jake, and then I heard fear in his voice when Jake mentioned the caskets—and the *Missal of Godwin*. Whatever Theron is hiding in that castle? He does *not* want us to know about it. And that excites me."

Scott could hear it in Aelryn's voice. "What are you expecting to find in there?"

"I don't know! I know it may sound crazy, but ever since we found each other, ever since I learned of Horvan and his mates, I have the inescapable feeling that something has... shifted. No pun intended. But now it's as if everything is holding its breath for something that is about to happen—something that will rock us to our core."

Aelryn's excitement was infectious. Scott could feel his own anticipation bubbling up inside him.

But it isn't only Aelryn. I've been feeling like this since I woke up this morning.

Maybe it was the thought of Aelryn coming home.

Enough. Scott had things to do.

"Okay, now you *have* to hang up. I need to go check on our new guests."

"I love you."

Warmth flowed through him. "I love you too. And I'll see you soon." And because he knew Aelryn wouldn't end the call, Scott finished it for him.

He had medical rounds to do—changing dressings, giving out medication, but most of all, being someone who could listen.

They've been through so much. The physical injuries would heal soon enough; the mental ones would take a good deal longer.

As Scott left his room, heading for the infirmary, he was aware of that blossoming feeling of anticipation again, only now it was stronger.

Something is coming.

DOCTOR RAMIREZ'S light touch on his shoulder made Scott jump. "Doctor, are you trying to give me a heart attack?"

The doctor frowned. "You need a break. You've been at it all morning. Get outside into the sunlight. Feel the breeze on your face. And that's my official prescription."

Scott chuckled. "Okay, I get the message." He closed the folder he'd been reviewing, stood, and went over to the fridge, where someone had left sandwiches and juice. He grabbed one of each, then headed for the doors that led to the school garden. He'd discovered it not long after they'd liberated the place. It was a tranquil spot, with trees, roses, and a fountain at its center, the tinkling sound of the water a soothing accompaniment to the pleasant perfume of the flowers.

Those students had everything.

Well, nearly everything. So many of their adoptive parents hadn't wanted them back. Scott's throat tightened. *And how do you deal with a thing like that?*

He strolled over to an empty bench near the fountain, sat, and turned his face toward the sun, his eyes closed.

Dr. Ramirez was right. This is exactly the medicine I needed.

The roses behind him gave off a heady scent, stronger than anything he'd ever encountered, and he wondered what species had been planted. Then the perfume changed, pervading the air all around him, becoming sweeter, yet at the same time there was an underlying spice that unfurled something deep in Scott's belly, an irresistible tugging that sent electricity zapping through him until he had to open his eyes to find the source of that incredible smell.

A familiar smell.

A woman stood in front of him, and Scott recognized her features from the lists of ex-inmates who'd arrived a short while ago. She was petite, with short, spiky black hair, and eyes so dark they were almost black too.

Then he realized the enticing scent came from her, rolling off her in waves, reaching for him, enveloping him, pulling him to stand, to step closer—

To hold her.

The woman gaped at him. "What are you doing to me?"

Scott gaped right back. "What am *I* doing to *you*? I'm just sitting here, enjoying the—" Then it hit him. *That scent.* The same scent that had assaulted him the day he'd walked into Aelryn's office for the first time—

And found my mate.

Bless her, she was trembling, and somewhere in Scott's head, a voice was yelling.

It's her! It's her!

Scott did his best to get his emotions under control. He smiled, holding up his hands. "It's okay, I know what's happening. There's nothing to be scared of." He stood, not moving any closer.

She didn't move but stared at him, wide-eyed.

"What's your name?" he asked in the gentlest tone he could manage.

"Kia. Kia Lombardi." She cocked her head. "I've seen you around here. Aren't you one of the medical staff?"

"Sort of. I'm here because my mate asked me to help out. You might know his name. Aelryn?"

"Aelryn? Yes, I've heard of him." She froze. Dear gods, her eyes were huge. "Your *mate*? Then the rumors are true?"

"Yes, but there's something I need to explain. You see—"

He knew the moment the penny dropped. Kia's mouth fell open, and her breathing quickened. "We're *mates*?"

He nodded. "Yes, but—"

"Wait, you already have a mate. so how can I—" Kia gasped. "I have *two mates*?"

Scott laughed. "I know. Isn't this amazing?" Then she was laughing too, and joy surged through him. "Hello there."

Her eyes sparkled like black diamonds. "Hey. I have so many questions."

"I was the same, when I found Aelryn."

Her breathing hitched. "But that's my first question. If you're together, doesn't that make you gay? And if you are, then—"

Scott stopped her words with a chaste kiss, and her arms were around his neck in a heartbeat. Their foreheads met, and she sighed.

"This feels...."

"Right. It feels right." He kissed her again, only this time with a little more heat, and Kia molded herself against him, as if she couldn't get close enough. Scott forced himself to break the kiss. "Aelryn and I are both bi."

Kia's soft exhale told him she liked that answer. Then she shuddered. "I... I have a confession." She swallowed. "Can we sit? My legs feel like they're made of Jell-O."

Scott took her hand, and they sat together on the bench. "Is something wrong?"

She swallowed once more. "In the camp, they... they...."

His intuition kicked in, and he decided to see if something else had too. *Did they use you in the breeding program?*

Kia stared at him. "How did you—"

You can do it too. It's part of being mates. Try it and see.

She shivered. *Oh my God, this is so cool.*

Scott stroked her hand. "I'm right, aren't I? About the Gerans and their breeding program?"

Kia's face contorted, but she nodded. "When they found out I was a puma, that was it. I was in the camp for three years, and in that time I had five babies, two sets of male twins and a little girl. Twins run in my family."

"What happened to your children?"

Her eyes glistened. "I have no idea. They were taken from me after a few weeks. They could be anywhere." Her face tightened. "When I was a teenager, my mom used to tell me I had to save myself for my husband, that my first time should be special." She sobbed, and the sound broke him. "I wonder what she'd say if she knew my first time wasn't even consensual."

Scott pulled her into his arms and cradled her. "Listen to me. I can't tell you to forget what they did to you, because I don't think you'll ever do that. In fact I'd go so far as to suggest you tell anyone who'll listen, because there are millions of shifters out there who need to know the ugly truth. But.... We took all the records from the Maine camp. And we're going to trace every child who was born as a result of their program." He lifted her chin with his fingertips. "We'll find your babies, okay? Aelryn and I will do whatever it takes."

Kia sobbed even harder, and Scott knew exactly what to do to dry her tears. He stood, removed his clothing, and shifted.

Her gasp of delight was the reaction he'd hoped for.

"Oh my God, you're a freaking red panda!" Seconds later, gentle hands stroked his fur, and he climbed up to nuzzle her neck, loving the giggles that spilled from her lips. She praised the bushiness of his tail and scritched behind his ears. When he was certain her tears were at an end, he shifted back.

"Oh." Kia averted her gaze, her face flushed. "Oh my. For such a small animal, you pack quite a—"

Scott chuckled. "Yeah, that has been mentioned." He dressed quickly. "But what I wanted to say was… your first time with Aelryn and me will be just that—your first time. And *eons* away from whatever happened before."

He bent down and kissed her on the lips, then whispered, "And we *will* be waiting for him to come home before we do… anything."

Kia's cheeks were scarlet. "Thank you. I'm going to need a little time to process all this, you know."

Scott smiled. "Take as much time as you need." He took her hand and helped her to her feet. "And now we're going to your dormitory, where you're going to pack whatever belongs to you, and then you'll move to my rooms." He squeezed her hand. "And just so you know? You get the bedroom—Aelryn and I will be on the sofa bed."

She laughed, and the sound thrilled him.

Wait until Aelryn hears about this.

"There's one thing you haven't told me. What is Aelryn?"

Scott grinned. "A lion." He couldn't resist. "Wait until you see him shift. He strolls around with me on his back."

Kia burst into a peal of laughter again. "That sounds like the cutest thing ever." Then her features grew solemn. "Were you serious about telling people what went on in the camps?"

"Hell yes. The Gerans have been fighting a dirty war in the shadows, and it's time we shone a light on all their dark deeds." He glanced at her. "Are you up for that?"

Kia's eyes blazed. "To quote you—Hell yes. I'm more than ready for a fight, especially if it means giving them a taste of their own medicine."

If Jake and Aelryn were right, they were about to deliver more than medication.

They were going to blast the Geran's world of lies and subterfuge into nothing but atoms.

Chapter Four

Horvan watched as the jet Duke had sent taxied to a stop at the end of the runway.

Going home. He wasn't sure how long he'd be there, but right then he yearned for his own bed, his mates on either side of him, their heads resting on his chest as they slept. He ached to bury his dick deep in Dellan's ass while Dellan did the same to Rael. Their bond connected them at all times, but nothing beat the feelings and sensations that always occurred when the three of them made love.

Can you not have thoughts like this while I'm talking to Mrs. Landon on the phone? Dellan groused.

The day I don't share how much I fucking need you is the day I die, so suck it up, buttercup.

Rael laughed. *In the dictionary under Telling it like it is, it says, See Horvan Kojik.*

Would you have me any other way?

The resounding *No* from both his mates was all the reassurance Horvan needed.

Do we have any idea how long we've got before we have to leave again? Dellan asked. *And yes, you heard right. I said we. If you're going on a mission to find Alec, you are* not *leaving me at home.*

I'd kinda assumed that. Besides, tigers have claws and teeth, and I like my balls where they are. Horvan might be top when it came to sex, but he wasn't stupid. He wanted it to stay that way.

Dellan's mention of Alec was a sharp reminder of how much they had yet to achieve. He knew it had to be on Dellan's mind too. *It must hurt like a son of a bitch, knowing the enemy has genetically modified your son to make him into a killer.* He also knew Dellan had high hopes of saving Alec.

Horvan had to be the practical one. *We don't even know if that will be possible.*

He didn't want to think about the upcoming mission, however. There was too much work to be done before he could do that. Hashtag was already on task, trying to locate the castle Seth had seen in his vision. Jake had been in contact with Orsini, who'd agreed to help them if they should find—

What, exactly? Horvan didn't know, but Jake clearly had an idea. Enough of one to tell Horvan this next mission could be the most vital yet. Horvan had thought *this* mission had been pretty vital. Another camp gone, sure, but more importantly, they had Seth, Jake, and Jamie.

Horvan grinned. *I guess Brick's gonna be busy once we get home.* Aric was a handful, and then some. And Seth? Horvan imagined Dellan had looked a lot like him when he was that age. *I bet Seth can be a handful too.*

Horvan didn't envy Brick.

Does that mean Rael and I aren't a handful?

Horvan chuckled. *You've seen the size of my hands, right?*

You know it's going to be awful crowded at home? Dellan added his own chuckle. *I know it appears to be a mansion, but the house only has five bedrooms. Of course, there are Mrs. Landon's rooms in the basement. I could ask if she wouldn't mind going to stay with her daughter, at least until Saul, Crank, and Vic's place is built. Unless you want Hashtag and Roadkill to move out and stay at the barracks with Eve?*

Horvan snorted. *Yeah, no. They're much better with us. What about Jamie? Has he said that he wants to stay with us?*

There was a pause. *He hasn't said a whole lot. If that's what he wants, then fine. But I get the feeling he might have other plans.*

And are you okay with that?

Another pause. *I guess. Whatever he decides, I don't think he'll stray too far from us. Not now my dad's back, and Seth too. And speaking of my dad... he'll need a room too. For the time being, at any rate.*

He saw through Dellan's words. *I don't know Jake's plans any more than you do, but I* will *make one suggestion. Give him some space. He's been through a lot.* Except thirty-one years was *way* more than a lot. Who knew what he'd been through?

And will those plans include Doc?

Horvan smiled. *You'd have to ask him.* It was kinda cute watching Jake and Doc circle each other. Since that first kiss—which had been a shock, but then again it wasn't: There was a rightness to it Horvan couldn't deny—they'd talked every minute they got.

You think they'll do more than talk?

Gods, I hope so. Horvan grinned. *I know I still want to be fucking when I get to their age. And enjoying it as much as I do now.* He caught Dellan's shudder. *Yeah, I know, you don't wanna think about your dad getting it on, but consider this. What's the only sex he's likely to have had during all his time as a prisoner? Hmm? Forced breeding, probably. So if he and Doc wanna bump uglies, more power to 'em. I say we give 'em some privacy and leave them alone for a while.*

Dellan laughed. *Okay, but they get the basement. Besides, it has a king, so they'll have plenty of room to... whatever. Now, suppose you tell me what's worrying you. I know my dad figures in there somewhere.*

Horvan sighed. *I can't hide diddly squat from you, can I? Have you talked with Jake recently?*

We talk all the time.

No, I mean really *talk. He seems... tired.*

The silence that followed spoke to the heart of Horvan's concern.

Dellan's heavy sigh said so much. *He hasn't talked about the camp or learning about Mom's death or how he's feeling. And that worries me. You said he's been through a lot. I don't think that even scratches the surface, and I don't know what to do about it.*

All you can do is be there for him. Like I said, give him some space. Let him readjust.

"Horvan, can we speak?" Aelryn's quiet voice broke into his internal conversation.

We can talk later, Dellan told him. *When we're home. And by the way? I can't wait to be sandwiched between you two either. Think we can talk Rael into taking both our dicks at the same time again?*

Horvan let out a mental growl. *Can you not say stuff like that?* He turned to face Aelryn. "Sure."

Aelryn's lips twitched. "I seem to have interrupted something. Is this not a good time?" His nostrils flared.

Fuck. Well, tough shit if he could smell Horvan's arousal. *Get a good whiff, because no way am I ashamed of my love for my mates.* He ignored Dellan's chuckle. *So you think this is funny? Wait until I get my hand on you.*

Don't you mean hands?

Horvan snorted. *Oh no, sweetheart.* And just for good measure, he sent Dellan a mental picture of him naked over Horvan's lap, his ass tilted, the shape of Horvan's hand-print clearly visible against the creamy skin.

Holy fuck, you fight dirty.

Horvan chuckled. *You know it.* Then he realized Aelryn was waiting. "No, it's fine, we can talk." He took another glance, noting Aelryn's wrinkled brow, his gaze that flitted, never settling on anything for long. "What's on your mind?"

"What's happening here?" Aelryn blurted.

His demeanor was so far removed from the unruffled leader Horvan had come to know and respect that it gave him pause. "What do you mean?"

"Scott is with the inmates. We took them to the school in Boston for the time being. And…." Aelryn swallowed. "He says he's found our mate. She was one of them."

Horvan beamed. "That's awesome." Something in Aelryn's manner checked his exuberance. "Isn't it?"

"Of course it is, but… why now?" Aelryn demanded. "Why are our mates suddenly emerging?"

Horvan got where he was coming from. "There *have* been a few lately."

"Yes, but…." Aelryn frowned. "Look at Hashtag and Roadkill. Military buddies for more than a decade, nothing more than friends, and no indication that they were mates. Then Eve comes along, and something clicks into place."

"I can't explain it either."

Aelryn locked gazes with him. "What if something in the universe has also just clicked into place? Because there has to be a reason. I can't believe this is nothing but mere chance."

Horvan couldn't believe that either.

"Maybe we'll never know why this is happening," he murmured. "Maybe we shouldn't try to come up with explanations, but accept it for what it is."

Aelryn's dark eyes met his. "But you want answers too, don't you?"

Yeah, he did.

"H, we're almost ready to leave," Brick hollered. "Unless you wanna stay here?"

Aelryn followed Horvan's gaze. "I don't blame him for what he did."

"We talking about him dispatching Fielding without orders?" Not that Horvan blamed him either.

"If truth be told, he solved a problem for us. I don't know how long we could've kept Fielding a prisoner." Aelryn glanced at Horvan. "You do realize there could be a price to pay, once Theron learns of Fielding's demise?"

"Yeah. We'll deal with that when the time comes. First thing on the agenda is to find wherever Theron is hiding—and *what* he's hiding." He grinned. "I've always wanted to visit the UK."

"When we know where we're headed, I'll organize a team to join forces with you. And I'll put you in contact with Derek Ferguson. He's a team leader, based in the UK. A good man. Maybe Richard Deveraux too, especially if you're going to be in the north of the country." He clasped Horvan's forearm. "Thank you again."

"You're welcome. Will I be seeing you in the UK too?"

Aelryn's eyes glinted. "When it could mean finally meeting the leader of all Gerans? Which is what Theron is, according to Jake. Not to mention uncovering whatever he's keeping in that room." He smiled. "I'll be there. I wouldn't miss it for the world."

Horvan had a feeling the contents of those stone caskets might turn their world upside down.

EVERYTHING IS moving so goddamn fast. And Jake was struggling to keep up.

Nicholas Tranter's presence was the one thing that anchored him, gave him something to hold on to.

He managed a smile. "I see planes haven't gotten any quieter in the last thirty years." He gazed out of the small window at the earth below. "Not that I remember a thing about the last time I was in a plane. One minute I was in Rome. The next? I was waking up in the US with one helluva headache and unable to shift."

All those years of not knowing what had become of his wife and son. Sure, he had Dellan back in his life, but learning the truth about Miranda had only caused more pain.

"It's over now," Nicholas murmured beside him.

Jake jerked his head to stare at him. "Do you really believe that?"

Nicholas sighed. "No, of course not. It's wishful thinking on my part. But it *can* be over—for a short while. At least until we know more about Theron's whereabouts." He smiled. "You've more than earned a break."

Jake didn't want to talk about Theron. All that did was twist his stomach into knots and give him one bastard of a headache. He twisted in his seat to peer at Nicholas. "Why did you never marry?"

He shrugged. "I finished my studies, I became a doctor—and then I was recruited by the military. There was no time to think of such things. Life got in the way."

"That's bullshit."

Nicholas arched his eyebrows. "Excuse me?"

"I trust my instincts, and they tell me you're not speaking the truth." Jake covered Nicholas's hand with his own. "If you can be straight with anyone, it's me."

That earned him a smile. "Except I'm not. Straight, that is. And neither are you, it seems. Have you always known you're bisexual?"

"Always." Jake couldn't hold back a second longer. "Just like I always knew you had feelings for me."

Nicholas's breathing hitched. "You... you knew?"

He nodded. "But what's really going to surprise the hell out of you? I had feelings for you too."

"But...." Nicholas swallowed. "You and Miranda...."

"Who also knew how I felt. Want to hear the shocker? She suggested I sleep with you."

His jaw dropped. "You're kidding."

"She thought I should find out what I was missing out on."

"Then... have you ever.... With a man?"

Jake bit back a smile. "Uh-uh. There's only ever been one lover in my life, and that was her. What happened in the intervening years since they took me?" He scowled. "It doesn't count."

"No, it doesn't," Nicholas agreed with some vehemence. He stared at Jake. "Okay, if you can be that honest, then so can I. The reason I never married? There was never anyone who made my heart beat the way you did. Anything else would have seemed like a poor substitute. It wouldn't have been fair to them, because I would always be comparing them to you. No matter who it was, they would have lost out. And I guess part of me always hoped for the impossible."

"And what was that?"

Nicholas locked gazes with him. "That one day I'd find you again, and that I'd have enough courage to tell you I... I loved you."

Warmth surged through him. "I loved you too."

"And now? Do you think you can still love me?"

Jake smiled. "I wouldn't be sitting here with you if I didn't." He paused. "I know it's been years, but I... I want to take things slow."

Nicholas chuckled. "You could've fooled me. That kiss was right off the blocks."

"I had to know." Jake cupped his face. "But I'm really an old-fashioned kinda guy. I want to get to know you all over again before we take the next step."

That hitch in Nicholas's breathing was all the sweeter the second time around. "Then we *are* going to—"

Jake cut off his words with a kiss, keeping it chaste. "Yes, we are," he whispered. "If that's what you want."

Nicholas nodded. "With all my heart." Then he laughed softly. "You know, it's my sixtieth birthday in a few days, but right now? I feel as though my life is starting all over again."

Me too. Gods, I love him.

Nicholas stiffened, his eyes wide.

"Hey. What's wrong?" Jake grabbed his hands.

"I just heard you in my head," he blurted.

Holy hell.

What about now?

Nicholas gaped at him. "I have no psychic ability. How can I be hearing you? How is this possible?"

Jake's heart pounded. *I think you know why. Why not put it to the test?*

Nicholas's chest heaved.

Please, Nicholas.

His Adam's apple bobbed. *I love you too.*

Tears pricked Jake's eyes, and his throat tightened.

"But why now?" Nicholas demanded. "Why not when we were younger? And why didn't we know this right away when we met again?"

Jake laughed. "You expect *me* to have all the answers? I'm as much in the dark about this as you are. And who's to say there are rules for this?"

Dad? Are you all right? Dellan's voice pierced the tumult of his thoughts.

Jake wiped his cheeks. *I'm more than all right. I just found one of my mates.*

The lack of response told him he'd stunned Dellan into silence.

Nicholas's mouth fell open. "*One* of…. You mean there's *another* one out there somewhere?"

Jake nodded.

The universe had opened a door and shown him how little he knew.

Now all he wanted was to open the door to that glass room and learn the truth.

Chapter Five

Dellan breathed easier as soon as he walked through the front door. He always did when he returned home. Maybe it was knowing Tom Prescott had built the house for his mom. He'd loved her, and while they were married, she'd been happy with him.

Mom had been on his mind a lot since Maine, and he knew why.

I never got to say goodbye.

He'd only learned of her death when he finally shifted back into human form, and that had been hard enough, but learning Fielding had murdered her had dealt him a body blow. Being home where she'd lived, laughed, loved….

That eased the pain a little. Not much, but it was a start.

They'd been home maybe half an hour before Mrs. Landon appeared. Judging by all the bags, she'd been to the store. She smiled as he walked into the kitchen.

"Oh, you're home. I'm sorry I wasn't here to greet you, but I had some last-minute groceries to buy. I've been dashing around ever since you called. I've only just finished getting all the rooms ready for your guests." She paused. "What's wrong?"

"Nothing's wrong," he lied. He peered into the refrigerator. "Oh my God. It looks as if you're feeding an army." There were plastic boxes stacked up, filling every shelf, and yet there she was, unpacking cartons of milk, butter, cooked meat, cheese, eggs….

"The downstairs refrigerator is stuffed too." Mrs. Landon laughed when he gaped at her. "Well, when you called to say there'd be fourteen mouths to feed, I got busy. I was up at dawn, making three casseroles, four meatloaves, and about six batches of cookies." Her eyes twinkled. "Except knowing all of you, that's probably not enough."

Horvan walked into the kitchen as she was speaking, and his eyes lit up. "Did someone say cookies?"

She shook her head. "They talk about the way to a man's heart. I guess the same is true of bears too." She hugged him. "Good to see you. And I baked the chocolate chip ones for you."

Horvan grinned. "You spoil me."

It was Dellan's turn to hug her. "Thank you." He released her, but to his surprise, she didn't move away but studied him for a moment. "Is anything wrong?"

"I was about to ask you both the same question." She frowned. "I can't put my finger on it, but I haven't been in the house five minutes and already it feels as though there's an atmosphere around here. Now I don't know what went on while you were away—and I don't expect you to tell me—but all I have to do is look at you to know something happened. I'm right, aren't I?"

He swallowed. "Yes, Mrs. Landon. It was a very intense experience, one I don't think we'll easily forget."

"If you ever need to talk...."

Dellan kissed her cheek. "That's a sweet thought, but I'm not sure we can."

"Sounds to me as though you all have a heap of emotions to deal with."

Horvan nodded. "And you'd be correct, but what's more important right now is reconnecting with our mates, to make the most of what time we have before...."

Before we need to go and do it all over again.

Dellan glanced at him. *She's right, you know. So much stress, so much tension, and then there were deaths to deal with.*

And we will deal with all of it. But like I said, not now. Later.

Then Dellan realized he had an unpleasant task to perform. "Mrs. Landon, while we were away, we... we learned something awful. I wasn't going to tell you, until I remembered that you knew my mom. You've been part of this house ever since Tom built it."

"Something to do with your mother?"

He nodded. "It... it wasn't a natural death."

She clutched her chest. "Oh no. That poor woman. Hadn't she been through enough in her life, not knowing what became of your father?" She wiped her eyes.

"There's a reason I'm telling you this. One of our guests? It's my dad."

Mrs. Landon's mouth fell open, and her eyes widened. "He's not dead? Then where has he been all this time?"

"That's a long story." And one he wasn't prepared to answer. She knew about shifters. They'd shared that with her because it would have been pretty difficult to explain why a bear, a lion, and a tiger were playing together outside behind the barrier Roadkill had erected, or why a Greenland shark was swimming in the lake. But Dellan hadn't gone so far as telling her what was going on in a world she knew nothing about. Mrs. Landon wasn't stupid. She knew Horvan and the others were soldiers of some kind, but she didn't ask questions.

"Is he okay?"

Only time will tell.

He gave Mrs. Landon a smile. "I'll introduce you. He went upstairs to freshen up. He's going to take Hashtag's room. Seth's going to be in Brick and Aric's room. And Jamie and Doc Tranter will be in the basement. Thank you again for understanding about the space issues." He knew he was changing the subject abruptly, but if he didn't he'd be crying too.

Mrs. Landon waved her hand. "It's no bother. My daughter is delighted to have me stay a while. Not that I'll be spending much time there, not with all of you to take care of."

"No!" Eve gasped as she walked into the kitchen. "Don't leave me, Mrs. L. I'm feeling outnumbered here."

Mrs. Landon beamed. "You'll be fine. You could wipe the floor with any of them. Except maybe Brick."

Horvan's expression grew pained. "Hey. What about me?"

She patted his cheek. "You? You're a sweetheart. In fact as one of you once said, you're practically a teddy bear." And with that she walked out of the kitchen.

"Who said that?" Horvan tried to look aggrieved, but Dellan wasn't fooled.

He laughed. "Wow. She knows you."

You okay?

Warmth flowed over him, and he knew that was Horvan's doing. *No, but I will be. All I need is time. And maybe a little therapy.*

Hey, we all need that at some point or other.

Dellan gave Eve an inquiring glance. "Where are your mates?"

"In H's office, where they've been ever since we got back here."

"What happened to making the most of your time on your own?" Horvan demanded.

Eve rolled her eyes. "Have *you* ever tried to drag Hashtag away from a laptop when he's searching for something?"

Horvan smirked. "He can be a little obsessive at times."

"A little?" She snorted. "Herding cats would be easier than distracting that man." Her eyes sparkled. "I did it, though."

Dellan chuckled. "I'm not sure my delicate ears are ready to hear this, which is a pity, because I happen to have a mate who can also be quite... driven."

Horvan gave a mock gasp. "You can't be talking about me."

Rael's laughter filled Dellan's head, and Horvan managed to appear offended.

Eve came over to where Dellan stood, leaned in close, and whispered, "Next time you want to grab his... attention? Crawl under his desk and go to work."

"You know I heard that, right?" Horvan said with a grin. "And thanks for the suggestion. I hope he puts it to good use. Soon."

Dellan snickered. "I'll remember you said that the next time you're doing a Zoom meeting with Aelryn."

Horvan narrowed his gaze. "And you remember what I said about getting my hand on you."

"Wasn't I in the middle of a progress report?" Eve said with a chuckle. "Hashtag's linked up to the satellite, still searching for that castle. Do you know there are about fourteen castles in Lancashire? They don't all have moats, however. But I think he's whittled it down to three. I'm here to grab them some coffee." She grinned. "And cookies, of course. Man cannot live by coffee alone, it seems." She went over to the pot and filled three cups. She glanced around the large kitchen. "Where's Jamie?"

"He said he wanted a nap before dinner," Dellan told her.

That sounds like a great idea. Rael chuckled. *Except sleep wasn't what I had in mind.*

Horvan's hand was on Dellan's back. *Jamie will be fine too. Stop worrying.*

Dellan wished it was that easy.

"I don't know about shifters being the only ones who have excellent hearing and a good sense of smell," Saul commented as he strolled into the kitchen. "I swear I could smell Mrs. Landon's cookies all the way from our room."

Behind him, Crank snorted. "You wanna be careful. What do they say? 'A moment on the lips, a lifetime on the hips'? I'm sure there was more for me to grab on to the last time we—"

Saul covered Crank's mouth with his hand. "I've got another one for you. Something about biting the hand that feeds you? Except we're not talking about food."

Crank blinked as Saul removed his hand. "Okay, I'm gonna shut up now."

Saul grinned. "Good boy."

Dellan watched the byplay between the mates. *Is it me, or are they all coping much better than I am?*

Horvan sighed. *They're dealing with it the only way they know how. And sometimes that means covering up their emotions until they have the time and the space to deal with them.*

At that moment Dellan's dad came into the kitchen. "This is a beautiful house."

"It was built for Mom." Dellan caught the flicker of pain across his face. "Have you got everything you need?"

"Yeah, about that… I love my room, but it feels wrong, having it to myself when there's a houseful."

Dellan couldn't help noticing the lines around his dad's eyes, the dark shadows under them, the air of fatigue that clung to him.

He really isn't okay, is he?

Give him time, Horvan said gently.

"Jamie's in the basement, and Doc too." Only, Dellan had a feeling Doc wouldn't stay there for long.

You and me both. Would you *be separated from either me or Rael?*

His dad chuckled. "Every time you say Doc, it reminds me of the Bugs Bunny cartoons you used to watch when you were little. I think of him as Nicholas. And while he's not here at the moment, it's his birthday in two days' time, and it's a big one. He'll be sixty. Can we do something special for him?"

Dellan smiled. "I'll get Mrs. Landon on the case. Not sure we have that many candles in the house, but we can always buy more."

Dad tilted his head. "If you'll excuse me, I'm wanted out on the patio." He headed for the French doors.

Dellan frowned. "Where's Brick?" He hadn't seen him since they'd walked through the front door.

Horvan laughed. "Do you see Seth and Aric? Where do you think he is?"

Crank smiled. "You remember the first time the three of us—"

"Yes, I do," Saul interjected. "And you can stop right there."

Dellan glanced at Horvan. *Remember our first time?* He sent a flood of images into Horvan's head.

Horvan let out a low growl. *Will you stop that? We've been in the house five minutes, and already I wanna take you upstairs and—*

Dellan almost choked as an image filled his mind—Rael, naked on their bed, lubing up his hole.

He grabbed Horvan's hand and dragged him from the room. "See you all later," he called out.

"Have fun storming the castle!" Crank hollered after them. Then Dellan caught his next words, spoken under his breath. "That's the last we'll see of *them* until tomorrow. Think Horvan can survive it?"

Dellan smiled to himself. He intended finding out exactly how far Horvan's stamina would take him.

"I don't know," Saul murmured. "But what a way to go."

"If we're not down for dinner, start without us," Dellan called out.

There were holes to be filled—and kisses to be shared.

Didn't you know? Sex can be therapeutic too.

Dellan chuckled. *I'm so lucky to have such a wise mate.*

A mate who's about to give you nine inches of therapy.

It wasn't until they reached their bedroom door that Dellan had second thoughts.

I can't just leave everyone to—

To what? Fend for themselves? They're all adults, Horvan reminded him.

What H said. Besides.... Rael's voice grew soft. *We can help you turn your mind off for a while, if you'll let us.*

Dellan sighed. *That sounds perfect.*

Time to close the bedroom door, shut out the world, and reconnect with his mates. It wouldn't diminish the worries and cares that awaited them, but it would remind him how far he'd come.

From a caged tiger, unable to shift, to a man with two mates who would go to the ends of the earth for him if he asked them to.

Then he realized they'd go without being asked.

That was love.

Chapter Six

Aric was a mess.

So far he'd unpacked Brick's duffel, filled the laundry hamper, and made room in the closet for Seth's things—until he realized Seth didn't have anything other than the clothes on his back. And while their sizes weren't too dissimilar, his clothes would fit Seth like a second skin.

He'd also showered—twice—taking special pains to make sure one region of his anatomy was squeaky clean, because hey, he lived in hope.

Brick chuckled. "We'll go shopping tomorrow, okay? Seth can have whatever he wants."

Aric rolled his eyes. "Be warned, Seth. Letting this man loose with a credit card? Fatal." Brick had taken Aric on a shopping spree when he'd first arrived in Homer Glen.

Brick's wallet—and his closet—were still in recovery.

"I don't want to think about shopping, not when I have something far more important on my mind." Seth crooked his finger. "Come here, kitty."

Aric's heartbeat raced as he walked over to him, drinking in the sight of Seth's lean frame—too lean, to be honest—his toned upper arms, the brown hair swept back like it always was, those dark brown eyes that had the power to melt him into a puddle of goo….

From the moment Aric had realized boys revved his engine rather than girls, and had taken his first tentative glances at porn, he'd known one thing for sure.

He was a bottom.

Porn had proved useful in one aspect—well, several, if he were honest. It had shown him being a bottom was nothing to be ashamed of. In fact he secretly believed bottoms had more fun. And once he'd met Seth, something else became obvious.

Seth might be a force of nature, but he was a bottom too.

Okay, so they'd never done more than kiss and indulge in some very hasty, very secret mutual masturbation in the camp, but he'd seen inside

Seth's head, and that left him in no doubt as to whose dick would be going where no man's had gone before.

That would be Brick's.

The same Brick who was staring at them as if they'd just walked into his life.

I get that. We're finally together, but damn, we came the long way around.

You okay?

Aric knew where Brick was headed. *Let's say I'm getting there.* He didn't want to think about Fielding—not that he'd ever forget him—but this was a time for being with his mates.

He chuckled. *Who am I kidding? This is all about handing in my V card.*

Aric had waited long enough. They all had. "So what comes next?" Aric asked.

"Me, I hope," Seth quipped. "Or both of us simultaneously, if it can be arranged." His eyes twinkled. "Except I don't think Brick's cock can be in two places at once, so we might have to draw straws."

"Wanna watch you undress each other." Brick sat on the bed, then patted the comforter. "On here, boys."

Seth grinned. "If we're going to give you a show, there'd better be some audience participation."

Aric glanced at Brick's crotch. "I think that's a given." He knelt on the bed, and Seth joined him, their lips meeting in a tender kiss. He leaned in, his forehead meeting Seth's. "Missed you," he whispered.

Seth kissed him, only this time it wasn't a fleeting embrace but a long, sensual connection that made him hot and cold at the same time. Their movements were clumsy as clothing was discarded, punctuated by frequent kisses, as though neither of them could bear to be parted for more than a couple of seconds. And as each new area of Seth's bare skin was revealed, Aric kissed and stroked it, reacquainting himself with Seth's familiar scent, the feel of warm, smooth flesh beneath his fingertips.

Neither of them made any effort to remove their underwear, and that felt right.

We're in no rush. They'd waited this long, right?

"Fuck, you two are cute."

Aric turned his head and lowered his gaze. He swore Brick was even bigger. He stretched out his hand and gave Brick's bulge a gentle stroke. "What have you got in there? A puppy?"

Brick laughed. "Why don't you find out?"

Seth shuffled on his knees across the bed, unfastened Brick's pants, and cupped the cotton-covered erection that lay like a thick steel rod, pointing toward Brick's hip. Seth gazed up at him. "Okay, so *not* a puppy—an anaconda."

Brick pushed his pants down to his knees, then overbalanced as he tried to remove them. Aric caught him, laughing.

"I know we've waited a while for this, but please, don't spoil it now by falling off the bed and breaking something."

Brick got rid of his clothing, leaving his briefs in place, and Aric couldn't stop staring at his crotch, the fabric stretched tight, hiding nothing. Then Brick reached into his underwear and adjusted himself, and now his cock jutted toward them, barely contained by the garment that pulled away from his body, revealing his balls.

"Can't tell you how many times I've thought about this moment." Brick's husky voice sent a shiver down Aric's spine. "I've dreamed of seeing your eyes widen, your mouths open… your bodies taking me in completely."

Seth moved closer, bent down, and kissed the head of Brick's cock.

Brick's shiver of anticipation was adorable.

Then Aric froze. "I think it's only just dawned on me. Me and Seth, we're both virgins—but then so are you when it comes to sex with guys."

"Why do you think I've been dreaming about this? And now you're both here—" Brick chuckled. "—I don't know where to start."

"I do." Seth cupped Brick's cheek and kissed him.

Aric followed Seth's lead and joined them, molding his body against Brick's, one hand on Brick's neck, the other on Seth's, the three of them joined in a single kiss.

That long, solid bulge in Brick's briefs kept tugging at Aric's concentration, however, pulling his gaze lower.

Brick laughed. "For God's sake, just *touch* it. I want to feel your hands on me."

Aric traced the stony length, his fingers straying to the edge where Brick's balls were attempting an escape. He couldn't resist. Aric pulled aside the cotton to release Brick's sac, holding it in his palm, testing the weight of the heavy balls, rolling them through his fingers. Then he leaned in and kissed one of them.

"Take it in your mouth," Brick whispered. "Suck on it."

Aric's mouth watered. He was conscious of Seth mouthing Brick's shaft through his briefs, low moans of pleasure tumbling from Brick's lips, growing in volume as Aric sucked first one heavy orb, then the other, dragging his tongue over the wrinkled skin.

Brick raised his dick with two fingers, holding it against his firm lower belly, his balls bifurcated by the fabric pulled tight. "Can you fit them both in your mouth?"

As if Aric could resist a challenge like that. He grinned. "Watch me." Then he took them both, and Brick cupped the back of his head, drawing him in until his mouth was so full.

His reward when he pulled free was Brick's kiss, a sensual, lingering embrace.

You did good.

Aric's chest was about to burst with pride.

"Can I take it out?" Seth pleaded.

Brick slid his fingers under the waistband and eased the cotton briefs lower, revealing his long, thick shaft an inch at a time before removing the garment and tossing it to the floor. Seth curled his hand around its girth, and Aric kissed the wide head, flicking his tongue over the slit.

Brick's gasp told him his instincts were on the money.

"Need to get you both ready for me," he ground out.

A moment later, Aric was kneeling between them on the bed, Seth in front of him, his lips around Aric's dick, and Brick behind him, his tongue in Aric's hole.

"Oh my God, that feels amazing. Where did you learn to do this?" Aric demanded.

"Been doing a bit of research," Brick admitted.

Seth snorted. "That means porn, right?"

"Porn?" he gasped, in what was obviously a show of offense that didn't fool Aric for a nanosecond. "I would *never*." Brick bit his lip. "Well, not much." Seth gave him a pointed stare, and he sighed. "Okay, I *might* have maxed out one credit card, but that was it." He kissed them both again. "And I have to tell you, being here with you? Nothing I saw was sexier than that."

Any comment Aric might have been about to add was swept away in the wave of pleasure that crashed into him when Brick renewed his efforts. He only knew the double assault on his senses was making him harder than he'd ever been, and he was torn between sliding his cock deeper into Seth's warm mouth and pushing back to get more of that talented tongue.

Brick broke off from his explorations of Aric's hole. "Spread your cheeks for me."

Aric reached back, pulled his cheeks apart, and was rewarded when Brick reapplied himself to his task with even more vigor. Their mental connection heightened every sensation, however, and Seth's obvious enjoyment sent Aric's need soaring.

Then it was Aric's turn to get his first taste of Brick's cock, and while he couldn't fit the whole thing in his mouth, he made a valiant effort. Brick moaned into Seth's kiss while Aric bobbed his head with enthusiasm, loving the thoughts that Brick couldn't hide.

"Can I be first?" Seth blurted.

Aric was fine with that. He wanted a ringside seat while Brick claimed Seth's hole for the first time. He loved the little noises Seth made when Brick kissed him, sliding his hands into Seth's briefs and squeezing his asscheeks.

"Gods, I wanna be in there," Brick announced in a hoarse voice. "Get on all fours, knees wide apart." Seth did as instructed, and Brick knelt behind him, pulling his briefs down and revealing his crack. He glanced at Aric. "Get the lube. It's in the nightstand drawer."

Aric had the tube in his hands mere seconds later.

Brick spread Seth's cheeks and gazed at his hole. "So the best way to get you ready? Is this." And then he dove, pressing his face into Seth's crease, pulling his cheeks apart.

Seth tilted his ass higher, pushing his chest into the bed, and the grunts of pleasure that poured from Brick left Aric in no doubt he was enjoying every second. Brick lubed up a couple of fingers and slowly pushed them into Seth's body. "So tight," he murmured.

Aric wanted to be more than a spectator, and once again his gaze strayed to Brick's impressive shaft.

Brick smiled. "Use your mouth to get my dick ready for him."

Moans filled the air, and to Aric's mind, it was a toss-up as to whose were the loudest. Then Brick slid his shaft through Seth's crack.

"Guide it into him," he told Aric. "Push the head against his hole."

Aric wrapped his fingers around Brick's cock and positioned it, the flared head pressed against Seth's pucker. He exerted a little more pressure, and the head popped in.

Seth groaned. "Oh God, I feel that."

Aric bent lower to kiss him. "And that's just the tip. Wait until all of him is inside you." He knelt once more at Seth's ass, kissing his cheek while Brick slowly filled Seth, taking his time. Aric couldn't tear his gaze away as Brick moved in and out, Seth's hole clinging to his shaft, Seth's moans and low cries increasing in frequency and volume.

"Want a better view?" Brick grinned. "Lie down between us, on your back." He gestured to the space below his balls. "Put your face right here."

Aric shuffled his way along the bed until he was staring up at where Brick and Seth were joined. Brick's balls were too much of a temptation, and he craned his neck to move in closer, kissing and sucking them while Brick slid deep into Seth's ass.

"Come on, Seth," Brick murmured. "Let me all the way in. Wanna fill you to the hilt."

Seth moaned. "I can feel Aric's mouth on your balls. Want to feel that too."

"Aric? Scoot around and lie under Seth. You know what sixty-nine is, right?"

Aric chuckled. "No, of course not. I've never watched porn. I'm a complete innocent."

Brick laughed so hard, he popped right out of Seth's hole.

Aric lay beneath Seth, his briefs pulled aside, his dick pointing to Aric's lips, Seth's mouth on Aric's shaft, while Brick mounted Seth and slid back into him, hips pumping as he went balls-deep into Seth's ass, the three of them connected, their emotions colliding.

When Brick paused, his cock edged in Seth's body, Aric let out a groan.

"Don't stop!"

"Oh. So you don't want me inside you, is that it?"

Aric stilled. "Where do you want me?"

"Swap places. Seth's gonna suck you off while I fuck you."

Aric had never moved so fast. He stripped off his briefs and knelt, his knees as wide as he could manage, ass tilted. "Go slow, okay?"

Brick's hand was gentle on his back. "I'll go nice and slow. Seth, play with his dick while I get his hole ready."

"You've already had your tongue in there," Aric complained. "Isn't it ready yet?"

Beneath him, Seth chuckled. "Don't be so hasty. You need prepping. Have you *seen* his dick? He's as hard as a rock."

"Don't you mean a brick?" Aric quipped. Then all humor fled when Brick pushed his thumb into Aric's hole. "Oh gods."

Seth laughed. "To quote you, wait until the rest of him is inside you." He stroked Aric's cock, sending delicious shivers through him.

It wasn't long before Brick's thumb felt just fine, and then two fingers stretched him out a little more. At long last, Brick eased into him, filling Aric with a warm, solid cock.

Aric bowed his head and closed his eyes, aware of Brick's hands on his shoulders and Seth's mouth around his dick, a circle of flesh, minds, and hearts, connected.

Bonded.

"Bend your leg," Brick told him. "Foot on the mattress."

Aric did as instructed, groaning when Brick slid deeper still and Seth swallowed his cock to the root, the three of them moving together, fluid and sensual, all heading in the same direction.

Brick flipped him onto his back, and Seth leaned over to kiss Aric, his tongue in sync with Brick's shaft as he moved in and out of Aric, hips rolling in a sensuous motion. Seth grabbed Aric's ankles, pulling them toward him and rolling Aric's ass up off the bed, allowing Brick to spear his cock deep into him, gaining momentum, his finger tight around Aric's scrotum, while Seth worked Aric's dick.

There was no way Aric could last long under that onslaught.

He shot hard, spattering his chest, and Brick gave a roar, back arched as he thrust into Aric. That exquisite throb inside him told him Brick had come too, and the kiss they all shared was the sweetest one yet.

Seth kissed his forehead, cheeks, nose, and lips. "You look amazing when you come."

Aric reached up to cup Seth's cheek. "And now I want to see you do the same." Brick eased out of him, still half hard, and Aric scrambled to his knees. "Your turn."

Seth lay on his back, his calves resting on Brick's shoulders as Brick slowly filled him again, only now Aric worked Seth's cock while they kissed, loving the mounting tremors that built and built, until finally Seth came, shuddering with each spurt of his dick.

Brick groaned. *I've never come twice that quickly. Ever.*

Aric chuckled. "I'd get used to it, if I were you." Brick blinked, and Aric shrugged. "Multiple mates, multiple orgasms… it's win-win, right?"

Then they lay on either side of him, their bodies damp, their thighs hooked over Brick's, their heads against his shoulders.

Brick kissed each of them on top of their heads. "Worth the wait?"

Aric grinned. "Ask me again in the morning. I think I need to experience more of this to help me make my mind up."

Brick snorted. "Oh really." Then Seth started laughing, and Brick gave him an inquiring glance. "What's tickled you? Apart from my dick, of course."

"I was thinking about what Aric said. 'Hard as a brick.'" He craned his neck to stare at Brick. "You have to tell us. Was this how you got your nickname?"

Brick's low, dirty chuckle reverberated through Aric.

"I wish. It was the weirdest thing. When I met the guys, Hashtag said I was as big as a brick shithouse. Thing is, back when I was in the military, the CO called me Brick because he said I was thick as one."

Aric snickered. "Gotta say, I agree with your CO." When Brick gave him an injured glance, he grinned. "Well, it felt that way when you were pushing into me."

Brick huffed. "He said I had to be thick as a brick because I couldn't read the signs in front of me that it was a no-win situation." He managed a shrug. "The name stuck. Oh, and that no-win situation?" He smiled. "I won."

"Looks like you won again," Aric remarked. "Only this time, you won us."

Brick pulled them against him until Aric could feel the steady beat of his heart.

"Best. Prize. Ever."

Chapter Seven

Whatever strength Jake Carson had drawn on to present a façade of a man coping with his reality, it was running out. The only thing keeping him going was the upcoming mission to locate Theron. Seth's psychic gifts were impressive, but Fielding's interrogation had left Jake with no illusions as to which of them possessed the greater skill. That... encounter had cost him a lot of energy, and he'd hated being so relentless, but he'd had no choice.

Horvan and Aelryn needed him. And they were going to need him again. All he had to do was keep going, keep pretending....

Jake wasn't sure how much any of them had guessed about his mental and physical state. He'd done his best to lock away his thoughts during the last few days, but while that prevented Dellan from seeing his inner turmoil, it hadn't kept Nicholas out.

Maybe that's as it should be. A mate should know the truth.

"And what truth is that?"

Jake gave a start. "You know, for a man who shifts into one of the largest animals on the planet, you move as silently as—"

"A mouse?" Nicholas offered as he rejoined Jake on the patio, handing him a tall glass of water. "And you're not the first to remark on it. I had a boyfriend once who claimed I was a secret ninja." He smiled. "I didn't dissuade him from that theory. It added to my... mystique." He sat on the chair next to Jake's and gazed out at the lake, the setting sun reflecting in its still waters. "This is a beautiful place. Horvan told me the first time Vic visited, he was out of the car and into the water in a heartbeat." He pointed to the piles of building supplies. "Do you know about the house Dellan is having built for them?"

Jake nodded. His son had grown into a thoughtful, loving, generous man.

Nicholas cocked his head. "But I'm not out here to talk about Dellan. I'd rather talk about you."

Jake's heartbeat slipped into a higher gear. "Oh?"

Nicholas's large warm hand covered his. "It's okay. I understand more than you think. Such as why you've been out on the patio most of the time since we got here. And I don't think you give your new family in there enough credit. *They* understand too."

"Understand what?" The lake was a sheet of molten golds, reds, and oranges, like oil flowing on the surface of water.

Nicholas cupped Jake's chin, and gently but firmly, he forced Jake to look at him. "No one gets out of captivity after thirty-one years and slips right back into a normal life. *No one*, do you hear me? Not even Jake Carson."

Jake's breath caught in his throat.

"I know you don't want to admit it, but there's a truth you need to accept if you're going to come through this."

Lord, the pain in his chest…. "What truth?" Jake croaked.

Nicholas took hold of his other hand and faced Jake. "You need to be right with yourself and everything that's happened to you before you can believe life is real again." He swung out his arm, encompassing the view. "That all this is real."

Jake had never felt so seen, and *God*, the relief. The damn burst, and he sobbed.

Nicholas knelt on the slabs and put his arms around him, Jake's face buried in his neck. "Let it out, love."

Jake's tears soaked into Nicholas's shirt, and it felt good to finally let go. Nicholas stroked up and down his back, a constant soothing reminder of his presence. When his sobs ebbed, Jake drew in a long shuddering breath and smiled.

"You need to get up and sit on a chair. At our age, concrete wrecks the knees."

Nicholas chuckled. He released Jake and retook his seat. "Now let's talk about sex."

Jake blinked. "Wow. You're a fast worker. Out here? Sure, I'd be up for that, but you *know* Crank'll want to sell tickets."

He laughed. "Idiot. Can you be serious for a moment? And don't think I can't see past that smokescreen of humor you put up."

Jake bit his lip. "Okay. No smokescreen."

"I know we've talked about taking the next step, and Lord knows, I want you inside me, but…."

Jake smiled. "The feeling is mutual. In fact, I thought about it a lot while I was in that camp." He sighed. "But the thing is? Mentally I need someone to help me get back into a good place. Don't get me wrong, please. I really *do* want you. It's just…."

Nicholas cupped his cheek once more. "What you need right now isn't sex but a real connection. Something solid to build on. So I thought that... maybe we could, you know, date for a while."

The sweetness of Nicholas's words and tone robbed Jake of breath for a moment.

Nicholas sighed. "A lot has changed for both of us, and we need to get to know each other all over again. We need to get back into the headspace where we're both safe and whole and holding on to one another, waiting for the storm to pass. And with time—and help—it *will* pass." He leaned forward and pressed his lips against Jake's in a chaste kiss. "Right now you need to work on being Jake Carson again. I understand that completely. And I'll stand by your side on this journey if you want me there. I've waited all these years to have you back, and I'll be honest, even if sex is never on the table, I'll *still* want you."

Jake smirked. "Sex on the table? Got some kinky fantasies going on there, Doc?"

He laughed. "And there you go with that smokescreen again. The only fantasy I have right now is of living the rest of my life with you. That's all I want. The rest is merely icing on the cake."

"Huh. First tables, now icing." Jake managed a grin. "I like the way you think." Before Nicholas could utter another word, Jake laid a single finger on his lips. "The humor helps, okay? It's a coping mechanism. And I love the idea of weathering this storm with you at my side. Because I get the feeling I'm about to sail into a shitstorm of epic proportions, and I'm going to need a port to come home to. I need *you*."

Nicholas squeezed his hand. "You've got me. I'll do whatever it takes to be there for you."

Jake swallowed. "Would that include giving up your single bed in the basement and moving into my room? At least while you're here. I don't want to sleep alone. And I think having your arms around me might quell some of the nightmares."

Nicholas grinned. "I'm going downstairs now to shove all my stuff into my bag and bring it to your room."

Jake had to smile. "You really like that idea, huh?"

He chuckled. "What gave it away?"

"You know what else is going to take some time? Catching up with the world. When I was first captured, phones were things that plugged into a wall, or else you found them in a phone booth on the street corner. I was gazing around the table this evening, and everyone has a cell phone. I mean, *everyone*. And as for the internet...." He shook his head. "What else have they come up with?"

Nicholas chuckled. "If you think that's impressive, wait until you see the new sex toys. Remote controls and everything." Jake stared at him, and he laughed. "And no, that isn't a joke. I could put something in your ass and with a touch on my phone, I could have it vibrating even if I was in a different state. Or on a different continent."

Jake was on another planet. It was the only explanation.

Nicholas chuckled once more. "So many things you need to learn about.... You missed the first Fleshlights, for one thing." Jake gave him an inquiring glance, and Nicholas waved his hand. "Don't worry about it now. I'll show you. I have one. And then there's the Magic Wand."

"That gizmo for massaging aching muscles?" Miranda had bought one for him.

Nicholas roared. "Oh, sweetheart, you really *do* have some catching up to do."

Jake smiled. "Sweetheart. I like that."

He could cope with everything this brave new world had to throw at him—as long as he had his family and Nicholas.

Don't forget. Somewhere out there, we have another mate.

Hearing Nicholas inside his head was easier to accept than the idea of a remote-controlled sex toy. Then a thought occurred to him.

"What if our mate is a she? Would you be okay with that?"

Nicholas smiled. "Why don't you ask Crank that question? Because while Roadkill—or maybe it was Hashtag—might have dubbed him the gayest straight guy ever, he'd never considered being in a gay relationship until he discovered Saul and Vic were his mates. And what's he like now? As the younger generation is fond of saying, he's totally loved up. So to answer your question, yes, I'd be okay with that. Because she would be our mate, and I can't believe some higher power would bring us together if there was even the merest possibility that we wouldn't be compatible." He rubbed his thumb in slow circles on the back of Jake's hand. "The same higher power that gave you your gifts for a reason." He looked Jake in the eye. "I also believe it's no coincidence we freed you at this point in time. You're supposed to be here. You have a very important task to perform, one that might change the course of shifter history."

The hairs on the back of Jake's neck stood to attention, and his arms prickled into a carpet of goose bumps. He couldn't argue that point.

Not when he'd had the same thought.

"Hey, you two. Can you come inside for a minute?" Dellan hollered from the French doors.

Nicholas held on to Jake's hand. "Let's go spend some time with our new family." He chuckled. "Funny how things turn out. I've been alone all these years, and now I have a mate, and by extension three stepsons and *their* mates." He led Jake into the kitchen—

"Surprise! Happy birthday, Doc!"

There was the *crack* of party poppers, a cacophony of noisemakers, and suddenly there was glitter everywhere. On the table sat a cake, and even though Jake had told Mrs. Landon what he wanted, he had to laugh when he saw it so well executed.

Nicholas guffawed. "It's an elephant wearing a party hat." Draped over its back was a banner bearing the words 60 TODAY. He turned to Jake, his eyes shining. "This is your doing."

Jake gave him as innocent a stare as he could manage. "Whatever gave you that idea?" He peered at the flickering candles and fanned himself. "Whoa. You could heat the whole house with those. Better blow them out fast before they burn the place down."

Nicholas placed his hands on the table and leaned forward.

"Make a wish!" Seth yelled.

He closed his eyes for a second, then blew out every single candle.

Horvan cheered. "Way to go, Doc. Amazing breath control." Dellan dug him in the ribs with his elbow, and Horvan blinked. "What did I say?"

Jake chuckled. "I think it's more a case of what Dellan didn't want you to say."

Any retort Horvan had planned was lost in the pop of champagne corks, and Dellan and Rael busied themselves filling glasses. When everyone had one, Dellan gave Jake a nod.

Jake raised his glass. "They say elephants can remember. So raise your glasses and join me in a toast to the man who not only remembered me, but also never forgot that he loved me." He locked gazes with Nicholas. "Happy birthday, Doc."

His words echoed around the kitchen, and there followed the sound of clinking glass. Jake took a sip, pleasantly surprised by its smoothness and flavor.

Nicholas picked up the cake knife from the table and gently tapped his glass. The room fell silent as he raised it.

"Thank you all for your kind wishes, and for helping me celebrate a day that… well, to be honest, I'd almost forgotten about. I also have a toast, but it has nothing to do with my birthday." He cleared his throat. "Let us drink to all our tomorrows. May each one be better than the previous, and may all our efforts be rewarded with success."

For a moment nobody spoke, and Jake noticed tears in the eyes of more than one of those people gathered around the large table. Everyone took a drink in silence.

Jake pointed to the cake. "And now you need to cut it."

Nicholas's eyes twinkled. "Only if you cut it with me."

Crank snickered. "Watch it, Jake. He'll be bringing out a ring box next and getting down on one knee," he quipped.

Jake opened his mouth to reply, but Nicholas got in there first.

"Two things about that. At my age, you only go down on one knee if you've dropped something and you're looking for it, because while getting down is easy enough, getting back up again takes more effort." He snickered. "And sometimes by the time you get down there, you've forgotten why the hell you were kneeling in the first place." Laughter ensued.

"What's the second thing?" Saul asked.

"I don't have a ring for Jake because I've already given him something more valuable and much more significant." He gazed at Jake. "My heart."

That was all it took to bring on Jake's tears. He put down his glass, Nicholas did the same, and they clung to each other while their friends and family patted them, cheered, whooped, and hollered.

Jake caught sight of Dellan's tear-streaked cheeks, and he smiled.

You're happy for me, right?

Dellan beamed. *As if you have to ask.*

It didn't matter that there was the possibility of danger awaiting them around the very next corner. That they were about to face a Geran who had the potential to be the greatest menace they'd ever faced, and in his own stronghold too.

We have the strongest weapon imaginable. We have love.

Nicholas tightened his arms around Jake.

Let's hope it's enough.

Chapter Eight

Eve lay in the darkened bedroom, listening to the cute sounds Hashtag and Roadkill made while they slept on either side of her. So far, sleep had proved elusive, and she had a good idea what lay at the root of her insomnia.

I need to tell them.

She'd been on the brink of sharing with them that afternoon, until Roadkill had gotten the idea of him and Hashtag skinny-dipping and roughhousing in the lake before dinner. Eve had been content to sit on the grassy bank, watching them and laughing her ass off.

There'll be another time.

Except with a mission looming in the UK, there really was no time like the present.

I still can't believe how my life has changed so drastically, and for the better.

Not everything was sunshine and roses, however. There were the nightmares to contend with, except she was careful not to let Hashtag and Roadkill anywhere near those. Hellish dreams where she was still a Geran officer, watching her military buddies stepping over the broken and bleeding bodies of the two men she loved.

It could have ended up like that if she hadn't learned the truth. Her mates could have died, and she would have walked over their corpses in order to spread Geran lies through violence. True, she'd already turned her back on all that by the time she met them, but that didn't quell the nagging feelings of what could have been.

And because of one decision to help the Fridans, everything had changed.

A far brighter future loomed in front of her, one where two men would do her bidding in the bedroom, and outside of it they would trust her to be strong enough not to need their help, but she'd still be grateful it would be there if she ever required it.

There was still one hurdle to overcome.

She hadn't known Roadkill and Hashtag all that long, so she had no idea if their masculinity would feel bruised when they discovered the truth. Eve had read a lot on the subject and knew being the breadwinner was central to many men's sense of self. Her experience of Geran males had shown her the mere thought of a woman breadwinning caused such a psychological burden for them that they would prefer women not to be employed at all. The old stereotype of keeping women barefoot and pregnant, chained to the stove, could have been written with Gerans in mind.

But Hashtag and Roadkill aren't like that. We're all soldiers. We're paid the same. We fight together. We're equal.

Except she knew her secret might change that perception.

"If you don't turn your brain off and go to sleep, I may have to spank you," Roadkill muttered.

Eve jumped. "Did I wake you up?"

Please, tell me you didn't see too far into my head.

"I wasn't enjoying my dream, so I woke myself up." He pulled her to him. "God, you smell good." He stroked down her arm. "Love the way your skin feels."

"Hey, no fair. Feeling left out here." Hashtag curled around her, and there she was, sandwiched between two hard bodies.

Getting harder by the second.

Eve sat up. "I'm going downstairs to make some hot chocolate." If she spent a moment longer in bed, she knew exactly what would happen, and while making love with them would provide a welcome distraction, it would only be putting off the inevitable.

Roadkill caught her hand. "We're coming too." He snapped on the bedside lamp.

"We are?" Hashtag exclaimed, rubbing his eyes.

He nodded. "And we're not coming back to bed until Eve has told us whatever it is she hasn't told us yet."

Hashtag blinked. "I think I must still be asleep, because that made no sense at all."

She should have known better than to keep it from them. "You're right. We need to talk." Roadkill passed her the silky apricot-colored robe he'd bought for her, and she slipped it on. They crept down the wooden staircase, as quiet as mice, and into the large kitchen that managed to feel homey.

Hashtag opened the refrigerator and grinned. "Leftover hamburgers and mozzarella sticks. Midnight snack time."

Roadkill rolled his eyes. "You're supposed to be handing me the hot chocolate, not feeding your tape worm."

And there's my cue.

"I can't wait for this mission," she said nonchalantly. "The first thing I'll do when I get you two to England is to feed you some proper food."

"What's wrong with hamburgers and mozzarella sticks?" Hashtag remonstrated.

Eve wrinkled her nose. "Really? When there's roast beef, Yorkshire pudding, roast potatoes…. And don't even get me started on breakfast." She grinned. "You both need some proper feeding up. I'm thinking a full English with a nice cuppa, followed by an absolutely amazing round of sex, then—"

"Wait—sex?" Roadkill's eyes gleamed. "*Psh.* I'll eat anything you want."

She smirked at him. "I'll keep that in mind." Eve swallowed. "But seriously? There's something I need to tell you before we go on the mission."

Roadkill leaned against the countertop, hot as fuck in nothing but his white shorts, hair sticking up as usual, glasses perched on the end of his nose, arms folded.

"The hot chocolate can wait."

Eve pulled out a chair and sat at the table. "You remember I told you my parents moved to the States when I was ten?" Both of them nodded. "Well, what I didn't mention was the fact that I still have a lot of relatives over in the UK. Actually most of them are in Lancashire."

Hashtag grinned. "No wonder you recognized the accent." His eyes lit up. "Oh, I get it. Do you want to visit your family when we're over there? I don't think H would mind. It might have to wait until after the—"

"Can you stop talking, please? Just for a minute or two?" She took a deep breath. "I'm sorry, but I've been building up the nerve to talk about this ever since we found each other, and it isn't easy, okay?"

Roadkill joined her at the table, Hashtag a moment later. Roadkill took her hand.

"Whatever it is, I guarantee it's not as bad as you think it's going to be."

Gods, she hoped so.

"Okay." Another calming breath. "The thing is… my grandfather's dying. And before you start commiserating? Don't. He used his home as a meeting place in the old days—for Gerans. It makes my blood run cold to think of what was discussed under that roof. But the reason I'm telling you all this? When I joined the military, Grandfather wasn't happy. He said my place was at the side of my future husband." She scowled. "I think he even had a few guys already picked out for me. I told him I wanted to serve. So he said he was going to change his will in my favor, so that when he passed, his home would belong to me. He didn't say it *implicitly*, but I think he figured I'd get a man who'd take care of the little woman and force me to stay home, waiting for my big, strong husband to save me. Thing is, I was never going to be that girl."

"Like fuck you would," Hashtag snapped. "You, my sweet thing, are a big, strong, independent woman who kicks ass and doesn't bother to take names."

Roadkill grinned. "What he said. We love you for who you are, not who you're expected to be. If we ever, and I mean *ever* act like that—"

"I'll kick your asses, promise." That earned her a laugh.

"So why are you telling us this now?" Hashtag asked.

She sighed. "My parents loved his idea. It meant they wouldn't have to worry about my future. It wasn't as if they needed the property—Mom had already inherited her parents' place. Even my brother loved the idea, because he certainly didn't want to be tied down to such a huge undertaking. I guess my grandfather intended it to be a sort of incentive for me to leave my career and become one of the ladies who lunch, who run charities, who support their husband's political campaign, who organize the tours, who—"

"Tours? What kind of tours?" Hashtag asked, his brow furrowed.

Another swallow. "Tours… of the house. People pay to visit it."

Roadkill blinked. "He's leaving you a house big enough to draw *tourists*?" He grinned. "It's not Buckingham Palace, is it?"

Eve pointed to Hashtag's laptop, which was never too far from him. "Fire that up. Then I want you to google something."

He did as instructed. "Okay. What am I searching for?"

"Gawthorpe Hall."

Keys clattered, and she knew the minute he'd found it when both men gasped in sync.

"Holy fuck!" Hashtag croaked.

"Welcome to my ancestral pile," she quipped.

"I don't think Buckingham Palace was all that far off the mark," Roadkill admitted.

"Listen to this." Hashtag read aloud. "'Gawthorpe Hall is an Elizabethan country house on the banks of the River Calder, in Ightenhill, a civil parish in the Borough of Burnley, Lancashire, England.'"

"My jaw dropped at Elizabethan." Roadkill stared at her. "And it's going to be yours?"

She nodded. "Well, more accurately, it'd be ours."

"It's got forty acres," Hashtag said with a low whistle.

Eve snorted. "It had more than that, but in 1955, the chairman of the local football team bought eighty acres of Gawthorpe land to set up a purpose-built training center."

"Oh my God, would you *look* at this place?" Hashtag sounded awed.

"I don't have to—I've seen it in real life," she told him.

"In the mid-nineteenth century," Hashtag read, "the hall was rebuilt by Charles Barry, the architect of the Houses of Parliament. Since 1953 it has been designated a Grade I listed building." He frowned. "What does that mean?"

She chuckled. "It means you can't change a damn thing about it, at least not in any way that alters the look of the place. Stuff like windows, heating...."

Hashtag slowly lowered the lid of the laptop. "I... I don't know what to say."

Her heart pounded, and her palms grew clammy.

"Well, *I* do." Roadkill grinned. "Our mate is an English heiress. Oh. My. God." He beamed. "Way to go, baby! Whatever will you do with it? It's way too big to live in."

"I haven't decided yet." Eve breathed a little easier. "Then you're okay with this?"

Hashtag gaped at her. "Hey...." He got up from his chair, walked over to her, and knelt beside her. "You were really worried about this, weren't you?"

She gave another nod.

"But why?" Roadkill demanded.

"I thought you might see me differently. Most of the men *I've* ever met would be intimidated. The rest would be drooling, like I was some kind of cash cow." She shuddered out a breath. "I should have known you two wouldn't be like them."

Hashtag kissed her. "I'll admit, I'm impressed. I can also understand that, given its history, you might not want to dirty your hands with it."

She sagged with relief. "There have been times when I'd thought seriously about razing it to the ground, except the local county council have a ninety-nine-year lease on the place, and together with the National Trust, they've forked out about half a million pounds to restore the south and west sides of the house. So I'd probably get my ass thrown in jail."

Hashtag stared at her. "And to think you sounded impressed when you got your first look at *this* house. It's probably the size of one of the garden chicken coops at Gawthorpe."

She chuckled. "I thought I sounded suitably amazed. But I'll tell you both something. There's more love within these four walls than in every inch of my grandfather's place."

"Can we go see it?" Roadkill asked. "You know, when we're over there?"

Her heartbeat quickened. "You'd like to see it?"

"Of course. It's part of your history." He cocked his head. "How long has it been in the family?"

"Oh, not all that long," she said with a shrug. "Only about four hundred years."

Their joint expressions of shock had her laughing.

Roadkill gazed at the packet of hot chocolate mix. "I feel as if we should be drinking champagne instead."

Eve wasn't in the mood for hot chocolate either.

She stood, holding out her hands. "Take me back to our bed, boys. I want to watch you two make love to each other." Eve smiled. "In fact, I want you to tire yourselves out so much that Roadkill falls asleep with his dick in your ass."

Hashtag's soft hitch told her he really liked that idea.

As they climbed the stairs, Roadkill squeezed her hand. "One thing you might want to consider...."

"Hmm?"

"Your grandfather used it for Geran purposes. Nothing to stop you using it for Fridan purposes when it's yours."

Whoever had brought the three of them together had certainly known what they were doing. Eve couldn't imagine two more perfect mates.

And we're going to need each other.

The storm that had begun with the raid in northern Maine now appeared as if it was going to develop into something far worse—with far-reaching consequences.

Chapter Nine

Roadkill gazed out over the lake, the smell of barbecue in the air accompanied by the sound of children's squeals as they played on the far side, audible even at a distance.

An ordinary summer's day.

Except, for the occupants of Dellan's house, it was anything but.

He'd had enough of waiting around to learn the details of their next mission. He'd tried to relax during the past week, like everyone else staying there, but he'd been on edge ever since Hashtag had located Theron's stronghold, and it was starting to show.

Hashtag and Eve's solution—fucking like bunnies—alleviated some of his tension, but it wasn't something they could indulge in all day long—no matter how much they wished otherwise—especially when Hashtag was spending so much time on his laptop, hooked up to the satellite.

Then he snorted. *Hashtag would try to qualify for a gold medal in fucking, given half a chance.*

Come inside.

Are you referring to the house or your ass? Roadkill chuckled. *We only fucked half an hour ago. I used to think you were insatiable. Man, you were tame compared to how you've been lately.*

Hashtag laughed. *Fine. Stay out there and miss the meeting.*

He whirled around. "What meeting?" he called out as he hurried toward the rear of the house where Hashtag stood by the French doors.

"Living room. Everyone's there." Hashtag's eyes twinkled. "We were waiting on you."

Roadkill stepped into the cool interior. "Is this it? Are we finally ready?"

Hashtag grinned. "Yup. Now kiss me before we go in."

"Why?"

He gave Roadkill a pained expression. "Do I need a reason?" Then he smiled. "Wait a minute. I have one." He closed the gap between them and stroked Roadkill's cheek. "I love you, and I need a kiss. Good enough?"

Roadkill's face was warm. "Good enough." Their lips met, and he lost himself in the intimate connection. Then Hashtag's words hit home. "That's the first time you've said it."

"Said what?"

His chest ached. "Don't do that. Don't take it back."

Hashtag locked gazes with him. "I'm sorry. I shouldn't tease." His hand was on Roadkill's neck. "I've loved you like a brother for years, you know that. We've had each other's backs more times than I care to remember. And now?" He smiled. "I love you in a totally different way, and it's… amazing." His eyes sparkled. "Plus now you have my back in a whole new way."

He caught Eve's internal groan.

I love you too, but if the pair of you don't get your asses in here, Saul is going to tear you both a new one.

Hashtag chuckled. *No thanks. The one I have is more than enough. Besides, Roadkill's still breaking it in.*

Roadkill's chuckle was pure evil. *Trust me, I plan on breaking it in for many years to… cum.*

He groaned. *I don't believe you went there.*

Can you two quit flirting and get your cute little butts in here?

Hashtag grinned. "She likes our butts."

They headed into the living room, where all Dellan's guests were squeezed into every chair, onto every couch, not to mention seated on floor cushions. Brick took up most of the small couch, with Crank sitting on its arm, but that didn't stop Aric and Seth from curling up in Brick's lap while he stroked their napes. Jake and Doc had grabbed two armchairs, and Eve stood next to the long window that looked out over the lake, Jamie at her side.

Horvan and Saul stood next to the TV screen. Dellan was perched on the coffee table, a laptop on his knee, and Rael sat on a cushion beside him.

Horvan arched his eyebrows. "Good of you to join us." He gestured to Hashtag. "Get over here."

Hashtag wove his way through the room to the front. He gave Dellan a nod, and an image filled the screen. "This is our objective—Thurland Castle, in Carnforth, Lancashire. It's set within ten acres of parkland, and yes, it has a moat." He paused. "Once we narrowed the search down to two possibilities, I contacted Milo and asked him to see what he could find out." Hashtag smiled. "This is definitely the place."

"What's the nearest airfield?" Brick asked.

"There's an airstrip in Penrith, about an hour's drive," Hashtag told him. "It's a remote location. The nearest inhabited place to it is Tunstall village, to the northwest." Another nod to Dellan. "Now I've taken a shit-ton of surveillance photos during the past week, and Aelryn sent footage taken by the drones." He pointed to the most southern point of the castle. "This is the only way in, through this archway on the other side of the moat."

"What have they got in terms of security?" Crank asked.

"I've seen guards, but not many. They walk the periphery three times a day, but that's all." Hashtag grinned. "Either Theron thinks he's impervious, or else he thinks no one knows about the place." Then he frowned. "But that presents us with a problem. We have no idea how many people are inside."

"We could've asked Fielding." Crank snorted. "Like *he* would've helped."

"But we wouldn't be where we are now if not for him—and Jake. Okay, so he didn't help us willingly." Doc's tone was grave. "Just like we wouldn't know about this place but for Seth being able to see it remotely."

"What movement have you seen?" Jake stared at the screen.

"None apart from deliveries. No one goes in, no one comes out. And before anyone suggests using the old Trojan Truck ruse again, forget it. After what happened in Maine, to quote The Who, they won't get fooled again."

Aric frowned. "The what?"

Brick leaned in. "British Rock band. Before your time. In fact, before the time of nearly everyone in here. And the only reason *I* know about them is my folks used to love them."

Jake snorted. "Careful. You're treading on my memories."

"And mine," Doc added.

Dellan shook his head. "*None* of you are going in there if we have no clue what—or who—is waiting for you."

"I agree." Horvan smiled. "But we have a plan." He glanced at Saul, who moved to stand in front of the screen.

"We're going to be working with a UK-based Fridan team, led by Aelryn. We have accommodations thanks to another Fridan leader, Richard Deveraux. Aelryn says there's plenty of space for us to use it as a base camp."

"Use *what* as a base camp?" Roadkill demanded. "Details, gimme details."

"We'll be staying at Leighton Hall. And if you think that sounds pretty grand, that's because it is. We're talking an English stately home." Horvan grinned. "You'd better be careful not to break anything, you got that?" He glanced at Saul. "Over to you."

"Once we're on the ground," Saul continued, "we delay incursion until we've sent someone in to assess the location and report back on numbers. *Then* we go in, probably the next day."

Roadkill widened his eyes. "And who exactly did you have in mind? Because getting inside will be the easy part. If they're caught, no way will Theron simply let them walk out."

"We have a plan for that too," Saul informed him. "A cover story. All we have to do is make sure Theron believes it."

Roadkill folded his arms. "Okay, but you still haven't said who."

Saul gazed at Eve, and Roadkill's initial instinct was to yell, *Absolutely not.*

"She's the perfect choice." Saul smiled. "She can sound like she belongs there. She knows what to look for. And she has an advantage—her experience with the Geran forces."

Eve glanced at Roadkill, but whatever she was thinking, she'd hidden it. *She learns fast.*

Brick gaped at Saul. "She can't go in there. They'll know who she is. And after the last mission, they'll know what she did."

"We've planned for that too," Saul announced. "And if all goes well, they *will* let her walk out of there." He met Roadkill's gaze. "Well? I'm waiting."

"For what?"

Saul smiled. "For you two to tell me you're not letting your mate stroll into the enemy's stronghold. That it's too dangerous."

Roadkill shrugged. "We don't like it. Of course we don't."

"But we trust Eve knows what she's doing," Hashtag said simply.

"And we'll be right there."

"To come running if she needs us," Hashtag concluded.

Eve grinned at Saul. "Told you."

Horvan laughed. "Well, that was easier than I anticipated." Then it was his turn to grin. "Now I *know* you're mates. The way you finish each other's sentences? Cute, guys. Like you're joined at the hip."

Eve chuckled. "Well… maybe not the hip, but definitely got some joining going on." She gave a devilish smirk. "It was kind of tight at the start, but with some patience and good lubrication, things started working much better."

Hashtag snickered. "Yeah, it's amazing what some good lube will do. And then—"

"TM freakin' *I*, guys," Horvan growled.

"Oh, *I* get it." Hashtag glared at him. "*You* can tell everyone you meet about my awesome tongue action—"

"Which it *totally* is," Roadkill interjected. He beamed. "Having been on the receiving end. H, you weren't kidd—"

Hashtag glared. "Dude?" He returned his gaze to Horvan. "As I was saying…. *You* can share about *me*, but I'm not allowed to share about my mates? And while we're on the subject—" Hashtag gave Horvan a pained stare. "—cute? Really?"

"Excuse me?" Horvan gaped at Hashtag. "It might have escaped your attention, but we've got a meeting going on in here. So if you'll let me continue…." He folded his arms. "Okay, this mission has three objectives: Rescue Vic, get Alec out of there, and find out exactly what Theron is hiding in that room." He inclined his head toward Jake. "That last part will be down to Jake, along with Luciano Orsini, the archivist. Aelryn is bringing him from Rome to the UK."

"I'm going too," Seth declared.

Judging by the lack of an argument from Brick and Aric, this wasn't news to them.

"So am I, but I'll be there strictly to oversee Alec's removal from that place." Doc's face was as serious as his voice. "But can I add a note of caution? From what Seth told us, Alec has aged since Saul first encountered him. That doesn't bode well. For all we know, he could appear older than his father by now. We know the Gerans tinkered with his DNA to speed up the aging process—and to bring about the mutation in his hands. What we *don't* know is if they've been able to halt the aging process. I think we must be prepared for the worst possible outcome."

Dellan said nothing, so Roadkill guessed this wasn't news either.

"I suppose you're going to leave me here." Aric sounded glum. "Especially with my track record."

Horvan studied him. "I don't know about that. As a kitty, you might be able to help us. You can get into spaces none of us can."

Aric jerked his head in Brick's direction, and Brick laughed. "You think H would've said that if we hadn't already discussed it? You're good to go, spy kitty."

Aric's face brightened. "Spy kitty. Yeah, I like the sound of that." Seth kissed his cheek, and he flushed. "Yay. I get to be useful."

Brick sucked in a deep breath, and Roadkill's scalp prickled.

Uh-oh.

"H? After we're done with all this? I'm out." Brick's tone was even, his breathing too, but Roadkill noted how he tightened his grip on Aric's hand. "My parents left me enough that I won't have to work for a while, so I'm going to get to know my mates properly." He shrugged. "Can't do that if I'm running all over the place while they're at home worrying, now can I?" He glanced at Seth. "I know you want to work in intelligence, so I guess we're gonna be having a few *high-level discussions* in the not-too-distant future."

Seth leaned into him. "Let's see how this mission goes, all right? I think we need to play this by ear."

Horvan gave them a warm smile. "Brick, you're a lucky man, you know that? Your mates are amazing." Then he sighed. "I figured this was coming, and I don't blame you. Thanks for letting me know." He swept his gaze around the room. "Okay, that's it. Now for the bad news. We leave tonight for the UK." He peered at the clock over the fireplace. "In about eight hours, to be exact. Transportation is arranged, so you need to go pack, then either chill or get a few hours' sleep." He gave Hashtag and Roadkill a mock glare. "Please note, I said *sleep*."

Hashtag grinned. "Oh, I heard ya." He glanced at Roadkill. *We'll need to keep the noise down.*

Across the room, Eve grinned at Roadkill. *Time for the ball-gag, I think.*

Roadkill returned her grin. *I like the way you think.* Then his thoughts slipped into a far more serious groove, and he locked them out of sight from Hashtag and Eve.

Some things needed to be kept hidden.

In the past, his military superiors had always known how much pre-mission fucking went on, but as long as the men were ready for action when the time arrived, they turned a blind eye. Roadkill had played the "but I might not be coming back" card more times than he cared to remember, and it had always earned him a hot night between the sheets.

Now? Everything had changed. Their mate was going to walk into the lion's den, and while he acted cool about that, Roadkill had no idea what Saul's plan comprised.

He was praying Eve—and a little kitty—walked out of there unharmed.

Chapter Ten

Hashtag peered through the windshield at the dismal gray clouds.

"Isn't this supposed to be summer?" The military vehicle sped along winding country lanes, the driving cab open to the back, where the team sat on two benches facing each other.

Next to him, Eve laughed. "Yes, but you know what they say about weather in the UK?"

"Wear layers? Forget sunscreen?" Crank cackled behind them. "Don't believe the weather reports?"

"They get four seasons in one day over here. You watch," she said, her voice ringing with confidence. "The sun will be out later."

Hashtag stared at the thick layer of clouds. "If you say so."

At the wheel, Roadkill chuckled. "Never mind the weather. You've got much more important shit to worry about. You're gonna be our eye in the sky, remember?"

"And *you've* got important shit to worry about too," Hashtag said, "such as making sure you're on the proper side of the street. They drive funny over here, remember? Keep your eyes on the road ahead."

"They do? Gee, I didn't know that." Roadkill rolled his eyes. He turned on the windshield wipers as heavy drops of rain splattered against the glass. "Now see what you did."

Hashtag rolled his eyes. "Oh, *I* see. The rain is *my* fault for daring to mention the crappy British weather." He glanced at Eve. "No offense."

"None taken. I haven't lived here in years."

"Sure you can still sound like a Brit?" Crank asked. "Or an even bigger challenge—a Brit from around here."

Eve said nothing for a moment, then smirked. "Will you stop mithering? Shut your cakehole an' stop harpin' on about t'weather. Anyone would think it were cowd out there. It'll be crackin' flags by two o'clock."

Stunned silence.

Hashtag twisted to take a look at Crank. "You okay back there?"

Crank blinked. "I think I understood about half of what she said. And that's only because they're normal English words."

Eve preened. "I've still got it." She blew on her nails and buffed them on her jacket.

"Wait—you mean we don't get a translation?" The passengers in Roadkill's truck burst out laughing, and Crank tore his attention away from the road ahead to stare at them. "Well, don't tell me *you* understood it either." More laughter ensued. He tapped Eve on the shoulder. "You made all that up, didn't you?"

She grinned. "Okay, Lancashire 101. 'Mithering' means complaining. Your 'cakehole' is your mouth, 'harping on' means going on and on about something, 'cowd' is how they say cold around here, and 'cracking flags' means it's going to be hot." She arched her eyebrows. "Want to hear more?"

"I think I've heard enough to know English is weird. Plus I can't be certain, but I think you broke my brain." That raised an even bigger laugh.

Hashtag appreciated the levity. Anything to take his mind off the upcoming mission.

Eve's hand was on his thigh. *Stop it.*

He sighed. *I really need to practice hiding stuff from you.*

I'm going to be fine.

He wasn't going to relax until he saw her walking back across that bridge, hale, hearty, and triumphant.

And definitely alive.

Eve snorted. *If I'm walking anywhere, it's a safe bet I'm alive.*

You know what I mean.

She squeezed his thigh. *Yes, I do.*

His phone buzzed, and he glanced at the screen.

Are we nearly there yet?

Hashtag laughed. "Horvan's trying to be funny." He typed. *Just follow the lead dog. We'll get you there.* Him and the other two trucks filled with the rest of the team.

Not that he had any idea where Leighton Hall was. Roadkill was the one with the map in his head.

ROADKILL STOOD in the doorway to Leighton Hall, staring out across rolling parkland. "This place is awesome. I can see for miles, and there's nothing out there." He squinted. "Except for some grayish-white blobs way over there." He froze. "I don't wanna worry anyone, but those grayish-white blobs I mentioned a second ago? They're moving."

Beside him, Horvan chuckled. "That's because they're sheep. And you're right. This place is awesome. Did you see the banqueting hall? I wanna walk through there with my elbows tucked in, in case I break anything historic. And these gardens are amazing." His breathing hitched, and he pointed to one of the stone pillars that framed the steps leading to the garden. "Do you see him? Of course, it could be a her."

"What are you talking—oh my God, would you look at that?"

A hawk sat on the pillar, its rich brown wings folded back, its long black tail feathers tipped with white as if it had dipped them in a can of paint. Roadkill imagined its curved yellow beak would make short work of a hot mouse lunch. And as for those bright eyes....

"I'm glad I'm not a mouse," Roadkill muttered.

Horvan was on his phone, scrolling. "It's a Harris hawk. Isn't it beautiful?" Then the hawk took off from its perch, heading their way. It landed on the ground in front of them, peering at them intently.

It was Roadkill's turn to catch his breath. "Either I'm paranoid, or that hawk is paying us way too much attention."

"That would be because you're standing in his doorway," Aelryn murmured behind them.

Roadkill didn't need to turn around to know Aelryn was smiling.

"*His* doorway?" He watched as the hawk took several bouncing steps toward them. He paused, and Roadkill stood aside quickly. "Sorry if I'm in your way."

The hawk bounced past them and entered the hall.

Aelryn smiled. "That was Richard Deveraux. This is his house. He's one of my most trusted leaders, and I'm grateful to him for offering us this space during this mission." He pointed to the thick green canopy to the east. "All this land belongs to him. You'll meet him later, at dinner." He touched Horvan's arm. "Can we talk?"

"Sure." Horvan gave Roadkill a smile. "Watch out for the sheep in case they decide to gang up on you."

"Is that likely? Do they carry flick knives or something?"

Horvan's eyes twinkled. "No knives, but they're all *baaaad* boys and girls."

Roadkill groaned. "Doing impressions of sheep now? Wow. There's no beginning to your talents."

Horvan was still chuckling as he walked back inside.

Roadkill strolled across the courtyard and down the stone steps to the meticulously laid-out gardens. Eve had said Leighton Hall dated back to the thirteenth century, and seeing its gray stone walls topped with crenelations, as if it was a castle, he could imagine battles being fought beneath its battlements, bloodcurdling cries rending the air, the *thud* of horses' hooves....

You always wanted to be one of King Arthur's knights, didn't you?

He laughed as Eve joined him. "Jousting sounds as if it was fun."

"Sure," Hashtag commented as he followed Eve. "You'd probably have gotten yourself run through with a lance. Mind you, you're the right size to fit into one of the suits of armor I saw in the hallway leading to the banqueting hall. They weren't big guys by the look of it."

Eve linked arms with both of them, and they ambled along the path, flower beds on either side. "I asked Saul if I could wear a tiny camera when I go into Theron's place."

Hashtag chuckled. "Confess. You always wanted to be James Bond. Or should that be Jane Bond?"

She grinned. "A spy? Sure. Who wouldn't want that? All those little gadgets...."

He shrugged. "We can do that. God knows we have the tech. But I don't think we should. They could be on high alert, for all we know."

"They'd better not be," she muttered.

He glanced at her. "Got your story straight?"

Eve's smile oozed her customary confidence. "Yup."

Roadkill loved that about her.

"You know we'll be listening. If you get into trouble—"

"What? You'll wade in there? You'll send in the marines? No. You stick to the plan. Thank you for worrying, really, but I'll be fine." She pursed her lips. "It's weird, you know? No one ever wondered if I'd be okay during a mission. Sure, they wanted me to make it out alive because that's how they'd get their information, but it was never about me." She smiled at them. "It feels good knowing you care."

Hashtag hugged her. "You are one awesome lady."

Eve bit her lip, and Roadkill stilled. He knew the signs. "What's on your mind?"

"When this mission is over, we need to have a conversation."

Hashtag's brow furrowed. "That sounds kinda serious."

"Because it is." Eve sat on a low stone wall, a sea of roses behind her, their subtle perfume carrying on the breeze. They perched on either side of her, Roadkill aware of Hashtag's heartbeat racing like his own.

"I'm assuming the day will come when you'll want to put your feet up," she began.

Roadkill blinked. "Retire, you mean? Sure, I've thought about it."

"Same here," Hashtag added.

"Well, maybe we should all think about it sooner rather than later." She paused. "If we're going to have kids."

Roadkill and Hashtag's voice rang out in unison. "Kids?"

"I figured I had to bring it up sooner or later."

Hashtag regarded her with interest. "You want kids?"

She shrugged. "I'm simply putting it out there as a possibility. Sure, I've thought about it quite a bit—lately." Eve bit her lip, and Roadkill found that adorable.

You think she's one thing, and then she goes and turns everything you thought on its head.

"Tell us what you feel," he urged.

"Honestly? I'm torn. I mean, I love my life the way it is. I really do. I love being able to wade into a fight and knock heads together."

Hashtag chuckled. "Yeah, I've noticed that about you."

Eve's smile was pure sunshine as she leaned into him. "But then again, I also love the idea of sitting in front of a fireplace, babies in my lap, while my mates rub my feet or back, and I'm there, content, with the kids sleeping against my chest." She sighed. "Is it wrong to want that?"

Roadkill kissed her cheek. "Nothing you want could be wrong."

She frowned. "Well, it is if my mates don't feel the same way. So I guess this is where I ask the million-dollar question. *Do* you?"

He peered at Hashtag, who stared at the flowers.

"I'll be honest, I never thought of having kids. I figured I'd be dead long before it ever became a thing. But then again, I also never considered I'd have what I do now." He met Roadkill's gaze. "For the first time in my life, I can actually see a future unfurling before me." Hashtag cocked his head. "What about you?"

Roadkill huffed. "If you'd asked me a couple of years ago, I'd have told you kids weren't part of the equation. But now?" He gave a shrug. "I'm not the same man anymore. And yeah, *this* man kinda likes the idea of tiny Hashtags and Eves clinging to my ankles."

Hashtag grinned. "Looking at the size of you, any offspring *you* produce? Yeah, we're *really* talking tiny."

Roadkill gave him the finger.

"Don't get me wrong. I haven't always felt like this," Eve told them. "When I was younger, I was dead set against motherhood."

"Any reason why?" Roadkill asked.

She flung out her arm. "Because it was what was *expected* of me. I wasn't supposed to join the military, remember? It was decided—without the slightest bit of input from me—that my role was to stay home and care for the kids. And honestly, I would have been okay with that if I'd been consulted, but I wasn't, and that bugged the hell out of me. I mean, really? This was *my* future they were planning. So I chose my own route, because I figured it would piss off my family. I was determined to show them I wasn't *just* a woman."

Hashtag gazed at her with affection. "You're not *just* anything. Never were, never will be."

"Are you enjoying my gardens?"

Roadkill turned to find a slight man with longish brown hair and the most stunning eyes he'd ever seen, bronze-green, bright, and alive with intelligence. "Mr. Deveraux? Unless you have a title, and if that's the case, my apologies, but no one has mentioned it."

"Yes, I do, but I don't use it." Deveraux smiled. "Which is why no one has mentioned it. And please, call me Richard. I'm happy to be of help." His gaze alighted on Eve, and he stilled. "And who are you?"

"Eve Duncan, our mate," Roadkill blurted.

Richard beamed. "Then I am delighted to meet the three of you. I dream of finding my mate."

Eve chuckled. "Be careful what you wish for. They seem to come in threes."

He laughed. "Even better. Are you comfortable in your rooms? Do you need anything?"

"You have a wonderful home, and we've got everything we could want," Hashtag affirmed.

"Then I'll leave you to enjoy the sunshine and the peace—while we have it." His eyes sparkled. "You never know how long it will last around here."

From someplace nearby, a riot of voices shattered the tranquility of the scene.

"Oh my God, you're being invaded," Hashtag gasped.

Richard laughed. "You're right, and most of the invaders aren't even four feet high."

"I *warned* H about those sheep," Hashtag remonstrated.

"It's the children from the local orphanage. They come here often to play in the open air, to run around where there's plenty of space, to help out on the farm." He pointed to the left. "Part of Leighton Hall is a farm with chickens, goats, pigs, horses...." Richard's face fell. "Life has given these children a rough start, so I try to give them some pleasant moments. One of the barns has been turned into sleeping quarters, and they love to come here on trips."

"You're a good man," Eve said in an earnest tone.

Richard flushed. "If any of you were in my position, I'm sure you'd do the same." He gave them a nod, then headed back into the hall.

"Nice man," Hashtag murmured.

Roadkill arched his eyebrows. "Nice as in merely *nice*—or as in, he's a good-looking dude?"

Eve gave a mock gasp. "I'm seeing a whole new side to you today."

"Me too." To Roadkill's surprise, Hashtag stood, hauled him to his feet, and kissed him, a no-holds-barred, toe-curling kinda kiss that sent heat surging through him.

To quote a song, I only have eyes for you—two! Hashtag added hurriedly.

Roadkill was too busy enjoying Hashtag's lips locked on his.

Care to make this a three-way kiss? Eve put her arms around them.

Only if we take this up to our room. Roadkill didn't want sheep for an audience.

"Making love in a four-poster bed? What a hardship. But I guess I can put up with it for a few days," Hashtag quipped. They walked toward the steps leading out of the garden.

Eve's phone buzzed, and she pulled it from her jeans pocket. She came to a dead stop.

"Something's wrong." Roadkill's senses went on high alert.

"Not *wrong*, exactly." Eve sighed. "It's a message from my dad. My grandfather died an hour ago."

"Does his death change anything?" Hashtag asked.

Her face tightened. "I'm sorry he's dead. I do have *some* pleasant memories of him, but they're overshadowed by what he stood for—or rather, who he stood with. As for what it changes?" She let out another sigh. "My future has a few more options, thanks to him." She linked their arms. "Would you mind if we just got into bed and cuddled?"

Roadkill kissed her soft hair. "We can do whatever you want."

Anything not to think about Eve walking into Thurland Castle.

"WE SHOULDN'T be doing this." Brick couldn't fight the feeling that he should be preparing for the incursion, checking his weapons, instead of lying in a gloriously comfortable bed, his mates curled up on either side of him.

"Yes, we should," Aric declared in a decisive tone. "Tomorrow's gonna come soon enough. Let's make the most of this." He gazed at the rich red velvet curtains hanging from the corners of the bed. "Talk about how the other half lives. I feel like I'm in a historical drama."

Seth chuckled. "I know. This is so wild. I love it."

Brick stroked Aric's back. "Are you sure you're okay with what I said the other day? About retiring?"

The glance Aric gave Seth told him there was a conversation coming.

"About that...." Seth sighed and leaned against Brick. "I know you told Horvan you want to retire, but, well, maybe think about it some more?"

He should have realized it wasn't as cut-and-dried as he'd thought.

"Why, baby? Don't you want me to be home with the two of you?"

Seth kissed him on the lips. "More than you know, but.... Okay, when you dream? Sometimes I see it."

Aw fuck.

"Your heart says you want to quit and stay home," Seth continued, "but I know that's not you." He smiled. "You're built to save the world, or at least people in it. Like you did for me and Aric. The thought that someone out there could be hurt or worse because you're not out there fighting for them? It kind of bothers me."

Somewhere deep in the recesses of Brick's soul, it bothered him too. "So what are you saying?"

Seth reached over him and took Aric's hand. "We talked. You *say* you want to quit, but neither of us truly believes your heart is in it. You're doing it because you think it's the right thing for us." Both of them snuggled against him. "But we can make it work no matter what you decide."

"Don't think I don't love the idea of you being a stay-at-home bear, because I do," Aric added.

Seth leaned over and kissed him. "That's because you're a stay-at-home kitty." He pressed his lips to Brick's chest, brushing them over his nipple. "But wherever we lay down some roots, we'll need a place near space where I can shift."

"We can do that." Brick shivered when Seth tugged on his nipple, and it sent ripples of pleasure all the way to his dick.

Seth chuckled once more. "Ooh, you like that."

"Can we be serious for another minute?" Lord knew the pair of them could distract him in a heartbeat.

"Of course." Seth sat up. "What's on your mind?"

"I just wanted to make sure Aric was okay about shifting and going into the castle."

Aric blinked. "It was your idea. Of course I'm okay with it. And I'll be fine. I'll be your everyday moggy, strolling through the hallways, hunting for mice."

"Moggy?" Brick frowned.

Aric laughed. "I got that from Eve. It's British slang for a cat." Then he slipped his hand around Brick's hardening cock. "And *this* moggy wants to take a ride."

Brick shivered at the thought of thrusting up into Aric's tight body.

"And while he keeps your dick busy...." Seth shuffled across the bed and straddled Brick's head. "*I'll* keep your tongue occupied." He grinned. "Can polar bears multitask?"

Brick was going to give it a damn good try.

Yeah, I could be knee-deep in preparations for the mission, but right now being balls-deep in my mates is more important.

There was always a shadow that hung over missions, a cloud of uncertainty about the outcome. And while it might *not* be his last mission, he was going to make sure he came out of it alive.

Chapter Eleven

EVE KNEW she wasn't walking into Thurland Castle naked. Okay, so she had no tech so the team could listen in, but she had Hashtag and Roadkill to relay everything Theron said.

That's if he'll see me.

Hashtag's voice was warm. *He'll see you, honey. But remember, stick to the story.*

She walked at a brisk pace along the road that led to the castle. Before she reached the imposing gray stone archway across the moat, she paused at the statues of two lions that flanked her way. She patted the head of one of them.

For luck, okay?

Eve hadn't been worried about this part of the mission, but she'd woken up with an unexpected case of the jitters.

This could all go horribly wrong.

She shoved the thought from her mind. Negative thinking was *not* going to help the situation. She marched up to the gateway, shoulders squared, back straight as she crossed the moat.

It's a beck. Give it its proper name, Roadkill quipped.

And who taught you that? Eve demanded. *Now is* not *the time for a geography lesson.* Then she caught herself and realized what she had just done. *I'm sorry. I guess I'm really nervous.*

We're always with you, Hashtag reminded her.

That helped calm the tremors. She shoved the thoughts from her mind once more and did her best to breathe evenly. A guard appeared, and she knew from the bulge in his jacket that he was armed.

"Can I help you? The castle isn't open to the public."

One sniff told her the guy was a shifter, and Eve recognized the moment he got a whiff of her.

"I'd like to see Theron, please."

The guard blinked. "There's no one here by that name."

She smiled. "I think we both know that's not true. So let's cut to the chase. Call the castle and tell Theron I was with Fielding when he died. Trust me, he'll want to see me."

The guard gave her a doubtful glance. "What's your name?"

"Eve Duncan."

"Wait here." He stepped out of sight, and Eve's stomach chose that moment to start churning.

What if he doesn't take the bait?

He will, Roadkill assured her. *His curiosity will get the better of him. You'll see.*

You know what they say about curiosity. It killed the cat. Is it too much to hope he's a kitty shifter?

The guard reappeared. "Follow me."

See? Worrying about nothing.

Eve wished she had half of Hashtag's confidence in that moment. Her own seemed to have packed its bags and gotten the fuck out of there.

She walked behind the guard into the large courtyard, the castle rising up before her, the main door to her right beneath a huge stone arch. She glanced at the smaller buildings around the yard, searching for signs that one of them was used as a barracks. She saw only two guards standing several feet away from the door, relaxed enough to be on their phones.

The guard in front pushed open the heavy door, and she stepped inside. The castle's interior was cool enough to chill the perspiration that had popped out on her brow. She followed the guard, crossing the worn stone flags that comprised the floor, the walls covered in oak panels adorned with shields, portraits, and the occasional head of a deer.

Nice. Cozy.

I think it needs swords on the walls. Suits of armor. An instrument of torture or two.

Eve mentally rolled her eyes. *Guys? Please?*

She needed all her wits about her right then. Going in there distracted was a surefire way to end up dead.

"In there." The guard pointed to a wide oak door.

Conversation isn't one of his strengths, is it? That was Roadkill.

Eve gave a snort. *I don't think he's here to indulge in small talk.*

She took stock of her surroundings, searching for something that could be used as a weapon if things went to hell. One of those swords Hashtag had mentioned, for example. Even a heavy vase would do in a pinch.

A stone fireplace dominated the room, and on either side were two heavily carved chairs, their wood dark and glossy from many years of care. The space was stuffed with furniture, none of it appearing remotely comfortable, especially the high-backed chairs beneath the leaded windows. An octagonal table stood in the center, its surface inlaid with warm veneers. Two dark green couches faced the fire, but again Eve doubted anyone ever sat on them. It was a cluttered room, claustrophobic despite its size, and she got the feeling nothing she was seeing had anything to do with the present owner.

"Eve Duncan. Served in our military from 2015 until six months ago, when you quit, supposedly to start a family." The words sounded as though they were accompanied by a sneer.

She turned. *Here we go.*

Theron was shorter than her, and so much older. He wore a suit, which kind of surprised her.

What was I expecting? Robes?

His bald head gleamed in the lamplight that caught in the white of his beard. Many lines crossed his brow, but what drew the attention were his eyes.

There were as cold as stone.

Then his gaze raked her body. He smirked, and Eve had to fight to hide the disgust that swamped her.

"Gorilla shifter, aren't you?"

"Yes, sir." She was grateful—and surprised—that her voice came out strong. Behind Theron, a guard stood at the door.

"And why would you leave for such a reason when you could have been part of the breeding program? With your strength, you could give us many powerful babies."

Fuck. She wanted to shift and rip into him right then and there. "Because at the time it was suggested that I be part of it, I preferred being on the front lines." The coldness of her tone matched his.

He shook his head. "Women are supposed to do as they're told."

She narrowed her eyes. "I managed to distinguish myself. Surely that's in my records too."

Theron waved a hand. "Whatever."

"But the reason I really left was—"

"Silence." Without breaking eye contact, he called out, "Bring him."

"Yes, sir." And then the guard was gone, leaving her alone with Theron.

A cold trickle of sweat slid down Eve's back. *What the hell are they up to? And how am I supposed to convince him if he won't even let me speak?*

Theron regarded her in silence, and she did her best to return his stare, back straight, shoulders squared.

I could take him out. End it right here.

We might need him. And you have no idea of the forces he keeps around him. Hashtag's voice was gentle. *You've got this, okay?*

A few moments later, the guard returned, followed by a huge man. One glance at his face told Eve he'd been in plenty of fights, some of them recent, judging by the bruises, not to mention a mélange of scars that made her think his face had been hamburger at some point.

Theron pointed a bony finger at Eve. "She will be your opponent. Do what you have to in order to win."

The hulking guy smiled at her, showing several missing teeth. "Of course, sir." He turned his head toward Theron. "Same deal?"

"Yes, yes," Theron replied with a touch of impatience. "Win, and your family will receive food and medicine. Lose, and they will suffer."

"I will not lose," the man vowed, his accent thick. Eve couldn't figure out where he was from, however.

Sounds Russian, Hashtag observed. *Or somewhere in that area.*

"Take her to the courtyard," Theron instructed. "The guards will be on standby. And I shall be watching."

Disgust seized her once more, tightening her throat. *They're forcing him to fight so his family would be cared for? That really sucks.* The guys had told her about Brick's parents, and she couldn't help wondering about this mountain on legs. *Who's to say his family is still alive?*

Then she realized she had more important things to worry about.

Like not dying.

He led her back into the courtyard that was easily the side of a football field.

Insane villainy apparently pays well.

The hulking man took a spot on one end, pointing to the other. "You stand there."

Eve had no idea what was going on, and right then she wished fervently for someone to explain the rules.

Theron appeared at an open window above that overlooked the courtyard.

"On my command you will each shift, then rush to the center to fight tooth and nail." His voice rang out in the still morning air.

As a gorilla she had an advantage. Or so she thought until the guy stripped down, revealing an ocean of muscles. Whatever he was, it was going to be massive.

Eve stripped off her clothes and tossed them aside.

"Duncan."

She raised her head to stare at him.

"If Victor wins, you will become part of our breeding program, and Victor will be the first to use you." Even at a distance, she caught the gleam in Theron's eyes. "And be warned, he's quite... animalistic in his approach to mating. Trust me, you'll likely end up wishing he had killed you."

"And if *I* win?"

Theron smiled broadly. "If *you* win, I'll listen to whatever it is you came here to say."

Victor can fuck right off. She heard the loathing in Roadkill's voice.

Then Victor shifted, and a hippo faced her, solid as a rock, a wall of gray flesh.

Well, my strength will be worth zip. The only thing I've got going for me is speed. A regular gorilla would have no chance in such a fight. She'd have to rely on her training.

Use your brains. That was Hashtag.

I remember reading once about animals that could beat a hippo. One of the answers had been both amusing and scary as fuck—a gorilla with the Infinity Gauntlet. Then a line came to her, and she had to smile. *Any hypothetical one-on-one battle will be won by the hippo, unless—*

Listen to me, Roadkill interjected. *Stay out of his reach. Keep higher than he is. And go for his eyes. His vision is poor, but you need to make it nonexistent.* He groaned. *Theron isn't looking for a matchup—he wants to see a slaughter.*

What he said, Hashtag added. *But if what I'm seeing from you is accurate, the guy has been in a lot of fights, so maybe he's not that good. Maybe they're relying on his size to intimidate you.*

Then it's working, Eve affirmed. *I've never seen a man his size before.*

Told you one day we wouldn't be enough to satisfy her. She likes the big ones.

She rolled her eyes. *Hashtag, remind me when I get back to kick your ass.*

Gladly. Get out of there in one piece and I'll be happy to let you do it. Or if you'd rather, give the word, and we'll abort the mission and come running.

Of course they would. Eve knew they loved her. She felt the warmth of that love flowing through her every time they glanced her way.

Nah, I got this.

One last thing, Roadkill added. *Keep him off balance. He's huge, yes, but he's not a true hippo. His human brain is in control, so just confuse the fuck out of him and stay away from his jaws.*

"Duncan!"

It was time.

Chapter Twelve

Eve shifted, and before Victor could move, she lunged toward him, propelling herself through the air to smash into his side with her shoulder. But as she moved back to repeat the assault, Victor recovered enough to slam into her, driving her toward the nearest wall, his head crushing her against it.

Fuck, this guy is strong. If he kept this up, he'd shatter her bones, which was clearly his intention.

His eyes, remember?

His head was so massive, she could scarcely reach them. She jammed a finger in, and he roared and backed off. It took Eve a few moments to catch her breath, but Victor wasn't going to give up. He rushed her again, this time knocking her into the air. She landed hard, and Victor was on her, using his bulk to hold her down.

Get up!

Now, woman!

"Not giving up," she growled. "Not with this much at stake."

It had to be the result of the adrenaline surging through her system, because no way could she move him on her own. She was able to push him far enough to get him off her.

I can't afford to get caught like that again. If Victor got her in his jaws, it would be game over.

You're good at this, Victor. But I'm better.

She pushed off the ground and launched herself up, her body protesting every move. It wouldn't stop her, however. She landed on Victor's head and dug her nails into his eyes, which caused him to bellow and shake his head, trying to dislodge her. Except now Eve had her balance.

Victor was fucked.

She rained her fists down on his head. Victor tried to slough her off but she held on, digging her fingers into his eye sockets.

He let out a strange roar that sounded more like a big cat growling, but Eve didn't slow her attack. She stayed on his back, beating his head with her fists, delivering blow after blow until her arms ached. Blood poured from his eyes, and loud, wheezing sounds escaped his huge jaws.

When he shifted back to human, crying out for her to stop, the suddenness of the shift shocked her into stillness.

He's lost focus. You've got him where you want him. Do it, Roadkill demanded.

Except she couldn't.

Eve climbed off Victor and shifted back, panting.

Theron shook his head. "Kill him."

Eve couldn't believe her ears. Or maybe she could. He'd lost the fight, right? Victor wasn't as strong as Theron had believed, and the Gerans had no use for the weak.

She gazed at him, bloodied and battered. Yes, she could kill him, but she wasn't that person anymore.

Even if killing him would be an act of mercy?

There's always the possibility Theron will kill Victor anyway for his failure.

She knew they were both right, but she couldn't bring herself to do it. She didn't know why, but she trusted her instincts. Not to mention that quiet little voice in her head that belonged to neither of her mates.

He has a purpose too, just as you do.

"Didn't I make it clear enough?" Theron called out. "I said kill him."

Eve lifted her chin and met his cold gaze. "No, I won't. Look at him. He's an incredible and apparently loyal asset. Killing him would only weaken your position. You have his family—"

"What family?" Theron snorted. "All but his youngest sister are dead. The promise of our protection has kept him in line—until now. He's of no use to me anymore."

Eve caught Victor's strangled cry, and she *really* wanted to be the one to kill this bastard. Nothing too painful, merely rending Theron limb from limb or chewing off his face.

Tears streaked Victor's cheeks, and Eve knew they were not for his loss in the fight, but for his murdered family.

"Then use him for your breeding program. That was the hardest fight I've ever had, and losing him would be a waste." Eve turned her back on Theron, picked up her discarded clothing, and dressed. When she was done, she glanced toward the window, but he was gone.

So was Victor.

The guard returned. "He wants to see you."

Apparently, Theron's curiosity needed to be sated.

She went back into the castle to the room where she'd met Theron to find him seated on one of the ornate chairs by the fireplace.

"Now I see why you left our ranks. You fight well, but you're soft," he said with another sneer.

"I *left* because as a woman, there was little advancement possible. So I chose to prove myself in a different way. And I succeeded."

"We'll get to that part in a minute. First, I want to know about Fielding. You told the guard at the gate you were with him when he died. I would know more of this. I would also like to know how you knew I was here. No one knows."

"Fielding did," she said simply.

He studied her in silence for a moment, and Eve had the weirdest feeling that he could see into her mind.

Gods, I hope not.

Then he gestured to one of the couches. "Sit."

Eve did as instructed. She'd been correct—the couch was as solid as a piece of marble and as uncomfortable.

"So you were in Maine. How did you come to be there?"

Her heart pounded. "I went in with a Fridan team on a mission to liberate the camp."

He froze. "And why would you do such a thing?"

"It took me six months to infiltrate the Fridans, but I did it. They believe me to be one of them."

"How did you manage that?"

She locked gazes with him. "Because I'm *that* good, that's how."

Theron arched his thinning brows. Then he leaned forward, his old eyes still bright. "Tell me of Fielding."

"I tried to help him escape. I got him past the gates of the camp, but he was shot. Then one of the soldiers shifted and tore him apart."

He winced. "All of which ties in with what was reported to me. Why didn't Fielding shift?"

"He couldn't, sir. He was drugged." She swallowed. "I managed to speak to him before... before the end. He spoke of you."

"What did he say?"

"That I was to come here and offer my services."

Lying had never been one of her strong suits, and she prayed Theron's ability to detect deceit wasn't working that day.

Theron pursed his thin lips. "You say you infiltrated the Fridans. Who was the leader of this group?"

"Aelryn, sir."

His face clouded. "A name I am familiar with."

"Fielding said I was to tell you… the Fridans know the location of all the Geran camps."

Theron's face tightened. "*All* of them? How? *How* could they know such a thing?"

"I wasn't taken into their confidence."

"Then it might not be true." His voice was tinged with hope.

Eve shook her head. "I saw the list, sir. Whoever aided them was very thorough."

And now safely out of your reach, reunited with his mate, and protected by Aelryn.

"But I *will* be involved in future missions," she confirmed. "I can still be useful." Eve still wasn't sure why Horvan wanted Theron to know about the camps, but she reasoned it was part of his plan.

He narrowed his gaze. "Where do they think you are at this moment?"

"Visiting relatives here in Lancashire." She bowed her head. "My grandfather has just passed."

Theron didn't bother to offer condolences, but then again she would have been surprised if he had.

"Tell me more of this team. Are they all shifters?"

"No, sir. Humans too."

He grimaced, not bothering to hide his disgust. "And why did they choose to raid that particular camp?"

"It was a rescue mission."

Another quirk of his brows. "All that effort to free one hundred fifty shifters?"

"Well, yes, but three in particular."

He frowned. "The information given to me about the actual raid has been sketchy at best. *Which* three?"

"They were tigers, all related."

He widened his eyes, and Eve was positive she heard a hitch in his breathing. "Would one of them be named Jake Carson?"

"Yes, sir."

There was no mistaking Theron's reaction. He could have been carved out of the same stone that surrounded him. "Then he's alive?"

"Yes, sir, and his sons, Seth and Jamie."

Those gimlet eyes narrowed. "But he was to have been eliminated. I was *told* he was dead. I had their assurance."

Eve looked him in the eye. "Then someone lied to you, sir."

Theron said nothing for a moment, and with every passing second, Eve's nerves increased. Finally, he rubbed his bearded jawline. "Very well. You say you wish to serve me?"

Holy fuck, he bought it.

"Yes, sir." She managed to keep her voice even, despite her racing heart.

"Then return to them. Watch them, learn of their plans—and report back to me." He stood, walked over to the octagonal table, and pulled out a drawer. He handed her a card. "Anything you send to this address will get back to me."

"Thank you, sir." Eve did her best to sound grateful.

"No—thank *you* for attempting to save Fielding. He will be missed."

His gratitude told Eve one thing—Fielding had been important.

Then Theron cocked his head. "This team you infiltrated. Have you heard any of them mention a shark shifter named Vic Ryder?"

"I *have* heard the name, sir. But he's missing, and no one knows where he is. He was on his way back from Rome when they lost contact with him."

"And what do they believe happened to him?" Theron's smile turned Eve's stomach.

"They think he was taken by your forces, sir. Someone suggested he might be in the camp in Alaska."

His smile widened. "Let them search for him in Alaska, then."

"You're sure you are safe here, sir?" Eve had never acted in such a sycophantic manner her whole life, but if it did the trick....

Theron's eyes gleamed. "My safety relies on secrecy, Duncan. I have a small force here to protect me, but to be honest, there is no need. Only a trusted few know where I am to be found." His smile faded. "Fielding was one of them. His murder has left a hole that I will find difficult to fill.

Nature abhors a vacuum, Duncan. Soon, the clamoring will begin as leaders jostle to assert themselves, to curry favor with me, all of them seeking to rise, to take his place." He shuddered. "And not one of them is even close to being half the leader Fielding was." He gripped the arms of his chair, and a moment later, Eve could see he'd regained his control. "But enough of such matters." He tilted his head to one side. "You were right. You chose a different way to fight, and as such you will be rewarded for your efforts. There is a place for you, should you choose to return to our forces. Gorillas always make the best soldiers."

"Thank you, sir."

Eve had never wanted a shower so badly.

Theron gestured to the guard. It seemed their meeting was over.

She left the room and walked toward the main door. Her way was blocked by a gray-and-amber-striped cat who wound in and out of her ankles.

The guard laughed. "How did *you* get in here? Come on, kitty." He picked the cat up and carried it to the door. As soon as he set it on the ground, the cat took off, running toward the gate. The guard straightened. "I guess he wanted to see what a castle looked like on the inside."

The guard outside the door snorted. "If it comes back, kill it. You know what they say: *Curiosity killed the cat.* It should know what to expect, then."

Eve said nothing but walked toward the road across the moat. When she reached the far side, she saw the cat sitting on top of one of the lions, curled up on its head.

She smiled. "Way to go, kitty cat." She glanced back at the castle. Theron's guards were pretty much like kitties too. Complacent, well-fed, relaxed—too relaxed, if they couldn't detect that Aric was a shifter.

Score one for the good guys.

Eve picked him up, and Aric rubbed his head against her chin. "Come on, Aric. Let's go find your mates. And mine."

The sooner she put some distance between her and Theron, the better.

Then her thoughts went to Victor.

I hope he doesn't stay here.

There were better forces to fight for, nobler wars to be won, and with people who would value him.

Chapter Thirteen

"Do you think he'll remember me?" Jake asked Nicholas. He'd been on tenterhooks all morning, ever since Horvan had told him Aelryn was on his way and Luciano Orsini was with him.

More than thirty years since we spoke. Orsini had been the last person Jake had seen before he'd been taken, and he'd burned their conversation into his memory, along with images of Miranda, of Dellan.... Anything to remind himself of who he was, what his life had been like.

I had no idea how long they'd keep me prisoner. Not that escape had been an option. He'd spotted way too many guns around for that.

Nicholas smiled. "You're not an easy man to forget." He studied Jake for a moment. "Want to tell me about it?"

He stiffened. "About what?" As if he didn't know.

"You tossed and turned most of the night. One of the drawbacks of sharing a bed, I guess—you get to know when your partner's sleep is disturbed." Nicholas chuckled. "And it's been far too long since I shared a bed with anyone. I'm not used to it." His gaze met Jake's. "Well?"

Jake sighed. "I had a bad dream, that's all."

Nicholas arched his eyebrows. "Only one?"

"There's no hiding anything from you, is there?" Jake rested his head against the back of the small couch in the sitting room Richard had given over to the team. It had a cozy feel, with portraits of the Deveraux family that dated back hundreds of years on the wood-paneled walls.

Jake shook his head. "Did you know Richard can trace his family back to William the Conqueror?"

"And you're avoiding the question."

He let out another sigh. "It was the same dream, over and over again. I tried to wake myself up, only to slip right back into it." He frowned. "I was standing in a long, darkened room. Suddenly I saw a light at the far end, and I moved toward it, only to have my way blocked."

"By what?"

"That's just it. I don't know!" Jake wrung his hands. "It was as if I'd run *smack* into an invisible wall. I could see that light, but I couldn't reach it." He gazed at Nicholas, his stomach churning. "What if it was some kind of prophetic dream? What if I keep having it because someone is trying to tell me I'm not meant to go any further?"

Nicholas said nothing for a moment, and Jake felt certain he was pondering how to tell him he was right. Then he smiled, and somehow that helped dissipate the waves of foreboding that had been with Jake since waking.

"I think a far more reasonable explanation is that whatever you're hoping to find in Theron's possession is on your mind, and you're worried in case you can't interpret it. You've built up our hopes to the point where even Aelryn is excited to learn what's in there, and now you're scared that either there'll be nothing there, or what we do find is worthless." He squeezed Jake's hand. "Anyone in your position would feel the same way."

Jake shuddered out a breath. "When you say it like that, you make it sound so plausible." He smiled. "Are you always this sensible and level-headed?"

Nicholas laughed. "Around you? Yes. Maybe that's why we fit so well." He glanced over Jake's shoulder. "And I think you have a visitor."

Jake turned, and his heart pounded to see the face he'd remembered all these years.

Luciano Orsini came toward him, arms held wide, and Jake didn't hesitate. He walked into them and hugged Orsini tightly. "I'm so glad you're here."

I'm going to give you two some space.

Jake broke the embrace and stared at Nicholas. "You don't have to."

Nicholas smiled. "Yes, I do. We've already done *our* catching-up—now it's time for some more." He bowed his head toward Orsini. "Signore, I look forward to speaking with you later." And with that, he left the room, closing the door behind him.

Orsini arched his eyebrows. "I am a little confused. Who is he? And why did that exchange seem so strange?"

"Probably because you only heard the part that was said out loud. Which allows me to answer your first question. That was Nicholas, and he's my mate." The words were easier to say now, but they still filled Jake with a sense of awe.

Orsini's mouth fell open. "But this is wonderful." He gestured to the couch. "May we sit? I have so many questions for you."

"Of course."

Once they were comfortable, Orsini regarded him with an intense gaze. "They took you as soon as you left the archive, didn't they?"

Jake nodded. "I never even made it across the bridge."

"I told no one of your presence, I swear."

He gaped. "No, please. Put that from your mind. It was nothing *you* did that caused this."

"But why did they do it?"

Although Jake had asked himself that same question many times during the last thirty years, it was only recently that he'd formulated a theory.

"You remember why my professor suggested I visit you?"

Orsini nodded. "He said your... skills would prove useful. And you were right, by the way. That document was—"

"A forgery?" Jake smiled. "Aelryn told me. Well, I think the Gerans got wind of my visit and were curious to see what I could glean. And maybe that's also why they've been testing the limits of my skills these last few years."

"And is there a limit?"

Jake smiled. "I think their testing has had an unforeseen consequence. It allowed me to hone my gift, to develop new ones." He cocked his head to one side. "Has Aelryn told you why I asked for you to be brought here?"

Orsini's eyes shone. "Indeed. I must be honest, I have slept little since Aelryn's call. And it is my first time outside the archive for many, many years."

"How long have you been there now?" Jake knew Orsini's father had brought him to the Castel Sant'Angelo when he was just a child, but he had no idea how many years ago that had been.

Orsini's lips twitched. "Long enough that I am not going to tell you. I prefer to keep my age a mystery. But tell me something... this Geran you saw in your vision. Aelryn spoke of this. It really is Theron?"

Jake nodded. "And I'm convinced he is the leader of all Gerans. Whatever artifacts we find in his castle, they will find their way to the archive. I want you with us to see to their safe passage. And I would like to come back to Rome with you to examine them."

Orsini beamed. "But there is no question of you not returning with me. I will need you." He clasped Jake's hands, his face tight. "I am sorry for all the losses you have suffered, but I rejoice that you have found your family again." He smiled. "I imagine you find the world a very different place from the one you left."

Jake rolled his eyes. "Understatement of the century. Can I ask you… with all the years you've spent researching shifters, have you found anything that has surprised you?"

He chuckled. "I have seen things that have completely changed the way I think."

"Such as?"

Orsini stroked his chin. "We're a diverse collection of shifters, yet we all—or almost all—share traits in common. While the bulk of us prefer human form, there are a large number who give themselves over to their animals, opting to live their lives on four legs—or no legs, in the case of some aquatic shifters—instead of being people."

"Why, do you think?" Jake couldn't imagine living his life as a tiger.

"Less stress, perhaps. But we all make choices that benefit *us*. We make our lives our own. In that respect, we're no different from humans, except that we have a few other options open to us." He frowned. "I think that is why this whole 'shifters are better than humans' perspective is, pardon the expression, crap. We *are* humans. We're just… a little special."

Jake had never heard it phrased so succinctly.

"Now, tell me about your family—and especially your mate. Is this a recent occurrence?"

Jake laughed. "So recent the shine has barely had time to wear off."

Then Orsini froze. "When you say you want me to come with you to help move the artifacts…. Does this mean I will be part of a mission?"

He stared. "Well, yes. I'd assumed Aelryn would have mentioned that part when he contacted you."

"He may very well have done, but I was so excited by the thought of leaving the archive that I must have missed it entirely. And please, don't assume I find the idea of being involved with the mission daunting." His dark eyes gleamed. "This is the most exhilarating thing that has ever happened to me."

Jake laughed. "Then welcome aboard, Signor Orsini." He stilled. "But is the archive safe without you to protect it?"

Orsini chuckled. "If you could see the shifters Aelryn brought with him, expressly for the purpose of guarding the archive in my absence, you wouldn't be concerned. It is in very safe hands. So… when do we leave?"

Jake was no military expert, but judging by what he'd seen going on around Leighton Hall during the last few hours, he reckoned it could be any time.

"Sooner than you think."

Fielding had been a nasty piece of work.

Jake had an idea Theron was going to be much, much worse.

Chapter Fourteen

An hour had passed since Eve and Aric returned from Thurland Castle, and Horvan had gathered all the team in Richard Deveraux's banqueting hall, everyone seated around the long table, grabbing sandwiches and cups of coffee. Aelryn was there too. He'd stayed after bringing Luciano Orsini to the hall that morning.

Speaking of Orsini, he, Jake, and Doc were talking up a storm at the far end of the table.

Horvan hated to break up their conversation, but it was debriefing time.

"Can I have your attention?" he called out. When silence fell, Horvan indicated Eve, who was sitting between Hashtag and Roadkill. Judging by the way they kept leaning in to kiss her or hug her, he guessed her mates were relieved to have her back in one piece.

"So… tell us what you found out." He and Eve had already spoken the minute she returned with Aric.

"As missions go, I didn't learn an awful lot," Eve grumbled. "I couldn't tell you how many guards Theron has beyond the few I saw. I couldn't see how well fortified the place was or if they had a security system in place." Her face brightened. "Okay, maybe it wasn't a *total* failure. I noticed there were a lot of open windows. We get another warm night, and that could play to our advantage."

Crank snorted. "What—we go in through the windows? They'll shut them at night and turn on the AC."

Eve laughed. "This is the UK. Firstly, Brits don't go for AC the same way Americans do."

Crank widened his eyes, clearly aghast. "How do you survive? Is that what made you so tough?"

She chuckled. "You need to know something. British summers are nothing like typical US summers. Sure it gets hot, but it only lasts a few days, a week at a stretch. Although if you believe the media, it's a heatwave and we're all going to die. Most of the year, it's a cool maritime climate, so there's no need for AC."

Crank's lower lip jutted out. "A week without AC? Babe, you know I'm like a flower. If we have to stay much longer, I'll wilt in that kind of weather."

Eve smiled. "Don't worry, you'll deal, I promise. Besides that, this is a listed building. They wouldn't be *allowed* to install AC. The most they could do is have fans all over the place. And I just thought of something else in our favor."

"And what's that?" Horvan was more than happy with the outcome of the visit to Thurland Castle. Aric's report had opened up all kinds of windows of opportunity.

"They were too complacent," Eve mused. "They seemed unconcerned, like they were untouchable. Even Theron."

Roadkill frowned. "If he'd been any more on the ball, you'd be hippo chow." When Eve didn't respond, he stared at her. "And you know I'm right, don't you? I saw Victor's maw, remember? He could've bitten you in half without much effort."

She stared back at him. "All I'm saying is, they're lax."

"And that's going to cost them, big-time." Horvan glanced at Aric. "Tell them what you told me."

Aric finished his mouthful of food. "I was able to go all over the castle. I counted about ten guards, and Eve nailed it—they're lax." He placed a roll of paper in the center of the table and unfurled it. "This is the layout of the castle, or as much as I can remember. The bits you need to know about?" He pointed to the sketch. "This small building in the courtyard is their barracks. And they're pretty comfortable in there. Couches, fridges, TV, showers…. There's even a fireplace, and where there's one of those, there's a chimney. Good for dropping gas bombs down, right?"

Brick's face glowed. "Nice one."

"Did you see where Theron sleeps?" Saul asked.

Aric nodded. "This room here, on the second floor. I went inside."

"How do you know it was his room?" Roadkill asked.

Aric wrinkled his nose. "Trust me, it was his. And talk about fancy. Four-poster bed, silk sheets…. Man, I came *this* close to shitting in his slippers. But I didn't," he added quickly. "One whiff of that and Theron would know there'd been a shifter in his room." He pursed his lips. "But *gods*, I wanted to pee on his sheets."

Everyone laughed.

"What about Vic? Where do you think they're keeping him?" Crank stared at Aric. "Did you see him? Hear him?"

Aric shook his head. "No, but there are a lot of rooms in the basement. He could be in one of those. I couldn't get into any of them." His face fell.

Seth kissed his cheek. "You're an awesome, brave kitty, and don't you forget it."

Aric flushed.

"Guys?" Horvan cleared his throat. "We're going in tonight." Heads jerked in his direction, and he saw in an instant he'd said the right thing. "Aelryn's team is standing by, and if Aric's right, we'll outnumber the guards."

Seth's eyebrows went up. "If?"

Horvan smiled. "Sorry. Since we're certain Aric's information is correct…. Better?"

Aric snuggled into Seth's side, sighing when Seth slid an arm around him. "Much."

"What time do we attack?" Hashtag asked.

"Oh two hundred. Everyone should be asleep by then, all tucked up in their nice comfortable beds having sweet, pleasant dreams." Horvan grinned. "And we're going to be their worst nightmare."

The murmurs of appreciation told him he'd read the room. His team was more than ready to kick ass.

"So here are the objectives. One, we find Alec and Vic. Two, we search for Valmer Cooper—*if* he's still being kept there. Jake saw him with Theron, but that was then. Three, we capture Theron. And four—"

"We remove the caskets Theron is hiding, and take them to a secure location," Orsini declared.

"Can't we just open them and see what's inside?" Hashtag frowned. "Those things are made of stone, Jake said. That's some weight to be carrying out of there."

Orsini shook his head. "We cannot open them in the castle. It must be done under controlled conditions."

"Which means the archive," Jake concluded. He glanced at Horvan. "Can you organize a plane to take me, Seth, and Signor Orsini to Rome? We'd need to crate up the caskets and get them to the airstrip where we landed. A cargo plane would do. Something that'll take the weight."

"I've already got Duke on it." Horvan reached for his phone to confirm the transport.

"I'd go with you, but…." Doc's voice faltered.

Jake took his hand. "I know, but you'll have a really important job to do. You have to take care of my grandson and see what can be done for him." His face tightened. "If indeed anything *can* be done."

Horvan's heart ached at the pain that surged through Dellan. He had to know this might not end well.

Wherever they take Alec, I want to go there.

Horvan sighed. *And you won't be going there alone. Me and Rael, we'll be with you.*

"I'm not happy about you going to Rome on your own," Doc murmured.

"I wouldn't let the three of them go without protection," Horvan announced.

"I'll go," Brick blurted, and Seth gave him a grateful glance.

"Are you sure you're up to this?" Doc peered at Jake, his voice laced with concern.

Jake smiled. "No, but I'm going to do it anyway. When we've got all the answers, *then* I'll rest. I have to do this."

"Can we go back a bit?" Crank's brows knitted. "What about Theron?"

"What about him?" Horvan asked.

"Well, are we gonna leave the bastard alive? He's *way* more dangerous than Fielding ever was."

"Theron will remain our captive." Aelryn's voice rang out. "But if Jake and Orsini are right, we're about to deal him a blow that will leave its mark. And we might yet have need of him."

Roadkill gazed at Aelryn. "You really believe that, don't you? That whatever Theron's hiding in those caskets is dynamite."

Aelryn nodded.

"I can't escape the feeling that in our world—the world of shifters, that is—this moment is where it pivots." Orsini shivered. "May the gods watch over all of us."

"We have medical facilities on the outskirts of Manchester," Aelryn told them. "There's a clinic where we'll take Alec."

"A clinic for shifters?" Crank arched his eyebrows.

Aelryn smiled. "For everyone, but yes, mostly for shifters."

Crank peered at Doc. "The ole secret shifter network strikes again, huh?"

Doc's eyes gleamed. "We're everywhere."

"Do you think the day will ever come when all humans can learn about shifters?" Saul asked.

"One day, perhaps." Aelryn sighed. "But not yet. You're not ready for it." He turned to Doc. "What facilities will you require?"

"A lab, for one thing. And isolation for Alec. We'll need to tranquilize him for travel. And glove up his hands as a precaution."

Horvan winced. *They turned him into a killing machine.*

Something you need to think about, Rael interjected. *They did this to Alec. Who's to say they haven't done it to other kids? What if there are more Alecs out there?*

Horvan didn't even want to contemplate such a horrific idea, but they had to know. "Aelryn, how are your people doing with the medical records we got from the Maine camp?"

"It's been slow so far. My tech team is examining all the laptops and data recovered. As soon as we find something, I'll report back to you."

Jamie cleared his throat, and Horvan gave him an inquiring glance. "Something on your mind?"

His face flushed. "It's just… look, I don't think I can be of much use to y'all. So if it's okay with you, I'm going to catch a flight to Boston and go to the school. I'm not a fighter, all right? But I might make a good teacher. And if there's a chance of that, I want to try."

"You won't stay away too long, will you?" Dellan's voice quavered.

Jamie smiled. "Don't you worry. Now that I've found you and Seth and…. Dad, I won't be away from you for too long. And I promise to stay in touch."

"I'll have one of my team take you to Manchester," Aelryn said. "You'll be sure of a flight from there." He glanced around the table. "Before you all disappear to get some rest, I would like to say…." He smiled. "It has been an honor to meet all of you. There are no finer fighters, even among my own men." He met Eve's gaze. "Men being a generic term, you understand."

She grinned. "I'd assumed as much."

"And to second Signor Orsini's prayer: May the gods watch over all of us."

Amen to that.

If Horvan had his way, he'd have them on speed dial.

VIC WAS usually a positive person, but after being kept in a cramped, windowless room, not another being in sight save for the guard who brought him his meager food ration, he was starting to panic.

I'm not getting out of here, am I?

He'd tried to connect with Saul and Crank, but so far his efforts had been fruitless. He'd become so disheartened, he hadn't even tried during the last two days. Theron's initial comment about using him as a pawn in whatever twisted game he was playing filled Vic with dread, but that paled into insignificance next to the inference that anyone coming to rescue him would find only a corpse.

Then he heard the click of a key in a lock, and he stilled. He'd already been fed—and that was far too generous a term to be applied to the hunk of bread and half a plastic cup of water they'd brought him that morning—so this was something new.

When the door opened and Theron loomed in the doorway, his heart sank.

I guess I've run out of time.

"Bad news, I'm afraid," Theron said in a light, cheerful tone, confirming Vic's fears. "They're not going to find you." He kept his hands behind his back, and that was enough to put Vic on alert.

"They'll never stop searching for me," Vic affirmed, his voice cracking.

Theron's cool smile sent shivers through him.

"Of course. Believe that if it helps. But you should know… they won't be looking here. Indeed, I have it on excellent authority that they're searching for you in Alaska."

"And how do you know that?"

That cool smile again. "I have my sources. In fact, I can have those sources feed false information to your Fridan friends. I could have them searching for you all over the globe."

A fucking mole. A traitor.

And there was no way of warning Horvan or Aelryn.

"It's very warm in here, wouldn't you agree?" Theron brought his hands out from behind him, and Vic saw a bottle of water.

You fucking bastard.

Theron cracked the cap and took a few sips. He grimaced. "Damn, I hate it when the water isn't chilled." He stared at Vic as he upturned the bottle and poured its contents onto the stone floor. Theron gave him an apologetic glance. "Oh, I'm sorry. Did you want some?" He pocketed the empty bottle with a cold smile.

You fucking monster.

"What do you hope to gain from keeping me here?" Vic demanded.

Theron buffed his nails on the lapel of his jacket. "Absolutely nothing. So enjoy your last breaths, because your time is about to run out." He pointed to the camera in the corner of the room, not that Vic hadn't spotted it about two seconds after they'd thrown him in there. "Your demise will be recorded for my amusement—and to torture your mates, of course." He let out a dramatic sigh. "To think they came so far and tried so hard, only to watch you die due to their failures."

And with that, he closed the door and locked it.

Vic took a deep breath.

I have to hold tight. I have to believe they'll find me.

He closed his eyes, fighting to calm his racing heartbeat, and opened himself up.

Saul? Crank? Can you hear me?

Then he choked back a sob when a familiar voice filled his head.

Baby?

Holy fuck.

Vic wiped his eyes. *Saul, where are you? Is Crank with you?*

Crank's voice came next. *Hey, sweetheart. We're only a few miles away from you. Sit tight. We're coming for ya.* There was a pause. *Fuck, it's good to hear your voice. Are you okay?*

No way was he going to reveal his present state. They'd only worry. *I'm fine.*

Then Vic recalled Theron's admission.

Guys, you need to warn Horvan. You've got an informer among you. I don't know who they are, but they're feeding stuff back to Theron. He was bragging about it.

Saul laughed. *Let him brag. Don't sweat it, baby. Theron's mole is one of us.*

Vic rolled his eyes. *You ever heard of the concept of a double agent?*

Sure, but you *ever heard of someone betraying their mates? Ain't gonna happen.*

He blinked. *What?*

We've got a lot to tell you. But it can wait. Crank's voice grew warm. *See you tonight.*

Wait—what?

Oh, didn't we mention that part? It's on for tonight.

Vic's eyes burned. He wanted to cry, but he had so little moisture left in his body. *Love you both so much.*

We know, Saul assured him. *And you'll be in our arms soon. So do what the man says and sit tight.* He paused. *Love you too.*

Then the connection was broken.

Vic's heart was dancing with joy.

They're coming. They're really coming.

He ached for the feel of cool water surrounding him. Sunlight on his back as he breached the surface. He'd gone too long without water sluicing over his body, and he was sure he'd pay the price. His skin was already dry and cracking. Too much longer and Theron wouldn't have to kill him. He'd likely suffocate or be crushed when he was forced to shift in a vain hope of not dying.

Not that he was ready to give up. There was too much to look forward to.

Four strong arms holding him.

Three mouths meeting in a kiss.

Two dicks ready for action.

One bed, complete with soft sheets and a whole lotta lube.

I'm going home, goddamn it, and nothing is going to stop me.

VALMER COOPER was starting to get a bad feeling about his incarceration.

For one thing, it had been a while since they'd filmed him with the intention of sending it to Rudy. The beatings had still continued, however.

For another, every time he asked about his release, he was met with silence.

They can't keep me here—can they?

His parents were getting on in years, and seeing as they hadn't heard from him in months, they had to be going out of their minds with worry.

And then there was Rudy.

Life fucking *sucked*.

He'd found his mate—his freaking *mate*, for fuck's sake—and in less than a day they'd been separated.

He must be going crazy.

Valmer had tried to find a way to link their minds, but it was no use.

Let's face it. I don't even know where I am. I could be anywhere in the world.

He hadn't seen Theron since they'd thrown him into this godforsaken room, but he wasn't about to complain about that.

Theron gave him a major case of skin-crawling terror.

The sound of a key turning in the lock startled him. There were no clocks in his room, but he had a fair idea of when they fed him.

So who is this?

Then goose bumps covered his arms as Theron walked through the door.

Valmer straightened, determined not to give the bastard the satisfaction of seeing him chicken. "Wow. What did I do to deserve a royal visit?"

Theron merely raised his eyebrows. "I see months of being locked away haven't improved your manners."

"Yeah, well, I forget my manners when someone waltzes into my hotel room, shoots me with a tranquilizer dart, then bundles me off to God knows where." He gave Theron a quizzical glance. "I don't suppose you're about to tell me I'm free to go?"

Theron smiled, and the sight sent a chill through him. "You'd suppose correctly. I am simply here to tell you to make the most of your final days."

Oh fuck. I'm going to die.

It was one thing to have a sneaking suspicion. It was something else to have that suspicion confirmed.

"You see, I set the Fridans an impossible task, and since I now have a new informant, I don't need your pitiful mate anymore. Which is probably a good thing, as I was beginning to suspect the information he was sending to me." Another chilling smile. "By the way, I thought you ought to know… there's been nothing in the news about your disappearance. No one seems to have missed you. What a sad epitaph. *He will not be missed.* All these years on this planet and no one will mourn your passing."

"You think my parents won't stop looking for me?"

Theron placed his hand over his heart. "Oh, I'm so sorry to be the bearer of bad tidings, but… they died. Last month, actually. Your mother went first, apparently. To be fair it seems she did miss you. Your father died a week or so later, of a broken heart, I believe. So no, there is no one left to mourn you."

Valmer choked back the tears. "And did *you* have anything to do with their deaths?" He'd mourn them later, when he didn't have an audience. His chest was tight, his eyes hot. *You fucking bastard.*

Theron arched his eyebrows. "Oh my, what a suggestion."

And it wasn't an answer.

"I still have a mate, whether you think him pitiful or not." Rudy wouldn't give up searching for him.

"Correction—you *had* a mate. I told you I didn't need him anymore." Theron smiled. "And now I'll leave you to enjoy your sleep—while you can." He turned and left the room, and the *click* of the key in the lock was too much for Valmer to bear.

He lay facedown on the bed and wept into his pillow.

What shocked him was that his tears were not for himself, but for his parents and for Rudy.

What happens when you lose a mate?

How long did he have left?

Chapter Fifteen

Horvan peered at the gateway through his night-vision goggles.

"No one on duty that I can see." If the guards had been under Horvan's command, they would have been out on their ear in a heartbeat.

Theron's complacency was their good fortune.

Beside him, Saul gave a snort. "So we're just gonna stroll across the moat? No incursion is *that* easy."

"We can hope, right?" Horvan tapped his earpiece. "Okay, we're good to go. Eve, keep Jake and Orsini close until I tell you it's safe to bring 'em in. Then head down to the basement. Take Aelryn's guys with you to bring out the caskets."

"Copy that. We've got a couple of bigass carts at the ready to remove them from the castle."

"Brick, you know the drill. Gas bombs down the chimney, then deal with the guards as they come out. Not *one* of them gets into the castle or across the moat, you get it?"

"Copy that."

Horvan glanced at Saul. "You and Crank get in through a window, then open the front door. If you meet any resistance, deal with it appropriately. Once we're inside, you two go find Vic and anyone else Theron is keeping locked up down there. But go quietly, okay? Like mice."

"Copy that."

"Mice like cheese, y'know," Crank interjected in a morose tone.

Horvan rolled his eyes. "Are you *still* going on about that?"

"All I asked was if we could go to London to this really bodacious American bar that has all-you-can-eat nachos and a cheese fountain, for God's sake. I mean, *cheese…*," he whined.

"Fine. If you can get through this mission without bugging me about it anymore, I'll give you some leave, and you can go to London and eat your little mousey heart out, okay? But right now we've got stuff to do…. You know, like taking down a bad guy and finding your mate?"

"Vic likes cheese too. Just saying."

Saul shook his head. "You and cheese. Are you sure you're not hiding something? You know, like you're really a mouse shifter?"

Crank frowned. "Us meeses, we like cheeses. Gives us a sad when there is no cheeses for the meeses."

Horvan gave up.

"Want me to wait too?" Doc asked quietly.

"Yeah. Hashtag'll bring you inside once we locate Alec. Then he's all yours. Aelryn's got an ambulance ready to take you and Alec to the clinic."

"Copy that."

Horvan smiled. "In case I forget to tell you… it's been good having you on my team. Kinda like the old days."

Doc chuckled. "And it looks as if you'll see a lot more of me, given the recent turn of events. Because if Jake is my mate, then Dellan is sort of a stepson—so what does that make you?"

He grinned. "We'll talk more about that later." He returned his gaze to the gate, but there was still no sign of any guards.

"I like that you saved the best part for you and me," Aelryn remarked in a low voice. "Taking down Theron. I appreciate being included in this."

Horvan chuckled. "You're with me to make sure I don't kill the bastard." He took a deep breath. "Okay, guys. The word is go."

They moved stealthily toward the castle, creeping across the road bridge and through the archway into the courtyard. Brick and Roadkill split off with their team, heading for the barracks. Saul and Crank moved around the exterior of the castle, where they'd spotted a few open windows during their earlier recon. Horvan and Aelryn went to the main door, accompanied by four of Aelryn's men.

"Well, goddamn." Saul's whisper filled his ear. "Not only do we have two open windows, they were kind enough to choose ones next to a drainpipe."

"Then get up there, you spider monkey."

Saul's snort was way too loud. "Funny man."

"Don't forget. Radio silence once you're inside, until you get the door open."

"Copy that. We're going in."

Horvan gazed across the courtyard to where Brick's men had positioned themselves by the door to the barracks. One of the team was already on the tiled roof, poised by the chimney pot. Some of the team were armed with tranquilizer guns, and all of them carried darts to prevent shifting.

It was poetic justice, using the Gerans' own tech against them.

Be safe, okay?

Horvan could hear the love in Rael's voice. *I will. And I'll be back there before you know it.* He focused, his muscles tensed, straining to catch any noises. No sounds carried on the night air, apart from the soft hoot of an owl—

Oh shit.

Horvan raised his head and sniffed. *Don't let it be a shifter.* Maybe Theron had them out on patrol. That could screw up everything. Fortunately, a moment later he saw it sail down into the forest and come back up with something in its talons, then alight on a tree and begin enjoying its midnight snack.

Paying them no attention whatsoever.

Thank fuck for that.

Then there was the creak of a door opening.

Horvan gestured to the rest of the team, and they crept inside. Horvan was thankful whoever owned the castle had kept the original stone flags rather than covering them with floorboards. He gave Saul and Crank the thumbs-up, and they peeled off, heading for the basement.

Horvan pointed to the ceiling, then led his team toward the staircase, its stone treads worn down by centuries of use. On the second floor, Horvan pointed to the room Aric had indicated. He and Aelryn stopped, tranq guns at the ready, the rest of the team lined up along the hallway, weapons raised.

The door was ajar.

Horvan pushed it slowly, before coming to a dead stop inside.

There was no one in the room.

BRICK CROUCHED behind the door to the barracks, waiting for Horvan's signal. His men formed a semicircle, ready to tranq the guards once they tried to escape from the gas.

Horvan's voice filled his ear. "Brick. The word is go."

"Copy that," he whispered. He signaled to Dex on the roof, and a moment later there was the muffled noise of an exploding gas bomb, followed by several roars.

The roars of animals.

Brick yelled, "Shift!"

The door went crashing onto the cobbled courtyard, torn off its hinges, and a lion bounded out, its jaws wide in a ferocious growl, followed by another lion and a cheetah.

They were met by two pumas and a panther who slammed into the guards, going for their throats. It was over in a matter of less than a minute. Roadkill and the others took aim, and those guards who tried to make a run for it were swiftly brought down.

When a brown bear burst out of the barracks, Brick didn't hesitate. He shucked off his clothing and gave chase, his heavy paws thudding on the hard cobbles.

You think you're gonna get away? Think again.

The bear didn't make it as far as the gate.

The final wave of shifted guards were the heaviest hitters of them all, five gorillas, as loud as they were fierce, and it took all Brick's team to subdue them. But at last the courtyard was silent.

Brick stood over the bloodied heap of brown fur and bellowed. He shifted back as Roadkill strode toward him. Brick pointed to the still forms lying on the ground.

"That's all of them, right?"

Roadkill nodded. "I thought it was gonna be a walk in the park until the gorillas joined in the fun." He handed Brick a pile of clothing. "Here."

"Thanks." He tapped his earpiece. "H, the guards are taken care of. They all came out fighting, already shifted."

"Any casualties?" Horvan spoke in a low voice, barely above a whisper.

Brick glanced at his team. "Minor injuries, mostly inflicted by the gorillas." He snorted. "Remind me never to piss Eve off."

"Good work. We're heading downstairs to the basement. Wait for us at the gate. I'll signal if we need you."

"Copy that." Brick gazed at the unconscious guards. "They were good, but we were better." He peered at Roadkill. "Sucks to be them, huh?" Brick signaled to his team. "Okay, guys. We're on standby in case they need reinforcements."

Except having him anywhere near Theron was *not* a good idea.

Horvan and Aelryn paused at the door they knew led to the basement.

"H, can you come down here?" That was Saul, speaking in his normal voice. "Last door at the end of the hallway. We've found someone you might want to talk to."

Bingo.

"On my way." Horvan glanced at his team. "When we get down there, spread out. Search every room. And if you don't find Alec down here, go search upstairs."

They had people to find.

Horvan descended into the cool basement, following the faint murmur of voices. In the hallway, he spied the unconscious body of a man in a robe, possibly a servant who'd heard the noise. When he and Aelryn reached the heavy wooden door, Horvan went inside to find Saul and Crank standing at the end of the long room with a vaulted ceiling, exactly as Jake had described it, right down to the walled-off section made of glass, a door set into it.

Then Saul moved aside, and Horvan saw an elderly man seated in a high-backed chair, glaring at him. On the table beside him were a book and a pair of glasses, and what appeared to be a glass of milk.

So this is the leader of the Gerans.

Horvan's skin crawled just looking at him.

"Found him asleep in his chair," Saul muttered.

Theron fixed cold eyes on Horvan. "What are you doing in my house?"

His voice was as glacial as his gaze.

Horvan ignored him and tapped his earpiece. "Eve? Bring them in. We're in the basement."

"Copy that."

He gestured to Saul and Crank. "We'll take it from here. Go find Vic. And see if you can find Valmer Cooper."

"Copy that." They ran from the room.

"You are remarkably well informed," Theron said in a dry tone.

Horvan aimed his gun at Theron. "Don't move. Shift and I'll put a bullet in you."

Theron arched his eyebrows but said nothing.

Horvan gestured to the medic who'd accompanied them. "Do it."

The medic approached Theron and removed a metal box from his backpack.

Theron stared at the syringe in the medic's hands, then gazed at Aelryn. "Are you going to sully your hands with my execution? I'm surprised you have the stomach for it."

Horvan frowned. "Who said anything about an execution? Is that what you think this is? Some kind of lethal injection? This is a dose of your own medicine, to prevent you from shifting." He watched as the medic rolled up the sleeve of Theron's robe, swabbed a patch of skin, then administered the injection. Theron made no movement when the needle pierced his flesh, his eyes locked on Horvan.

"Is that stare supposed to intimidate me?" Horvan chuckled. "You need to work on it."

Aelryn touched Horvan's arm. "They've found Alec. I've had someone send for Doc."

"Thanks." When Aelryn didn't remove his hand, cold flushed through Horvan. "What is it?"

Aelryn's eyes were filled with compassion. "It doesn't look good."

Let me know when you see him. Dellan sounded anxious.

I will, I promise. In the meantime, you and Rael take the first train to Manchester. I'll have some of Aelryn's men meet you to bring you to the clinic.

Horvan prayed they'd be in time.

Theron opened his mouth to say something, but fell silent when Eve entered the room. Jake and Orsini followed her, and Theron blinked. "You're a long way from Rome, Signor Orsini."

Orsini shuddered. "I remember you. I knew the day you came to the archive that you were trouble."

Theron snorted. "I have nothing to say to you. To any of you." He scowled at Eve. "And especially you. Traitorous bitch."

"Flattery will get you nowhere," Eve said with a smile.

"It's okay if you don't feel like talking." Jake stepped forward, and Theron's breathing hitched.

"Don't you touch me." His words were more like a growl.

Jake huffed. "I don't have to touch you. Fielding gave me everything I needed."

Theron froze. "You lie."

"How do you think we found this place? We couldn't have done it without him."

"He would never have—"

Jake cut him off with a wave of his hand. "For the record, we're not interested in anything you have to say. You're not the reason why we're here." He glanced at the wall of glass, just as eight men came into the room, pushing carts on which sat packing crates. Then he returned his gaze to Theron. "*That's* why we're here. Whatever you're hiding in those caskets."

Theron paled. "No!"

Jake widened his eyes. "Whoa. He's scared to death. I mean it, Horvan. He's not faking this." He cocked his head. "What's in there?"

"Nothing," Theron said with a snarl.

Jake walked slowly toward him and stopped, his body rigid.

"You're lying. That forgery I saw all those years ago? That's why you had me taken, wasn't it?"

"Forgery?" Theron's eyes blazed. "I have no idea what you're talking about." He gaped as one of the team opened the glass door and went inside. "No. You can't *do* this."

Jake smiled. "Correction. We're *doing* it."

Aelryn spoke into his mic. "We're ready for you. Come and get him."

"What are you going to do with me?"

Horvan nodded to the medic, who stepped forward, a syringe in his hand. "All you need to know is when you wake up, you'll be somewhere safe—but nowhere near as swanky as a castle that dates back to the eleventh century."

"A castle nearly as old as the oldest shifter records," Aelryn added. "When they started building this place, Ansfrid and Ansger were alive. They might even have visited here."

Horvan didn't miss the flicker of fear that flashed across Theron's face, and he couldn't resist. "So what do you think the Gerans will say when they learn the truth? That there was no animosity between the brothers? That everything they've been told is a lie? Because that's what we're going to discover in those caskets, isn't it?"

The medic injected Theron in the neck, and within seconds, Theron's eyelids fluttered and his breathing changed. Before he slipped into unconsciousness, he fixed his gaze on Horvan.

"It doesn't matter what you discover. No one will believe you. No one." Then his eyes closed and his chin slumped to his chest.

"They'd better," Horvan muttered.

Everything was riding on this.

Two of Aelryn's men lifted Theron from his chair and carried him from the vault. Horvan glanced at Aelryn. "Keep him unconscious until he reaches Leighton Hall. Has Deveraux given you any idea where you can store him until you're ready to leave?"

Aelryn's lips twitched. "Apparently, there are dungeons at the Hall. I think that's a fitting place for a makeshift prison, don't you?"

Horvan grinned. "Perfect. Does it come with instruments of torture?"

"Alas, they're all long gone."

"Pity." The thought of putting Theron in an Iron Maiden.... He cocked his head. "Does Amazon sell them?"

SAUL STOOD in the middle of the hallway, confronted by a line of doors, all of them locked. *Sing out, baby. We're close.*

"In here!"

Vic's voice was faint, coming from the door at the foot of the narrow staircase.

Crank was there in a heartbeat, kicking at the base of it, slamming into it with his shoulder. "Vic, step away from the door!" he yelled before aiming his Sig at the lock.

"That doesn't work, remember? Only in movies," Saul yelled as he ran to join him.

Crank gave one more slam into the door, and it broke off its hinges. "Oh fuck. Saul, get in here."

Saul double-timed it into the room to find Vic bound to a chair. He looked like shit, his skin dry and cracked so badly that it had bled. "Goddamn it. I'll kill that son of a bitch." Saul's voice quavered.

"What's wrong with him?" Crank crouched next to Vic's chair.

"He's been out of the water for too long." Saul tapped his earpiece. "Bring my bag. Now!" He wrapped his arms around Vic's neck. "We've got you, baby," he crooned. Then he quickly undid the ropes and stripped off the grubby clothes, his heart quaking at the sight of Vic's body.

Hold on, baby. You hear me?

A soldier came running into the room, carrying a hefty duffel that he handed to Saul, who ripped it open. He handed Crank a bottle of water, then grabbed another and snapped off the top. Crank, fortunately, followed suit. Then, very carefully, Saul poured the liquid over Vic, making sure it went everywhere.

"Oh, thank the gods," Vic croaked.

Crank emptied his own bottle over Vic while Saul picked up another. "I don't understand."

Saul didn't take his eyes off Vic. "Aquatic shifters need to be near water all the time. Even if it's just a shower or bath. They kept him locked up in here, and his body is going into shock. We need to hydrate him, then get him medical help."

"I'm fine," Vic croaked. Saul brought the bottle to his cracked lips, and Vic swallowed, although more ended up on him than in him.

"You're a fucking liar," Saul snarled. "Your blood is pooling on the floor." He jerked his head toward Crank. "Tell Horvan to get that fucker Theron out of here or I'll kill him, even if I have to take out our own guys to get to him."

"And I'll be there with you," Crank vowed.

Saul cupped Vic's chin. "Will it hurt you if I lift you?"

"Just get me out of here."

He hoisted Vic into his arms, wincing when his lover gave a shuddering cry. He turned to ask Crank to help, but he was already storming toward the door.

"Where the fuck are you going?"

"To kill that son of a bitch," Crank snarled, his voice breaking. "He has to die."

"And do you want *Vic* to die? I—we—need you right now. Please. Wendell… don't leave us."

Crank turned back, grinding his teeth, his fists clenching. "I'm sorry. I lost my head."

"Thank you. I love you."

Crank calmed at the words, but there was still such anger in him. Saul wondered if it would ever heal.

"We're going to get you out of here," he said to Vic.

Vic managed a faint smile. "I knew you'd both come. Leave no man behind, isn't that what you always say?"

Then he passed out in Saul's arms.

Saul held him tightly. *You're going to be okay.*

He had to be.

DOC WANTED to find Theron and choke the life out of him.

He stared at the man asleep on the bed. There was no mistaking him. Alec resembled Dellan strongly. What shocked the hell out of him was that he appeared to be the same age as his grandfather. His face was gaunt, his cheeks sunken. One hand rested on the pillow, and Doc shivered to see it. The long fingers curved into claws instead of digits.

"Oh my God," Doc murmured. "What have they done to you?"

This is going to kill Jake and Dellan.

"Doc, I'm not sure about this," the medic at Doc's side muttered. "Do we dare tranq him for the trip?"

"We have no choice. We don't know what we're dealing with." He prepared the syringe, then swabbed the skin on Alec's inner arm. Skin that felt and looked paper thin. "Be careful not to touch his hands. Wrap them in towels before we move him."

"You've got this wrong, Doc. This guy is sixty if he's a day."

"And yet he was born last year, at a guess."

The medic gasped. "Those fucking bastards. Let's hope he's the only one they've done this to."

Doc would have a better idea of that once Aelryn's team had finished going through all the records taken at the Maine raid.

How does the saying go? If at first you don't succeed....

What worried him was how many times the Gerans would try again.

AELRYN WALKED into the bedroom on the third floor, a guard stationed at the door.

On the bed sat a tall man with short hair and piercing blue eyes surrounded by circles of dark flesh. His face bore the trace of faded bruises and healing cuts, as did his hands.

He regarded Aelryn with interest. "Who are you?"

"That doesn't matter. What *does* is who sent me to find you." Aelryn smiled. "I believe you're acquainted with one of my team leaders—Rudy Myers."

Valmer's mouth fell open. "Rudy? He's alive?"

Aelryn frowned. "You thought he was dead? What gave you that—?" He growled. "Theron, of course. Believe me, your mate is alive and well."

"He told me my parents were dead too."

That look of hope nearly unraveled Aelryn, and he hastened to put Valmer's mind at rest. "That was a lie too. Rudy contacted your parents when you first went missing. He had me place them in a safe house, in case the Gerans wanted leverage. I assure you, they're quite well. Worried about you, but delighted to meet Rudy." Aelryn paused. "He never gave up hope of finding you. And he did some terrible things to keep you safe, to get you back."

"I begged him not to tell them anything."

"And your captors made sure he saw the mess they made of you."

Valmer stuck out his chin. "I didn't make for an easy target. I gave as good as I got." His Adam's apple bobbed. "Where is Rudy?"

Aelryn smiled again. "Waiting for you not far from here."

His lower lip wobbled. "I... I don't deserve him."

"Yes, you do. You're mates." Aelryn sat beside him. "You were made to be together. And all those things you couldn't tell him because you feared you would put him in danger? They're about to come to light."

"The tomb? You... you found what was in there?"

"All the artifacts are on their way to a safe place, where they'll be examined... studied."

"And Sarah Delaney? Have they found her too?"

Aelryn frowned. "The archaeologist who discovered Berengar's tomb?"

"Yes. She disappeared."

"Then we will find her." He tilted his head. "You could help us."

Valmer blinked. "Me? How?"

"You're a Geran."

"Correction. I *was* a Geran. As soon as I realized they were lying to us, I couldn't do this anymore. It's why they had no problems torturing me."

Aelryn scowled. *They did this to one of their own.*

"I can understand how that might change your mindset. As for the artifacts, if we're right, we're about to uncover truths that many Gerans won't accept, no matter how overwhelming the evidence. *You* could spread the word, seek out like-minded Gerans who can be swayed. Who would in turn spread the word." Aelryn sighed. "It isn't a task that can be accomplished overnight. It might take years. But we won't give up."

Valmer straightened. "I'll do everything I can, I swear."

Aelryn stood. "Then let's get out of here and reunite you with your mate."

The battle of Thurland Castle might have been won, but Aelryn feared the war had only just begun.

Chapter Sixteen

Dellan stared through the window. Beyond it was a single bed, surrounded by monitors and other medical paraphernalia. Doc stood next to it, talking quietly with another doctor.

Dellan didn't need to hear what they were saying. Their expressions said it all, and Doc had already given his verdict half an hour ago.

Nothing had changed in those thirty minutes. No miraculous recovery, no sudden change in Alec's condition.

What happened next was up to Dellan, except he couldn't make a decision. He'd been a wreck ever since he walked into the clinic.

As for the room's occupant, he was oblivious to the discussion.

He doesn't even know who I am or that I'm here.

Horvan's arm around Dellan was a welcome intrusion, as was Rael's hand on his back.

"We heard what Doc told you," Rael said in a low voice.

Dellan could still hear him. The words were burned into his brain.

"We can't reverse it. And now the aging process seems to have speeded up, he's in constant pain. The venom he secretes in his claws? It's consuming him." Doc had looked Dellan in the eye. "You have to be the one to decide."

There lay his dilemma. He couldn't bring himself to give the word.

Sobs racked his body, and he buried his face in Horvan's chest. "I can't. I just can't." Horvan's solid frame muffled the words.

Horvan held him close.

"Let me ask you something. Why is this hitting you so hard? You never met Alec until yesterday. You know nothing about him. What is it about him that's tearing you apart?"

Dellan peered up at him, letting his tears fall. "He's—he *was*—my son. I never got to know him. I never even knew he existed. And now? I have to watch him die. I have to sit there and be helpless. I can't even hold his hand when he takes his last breath. Hell, I never even got to see him take his first one. The fucking Gerans saw to that."

He sobbed again, only this time both his mates enfolded him in their arms, giving him all the warmth that had been sucked out of him since that stark conversation with Doc.

"What do I do? Help me decide."

Horvan raised Dellan's chin with his fingertips. "Love, you heard what Doc said. Alec can't survive this. So the way I see it? You have two choices. You let Alec suffer until his body finally breaks down, or you help him go out peacefully, knowing love for the first time."

Dellan gazed at the man in the bed. Yes, he resembled Dellan's dad, but apart from that, he was a stranger.

I can let a stranger go. I can give him peace.

Dellan swallowed hard, then released Horvan. He opened the door and walked over to join Doc at Alec's bedside. Dellan stroked Alec's forehead.

"Okay, Doc. Take the pain away."

He didn't watch Doc's ministrations. He kept his gaze focused on Alec's face. He didn't need to see—he knew the moment the drug took effect.

Alec let out a sigh, and he was gone.

Then Horvan and Rael were there, holding him, loving him, and he leaned into them. Dellan didn't weep—he'd sobbed enough.

I couldn't help you.

Rael kissed his forehead. *But you can help the others.*

Dellan stared at him. "Others?"

Horvan nodded. "Alec is the first child of yours that you know about. But there must be others. And not just *your* children—all the kids born to mothers who were forced into their wretched breeding program."

"Kids that need your help too," Rael added. "And their mothers and fathers."

Dellan's mind raced. He'd been so mired in what *he'd* lost, he'd never even considered other people. Mothers who'd given birth, then had their child ripped away, never to hold them. Fathers who'd been forced to mate, planting the literal fucking seeds to bring life to this world but never having a chance to be the father. And worse, far worse than that, the fucking straw that broke the camel's back, was the fact that almost none of these children had a chance to grow up knowing they were loved.

What they received from the households they were implanted into wasn't love—it was indoctrination.

Shifters are better than humans.
Shifters are born to rule over humans.
Our feet belong on their necks.

First at home, then in school, a never-ending litany of superiority and entitlement.

And it was about time someone stopped it.

Dellan nodded slowly. "You're right."

He *could* make a difference to their lives.

All he had to do was work out how. And focusing on a new goal was better than dwelling on the past, on events he couldn't change.

Dellan had a chance to change the future for a great many shifters.

CRANK TOUCHED Saul's shoulder lightly. "Take a break. Get some air. You've been sitting there for three hours." Not that *he* could talk. The only things to drag him away from Vic's bedside had been the need for coffee and the subsequently greater need to pee.

"When he wakes up."

Crank stroked Saul's head. "Look at him. They've given him baths, he's on a drip…. He's a million times better than when we found him." Vic's skin was healing already.

It had to be a shifter thing.

"It is." Saul managed a smile. "I always tease him about how quickly he heals."

"It pisses you off, you mean," came a murmur from the bed. "Your teeth marks never stay long enough for me to show them off."

Crank beamed. "Hey, you're awake."

Vic chuckled, then gave a harsh dry cough. Saul picked up the cup of water and held the straw for Vic, who drained the cup. Crank quickly refilled it.

"I was *trying* to sleep, but with you two around? Even your thoughts are noisy."

They each took a hand, careful of the tubes. "We were so scared." What shocked Crank was the hoarse, broken sound of his own voice.

"That fucker Theron. He enjoyed it," Vic rasped. "Psychologically torturing me was a kink for him. But please… tell me you didn't kill him. I wanted to be the one to do that."

"We wanted to," Saul replied. "We were ready to tear into our friends to get to him."

"I'm glad you didn't. I wouldn't want him to have the satisfaction of knowing how close he came to breaking us."

Saul let go of Vic's hand to run his fingers through Vic's hair. "Hey, you," he said softly.

Vic smiled. "Can't get rid of me that easily." He glanced at his room. "Where am I?"

"In a clinic north of Manchester. Aelryn had you brought here. He said it was the least he could do after everything you did for him."

Crank recognized that soft gleam in Vic's eyes. It usually spelled trouble. "And what just crossed *your* mind?"

Vic casually rolled one shoulder. "Nothing. It's… well, I've heard there are some great BDSM bars in Manchester. Maybe we can check a few out while we're here."

Saul snorted. "I might've guessed. I should never have taken you to that club in San Francisco. It's given you ideas."

Vic grinned. "Yeah, but really *good* ideas."

"Well, you can forget it. You're confined to the bed until the doctors give you the all clear." Crank ran his fingers through Vic's hair. "But we can come back, if you want."

"No, I just want to go home." Vic's sigh came from someplace deep. "That mission to meet the leaders seems like a century ago. So where did I end up?"

"Lancashire, in the UK." Crank grinned. "And do we have news for you. Since you've been gone, mates have been crawling out of the woodwork."

"Oh?"

Saul glared at Crank. "He needs to rest."

Vic scowled. "No, I need to catch up. What have I missed?"

"Sleep. You've missed sleep. Now shut up," Saul insisted.

He smirked. "I swear, it's like you two don't know me at all."

Crank settled in the chair next to Vic's bed and filled him in about Jake and Doc, and Eve, Hashtag, and Roadkill, loving Vic's comical expression of surprise, especially when Saul revealed Eve was capable of wiping the floor with both her mates, probably at the same time. When Crank told him about Fielding's death, he went quiet for a moment.

"Is it wrong that I'm glad he's dead? After the way he had Saul tortured?"

Crank squeezed Vic's hand. "I'd be worried if you showed any sign of grief. The guy was a fucking—"

"Whatever he was, it was thanks to Jake's interrogation, and his and Seth's gifts, that we discovered where you were," Saul interjected. "Not to mention what Theron was hiding."

Vic stilled. "Would that have anything to do with artifacts?"

Crank nodded. "Jake and Seth have gone with them to Rome with that archivist."

"Orsini?" He smiled. "This is great news." Then he yawned.

"And we've talked too much. Saul's right. You need sleep." Crank caressed Vic's cheek. "What are you looking forward to most about getting home?"

Vic smiled. "Going for a swim in the lake. Preferably with you two." He closed his eyes. "And having a batch of Mrs. Landon's oatmeal raisin cookies all to myself," he murmured.

Seconds later, he was fast asleep.

"*Now* will you take a break?" Crank demanded.

Saul stood. "Yes." He gave Crank an inquiring glance. "You think Brits can make decent pizza?"

Crank laughed. "Anyone can make decent pizza. Let's google it, though. Just to be sure. I've seen what these people eat for breakfast, and I worry about what might end up as a topping." He cast a last glance at Vic as they left the room.

It's going to be okay.

VALMER DIDN'T spare the awesome surroundings of Leighton Hall a second glance.

He only had eyes for Rudy.

He caught Rudy's scent the moment he crossed the threshold, and sure enough, there was his mate, waiting for him with open arms.

Valmer didn't hesitate. He grabbed Rudy and swung him around, unable to restrain the joyous laughter that tumbled from his lips. Rudy locked his arms around Valmer's neck and his legs around Valmer's waist, their mouths fused in kiss after kiss.

"Oh my God, you're really here," Rudy murmured between kisses.

"Me? I'm the proverbial bad penny. I keep turning up," Valmer teased, before claiming Rudy's lips in another passionate kiss. "Fuck, you smell good. You taste good too."

A cough behind him reined in Valmer's exuberance, and he lowered Rudy to his feet. Aelryn stood by the door, smiling, his eyes bright.

"That was a pleasant sight at the end of this day." He came forward. "We have a few days here before we leave for the US. Enjoy the hall—and each other's company, of course. Richard's cook is amazing. I promise you will not go hungry within these walls. The gardens are beautiful." Aelryn gave a short bow. "And now I'll leave you alone."

"Aelryn," Valmer blurted. "Thank you. For rescuing me. And for sparing Rudy."

Aelryn's face glowed. "I too have mates. I'd like to think someone else in my position would have done the same thing." And with that he left the hall.

"They've given us a beautiful room," Rudy told him. "A few days R and R is exactly what you need."

"What I *need* is to call my parents." Valmer grabbed Rudy's hand. "Thank you for thinking of them. I was going out of my mind worrying about them—and you."

Rudy flushed. "They were startled to learn we were mates, but they soon adjusted to the idea." He bit his lip. "I'm sorry, but they asked me where you were and what had happened to you, so… I told them. They know it was the Gerans behind it."

"Did they believe you?" Valmer imagined his father would be difficult to convince.

Rudy frowned. "I thought they were going to give me a hard time at first, but no, they accepted what I told them." He smiled. "Word is getting out. People are starting to learn what the Gerans have been doing in secret."

Valmer huffed. "Whatever's gotten out, I suspect that is just the tip of the iceberg. There's a lot more to come."

And when it's finally out there, I'm going to do my damnedest to make sure every shifter on the planet learns the truth.

Chapter Seventeen

Jamie wasn't surprised to find he didn't have an apartment anymore. What else was his landlord expected to do when there'd been no word from him for months? The lease should have been renewed a month after the Gerans had snatched him. At least all his stuff had been packed up and stored: Jamie knew that had to have been Lauren's doing. As the landlord's wife, she was the one who took care of the tenants, took in packages when they were out, and generally acted like a mom to everyone in the building.

The hug she gave Jamie when she opened the door almost brought him to tears.

I might never have seen her again.

He owed Horvan, Aelryn, and their teams big-time.

"So where have you been?" Lauren asked as she poured him a cup of tea. "I was worried when I couldn't get through to you either by phone or email. It was as if you'd dropped off the face of the earth."

He glanced around her kitchen with its pale cream walls, cherrywood cabinets, and gleaming pots and pans hanging from hooks over the kitchen island, and he had to fight to maintain his self-control. It all seemed so… normal, and a universe away from what he'd been through.

"I can't tell you," he said at last. "I do understand why Craig gave my apartment to someone else when the lease was up. And thanks for storing my stuff. I don't suppose there's another apartment going empty right now?"

She shook her head. "And no leases up for renewal either, so there won't be anything for a while." She gazed at him, her eyes warm. "What will you do?"

"Oh, don't worry about me. I'll find something," he said nonchalantly.

There *was* one route open to him—Aelryn had said he could stay at the school for a while. And if he did get a job there, that would be his accommodation taken care of.

"Well, when you find a place, let me know, and I'll have Craig bring over all your things." She chuckled. "That man needs to be kept busy. Now drink your tea, and help yourself to some of my shortbread. You look as if you need fattening up a little. Wherever you've been, they obviously haven't been overfeeding you."

If you only knew.

Jamie stilled. He didn't like the negativity that had forced its way into his thinking of late.

Well, no more. I'm going to put the last months behind me and try to forget them.

Except he knew it wouldn't be *that* easy.

"So you've worked for the school before?" The new principal, Gina Payton, seemed easier-going than the previous incumbent, but they hadn't gotten to the awkward questions yet.

The ones where he told her he used to be a Geran, and exactly what he did for the school. Two items that were sure to blot his copybook.

"Yes, but not as a teacher. My job was to interview parents who wanted their child to attend here. I realize that while this is still a school, it's changed dramatically since—"

She held up her hand. "Mr. Matheson, I don't want to dwell on the past. Since I was brought in to run this institution, I've made it my goal to provide a safe, positive environment. Every student here was previously in a school in Texas. They've been brought here to start a new life, and this administration is currently seeking foster families for them."

"Does the school provide therapy for the students? Because I imagine many of them will need it."

She arched her eyebrows. "Why yes, we do." She paused. "Where have you been since you last worked for the school?"

He looked her in the eye. "In a Geran camp in northern Maine."

She studied him for a moment. "Then I should think you might need a little therapy yourself."

"Let's just say it's on my to-do list."

Gina leaned forward, her hands clasped. "You said in your email that you want to work here. In your previous capacity?"

He shuddered. "Oh gods, no. The way I described my previous employment made it sound quite innocuous. I don't want to tell you what the school did with the information I gave them—a process I knew nothing about until someone opened my eyes to what was really going on." He paused. "I have a degree. What I lack are teaching qualifications." And now he'd finally gotten to the point, his courage failed him.

Why would they want me? What benefit could I bring to the school?

Gina didn't break eye contact, and he squirmed under her intense scrutiny. Finally she sat back in her chair. "I'd like to propose something rather unorthodox. You don't have to say yes, but maybe you should consider it."

Jamie blinked. "I'm all ears."

"Suppose I were to offer you a place here as a teaching assistant. We'd train you on the job, as it were."

His heart hammered, but before he could tell her what a wonderful idea it was, she held up her hand.

"However... I would also like you to work with our two counselors, to be involved in their sessions with the students. And I'd like you to consider taking a course in counseling. I think you have a lot to offer our students." She smiled. "I know this isn't how things are done in human schools—I've worked in a couple of them—but these are no ordinary students. They've been brought up to believe they have a particular place on this earth, and—"

"I was brought up the same way," Jamie blurted. "I believed what my parents and teachers told me. I was a student here too."

She smiled, and it reached her eyes. "But you know the truth now, don't you?"

He returned her smile. "Yes, ma'am."

"So *you* have been where they are now. You *know* what is going through their minds. They need support, encouragement, and while the staff and counselors can give them that, *you* can give them something unique—understanding and insight."

Jamie swallowed. "I like your unorthodox proposal, Ms. Payton."

Her eyes sparkled. "I thought you might. Your salary wouldn't be large to begin with—that will grow as you gain experience—but we'd provide you with all your meals, accommodation, laundry facilities...." She paused. "Although I should warn you about the two counselors you'd be working under. They already have a bit of a following around here. They're rather exuberant characters, and the students adore them."

"Would it be rude of me to ask what they are?" He was dying to know.

She chuckled. "I don't see that as an issue, seeing as you'll be working with them. Shawn is a grizzly, and Brandon is a North American cougar.

And one thing more…." She gazed at him. "I don't know if you've ever met any shifters like them before."

Jamie raised his eyebrows. "What makes them so different?"

"It was the first time I'd come across this, but since then I've met more, so—"

"They're mates, aren't they?" Jamie smiled. *What is there, something in the water?*

Gina stared at him. "You know about this?"

He laughed. "My half brothers have mates, their friends have mates, my dad has a mate. I guess you could say I know a bit about it."

She beamed. "That's something else you can discuss with the students. Word is getting around, and they have so many questions."

"I'm not sure I have the answers, but I'll do my best." He tilted his head to one side. "Is that why they have a following? Because the students know they're mates?"

"Partly." She chuckled. "It might also be because they're rather good-looking gentlemen, and they have a lot of admirers—girls *and* boys." She extended a hand across the desk. "Welcome aboard, Mr. Matheson."

"Delighted to be here, Ms. Payton."

Gina stood. "I'll show you the way to the staff accommodations and we'll find you a room. Then we'll come back and sort out the paperwork."

For a while at least, Jamie had a home, and possibly two careers.

He was content.

JAMIE CALLED Dellan as soon as Gina had finished with him.

"Hey, how did the mission go? Are you still in the UK?"

"Yeah, we're still here. Vic's okay. Saul and Crank are with him at a clinic. Theron's locked up in Richard's dungeon until Aelryn moves him. Dad's going to Rome with Seth, Brick, and Orsini. And… we lost Alec."

Jamie's throat seized. He'd hoped they could've done something, but….

"He was too far gone and in so much pain." The tremor in his voice told Jamie how hard Dellan was fighting to keep his emotions under control.

"I'm so sorry."

"But enough about us. What about you? What's going on in Boston?"

Jamie told him the good news, and the joy in Dellan's voice reminded him what a generous, kind man he'd gotten for a half brother. *He's going through hell, and he can still be happy for me.*

"So what are they like, these counselors you're going to be working with?"

"I only just signed my contract! I haven't met them yet. In fact, all I've seen is my room." Which was more than satisfactory. He'd call Lauren later and make arrangements to move his stuff.

"Well, let me know. And tell me how things are going, okay?"

"Of course. As long as you keep me informed about whatever Dad discovers in Rome."

"I will. Visit as soon as you can, all right?"

"I promise. Give my best wishes to Horvan and Rael." He hung up.

It felt strange being back in the school, a place he'd known since childhood. He had to admit, he liked the atmosphere.

They're doing something right, obviously.

He walked through the hallways as the bell rang for lunch. Doors opened, and kids of all shapes and sizes poured out from the classrooms, chatting, laughing like kids anywhere in the world. Here and there he noticed a few students who didn't appear as carefree as most of their classmates, their brows knitted, their eyes dull, but he also noticed how it wasn't long before another student joined them, talked with them, linked arms with them.

They're looking out for each other.

Which was as it should be. And *much* better than listening to the pessimistic voice in his head that told him to take nothing at face value, that they could just as easily be espousing Geran garbage to try and persuade others that nothing had changed, that they didn't like the idea of Fridans in charge of the school.

I can't hear you. Jamie would have stuck his fingers in his ears but for the fact that it would have drawn weird glances from those around him.

He headed for the staff quarters. Dellan had told him to visit the infirmary, where Aelryn's mate, Scott, was working, and he planned on doing that after lunch.

The staff bedrooms were in the oldest part of the school, with high ceilings and tall windows. His room was on the top floor and so far was the only one of four that was occupied. No one had thought to install elevators, so he figured the stairs would keep him fit.

Maybe I should look for a gym too. Someplace local. Not right away, though. He still needed to get back into a regular schedule of meals. Lauren had nailed it—he'd lost a lot of weight.

He passed teachers on their way down the stairs as he climbed, and everyone gave him a nod or a smile. Once he was inside his room, he closed the door and took a deep breath.

I have a home again. And when his stuff arrived, it would start to feel like a home.

His phone buzzed, and he smiled when he saw it was his dad.

"So, you finally got yourself a cell phone, huh?" Jamie said teasingly.

"Don't even go there," he growled. "I saw a little kid using one this morning. A *kid*, for God's sake. That was the last straw. I got Orsini to take me to a store. An Italian phone will still work in the US, won't it?"

Oh, bless him.

"Dad, it'll work anywhere. Just change the SIM when you get back to the States."

"The what? Never mind. How are you?"

"I'm fine." Then he smiled. "Actually, I'm better than fine." He told him his news.

"That's awesome! I'm so happy for you. So I guess this means your life is finally coming together again."

Almost. There were still a few holes to be filled.

One hole in particular.

"When do you get to look at whatever you found in the UK? And what time is it in Rome now? Dinnertime?"

"That's right. And we're going to the archive in the morning." He paused. "To be honest, I'm a little nervous."

"Dad, you've got this." Jamie was in awe of his dad's gifts.

"You don't understand. What makes me nervous isn't that I might not be able to glean anything from the artifacts, but rather how much we're about to discover—or how little. I've built this up in my mind, and if I go in there and find a thousand-year-old shopping list, I'm going to be a bit disappointed, you know?"

"What does your gut tell you?" Jamie was trying to listen to his more and more.

Another pause, followed by a sigh. "That it's going to be a helluva lot more than that."

"Hey, Dad? You want to sound like you're living in the twenty-first century? We'd say hella more."

"What? That sounds awful."

"Here's what I suggest. Get Orsini to take you, Seth, and Brick out for some delicious pasta—or even a pizza, because a pizza in Italy has to be good, right?—drink a couple of glasses of wine, and get some sleep. In the morning you're going to be the incredible man I know you are."

"Love you." His dad sounded a little choked.

"Love you too. Now go find some pizza."

Dad laughed. "I'm on it. Good night, son." He hung up.

Jamie couldn't escape the feeling that he'd helped, and *damn*, that felt good.

He glanced into the small bathroom, and the sight of the shower was enough to have him remove his clothes and climb into the enclosure. The water was warm, so good against his skin, sluicing away the sweat brought on by the day's heat. He didn't have a change of clothing, but he was cleaner, and he smelled better.

His stomach rumbled, and he wondered if anyone would mind if he grabbed a bite in the cafeteria. He left his room and headed down the stairs. As he approached the floor below, he caught the sound of two deep, gruff male voices in the middle of an argument.

"All I said was he was cute. Doesn't mean I wanna do anything with him, okay? And you *know* I wouldn't."

"Then why all the puppy-dog eyes? Hmm?"

Jamie chuckled. *A lovers' tiff. How sweet.*

Then he rounded the corner of the stairs and saw the speakers. Both men were muscled to the hilt, sporting healthy beards, and they had to be at least six feet.

Two walking mountains, he mused. Who had the best taste in cologne, because they smelled amazing.

The older of the men jerked his head in Jamie's direction, and he dug his elbow into the other guy's ribs. Both stopped and stared at him, their chests rising and falling rapidly.

"Are you okay?" Jamie asked as he approached them. Their cologne grew more overpowering the nearer he got, and it went straight to his head—

And his dick.

The older guy grabbed Jamie and shoved him against the wall. "Mate!" Then the other guy got in on the action, two hard bodies crushing him.

What the fuck?

Chapter Eighteen

"Names would be nice," Jamie gasped. "You know, before you drive all the air from my lungs." Not that he was complaining. Every cell in his body felt as though it was vibrating, and the feel of their hands on him amplified the reaction.

The guy with the shaved buzz cut hoisted Jamie into his arms, his huge hands supporting Jamie's ass. "Get the door, B."

"Hello would be good too," Jamie called out as the younger guy led the way along the hallway to a door. "You know, instead of coming across as full-on Neanderthals?" His heart pounded, and his breathing was ragged.

And damn it, his boner would *not* quit.

"We can talk in here," the older guy said as the other pushed open the door.

Jamie had a feeling they were going to do more than talk, and his hole clenched at the thought.

The guy lowered Jamie to the ground, then leaned in and nuzzled his neck. "Fuck, you smell good. Like apple pie and curry, rolled into one."

The younger man was at Jamie's back in a heartbeat, inhaling deeply. "No, he's more like a cinnamon roll. All sugary and warm spiciness."

"You both sound as if you're about to eat me," Jamie quipped.

The older guy's eyes gleamed. "Well, I know where *I* wanna start."

Despite his eagerness to have at least one of them plowing him, there was something much more important to address first.

Mates?

One way to find out.

Jamie took a deep breath. *Whoa there. Slow the fuck down, okay?*

They both froze, and there it was, the confirmation Jamie needed. *You really are my mates, aren't you? Because you can hear this.*

Buzz Cut Guy gaped at him. "How the fuck did you do that?"

Jamie rolled his eyes. "I just told you. Mates can do this. I know, it messes with your head. The first time I heard about it, I didn't believe it, but—"

He pressed two fingers to Jamie's lips. "Let's start again, what do you say?"

Jamie grinned. "Works for me. Can we get to the part where you tell me who you are?" He took stock of his surroundings. They were standing in a room that served as both living area and bedroom. There was a large couch that took up most of the wall space on the window side, and the bed was a king.

"Biggest we could squeeze in here," the younger man informed him.

Jamie took stock of him too. His dark brown hair was short at the sides and full and wavy on top, his eyes an equally dark brown. His neat beard made Jamie's fingers itch to stroke it.

Well, one of us needs to get this ball rolling.

"I'm Jamie, Jamie Matheson."

Buzz Cut Guy stared at him. "The guy we just got a call about? The one who's going to be working with us?"

No. Fucking. Way. These were the counselors Ms. Payton had spoken about? The ones he'd be working under.

Literally, it seemed.

Jamie's mouth fell open. "You're Shawn." His beard was thick and full, reaching his chest, and the way his biceps bulged made Jamie's mouth water and his tongue ache to lick the firm flesh.

Jamie imagined he was a magnificent grizzly.

"How did you work that out?"

He smiled. "You called him B, which makes him Brandon. Process of elimination." Which also made him a North American mountain lion.

Yeah, Jamie could see that too.

Shawn grinned. "Hey, looks like we got ourselves a smart one, B." He gestured to the couch. "Wanna sit while we talk?"

Jamie chuckled. "So you do actually plan on talking to me?"

"Well...." Brandon shrugged. "For a couple of minutes. Then the clothes are coming off."

"What he said," Shawn added.

He laughed. "Can you both get your hormones under control, please?"

Shawn sniffed, and his grin widened. "From the smell of you, I'd say you're in the same condition. And if you knew how long we've been waiting to get laid, you'd be more cooperative."

Brandon snorted. "You make it sound as if we're in need of a pity fuck." Then he chuckled. "Which I guess we are. I haven't had sex for two months."

"Hell, it's been four months for me."

Jamie frowned. "But… you're mates." He stared at them. "You mean… you two haven't…?"

Shawn rolled his eyes. "With him? Fuck no. I'm a strict top. Ain't no one's dick getting within an inch of *this* ass."

"And I'm the same," Brandon added.

Jamie was struggling to follow the conversation. "Then why not go out and find someone? You're both gorgeous. There has to be a guy out there who'd be more than happy to accommodate you."

Shawn's brows knitted. "Unfortunately, there appear to be rules."

"Which we didn't know about until the first time we got invited back to a guy's place."

"What happened?"

Brandon scowled. "He took his clothes off, and Shawn threw up. Then I got a whopper of a migraine. We made our apologies and left."

"The second we hit the street? We felt fine. When it happened again the next night, we got the message." Shawn sighed. "We're mates. Which apparently means we can't be with anyone else. So we've been watching porn together—"

"*So* much porn," Brandon added.

Jamie smirked. "Is that ever a bad thing?"

"And jacking off separately," Shawn said with a glum expression.

He gaped. "You don't even, um… lend each other a hand?"

"That feels weird as fuck," Brandon told him. "*Some* things seem to be okay. Kissing works. Go figure. So we've been doing a lot of that." He cackled. "We're thinking of buying shares in lip salve. Anyhow, we assumed Fate screwed up. Then we heard mates come in threes, and we held out hope that we'd meet ours and things would change." He leaned in and sniffed Shawn's throat. "Well, what do you know about that? You smell different."

"A good different?"

Brandon grinned. "Oh yeah."

Jamie loved how they didn't hesitate to kiss, cupping each other's faces, lost in one another for a moment. When they parted, Shawn cleared his throat. "Sorry about that, but I had to know." He cackled. "Still don't wanna fuck him, though."

He couldn't resist. "And what if *I* said I was a strict top?"

Brandon smirked. "You've got big bottom energy written all over you." He kissed Shawn's throat. "And we'll be using that bottom a lot."

Shawn snorted. "Every fucking day. Maybe multiple times."

Jamie couldn't believe his good fortune. Fate finally got it right.

Then something Brandon said registered.

"Who told you mates came in threes?"

"We met this guy who's working in the medical wing here. Scott. He said the whole not messing with each other part was unique, because he had a mate, and they worked perfectly in the sack way before their third turned up."

"Which *we* thought was total crap, but what did we know? And then he told us he'd found her, which *really* threw us for a loop."

Brandon shook his head. "The idea that someone might have put us with a girl? Dude, I'm gay from the hairs on my head right down to my toes. If you cut me in half, through the middle it would read Gay AF."

Shawn let out another sigh. "So we've gone out every weekend for the last three weeks, searching every gay bar in Boston, hoping to find our third."

"How long have you guys been together?"

"A month," Brandon told him. "Shawn walked in and *boom*, I knew." His eyes gleamed. "Just like when we walked around that corner and there *you* were." He stilled. "And by the way, *what* are you?"

"A tiger."

Brandon beamed. "Another cat. I love it."

"And you were right. I like bottoming. I enjoy it more than topping, if I'm honest." He raked his gaze over them. "And I think I'm going to enjoy it a whole lot with you two."

Shawn studied him. *So do we get to hear* your *life story now? Or do we all get naked and learn what makes each other tick?*

Jamie felt as though he was in one of the cartoons he used to watch as a kid, when there was an angel on one shoulder, a little devil on the other. A sweet voice inside his head was telling him to go find his lunch, that this could wait, that he needed to go slow, talk, bond....

And a raw-as-fuck voice was urging him to forget about eating, waiting, conversation, the social niceties, and get down and dirty.

Which voice are you gonna listen to? Brandon licked his lips.

Lips that would look amazing wrapped around his cock.

Shawn grinned. *And we have a winner.*

Before Jamie could come up with a suitable response, he found himself between them, both men busy with the task of removing his clothing, no words uttered as they bared his skin, their breathing the only sound in the quiet room.

It was heady as fuck, and Jamie's dick pointed to the ceiling like a flagpole.

Shawn sat on the couch, tugging Jamie into his lap, and their lips met in a fierce kiss.

What about your clothes? Aren't you getting undressed?

Brandon's chuckle filled his head. *Later. Right now I have a cock to suck.*

Jamie moaned into Shawn's kiss as Brandon pushed Jamie's legs toward his chest before reaching under the seat cushion and bringing out a bottle of lube.

A second glance revealed it to be edible lube.

"Cherry-flavored?" Jamie stilled. "But...."

"What are we doing with edible lube when we don't play with anyone else?" Shawn chuckled. "I don't know either. I saw it at the supermarket, and something told me to buy it. So I did."

"And we're going to need it," Brandon said in a husky voice.

Shawn's breath tickled his ear. "Are we good to go bare? Our latest results are on our phones."

"Mine too." Thank God he'd had a full physical once they'd freed him from the camp.

Then Shawn claimed his mouth once more, and Brandon slid a slick finger into his hole while he bent down to lick the head of Jamie's dick.

Jamie groaned and arched his back, Shawn's tongue exploring him as Brandon swallowed him to the root.

It felt illicit, being naked while they were dressed, Shawn tugging on Jamie's nipples with his teeth, Brandon's finger fucking his ass, his hand curled around Jamie's rigid cock. Jamie looped an arm around Shawn's shoulder and clung to him, battered by the double sensual assault, his shivers multiplying as his mates' enjoyment washed over and through him.

He could feel everything they felt. It was glorious, delicious, and he wanted more.

And then Shawn added his finger to Brandon's, and Jamie couldn't rein in his fervent groan of pleasure.

"Let's move this to the bed," Shawn murmured.

Brandon reacted a second later, lifting Jamie into his arms and then carrying him toward the wide bed covered in a rich gold comforter, pillows in matching cases scattered against the headboard.

Shawn climbed onto the bed. "Kneel facing me."

It took Jamie only a heartbeat to realize he liked being told what to do.

Behind him, Brandon nuzzled his ear. "You didn't know this about yourself?"

He shook his head.

Shawn chuckled. "Which only goes to prove someone knew what they were doing when they put us together." He stroked Jamie's neck while he kissed him, one hand moving down his chest until he reached his nipple.

The tug on the nub of taut flesh went all the way to Jamie's dick, and he moaned into the kiss, the volume increasing as Brandon spread his cheeks and dove in, his tongue demanding entry. Jamie tilted his ass, and Brandon pulled back, laughing.

"Our boy likes his ass eaten."

Fuck. Brandon's words were as hot as his tongue.

Jamie had no idea how long they spent in that position on the bed, him kissing Shawn while Brandon loosened Jamie's hole with his tongue. He only knew that by the time his mates removed their own clothing, he was more than ready to be fucked.

Shawn knelt in front of Jamie, who was on all fours. "I want to watch him slide into you." He grabbed his own thick cock and smacked it against Jamie's cheek, and a moment later, Jamie's mouth was fuller than it had ever been, his nose pressed into wiry pubes. He groaned around its girth, only to moan louder when the head of Brandon's cock popped through the ring of muscle, and there he was, filled from both ends.

And happier than he'd been in a long time.

They fucked him together, Shawn leaning over Jamie's back, and judging by the sounds above him, they were kissing. Then Shawn groaned.

Holy fuck, that looks so hot.

Brandon moaned. *The feel of his ass when I drive into him. So warm, so tight. You need to feel this too.*

Jamie wanted to yell at Brandon to stay where he was, and his hole ached as Brandon pulled free of his body. Then Brandon flipped onto his back, tugging Jamie to straddle him, his face inches from Brandon's slick cock, his own shaft pointing toward Brandon's lips.

"You know where this has just been?"

The raw edge to Brandon's voice was a total turn-on. "I couldn't miss it. You're not exactly small."

"So if I tell you to suck it, what are you gonna do?"

An illicit shiver coursed through Jamie as he engulfed Brandon's dick with his mouth, and then a wave of pleasure washed over him as Brandon mimicked him, the pair of them settling into a rhythm—

Broken when Shawn penetrated him, stretching him wider than ever.

Jamie moaned around Brandon's cock, lost in the sensations that flowed through Brandon as he looked up and watched Shawn's dick driving into Jamie's hole.

He could see what they saw, feel what they felt, and all of it was pushing him ever closer to his orgasm.

"Want you to ride me," Shawn said in a gruff voice.

Jamie pulled free of Brandon's dick, chains of saliva falling from his lips. Shawn lay on the bed, holding his shaft steady around the base. Brandon wiped slick fingers over it before Jamie sat astride him, easing the wide head into him. He bent over to kiss Shawn, his breath catching as Brandon fondled his cock.

"Fuck yourself on it," Shawn growled.

Jamie rolled his hips, Shawn's dick going deep as he rocked back and forth.

Can you both see this, if I do? Brandon asked.

Jamie's head was filled with the image of Shawn's glistening shaft sliding in and out as Jamie impaled himself on it over and over again. The sight, coupled with the physical sensations, propelled him closer to the precipice, and he rocked faster, his moans punctuation for each thrust of Shawn's cock.

Then Brandon climbed onto the bed behind him, and there was the unmistakable feel of a warm, solid dick smacking against his asscheek.

Jamie stilled. "Are you going to...."

Brandon's throaty chuckle made his heart beat faster.

The image Brandon sent surging over him almost stopped it.

Oh gods. I've never....

Brandon nuzzled his neck again, and that was *really* fighting dirty. His neck was a hot spot.

But you know that, don't you?

Another throaty chuckle. *Oh yeah. And I know something else too. You want this. You want both of us inside you, stretching you, filling you....*

It was useless to deny it when both his mates could read him like a book.

He gasped when Brandon eased a slick finger into his hole, Shawn stilling for him. "How's that?"

Jamie's heart hammered. "G-good."

Then he added another, and Jamie moaned.

"Gotta loosen you up a little. We're not exactly small," Shawn said with a chuckle.

"Really? I hadn't noticed," Jamie lied. His mates' packages were in proportion to their size.

And there was Brandon once more, tapping against his asscheek.

Gonna let me in there?

There was nothing Jamie wanted more. He'd watched three-ways on his phone, his laptop, and every time a guy took two dicks at once, the same thought had sent shivers through him.

I want to know how that feels.

It seemed Someone had been listening.

Shawn pulled him lower until Jamie's chest met his, Shawn's hand on his nape.

Look at me, he urged. *I want to watch your face when he enters you.*

Jamie stared into Shawn's eyes, his breath stuttering as Brandon eased his cock into Jamie's hole, sliding alongside Shawn's.

Oh holy, holy fuck.

Shawn gazed up at him, his mouth open, and with such an awed expression that Jamie's heart quaked to see it. "You're our beautiful boy."

"Yours," Jamie croaked.

"And we're yours." Brandon's breath was warm on his neck.

"Mine."

The words sounded like a vow, and that felt so fucking *right*.

Brandon and Shawn worked together, taking turns to slide in and out, slowly to begin with, then gaining momentum, their breathless moans filling the air as surely as their shafts filled Jamie's body. Brandon was the first to shoot his load, and Jamie cried out to feel both the throb of his cock and the wave of ecstasy that surged through his mate.

And then Shawn came with a roar, hips tilted as he thrust up into Jamie's hole, before he grabbed Jamie's head and pulled him down into a brutal kiss.

I don't think I can....

With a cry, Jamie came, his cock pulsing onto Shawn's chest, his body shaking as they cradled him, kissing him, murmuring words that made no sense—and yet they did, soothing sounds that spoke of exquisite pleasure.

Of love.

They lay on the bed, limbs entwined, a puzzle made of flesh. Jamie wanted to tell them how wonderful it had been, how no one had ever taken him to such heights.

Then it hit him.

They already know.

"I have so much to tell you," he whispered. Then his stomach grumbled, and he chuckled. "Except that might have to wait."

"Let's get cleaned up, and then we'll feed you."

Brandon regarded him thoughtfully. "What's wrong?"

Jamie sighed. "There's a whole lot of stuff going on out there, and you need to know about it."

"What kind of stuff?" Shawn asked.

There was no use trying to hide it.

"Things that could change our world."

Chapter Nineteen

"Want to tell me where I'm going?" Roadkill stared through the windshield.

Hashtag snickered. "You need to trust her. She's giving you clear directions, isn't she?" He was as curious as Roadkill—he just wasn't about to show it.

"What he said. I won't steer you wrong." Eve had been a little bouncy all morning, and while he might not have known her all that long, he knew enough to get the feeling she was hiding something. Not that she'd given anything away in her thoughts, which made him all the more certain she was blocking them.

What are you up to?

"I'm amazed you got Horvan to okay this trip to… wherever. You must've caught him on a good day." Roadkill frowned. "We must be nearly there. We've been driving for over an hour."

"Not far now. When you see Tesco's, look out on your left for Stockbridge Drive shortly after."

"What's Tesco's?" Hashtag inquired. It still gave him the shivers to drive on the left.

"It's a supermarket." Eve pointed. "There it is. Now watch out for the turn."

Roadkill smiled. "Got it." He turned off the main road, and they were on a narrow lane, a fence to one side and open fields lined with trees to the other.

Hashtag caught sight of a white sign. "National Trust: Gawthorpe." He gasped. "Why didn't you just say we were going to visit Gawthorpe Hall? I assumed you'd want to do that while we were in the neighborhood."

Eve laughed. "I hate to break it to you, but for Brits, a drive of one hour and—" She checked her phone. "—thirty minutes is not 'in the neighborhood.' You know the main difference between the US and the UK?"

"They can't speak English properly?" Roadkill quipped. Eve smacked him on the arm, and he gave her a mock glare. "Hey! Don't hit the driver!"

"I was *about* to say, in the UK, a hundred miles seems like a long way, and in the US, a hundred years feels like a long time."

The fields gave way to trees on both sides, and Hashtag chuckled. "Well, you could always ask the owner of these woods for permission to chop down some trees if the fuel gets too expensive."

Eve coughed. "That would be me."

He gaped. "This is all part of the estate?"

She laughed. "I told you it has forty acres, right? Do you know how much land that is?" Then she straightened. "Turn left into the parking lot."

Roadkill did as instructed and then drove into a space. He switched off the engine, and they got out. "Where now? I don't see anything."

Eve led them back onto the lane, then pointed ahead of them. "This takes you straight to the Hall, but I want your first view to be the best, so follow me."

They walked with her along the tree-covered drive, and then she took a path to the right. "This brings us out at the far end of the lawn. Now, don't look to the left until I tell you, okay?"

Roadkill chuckled. "This is like a mystery tour."

Hashtag was dying to take a peek, but he knew this was important to Eve. At last they came to a halt.

"Okay, boys. *Now* you can turn to the left."

He turned—and gasped.

"It was impressive online, but now I see it in real life...."

Hashtag was officially blown away.

Gawthorpe Hall was a square stone-built edifice with a four-sided tower rising from its center. It was three stories high, topped with an intricately carved rampart. The main door sat in a portico, with four steps leading up to it and stone pillars on either side. A curved, gravel-covered driveway cut into the lawn, and Hashtag could imagine carriages driving up to the front of the house and footmen opening doors and helping richly-dressed ladies out of them.

"How old did you say this place was?" Roadkill sounded awed, not that Hashtag could blame him for that.

"It's Elizabethan," Eve reminded them. "On the other side, there's a beautiful garden laid out in a semicircle, overlooking the River Calder."

"Eve, it's… it's awesome." Hashtag climbed the flight of stone steps that led up to the vast front lawn. "Okay, I was crap at history in high school, but Elizabethan… as in Elizabeth the first? Early sixteen hundreds?"

She nodded. "It was originally a tower, but it was developed into an Elizabethan mansion round about then, yes. Then in the eighteen fifties, it was redesigned." She cocked her head. "Have either of you seen that TV show, *Downton Abbey*?"

Hashtag beamed. "I loved it."

"Well, the architect who designed Highclere Castle, where it was set, was also the one who worked on Gawthorpe. He did the Houses of Parliament too." She widened her eyes. "And I told you that too. Is this going to be a thing, you two not listening to a word I say?"

"We *heard* you," Hashtag remonstrated. "But hearing is one thing—finding yourself confronted with a piece of history is something else."

"What he said." Roadkill shook his head. "This blows my mind."

She grinned. "Wait until you see the inside."

Walking through the wide wooden front door, set into beige-colored stone, through an archway hung with richly tapestried curtains, gave Hashtag a thrill.

"You get the full tour," Eve told them before taking them through a long gallery with varnished floorboards and a molded ceiling. Paintings hung every few feet, covering wallpaper decorated with a rich brocade, and on either side were chairs, tables, chests, all of them made from a dark glossy wood that spoke of centuries of use.

Every room was a revelation, from the dining room with its huge stone fireplace and chandeliers over the table, its upper minstrels gallery on which was mounted a stag's head, the winding staircase at the corner of the Hall, its worn stone steps recording the passage of time, ending in a balcony from which Hashtag stared down at the linen-fold wood panels and the tiled floor with its intricate design.

"I don't know what to say," he said at last.

"Do you like it?"

He laughed. "Are you kidding? It's amazing."

"How many bedrooms does this place have?" Roadkill asked.

"I don't know. I never counted them." Eve cocked her head. "Would you like to see the master bedroom?"

"Lead the way."

Eve took them along the hallway, Hashtag and Roadkill following, their steps slower.

"Do you believe this?" Roadkill muttered. "I feel like freakin' royalty just walking up those stairs."

"Up the stairs? How about through the front door?" They went into the bedroom, and Hashtag let out a gasp. "Oh my fucking God."

The bed looked as if it belonged in Buckingham Palace. It was made of the same dark glossy wood Hashtag had seen in the long gallery, covered in ornate carvings, its four posts supporting the roof of the bed with its sculpted edges. Deep cream and floral curtains framed the headboard that went all the way to the ceiling. A padded footstool sat on the warm rug next to the bed, clearly to help its occupant gain access.

"You couldn't sleep in a bed like that," he remonstrated.

"Why not?" Eve's eyes sparkled. "We could give it a try."

"Okay, can we be serious for a minute?" Roadkill stared at the opulent room. "You said once that you'd have been happy to burn this place to the ground, because of its associations with your grandfather and his support of the Gerans."

"Yeah, I did. I've changed my mind." Eve sat on the couch at the foot of the bed. "There's so much space. Most of it was taken up with servants in Grandfather's day. I think they outnumbered the family three to one. Way too much space for the three of us."

Hashtag blinked. "You want us to *live* here? I thought the county had it on a lease."

"They do, and it's about to expire. And as for living here...." Eve wrung her hands. "I don't know, all right? I need time to process all this."

Hashtag had waited long enough. "What is it you're not telling us?"

EVE SWALLOWED. "I've had an interesting offer." She'd been meaning to bring it up ever since Richard had taken her aside. She should have told them right away, and God knew blocking them had been pure torture, but she wasn't sure how she felt.

This seemed like the perfect time.

"Told us *what* right away?" Roadkill demanded.

"I would *never* ask you to stop doing what you're doing, okay? You're both awesome, and—"

"Eve, if you don't spit it out, we may have to kill you," Hashtag teased.

She snorted. "You could try." Then she let out a sigh. "How would you feel about... working for another leader? In another country?"

"You're talking about here, aren't you?" Roadkill locked gazes with her. "In Lancashire?"

She nodded. "Richard Deveraux spoke with me this morning. He asked if I would join his teams. Actually, he wants me to *lead* a team." Eve grinned. "Apparently my ability to remain cool under pressure during my visit to Theron impressed him. I told him having you two in my head was what gave me the edge. He said I could have whomever I wanted on my team. I'd like for it to be you—if you want. I mean, there's no AC, but could you live here?"

"Can we think about it?" Roadkill quipped. She gasped, and he laughed, grabbing her and spinning her around in his arms until she was dizzy. "Silly woman. Wherever you are, that's home."

"Besides, aren't Horvan and Aelryn joining forces permanently?" Hashtag reminded her. "And Richard is one of Aelryn's leaders, right? So we'd still see the gang from time to time."

"The gang?" She smiled. "They're your family."

Roadkill glanced from Eve to Hashtag, then back to Eve. "Then I guess we're moving."

Hashtag shrugged. "Okay by me." He grinned. "Besides, you know how much I fucking *love* that accent. I may even end up sounding like a Brit. Well, that or Dick Van Dyke."

"Hey, I always thought his accent was spot on," Roadkill remarked.

Eve wanted to dance, she felt so fucking *light*.

"Thank you. And at least we won't have to worry about a roof over our heads." She gestured to the bed. "We still have time to try it out." Then she beamed. "Except what I really want to do is hightail it back to Leighton Hall and give Richard the good news."

Hashtag smiled. "Then that's what we'll do."

"There's one more thing." She squared her shoulders. "Neither of you get to leave this room alive until you've given me some very important information."

"Such as?" Roadkill gave her a quizzical glance.

Eve narrowed her gaze. "I want to know your real names."

They laughed.

Hashtag took hold of her hand. "Delighted to meet you, Eve. I'm Donal Phillips."

Roadkill took her other hand. "And I'm Hiroshi Ogawa."

Eve smiled. "I love your names." She pulled her hands free and looped her arms around their necks. "Now kiss me."

"Bossy woman," Roadkill murmured as he leaned in.

"What he said," Hashtag added before all their lips met in a sweet kiss. *You know you wouldn't have me any other way.*

Their chuckles were all the answer Eve required.

"Now I'll show you the rest," she said when they parted.

Hashtag blinked. "Wait—there's more? And what happened to hightailing it back to Leighton Hall to see Richard?"

She rolled her eyes. "I think we've got time for a quick tour. There are lots of outbuildings, and if you go out the front door and follow the driveway to the left, you'll come to a walled part of the estate. It used to be the stables, and there's a huge grassy area with stone buildings along two sides. It hasn't been used for that purpose for years, of course." She smiled. "If you'd both thought the Hall too grand to live in, I was going to suggest that we convert the stables into something cozy for us."

"I wouldn't say it's *too* grand," Roadkill mused. "But we'd rattle around like peas in a pod, it's so big. Maybe we could live in one wing?"

"Can I see the gardens?" Hashtag asked.

Eve smiled and took his hand. She led them out of the Hall through a side door, and his first thought was that the front of the Hall was far prettier than the rear. A low gray stone wall followed the curve of the semicircular flower beds, urns sitting atop the wall at regular intervals. The beds were laid out in the shape of a flower, its petals open, containing a mix of yellow-leaved shrubs and purple lavender.

Roadkill inclined his head toward the wall. "I can hear the river."

Eve sighed. "This was always my favorite place when I was a little girl. I loved that I could hear the running water from my bedroom whenever I came to visit Grandfather." She smirked. "Which was probably why I had to run to the bathroom a lot."

Hashtag put his arms around her. "You feel better about the place now, don't you?"

She gave him a warm smile. "Yeah, I do. And I think that's down to you two."

They'd helped her see the Hall with fresh eyes.

"So *now* how about we drive back to Leighton Hall and give Richard the good news?" Roadkill suggested.

"Sounds good to me."

"Can we stop off on the way there?" Hashtag inquired.

"Sure. Is there someplace particular you want to go?" When he didn't reply right away, Eve gave him a quizzical glance. "Hey, we can go anywhere you like."

Hashtag bit his lip. "Can we go to Tesco's?"

It was Eve's turn to blink. "Of course, but why?"

He shrugged. "I wanted to see what an English supermarket is like, that's all."

Roadkill snorted. "And the rest. I know what *you're* after."

"I have no idea what you're talking about," he said with a huff.

"Yeah, right." Roadkill grinned at Eve. "You might as well know this now. He's a chocoholic, and he hasn't had a fix for days."

Eve let out a sigh of relief. "Oh, thank God I'm not the only one." She linked arms with them. "Come on. Let's go shopping."

As they walked along the lane to the parking lot, Eve felt happier than she'd been in a long time.

I was worrying about nothing.

They like the idea.

Even better, she'd brought up the possibility of having kids, and they hadn't balked. That plan might have to go on the back burner until she felt the time was right, but she had no doubt they'd make great dads.

This is so strange.

And yet it was a good strange. All her life, she'd been searching for a place where she belonged. At first it was with her family, though they'd seen her as nothing more than a housewife. The Gerans saw her first and foremost as a female, but once she'd established herself, they came to view her as a warrior.

Except they weren't prepared to give her the advancement she so deserved.

Hashtag and Roadkill saw all of her, and they didn't want her to be anything other than who *she* wanted to be.

Heaven help her, she loved the feeling.

Almost as much as she loved her mates.

Yet despite her growing contentment with her changing situation, she couldn't help but wait for the other shoe to drop. It felt too easy. Things like this just didn't happen.

So what was waiting around the corner for her?

For all of them?

Chapter Twenty

Roadkill turned off the car engine and frowned. "Can you hear screaming?"

What Eve loved was the way he tensed his muscles, ready to take action if needed.

Ready to protect us.

Eve laughed. "It's not screaming—it's kids. Richard regularly invites children from the local orphanage to spend time at Leighton Hall. They look after the farm animals, they learn about nature, and they get to be in beautiful surroundings." Then her face tightened. "Except *these* kids are different. Poor things." Richard had told her about the activities planned for that afternoon, but it had slipped her mind.

"Why poor?"

"They were liberated from that camp in Texas." She peered at them. "Weren't *you* part of that mission?"

Hashtag nodded. "That was the second camp we raided. The first was in Montana." He shuddered. "Only Texas was worse."

"Why?"

"The fucking Gerans and their fucked-up breeding program, that's why." The bitterness in Roadkill's voice surprised her. He was usually so easygoing. "We found so many kids there, kept apart from their mothers. God knows what the Gerans were doing to the poor little mites."

She took hold of Roadkill's hand and squeezed it. "But you saved them. That's got to be worth something. And then Aelryn took them out of there."

"How do you know all this?" he asked.

"Richard told me when we talked this morning. He said some of the kids stayed in the US and some came to the UK, to give them a new life over here. That's when he became involved with them. He's helping to find families for them all."

"Their parents didn't want them?" Roadkill seemed horrified. "It's not the kids' fault. They didn't ask to be born. So they were abandoned? How many kids are we talking about?"

"I think he said about twenty in this part of the UK." She tilted her head to one side. "Want to see them? I told Richard we'd help out. You know, playing games with them…."

Hashtag smiled. "We can do that." Then he grinned. "We should get Horvan out here. He could shift and give them rides on his back. I bet they'd love to ride on Mama Bear."

"Or a lion. Or a tiger." Roadkill's eyes widened. "And that might be something Dellan could do too. I know it wouldn't take his mind off things, but it would give him something to focus on."

"Excuse me? Can we go back to… Mama Bear?" Eve bit back a laugh. "Horvan? I can't think of anyone less like a mama bear."

Roadkill rolled his eyes. "Oh gods, don't tell him I said that. He hates it when we call him that."

"No, what he hated was when someone painted his claws with sparkly nail polish while he was taking a nap."

"They didn't." Eve snorted. "Oh, I wish I'd seen that."

Roadkill chuckled. "Don't worry, I have pictures."

"What?" Hashtag squawked. "You never told me that."

"Duh. Because if I had, five seconds later Horvan would have found out, and then he'd have made me delete them."

"I would never tell." He smirked. "Okay, yeah, I probably would have before. But not now. Mate's honor." Hashtag got his phone out. "Let's see if H can spare the kids some time."

Eve and Roadkill left him to his call and walked into the gardens where children of all ages ran around shouting and laughing, the late afternoon sun lighting up the tops of the trees, making them glow. To listen to the happy sounds, no one would ever have guessed the miserable circumstances that had brought the kids to this spot.

Hashtag joined them a minute later. "He loved the idea. He said he'd be right out."

The words had barely left his lips when screams of delight filled the air.

"Kitty!" one little girl hollered and made a beeline for Dellan, who lowered his chest to the ground to allow her to clamber on his back. Then he padded carefully across the lawn, followed by a group of three little boys, all clamoring for their turn to "ride the kitty."

Rael lay on his back while a boy and girl rubbed his tummy.

Eve chuckled. "So that's what a lion sounds like when it's being tickled."

As for Horvan, he was playing tag with five or six children, and judging by the whoops and yells, they were loving every minute of it.

"Wouldn't you love to know what kind of shifters they are?" Roadkill mused. "We could be surrounded by snakes, mice, bunnies—"

"Bunnies?" Hashtag snickered. "Cute, Roadkill, very cute."

A young woman approached them. "I'm Mary Edwards. I take care of the children. I don't know whose idea this was, but it was a masterstroke." She watched the children engaging with Horvan, Dellan, and Rael, her smile constant. "They're so good with children. Do they have any of their own?"

Eve's chest tightened. "No, they don't." *At least none that we know about.* Something in a nearby tree caught her eye. Nestled in the branches, its tail caught between its paws, was an adorable red panda.

"Oh, look at that," she said softly.

Mary followed her glance. "Oh my," she said with a sigh.

It was such a change in her demeanor that it pricked Eve's senses.

"Is everything okay?" Then it struck her. "Why isn't he—or she—playing with the others?"

Mary let out another sigh. "His name is Logan. He's four, and he's scared to death of everything and everyone. We'd hoped bringing him here, letting him touch grass and climb the trees would help, but he's so scared he just stays up there and screams if we try to take him down."

Roadkill growled, and it vibrated through Eve and Hashtag. *Those fucking monsters.*

"You don't know the half of it," Mary muttered.

Oh hell. I said that out loud, didn't I? "Then tell us the rest."

"We've only recently learned about him. Aelryn's people have been going over the records they found in Texas. It seems as though Logan was kept in isolation for most of his life."

"But why?" Eve demanded, aghast.

Do you need to ask? Hashtag snarled. *Why did they do any of the atrocities we've discovered? Because they could. Because no one knew what they were doing.*

Mary regarded her with troubled eyes. "He was rescued from a lab of some sort. He was locked in a cage, crying. When they took him out, he panicked. Even when they tried to talk softly, he screamed. In the end, they had to tranquilize him. The file we found for him had no name listed, so one of our people called him Logan. The name stuck. But if he's ever adopted, his new parents are welcome to change his name."

"What was he doing in a lab?" Not that Eve didn't have her own ideas. She just didn't like them.

"They were doing experiments on him, injecting him with the DNA of other shifters in an attempt to make him viable for… something. And don't ask me what, because they didn't say. One report said he should be culled, but another argued he could be useful."

"Useful." Hashtag's tone was bitter. "They're talking about a little boy."

"In the end, they kept him and subjected him to horrific things. It seems they took his DNA and tried to splice it with the DNA from shifters who exhibited psychic powers. I can only assume they wanted to know if it could be done, and I have no idea if they were successful or not. I didn't think psychic powers could be passed down through the genes, but what do I know?"

"Oh, you'd be amazed by what they've accomplished." Eve shivered. "Except 'horrified' is probably closer to the mark."

Hashtag jerked his head in Roadkill's direction. "You don't think they used Seth or Jake, do you?"

Roadkill frowned. "I don't know how many other psychic shifters they had, so maybe?"

"It doesn't matter," Eve said flatly. "In fact, the only thing that matters is *this* little guy needs help." She crossed the yard and stopped at the tree. The red panda didn't so much as glance at her.

Eve wasn't going to be put off.

"Hey, sweetheart. How are you? My name is Eve." She gestured to the guys, who came over to join her. "And these are Donal and Hiroshi, my mates."

"Hey, big guy." Hashtag kept his voice low and soothing. "It's good to meet you." He reached up and scratched the tiny ears. "Can we call you Logan? You seem like a Logan to me. I love that name."

The little panda shuddered. Hashtag sat at the foot of the tree. "You know, I bet I'm way more comfortable than that branch." He patted his lap. "Why not come down and see if I'm right? You can sit here with us."

Logan gazed at them, almost as if he was trying to judge the sincerity of their words. Finally he stepped gingerly across the branches until he reached the trunk, then moved down the tree head first and dropped onto the ground.

"That a boy," Hashtag said, smiling. "Come on over."

Instead, Logan turned and rushed toward Eve, who swooped him into her arms and held him close. His warm soft fur smelled amazing, but the way he clung to her?

That felt... right.

"It's okay," she whispered. "I swear, it'll be okay." She gazed at her mates, her heart hammering. *I want to help him.*

Roadkill smiled. *Then that's what we'll do.*

Eve blinked. *You don't think it's too soon for us to be adding a child to our practically new relationship?*

No, sweetheart. We know we're bound by fate. Maybe that's why we found this little one now. Fate has more in store for us.

She glanced at Mary. Before Eve could get a word out, she beamed. "All of these children are available for adoption, you know."

See? Hashtag teased. *Fate brought us here for a reason.*

He's right. Roadkill smiled. *And that reason is sleeping in your arms.*

Eve glanced at Logan. Sure enough, he'd fallen asleep, still clutching his tail.

She knew one thing for certain. Fate knew exactly what it was doing when it brought her to Horvan's team.

And speaking of Horvan, he was lumbering over to them, a little boy on his back, his tiny fingers clutching the brown fur around Horvan's neck.

"Way to go..., Mama Bear," she murmured.

That was the first time she'd ever seen a bear roll its eyes.

Eve squared her shoulders and turned to Mary. "Who do we talk to about adoption?"

HORVAN HAD only just shifted back when Aelryn stormed into the hall, his eyes blazing, his cheeks flushed.

"What's happened?"

"It's taken longer than we anticipated, going through the Geran records and data, but details are starting to emerge." Aelryn gritted his teeth. "Monstrous doesn't even begin to cover it. I think if the rank-and-file Gerans knew what was happening, they'd defect in droves."

Horvan had never seen Aelryn so riled up. "What have you found?"

"The breeding program? It wasn't cranking out the foot soldiers fast enough." He widened his eyes. "Do you know they were actually discussing the possibility of implanting embryos in men. Seriously? And what makes this ten times worse is the people they were going to use? The Gerans knew they'd never survive the attempt, and they didn't give a crap."

Horvan went cold. "Tell me this is a joke."

"Oh, I wish it were, but it gets worse. They wanted to see how soon children could be impregnated. Children!"

"But… that would've killed them."

"Exactly. Their bodies wouldn't be able to handle the surge of hormones, not to mention a life growing inside them, or giving birth to a child that might have been huge. Then it gets really interesting. The Gerans had a 'preferred ability' list and wanted to see if they could increase the pool of shifters with those abilities."

"What sort of abilities are we talking about?"

"Things like telekinesis, pyrokinesis, etc. Stuff that *we're* not even sure exist, *they* wanted to try and make reality. And the scariest part? On paper it seems like they were really fucking close on some of these things." Aelryn shivered. "I hope and pray Jake finds what he's looking for, because this needs to end—*now*."

HORVAN FELL back against the pillows, utterly exhausted. Playing with the kids had been fun, and even Dellan seemed to be having a good time, although there was clearly something on his mind he was keeping locked away. When he'd dragged Dellan and Rael to the bedroom, Horvan's intention was to find the perfect way to exhaust them all, allowing them to shut down their brains for a while.

He still couldn't believe what Aelryn had told him. He knew the Gerans were monsters, but he never would have guessed there wasn't a shred of humanity in some of them. *Children, for fuck's sake.* He'd rolled around with those kids, and he'd seen their smiles, heard their laughter, felt their need to be shown they were loved.

And the fucking Gerans had exploited that. When Eve had told him about Logan, Horvan wanted to hit—or kill—something. Maybe someone.

Possibly a lot of someones.

"If three rounds of sex didn't wear you out, we'll need to get some warm milk and cookies, because I don't think I have another go in me," Rael said, stroking his fingers over Horvan's chest. "Or a drop of spunk, if it comes to that."

"I'm sorry. I don't mean to keep you awake."

Rael sat up. "You *do* know the darker your emotions, the harder it is to blot them out, right? Who's got you pissed off?"

He didn't want to tell them. Better they remain somewhat innocent.

Except that's wrong. They're my mates, and I have to trust them to make up their own minds.

Horvan sighed. "What I have to say is hard. Like enough to put you into an anger-induced frenzy kinda hard. That's what has me so worked up." He kissed the top of Dellan's head. "It will be worse for you."

Dellan craned his neck to look Horvan in the eye. "It has something to do with kids, doesn't it?"

"Yeah." Horvan took a deep breath. "It seems as though Alec wasn't the only one. The Gerans did horrible things to a lot of people, kids included. And we might never know the full extent of it all."

Then he told them about Logan, and Eve's intention that she and the guys would adopt him. Even knowing that his life might be shortened, like Alec's, by something the Gerans had done.

Dellan snuggled against Horvan's side. "I wish I didn't want all the Gerans to die. I never thought I had it in me to yearn for harm to come to people like that. But God help me, I want them all to be turned into rock, then ground to a fine powder. I want them put on an island, then have the military nuke the fuck out of them. Like brainwashing the kids wasn't bad enough, they had to dig deeper to show how low they could *really* go."

Rael reached over and stroked Dellan's side. "We're going to win this. It won't fix everything, I know, but we can at least put some things right. The kids they were indoctrinating are being deprogrammed and shown that life as a kid can be—*should* be—fun. We can only do so much. We need to get everyone on the same page and working together."

"Sounds like a perfect job for you, Rael," Horvan suggested.

His eyes widened. "What?"

"You're smooth and confident. You're used to getting people to gather around a problem and solve it. This fight isn't just a war of weapons. It's a war of words. Of winning over the people who aren't sure which side to believe. We have a few others, but they need a leader to help them band together. That could be you." Horvan smiled. "Rael Parton, photojournalist. Who writes books. Perfect."

"And what about Dellan?"

"I have my own ideas," Dellan said in a firm tone. "And I need to pursue them."

"Then I think we have a plan in place," Horvan announced. "Each of us is going to attack this situation from a different angle, and when you add it all up, everyone benefits."

"But...." Rael blew out a sharp breath. "I don't know if I can work with former Gerans."

Dellan sat up and joined hands with Rael and Horvan. "We have to keep one thing in mind. Not every Geran will be bad, like not every Fridan will be good. We have a few Gerans now that we can trust with our lives. We shouldn't harden our hearts against them all just because their leaders are assholes."

"I hate to admit it, but he's right. Eve has proven herself invaluable, and so has Milo. Fine, he wasn't convinced until he found his mate, but he did come around. And what about Valmer Cooper?" Horvan sighed again. "Sometimes all we need is to see the war through someone else's eyes. Don't be the one that closes them to everything."

Rael said nothing for a moment. "You're right. And I'm sorry."

"For what?"

His eyes gleamed. "I think I'm going to need that fourth round."

Horvan chuckled and pulled the blanket back, revealing his hard cock. "I think we can arrange that." He blinked when neither of them made a move, but stared at it. "Hello? You waiting for a written invitation? Get those lips and tongues into gear."

He sighed when both his mates leaned over and began worshipping his aching shaft. But even their sensual adoration didn't take his mind instantly from their conversation.

We're gonna make this work. We have to.

Shifter and human lives depended on them.

Chapter Twenty-One

Jake paused at the scrolled iron gate that marked the entrance to the archive.

"Good to see some things don't change."

"I still can't believe we're here," Brick murmured behind them.

"In Rome?" Seth asked.

"No—in *this* freakin' place. Didn't you see the movie *Angels and Demons*? They filmed in here. Tom Hanks was *here*, goddammit."

Jake frowned. "The actor who was in *Big*? *Splash*? *Dragnet*?"

Brick snorted. "Those are some of his early stuff."

Seth touched his arm. "But not for my dad. Where he's been, there were no movie theaters, remember?"

He flushed. "Yeah. Sorry."

Jake smiled. "It's okay, Brick. I can see I have some catching up to do."

"I have made *some* changes since your last visit." Orsini opened the gate and led them to the door Jake remembered. Once inside, however, he realized the only air in the room came from vents. There were no windows.

"You weren't kidding." He walked over to the panels on which were painted the shifter family trees. "You've added some names too." He scowled when he saw Theron's. "Would it count as wishful thinking if I drew a big red cross through his name?" Then he saw the caskets at the end of the long room, and the sight provided him with a burst of energy—and excitement—despite the fact that he was tired.

Bone tired.

He'd resisted the urge to touch them during the flight to Rome. Instinct told him that once he gave in to that impulse, he'd have been unable to tear himself away.

And why didn't Theron want anyone to learn their secrets?

Jake approached them, still not daring to touch the stone caskets.

Orsini stood beside him. "Before we examine their contents, I would like you to do something for me." His eyes shone. "Remember your first visit here when you held that artifact and you told me it felt wrong? You knew it wasn't the age it purported to be. So before we examine whatever lies within them in any great detail, I want you to touch what we find—without the protection of gloves. Tell me what you feel." He glanced at Seth. "Do you possess the same gift as your father?"

Seth shook his head. "Psychometry isn't one of my skills. But Dad is amazing."

Orsini smiled. "He was amazing when he was *your* age. I long to see what he is capable of now."

Jake pointed to the carving of a bear holding a spear on the side of the nearest casket. "That's on three of them."

"It would be. Those would have been taken from the tomb of Berengar, an ancient shifter. His name means *bear* and *spear*."

"When was he alive?" Jake loved Seth's tone of awe.

"According to records, he lived in Germany in the mid twelve hundreds." Orsini's hand trembled as he stroked the lid.

Jake didn't want to wait a second longer.

"Help me move this, carefully," he asked Brick. Together they lifted the lid, then set it down on the rug. Jake peered into the shallow casket, his breath catching in his throat at the sight. Nestled in layers of cloth was a sheaf of thick, fluffy sheets of paper, a deep cream in color, almost yellow in places. A woven strand had been tied around them.

"Is that paper?" Brick asked.

"Yes. Probably the oldest form of paper we have," Orsini told him.

"Why does it look like that?"

"If it's the same as the paper on which the *Missal of Godwin* was recorded, it's made from flax and a small amount of straw. The paper appears thick and fluffy because the fibers had been chewed and beaten."

Jake touched the top sheet, and an electric shock zapped through him.

"Oh my God," he whispered. He focused his senses, concentrating on the image that filled his mind.

"What? What do you see? What do you feel?" Orsini's rapid breathing betrayed his own excitement.

"I see a man. He... he's huge. Even bigger than Brick, and that's saying something. He's wearing a robe with a fur collar." The light that fell on him came from torches and shallow metal bowls suspended on chains, in which flames flickered.

"You could be seeing Berengar himself. Where is he?"

Jake fought to control his elation. "He's in a room. The walls and floor are stone. The three caskets with the carvings are there too." He shivered. "So old…."

"The sheets of paper?"

"Not just them. Everything." All he saw had to have taken place long, long ago. The robes the guy wore, the swords on the wall, arranged in a semicircle, the decorations…. Jake swallowed. "I think you're right. This could be Berengar."

"*Ohhh.*" Orsini gasped. "What I would give to see with your eyes."

"Can we open another casket?" Seth was like a little kid on Christmas morning.

"I was about to ask the same thing," Brick added. "The hairs are standing up on the back of my neck."

Jake totally got that. He was bubbling inside.

They removed another lid to find another sheaf of papers, nestled in several layers of fabric. Jake laid his hands on them, and the emotions that washed over and through him were intoxicating. "These were written a long time ago." Then he paused. "Wait." Something tugged at his mind, and he closed his eyes to focus.

"What is it?" Seth demanded.

"It's Berengar again… but this time he's focused on a document. Whatever is on it has really shaken him."

"Can you see what it is?" Brick asked.

Jake shook his head. "Not clearly. All I can make out is a painting. He isn't looking at text." He opened his eyes, his heart pounding. "Let's open the last two. Then we can get started."

What drew him, however, was the casket with no carving.

What are you hiding?

When they opened it, Jake recognized the writing immediately. "This resembles the *Missal of Godwin*," he told Orsini, who joined him, staring at the top sheet.

Orsini's breathing caught. "That's because it was probably written by him." He grabbed a tablet from the table and scrolled. "Look. This is what we have." He showed them an image of a similar yellowed sheet of paper, covered in writing.

Jake peered at it. "That's what you showed me, isn't it? The one that's real." When Orsini nodded, Jake turned to Seth. "The *Missal of Godwin* tells us that Ansfrid.... Wait, let me see if I can remember this right." He closed his eyes, and in his head, he heard Orsini's voice from more than thirty years ago, translating the document from Latin into English.

"'*My Lord Ansfrid is beloved of his people, counting among those he loves both humankind and versipelli.*' That's Latin for shifters, by the way. Then it went on, '*But Lord Ansger shows his countenance to versipelli alone, shunning the company of humans.*'"

Orsini beamed. "Your memory is phenomenal. Now look here at the number in the top corner. One. But this new sheet has the number two. This one came *after* the page we already have from the *Missal*. So whoever originally got their hands on the *Missal of Godwin*, they only took the first page."

"What does it say?" Jake demanded.

Orsini took the sheet in his trembling gloved hand and read in silence. His mouth fell open, and goose bumps erupted on Jake's arms. At last Orsini lowered the sheet, his eyes wide. He gazed at Seth and Brick.

"All those years ago, I showed Jake a document purporting to be Ansger's condemnation of his brother's belief that shifters and humans were equal. The basis for the rift between shifters, in fact. The very act that caused the Gerans and Fridans to exist. Jake said it didn't feel old enough to have been written in the time of the brothers, and when we dated it, he was proved right. It had been produced in the early twentieth century. But *this*…. This *proves* that document was a forgery." Orsini's voice rang with triumph. He peered once more at the ancient paper. "This tells of an accident that befell Ansger. Godwin writes that Ansger went out riding and did not return. They searched for him, but to no avail. Then after seven days, he was brought to the home he shared with his brother." Orsini's eyes gleamed. "A human brought him, the same human who had found him when Ansger's horse threw him. He'd tended to Ansger's wounds, taken great care of him, and nursed him back to health. Godwin writes that Ansger was extremely grateful." He paused and read further. "The physician who treated Ansger on his return said that without a doubt, Ansger would have died if not for the human."

"Ansger being so grateful doesn't mesh with the idea of a guy who'd think all humans were the lowest of the low," Seth observed.

"I would agree." Orsini smiled. "Especially since Godwin goes on to say Ansger and this human—Elric, that was his name—grew to be the best of friends." His face flushed as he continued to read. "Oh. I stand corrected. They were *so* much more than friends."

"They were lovers?" Jake stared at Orsini. "So *not* as averse to humans as that forgery would have us believe."

Orsini nodded. "It doesn't say how long they were together. Maybe that's something we'll find in the rest of this, or else in the other caskets. But it does relate a conversation between Ansger and Ansfrid. Listen to this." He cleared his throat. "Okay, I'm paraphrasing, because Godwin uses fifty words to say what could be said in about ten. Ansger admitted he was wrong to shun the company of humankind and that Ansfrid had the right idea all along. Humans and shifters were meant to dwell side by side with each other, and that when the prophecy came to pass, shifters would be free to step into the light and show themselves, and there would be peace in our world. And by 'our' I mean shifter society, not the world at large. At least, I *think* that's what it means."

"Prophecy? What prophecy?" Jake gaped. "Do *you* know what Godwin was talking about?"

"This is the first I've heard of such a thing." Orsini frowned. "It sounds as though he's talking about humans learning of the existence of shifters."

"So something's supposed to happen that will bring this about?" Seth gazed at the sheet in Orsini's hand. "Does it say what's in the prophecy?"

"Has anyone else still got goose bumps?" Brick rubbed his arms briskly.

Jake chuckled. "That makes two of us. I've had them ever since we opened the first casket."

Orsini perused the sheet, then read the next, and the next, until he'd gone through all the sheets in the casket. He sighed. "It goes on about feasting, the weather, riding…. Boring accounts of Godwin's stay with the brothers. There's nothing else in these documents that mentions a prophecy."

Jake glanced at the three caskets whose contents they had yet to examine in any great detail. "Maybe what we're searching for is in those."

Seth grinned. "Then let's start looking."

JAKE WAS beginning to feel as though he was on a wild goose chase. They'd gone through two of the three remaining caskets, whose documents appeared to have been written in the thirteenth century. Thus far there was no mention of the brothers, a prophecy… in fact anything that was of any interest. Orsini was delighted, however, and told them even one of the caskets represented a lifetime of research to keep shifter historians and scholars busy.

But none of it helps us get any nearer to knowing what Godwin was talking about.

Jake could understand why Theron had kept the rest of the *Missal* a secret. Peace? Humans and shifters living side by side? That didn't fit the Geran agenda. Instead, they'd manufactured an artifact to show just the opposite, a reason for the split, the beginnings of a chasm between Fridans and Gerans that they sought to widen.

So why did Theron hide the Berengar caskets?

"Only one more casket left," Brick commented. "If it's like the first two, it might contain recipes, or something equally unimportant."

"Hey, some people might *want* to know what shifters ate back then," Jake teased. His humor served to mask his own frustration. What they'd discovered in that first casket was groundbreaking, and if they could share their knowledge, it would rock the shifter world to its foundations.

He and Brick removed the final lid to reveal yet another tied sheaf of papers, not as thick as the first bundle. Orsini unraveled the knot with care, then read the first sheet.

Jake noticed the change in his breathing instantly.

"What is it? What have you found?"

"This is not like the other caskets," he said breathlessly.

"What makes it different?"

Orsini swallowed and pointed to the first line, where the initial letter of each word was written in red ink. "This says, *The Chronicles of Ansger*."

Jake caught his breath. "Ansger *wrote* this?"

"Unless it's another forgery."

"Can… can I touch it?" Orsini nodded, and Jake laid his hands on the sheet of thick paper. He closed his eyes, opening himself up once more.

"Well?" Seth demanded. "Is it real?"

Jake took several deep breaths in an effort to calm his racing heartbeat. "It feels as old as the *Missal*, if that helps." In his head he saw the same sheet, and he concentrated on the hands holding it but couldn't see more of the owner of those hands. "Damn."

"What's wrong?"

"Nothing. I just wanted to see what Ansger looked like, that's all." He opened his eyes. "But it *was* him. I feel it."

"There are no records of the brothers' physical appearance," Orsini told him. "Please, try again."

Jake closed his eyes and focused on the feel of the paper beneath his fingertips. He prayed to whoever was listening.

Let me see them. Just this once.

Dizziness overcame him, and he took several deep breaths. He could see the hands again, only now he could make out a gold ring on the left hand. Jake concentrated, mentally taking a step back in an effort to see more.

Only to find the owner of those hands was staring right at him.

Chapter Twenty-Two

"Oh my God, I'm looking at one of them," Jake whispered. "Except it'd be more accurate to say one of them is staring right at *me*, as if I'm there in the room with him."

"Which one?"

"I have no idea." The man in front of him was tall, with long dark brown hair tied back from his shoulders. He wore what appeared to be a linen shirt and breeches, and around his shoulders was a warm red wool cloak, fastened on the left with a brooch in red and blue enamel, with intricate patterning worked over it in gold. His shoes seemed to be fashioned from soft leather. He gazed at Jake, his eyes bright with amusement, and Jake knew this was an intelligent man.

Then he saw the stick clasped in the man's left hand, and a wave of shock rolled over Jake when he realized who he was seeing.

"It's Ansger, after his accident." Jake hardly dared breathe in case his words caused the vision to disappear. "It must be. He has a cane to help him walk."

Ansger spoke, and Jake struggled to understand what he was saying, until he realized it sounded a little like German.

"This is so weird. He's *still* looking at me as if I'm right there with him, but that can't be." Jake let out a sigh. "Where's a mirror when you want one? I have to see if it's me he's staring at."

"You won't find one," Orsini told him. "There were none at that time. They believed the devil was watching the world from the opposite side of glass mirrors."

Jake scanned the room. "Wait a sec." On the wall was a burnished shield placed over a pair of crossed swords. He walked toward it, and caught his breath at his reflection.

"I don't look like me." But he did resemble Ansger. The same shape of the nose, the same eye color, even the shade of hair.

Holy fuck.

He was looking at Ansfrid. It had to be.

"How can I be Ansfrid?"

"There is only one explanation. You must be a direct descendant," Orsini told him. "Perhaps you are seeing Ansger through his eyes."

"Ansger… thinks I'm his brother?"

Gods, I want to understand what he's saying.

Jake stilled and opened himself up to the universe.

Look, whoever You are who gave me this gift… if You're the same power that brings mates together, that is showing me truths long since hidden, please… let me hear their words? Give me wisdom enough to interpret what I'm hearing? Because I believe there's a reason I'm meant to see this… vision.

He could do no more.

Ansger spoke again, and judging by his tormented expression, whatever he was saying gave him pain to utter it. Then the image rippled, almost as though Jake was seeing it through water, and when all became still again, it was as before.

"Can you ever forgive me?" It was a deep voice, rich and slow.

Holiest of Holy Fucks. That was English. Ansger was suddenly speaking in English, except it was like one of those dubbed kung-fu movies, when the lips didn't match the words.

"There is nothing to forgive, my brother."

That was Ansfrid. His voice was higher than his brother's, with a sweetness to it that was almost musical.

This is…. Jake was beyond words. He couldn't relay what he saw because he was too caught up in the magic of it.

Ansger clasped Ansfrid's arm. "I was close to death, but I prayed to be spared. I had to see you, to tell you…."

Ansfrid cupped his brother's cheek. "Hush. You are alive. And now you are not alone." A pause. "I am right? He finds favor in your eyes?"

Ansger flushed. "You see much. You saw how there should be no divisions between us, and I did not. But you saw the truth." He glanced to the right—at what, Jake couldn't see, but Ansger's smile lit up his handsome face. "And yes, Elric finds favor in my eyes."

"Then he shall dwell with us." Another pause. "Could he be your mate?"

Fuck. Jake's heart went into overdrive.

Ansger shook his head. "I do not think that time is upon us yet. And if he were, I think I would know it."

Ansfrid sighed. "So when will it come to pass? Shall we live to see it?"

Then the image rippled again, and Jake cried out, desperate to hold on to the vision for a little while longer, but he knew it was fading.

He was standing beside Orsini, the *Chronicles* still beneath his fingertips, tears streaming down his cheeks.

"I was there. I was with them. I could smell roses, lilies, sage, rosemary.... Oh my God, the brothers.... They were so real, so solid. And I heard them. I understood them." He wiped his eyes.

Orsini brought him a chair, and Jake sat, his legs weak as a newborn foal's. Seth crouched next to him, his hand on Jake's knee, and Brick handed him a tissue.

"What did they say?" Seth asked.

Jake took a moment to breathe, to calm his racing heart, before delivering word for word the conversation he'd been privy to.

Orsini gasped. "He spoke of mates? Truly?" He glanced at the *Chronicles*. "Then give me time to read this. I would know more." He was bristling with excitement. He patted Jake on the shoulder. "I can have food brought for us. None of us have eaten for hours."

"Food would be good," Jake admitted. He was also in a hurry to know what the document contained.

Seth opened his mouth to add something, but the only sound escaping him was the loud grumble of his stomach. Then Brick's got in on the act, only louder.

Orsini chuckled, then picked up the phone to give instructions. When he was done, he replaced the handset. "It will be here shortly. Now, back to the *Chronicles*." And with that he took the slim sheaf of papers and sat in his armchair, a notepad at his side.

Jake's head was still reeling.

"What you heard.... Let me know if I've got this straight." Brick took a breath. "That was them making up after their disagreement, wasn't it? Ansger admitting he was wrong that humans and shifters shouldn't be together?"

Jake nodded. "And whenever that conversation took place, it sounds as if they already knew about the prophecy." He gazed at Orsini, who was muttering under his breath as he scribbled notes. "I hope he discovers more about it."

"This is excruciating," Seth whispered. "He's holding what could be the equivalent of a shifter bible, you know that, right?"

He laughed. "I feel the same way, but patience, okay? Let the man work. Haven't we made enough earth-shattering discoveries for one day? For all we know, this could be Ansger's diary. *You* know the kind of thing.... *Got up. Had coffee. Brushed my teeth. Walked the dog. Ate lunch.*" Except his gut instinct told him what Orsini held in his hands was far more consequential than that.

Brick snickered. "Okay, that's funny. And they didn't have coffee back then."

Jake peered up at him. "That's all *you* know. Coffee beans have been around since about eight hundred AD. Okay, so we didn't start roasting them and drinking it until the fifteenth century, but—"

"You need to hear this," Orsini interjected.

The tremor in his voice was enough to bring about another carpet of goose bumps.

Jake brought his chair over to Orsini and sat facing him, Seth on the floor at Jake's feet, Brick behind him.

Orsini leaned against the seat cushions, the sheaf in his gloved hands.

"This tells the story of how Ansger and Elric met, thus corroborating the *Missal of Godwin*. It seems to have been written at the end of Ansger's life. He and Elric—who became his husband—lived to a ripe old age, and he continued to be friends with both shifters and humans. He and Ansfrid ruled together, lords of their land, and when Ansfrid died first, Ansger was devastated. So were their subjects. It was a time of great mourning, for humans *and* shifters."

"Then what happened? How come we've become nothing more than a myth?" Jake figured something cataclysmic had to have taken place to have wiped the knowledge of shifters from the minds of men.

"I don't have the answer to that question. But I did learn something I had not known until now." Orsini looked Jake in the eye. "The brothers... they were both tigers."

Seth's breathing hitched. "That fits. If you saw through Ansfrid's eyes...." He swallowed.

"What—that my family line descends from the brothers?" Jake still found that hard to swallow.

"Hey, if Aelryn can trace his line all the way back to Ansfrid, then I don't see why you can't do the same." Brick cocked his head to one side. "Don't you *want* to know?"

"Can we discuss this some other time?"

The urgency in Orsini's voice grabbed Jake's attention.

"You found something about the prophecy." Jake's chest tightened.

Orsini nodded. "Everyone knew about it, or that's how this reads. In fact they were waiting for it to come to pass. They felt as if it would be soon. Much like in the human book of Revelations in the Bible, predicting the second coming. All the believers thought it was imminent."

"But what were they waiting *for*?" Brick asked.

"It seems the prophecy had something to do with the future of shifters. There was no indication of when it would happen, only that an event would occur that would herald the way to peace between shifters and humans. And as I've never seen any mention of this, I can only assume the event hadn't come to pass. From what you witnessed, it hadn't happened by the time of their conversation. They must have given up waiting." Orsini's eyes widened. "Perhaps this is where man found the only references to shifters—in a prophecy long forgotten."

"But does it say what the event would be?" Seth demanded.

Orsini paused. "That's the interesting part." He walked over to the casket and laid three sheets on the layer of fabric, then stared at the remaining sheet in his hand. "This speaks of mates, as Jake did. In fact it's the first mention of mates that I can recall seeing in these artifacts."

Jake drew in a deep breath. "We've always assumed there were mates in the past, but that somehow they all disappeared, becoming merely a myth." A myth so lost in the past that all shifters assumed it might not even be true.

Orsini shook his head. "No. We got that all wrong. The *Chronicles* tell of a mystic who met with Ansger after his accident. He told him a time would come when all peoples of the world would find the ones fated to be with them. Note I said peoples—it doesn't say just shifters. And he was very specific about one thing—mates came in threes."

Jake gaped at Orsini. "Then whatever was in this prophecy, it must have happened. It seems like everywhere I look, there are triads of mates appearing."

"But that isn't even the interesting part—*this* is." Orsini held up the remaining sheet. "The emergence of mates would have a beginning, and that would be marked by the arrival of the first triad." He held it out to Jake. "Tell me this is a coincidence."

Jake stared at the painting on the thick paper. "Oh my fucking God."

Seth moved in to take a closer look. He blinked. "But…. No. It can't be. This has to be a mistake." Brick peered over Seth's shoulder and made a strangled noise.

"Jake said he saw Berengar staring at a painting in his vision." Orsini met Jake's gaze and shuddered out a breath. "I believe *this* is what you saw. It's an image of a triad. As for why Berengar appeared so agitated, maybe he saw this and believed that somehow he was part of the prophecy. An understandable conclusion to arrive at, given the evidence."

Jake's world had been turned upside down for the second time.

The sketch was crude, the colors faded, but there could be no mistaking its subjects. He was looking at three animals standing together, their heads meeting, their eyes closed.

A lion, a tiger, and a bear.

Chapter Twenty-Three

"It all fits." Orsini's eyes shone. "Your son is part of the prophecy. The two men who freed him are both his mates. *Your* gift allows us to confirm the age of these artifacts. And Theron knew."

"What could he know?" Jake's head was spinning again.

They are not going to believe this. He wasn't sure *he* did, not completely. It was all a bit… mystic?

And what do you call seeing a vision of two brothers who lived a thousand years ago? Hmm?

"You're aware Theron had Dellan in captivity, forcing him into their breeding program, correct?" Jake nodded, and Orsini tilted his head to one side. "How did that come about?"

"Dellan's stepbrother, Anson, did a deal with the Gerans. He was to hand over Dellan, in return for the rights to manufacture the drug that forces shifts."

"Well, supposing Theron knew about the prophecy, he *knew* the three shifters depicted needed to get together, but there was no way for him to know Dellan was the tiger in the prophecy. When Rael turned up, it set in motion a chain of events that led Theron to learn about the three mates."

Jake nodded, excitement surging through him like electricity. "Horvan said whoever he spoke with when Anson was murdered, he was very interested to learn they were mates."

"Exactly. Imagine what must have been passing through Theron's mind. What if these were the triad from the prophecy? What if it was *finally* about to come true? That would signal the end for the Gerans."

"So he hid all knowledge of the prophecy." Jake scowled. "God forbid you have shifters *not* living in a climate of fear."

Orsini sighed. "And now the hard work begins."

"What do you mean?" Brick frowned. "This is dynamite. We *know* the Gerans have been lying to us. We *know* there was no split between the brothers. We know—"

"And who do you think people are going to believe? Jake, who they don't know at all, or their leader they've been following for years, who's been telling them of their great and grand destiny?"

Jake goggled. "How can they do otherwise, when they see—"

"See what?" Orsini cut Jake off. He stared at him for a moment, then sighed once more. "I keep forgetting. You've been out of the world for such a long time. Well, Jake, I hate to be the one to disillusion you, but you speak as if people are logical beings, capable of recognizing the truth when they see it. And man today is the most illogical creature imaginable, who never sees what is right in front of him."

Seth was peering at the drawing. "Guys? What does this say under here?"

Orsini stared at the sheet. "I didn't read it. I got as far as the painting and my mind unraveled." He scanned the page, muttering under his breath. Then he dropped it, his breathing rapid, his eyes huge. "We need to share this. We need every shifter to learn the truth."

"But what does it *say*?" Seth whined.

"It reads like a series of events that will happen." Orsini met Jake's gaze. "Oh my. This has to be the prophecy."

"Read it," Jake croaked.

Orsini took a deep breath.

When he who can see is freed from his shackles
When his sons find him once more
When the tiger is freed by the lion and the bear
Then shall versipelli find the ones who complete them, be they versipelli or humankind.
Three hearts, beating as one.
Three bodies, joined in love.
Three souls fated to be together.
Then all things shall become possible.

Brick made a choking sound. "Holy fuck."

Seth's jaw dropped. "That first line… that has to be you, Dad."

Jake shook his head. "This… this can't be."

"'*When his sons find him once more*'? You mean like me and Jamie and God knows how many other shifters who walked up to you in those camps and said, 'Hey, I think you're my dad'? And there's no mistaking line three, is there?"

"Vic, the young man who visited the archive… his mates are both human, aren't they? And Eve, that remarkable fighter—she too has human mates." Orsini's eyes glistened. "The prophecy is finally being fulfilled, and I shall live to see it."

"You were correct, though. We still have to convince people." Jake had a feeling some Gerans out there would not believe what was right under their noses.

"Then you need to show them. Talk to them."

"Wait a minute here. Weren't *you* the one a few seconds ago telling me people wouldn't believe me?"

"That was before we found this!" Orsini pointed to the final lines on the paper. "They *must* believe this. They have to."

Jake couldn't tell Orsini what lay on his heart—not a desire to spread the word but a deep longing to find a home with Nicholas. A chance to share love again. To rest. To shut out the world that had thrown so much at him in the last thirty years.

But isn't that just being selfish? When I could make a difference?

Could he really turn the tide?

Orsini regarded him with affection. "Think about it, that is all I ask. Besides, your first task is to return to Dellan and his mates." His eyes sparkled. "You have quite the tale to tell."

"But don't do a Godwin on them," Brick murmured. Jake glanced at him, and he flushed. "You know, don't drag it out like I saw on a reality TV show once."

Jake blinked. "What's a reality TV show?"

Brick grinned. "You're much happier not knowing. But Orsini is right. We should go home." He bit his lip.

Jake hugged him. "You need your mate, and I need mine."

"And I need to drag as many scholars as I can find in here," Orsini added. "We have a lot of work to do."

"Here's a thought," Brick interjected. "Why not invite some *Geran* scholars onto your team? You know, to get the ball rolling?"

Orsini's eyes gleamed. "Excellent idea."

Jake couldn't wait to see the faces of Dellan's found family when they heard this.

As long as I only have to tell the story once.

Except deep down he knew this was a story he would be telling for many years to come, and to a great many people.

"So what's the hotel like?" Aric asked. "And why can't you catch a flight tonight?"

"You're flying back to Chicago tomorrow, right?" Seth confirmed.

"Yeah. Horvan says there'll be a plane waiting for us at the airstrip where we landed." He huffed. "Great. *We* get to leave here at the crack of dawn to get into a flying tank, while *you* get to have breakfast in your room, and a commercial flight—"

"That'll take more than ten hours. We land at two thirty tomorrow afternoon. By that time, you'll already be home, waiting for us." He smiled. "Have you missed us as much as we've missed you?"

"You know it. And you still haven't told me what your room is like."

Seth glanced at his surroundings. "It's okay." Except La Residenza Dell'Angelo was *way* more than okay. He'd been blown away from the moment Jake led them into the hotel lobby. There was marble everywhere, and *oh my God*, that bed looked comfortable. They were staying across the river from the archive. Seth could see it from their window. Night had fallen, and the Castel Sant'Angelo was lit by golden lights, brilliant against the dark sky.

The hotel was a blend of the old and the new. Their room's furnishings were modern, but there was the cutest little old-fashioned elevator, rising in a wire cage up the middle of the winding staircase, and it had required two separate trips to get the three of them to their floor: Brick had to make the journey solo.

Speaking of Brick, he seemed to be taking his time in the shower.

"You're very quiet," Aric observed.

"Yeah."

"Would that have something to do with whatever you guys found in those caskets?"

"It would. Only… don't ask me to talk about it now, okay?" He was wiped out.

And if I'm tired, Dad has to be exhausted.

"But you will tell me?"

Seth managed a smile. "Tomorrow. When we've had some sleep and a bit more time to process it all." He heard the water shut off. "Wanna say good night to our bear?"

Aric snorted. "I thought you'd never ask."

Seth held out his phone to Brick as he emerged from the steam-filled bathroom in nothing but a towel. "There's a kitty waiting to talk to you."

"Hey, baby. Can't wait to see you tomorrow. Anything you want from Rome?" Brick laughed. "I think I can manage to find some chocolate. Now get some sleep. … Yes, I know what time it is. We're only an hour ahead of you, remember? And you're up early in the morning." Brick sighed. "Love you." He handed the phone back to Seth.

"And I love you too." Seth blew him a kiss. "See you tomorrow." He hung up.

Brick sat on the edge of the king-size bed. "I can't stop thinking about it."

Seth didn't have to ask what "it" was. "I know. It's all so much to take in." He pulled back the sheets and climbed into bed. "I'm hoping a good night's sleep will help me get my head around it."

That was if he *could* sleep.

He watched Brick towel off the remaining drops of water. "Does it make you view them differently?" He'd thought of little else ever since he'd seen that painting, and read the lines beneath it.

Could it really be talking about Horvan, Dellan, and Rael?

Brick got into bed. "Part of me thinks we've gotten it all wrong and it's talking about three other shifters."

"And the other part?"

Brick shivered. "Is asking me what the hell is going on."

JAKE STOOD at the open window, listening to the noise of the traffic below. The hotel had to have triple glazing, because the room had been quiet until that point. He stared at the castle.

I wonder if Orsini feels like sleeping?

He wasn't sure he could turn off his brain.

His phone buzzed on the nightstand, and he went to investigate. He smiled when he saw Nicholas's name. "Hey, you."

"You okay to talk?"

"Sure, as long as we stick to the weather, what I had for dinner, how noisy Rome is…. Anything more than that and I might blow a fuse in my head."

There was silence for a moment.

"Nicholas?"

"I already know what the weather's doing because I checked, I hope whatever you ate was suitably delicious, and yes, I *am* jealous as hell because you're in Rome, and I freaking *adore* pasta. And as for the traffic, I packed you a set of earplugs." He paused. "So is that all I get?"

"It's all I can give you right now. To be honest, this is one story I need to tell only once. You'll understand tomorrow."

"Wow."

Jake chuckled. "Yeah, that about covers it. I'm glad you called, though. Have you ever been here?"

"I attended a conference there once, decades ago. I'd like to see it through the eyes of a tourist. I'd liked to stand beside you at the Trevi Fountain, toss in a quarter, and make a wish."

"And what would you wish for?"

Nicholas sighed. "That might surprise you."

"Try me."

"How about 'Peace on Earth, and good will to all men,' shifters included?"

Right then Jake really liked the peace part. As for the good will….

He sighed. "I've got a lot of work to do when I get home." Orsini was right. He needed to tell as many shifters as would listen.

"I figured that might be the case. As long as you know I'm here for you, okay?"

"I know. And I wish you were here."

"You missing my hugs?"

Jake said nothing for a moment. "And the rest."

"Jake?"

"When I get back… let's move things to the next level."

"Are you sure? It *was* you, less than two weeks ago, saying you wanted to take things slow?"

"Yeah, but a lot's happened since then." Jake smiled. "I think I've waited long enough. Now go to sleep and dream of me."

"I've been dreaming of you for years. Don't see any reason to change the habit of a lifetime. Love you."

"Love you too. And yeah, I can't wait for my next Nicholas hug." He hung up, then placed the phone back on the nightstand. He walked over to the window and gazed at the castle.

Your secrets won't be secret for much longer.

Chapter Twenty-Four

Roadkill came into the bedroom. "You finished?"

"All done." Eve pointed to the bag sitting on the floor beside the door. "Except I'd rather still be in bed. The sun isn't even up yet." She let out a sigh. "Well, Leighton Hall was certainly several steps up from some of the accommodations I've had to stay in." She glanced at the four-poster bed. "My only regret is that we didn't get to play with that the way I wanted." She met Roadkill's gaze, and he made a choking sound.

"*Now* you tell me. Why didn't you mention this before?"

"I had stuff on my—"

Holy fuck.

Eve laughed. Their mental image had grabbed Hashtag's attention in record time.

Why are you two picturing tying me to the bedposts?

She laughed. *Are you saying "no no no"?*

Fuck that. I'm pissed that you're telling me about it now when it's time to go home. Hashtag paused, and his voice changed in a heartbeat. *Eve, get down here, ASAP.*

She hurried out of the room and down the grand staircase, Roadkill following. *Where are you?*

Kitchen.

She pushed open the door and almost ran into Richard's cook and butler, who stood with their backs to her. Hashtag was crouched on the floor next to—

Oh my God.

"Victor?"

He looked like crap, only it was crap that had been savagely beaten. His eyes were practically swollen shut, he was missing a bit of his ear, his mouth was ripped open, and more teeth had been removed.

Whatever state she'd left him in after their encounter, this was worse.

"Someone call for a doctor!" she hollered, falling to her knees beside the wreck that had been Victor.

"They already have," Hashtag told her. "Richard says there's a hospital ten minutes from here."

Victor grabbed her arm. "I don't wish to be a burden." His voice was raw.

Eve cupped his bloody cheek. "Hush now. We're going to take care of you. Who did this? Theron?"

"He... he didn't...."

Roadkill growled. "I'll bet. He probably ordered someone else to do his dirty work."

"I need... I need to ask you for a favor," Victor wheezed. "Please. I beg you. I don't know how much time I've got left, and I have to make sure she's—" He erupted into a fit of coughing, and the sound made Eve wince.

She already had an idea of what was on his mind. "You want me to save your sister."

He managed a nod. "She's all I have left in the world. As soon as you crossed the moat, Theron decided I should be made an example. He had his men do this to me, then tried to lock me up."

"But you escaped," Hashtag observed.

Victor gave another nod.

"How did you find me?" Eve asked.

He gave a gapped-tooth smile. "I'm a hippo. We have a keen sense of smell, which helps when you're searching for tasty treats. Your blood was on me, so I followed the scent. It wasn't easy, and I lost my way a couple of times, but I made it."

"But only just," Roadkill told him. "We're about to leave."

"Dude, we're gonna fix you up, okay?" Hashtag grasped Victor's hand. "And then you come work for us. Yeah? Work for the good guys."

Victor scowled. "I hate the Gerans. Even more now that they... hurt my family. Theron used them to make me do what he said. I never wanted to hurt anyone. And then he tosses out the fact that he's had them all killed like it was nothing."

Eve crouched lower and whispered, "What's her name?"

"Irena."

She gave him the most confident smile she could manage. "I will find her, okay? And I'll make sure she's safe. But you know what? You're going to be around for a while yet." She sat on the floor with him, simply holding his hand, trying not to panic about his wounds. Eve glanced up at Roadkill. *They really made a mess of him.*

I've seen worse. And those guys survived. He will too.

Yeah, you should've seen Saul, Hashtag added. *I didn't think he'd make it.*

As wrong as it sounded, that comforted her. She didn't wish harm on Saul at all, but knowing he survived gave Victor a good chance. Then she caught the sound of a siren from outside.

Help had arrived.

Richard Deveraux appeared in the doorway. "Don't worry, one of my men will go with him. I know you have little time."

She smiled. "Thank you."

Victor held on to her hand. "Thank you for saying you would find Irena. And by the way... you're one hell of a fighter."

"She is, isn't she?" Hashtag's voice brimmed with pride.

Medics came into the kitchen, and Roadkill tugged her toward the door.

"Let them do their thing. We have a plane waiting for us."

"I'll keep you informed of his progress, I promise." Richard patted her on the back. "And I'll be in touch to discuss your move."

Eve nodded, then gave Victor one last glance. "I'll see you again, you hear?"

He nodded. "Thank you."

Hashtag and Roadkill ushered her from the room, and Roadkill bounded up the stairs to grab their gear. Eve stood in the entrance hall, her hands at her sides, clenched into fists.

That fucking bastard Theron. Imprisonment is too good for him.

Part of her wanted to stay long enough to bring Logan back with them, but the adoption procedure was proving slower than she'd either anticipated or wanted. She had to be content with a return trip when all the paperwork was signed, sealed, and delivered.

Then Logan will be ours.

ARE YOU sure you want to do this?

Valmer Cooper heard the distress in Rudy's voice. He held him close. *I have to see Theron, okay? I have to tell him what I think of him.*

"But why?" Rudy stroked Valmer's cheek. "You're safe now. That nightmare is over."

Valmer smiled. "He's in the dungeon. He can't shift. What's he going to do—melt through the bars and strangle me? And besides, this is my last chance to face him. Aelryn's having him moved tomorrow, and once that's done, *no one* will know where to find him." He was still surprised Aelryn had consented to the visit.

Maybe he understands why I need to do this.

Then again, maybe he understood a lot more than Valmer gave him credit for.

His heartbeat raced. *Oh gods, I hope not.*

"But what if he tries to…." Rudy's voice faltered.

"To what? Influence me? Convince me I should stick with the Gerans?" Valmer raised Rudy's chin with a couple of fingers. "You've heard the rumors, the same as I have. They're finished. Maybe not today, but it's coming. The Gerans built their world on lies and hatred, and once word gets out—once the *truth* gets out—it'll collapse."

"I still don't see why you have to—"

"I won't be long. I just have to let go of all the anger and hate that's been building up inside me ever since he took me hostage." He kissed the tip of Rudy's nose. "That's no way to begin a new life together, is it? On a foundation of seething resentment and pent-up rage? So this is for the best. I see him, I vent, and he can't do a thing to stop me."

Rudy sighed. "I guess you're right. It makes sense when you put it like that." He kissed Valmer on the lips. "I'll be waiting for you."

Valmer pressed Rudy to his chest. "And that's my incentive to get this over with." He released his mate. "Like I said, I won't be long."

And with that he turned and headed through the door, down the narrow stone steps that led to the dungeon in the basement, and along the hallway to the room Aelryn was using as a temporary cell.

With only one occupant.

Valmer stopped at the door, a guard positioned outside. "I have permission," he began.

The guard held up one hand. "It's okay, sir. I've been informed. Knock on the door when you're ready to leave." He shivered. "Rather you than me. That guy gives me the creeps."

Valmer said nothing, but waited as the guard unlocked the door. He stepped inside and heard the *click* as it shut behind him.

Theron was seated at a small square table on which sat a jug of water and a plastic cup. A single bed stood beneath the barred window below the ceiling, the thick wall sloping toward it. There was nothing else in the tiny room that had once been for storage. A wall of bars separated them.

Theron arched his eyebrows. "Didn't you have enough of my company? I thought I'd seen the last of you. Couldn't stay away, huh? How sweet."

Valmer stared at him in silence.

He gestured to his surroundings. "I suppose I should be grateful not to find medieval instruments of torture in here, ready for me. The rack, for example. Or maybe some fiendish machine designed to slowly dismember me."

Still Valmer said nothing.

Theron frowned. "Well? Why are you here? To gloat? Is that it? Or maybe it's to find out how they're treating me? Lavishly, as you can see." He smirked. "I provided better accommodation for my guards."

At last he found his voice. "I wanted to see you one last time."

"Ah, before you shoot me? I've been expecting *someone* to carry out my execution." He sneered. "How disappointing that they chose you. I suppose Aelryn couldn't bring himself to do it. Ansfrid must be rolling in his grave to see his descendant so lacking in courage."

"I wish I *could* be the one to execute you. God knows I have reason enough." Valmer's throat seized, and he swallowed. "You threatened my mate. You made him betray his friends. You had me beaten up so he'd comply. So yes, nothing would make me happier than putting a bullet in your brain."

"Then why not do it?" Theron waved his hand. "Oh, I forgot how weak you are. How pathetic. Well, if you're not here to shoot me, why *are* you here?"

"I had to see you before they ship you out of here. Before they put you somewhere you'll never see the light of day again." Valmer moved closer to the bars. "You're going to rot, alone and unloved." He forced the words through gritted teeth. "Even the rest of the Gerans will forget you as they learn the truth."

"Never," Theron snarled.

Valmer smiled. "It's already begun. Soon every shifter on the planet will know what you did. What the Gerans did. You're about to become irrelevant, insignificant, unwanted." He grinned. "Forgotten, unlike the artifacts you tried so desperately to keep out of sight. Now they will *never* be forgotten, and that's because of you."

Theron's face tightened.

"But I wouldn't worry if I were you. I mean, *how* old are you? How many years do you think you have left to spend them in a cell? Because the Fridans will *never* let you out. And unlike you, they're very good at keeping people alive. You might even survive another thirty years."

Theron glared at him, his lips twisted into a snarl.

Valmer glanced at the walls. "This—or something like it—is going to be your view for the rest of your life. And don't expect them to put an end to your misery. They won't execute you. It's far more satisfying to keep you like this."

Theron narrowed his gaze. He stood and walked toward the bars. "I won't be kept a prisoner. I'll escape."

Valmer barked out a laugh. "How? You can't shift. Your food probably takes care of that. You know, the way you kept *me* drugged? And now I'm wondering how long they'll keep you like that. Who knows? You might never shift again." He smiled, knowing that would probably be the barb that found its target. "Payback really is a bitch, isn't it?" He paused. "But there *is* an alternative." Valmer's heart pounded.

Theron arched his eyebrows again.

Valmer reached into his pocket for the small metal box. He held it out to Theron between the bars. "It's only a tiny bottle, a mouthful, really, but there's enough in it to be fatal. As strong as you think you are, it'll even kill you."

"And why would I do that?" Theron kept his hands at his sides.

"Because I don't think you want to be caged for however many decades you have left." Valmer tilted his head. "I'm right, aren't I? And although this *might* feel as though you'd be taking the easy way out, you'd deprive Aelryn of his victory. His prize." He smiled. "And part of me thinks you would rather do that than put up with what your life will become. Imprisonment... locked into your human form. Daily visits from Aelryn to remind you of your crimes. Though I'm sure you'd come to look forward to such visits, because apart from your guard, he'd be the only visitor you'd receive." Another pause. "So... do I put it back in my pocket and walk out of here?"

Theron snatched the box from his hand in a flash. "Now get out of my sight."

Valmer smiled. "With pleasure." He turned and went to the door. He rapped on it, and a moment later, the guard opened it. Valmer didn't glance back as he exited the cell.

"That was short and sweet," the guard observed.

If Theron drank the contents of that vial, it would be sweet indeed. Valmer had pushed Theron as far as he could. Now it was his choice.

That's it. I'm done.

Valmer had a mate and a new life. And somewhere out there was their third.

He pushed all his memories of Theron into a mental lock box and tossed the key deep into the recesses of his mind.

That chapter was over.

MILO FLOPPED onto his back, sweat covering his chest. "Oh my God," he said weakly.

Jana leaned over him in a heartbeat. "Are you okay?" That note of anxiety in her voice touched him.

"I'm fine. Exhausted, but fine. I never thought I'd have someone as perfect for me as you are. I owe Fate big-time." He peered at her. "I do have one question, however. Are all otters as insatiable as you, or did I get lucky?"

She chuckled. "I'm just getting warmed up."

He gaped at her and let out a gasp of mock horror. "I may not survive this." Then he grinned. "But what a way to go." He held his arm wide, and she laid her head on his shoulder.

Jana tilted her face toward his and smiled, and the sight did things to Milo's stomach. Good things. Right things.

"Wait until we find our third mate. I have a feeling the two of us are going to run you into the ground." Her eyes twinkled. "I also have a feeling you'll love every minute of it." Then she laid her head back down, her hand on his damp chest.

He stroked his fingers through her hair. She was beautiful, breathtaking, sexy, and so much more.

I fell for her so fast.

He knew there was another out there for them, and he was eager to meet them. It didn't matter to him if it was a man or woman, because they'd be welcome. He'd even learn to love being on the receiving end if necessary.

There was still space in his heart waiting to be filled—space big enough for their mate.

Did you mean that?

Milo blinked. "I'm still getting used to you hearing my thoughts. Did I mean what? That I can't wait to meet our third?"

Jana craned her neck to stare at him. "No, I meant the part about being willing to try being on the receiving end."

He laughed. "Oh, so you'd like to see our mate taking my anal cherry, would you?"

She bit her lip. "Yes, assuming it's a he, but if not, there are other possibilities too."

"Such as?"

She grinned. "Ever heard of a strap-on?"

Milo stared at her. "I was right. You *are* insatiable."

"And curious. I've always wanted to try that. So… *can* we? Can I?"

He laughed. "Sure."

She snuggled against him. "Boston has been okay, but I'm happy to be moving. Have you ever been to Galveston?"

Aelryn's people had found them a house near the Gulf Coast of Texas, and Milo and Jana would be training with a team there.

"No, but I'm looking forward to it. Apparently it's a good place for otters." And their future team leader had a sprawling estate with plenty of trees and green pastures, where a gorilla could feel at home.

Maybe our mate is already there, waiting for us. Excitement bubbled up inside him. So what if the war to win over the Gerans was only just beginning? So what if there would be minds that would remain shut to the truth?

Milo was on the brink of a whole new life, and he couldn't wait for it to get started.

Chapter Twenty-Five

It didn't matter to Dellan that he was home. The familiar, comfortable surroundings only reminded him that he didn't *want* to feel comfortable. He didn't want anyone to see him in his present state either, and that included Horvan and Rael. They'd tried to do whatever they could to make him feel better, but right now he didn't *want* to feel better. He wanted the pain, the agony.

I never got the chance to know Alec.

Would things have been different if he had? What could have come of it? Alec was still nothing more than a science experiment, destined to die young.

Gods, this fucking *hurt*.

He wanted to hit something. Someone. He wanted to go into Horvan's weapon box and pull out a gun, then force the barrel down Theron's throat, empty the clip, then reload. *Who could do this to a child? What kind of fucking monster was he?*

Except Theron was God knew where, and as for Dellan getting within an inch of him? That wasn't going to happen.

So many questions filled his head.

How many of the Gerans knew what their leaders were up to? Eve had known about their breeding program, but not about the forced mating, so would anyone else?

Would they have a change of heart once they heard about the child they'd mutilated?

He wanted to believe they would. Because the alternative made them as monstrous as Theron.

And speaking of monstrous....

The news that the Gerans had conducted more experiments hadn't been a surprise. *Since when do scientists conduct only one experiment?* What shocked him was the nature of their research. Eve had related what she'd learned about Logan, who was the dearest little creature ever. She'd shown them the photos, and it was hard to marry up the image of an adorable red panda with the knowledge that scientists had tried all kinds of DNA experimentation on him.

Because they could.

Just to see what happened.

He was a goddamn baby, *for fuck's sake.*

Like Alec. And probably like countless others. Dellan doubted they'd ever know the true extent of the Geran's manipulations, and to be honest, he wasn't sure he wanted to know. It was too hard. Too painful. The memory of his son as he took his last breath, of seeing him die. Of feeling the pain of a child he never even knew existed until it was too late to save him. Why couldn't he get Alec's face out of his mind? He didn't know him, but now he would never forget him.

"Dellan?" Eve's low voice shattered the quiet of the small living room where he'd holed himself up.

He stifled a groan. "Not now, Eve. Please… leave me alone, all right?"

The next moment, he found himself engulfed in a hug.

Dellan struggled to break free, to keep his cool, but his emotions overwhelmed him, and he broke down, gulping huge breaths in an attempt to get himself under control. Eve sat beside him on the couch, her arm around him, making soft crooning noises that soothed him, eating away at his anger, lessening it.

Dellan laid his head on her shoulder. "I'm sorry," he choked out.

"It's okay to let it all out," she said softly. "And I'm sorry for disturbing you when you wanted to be alone, but I couldn't stay away."

He breathed in her warm, comforting scent. "No, you're good. I needed to break out of that pity party I'd gotten myself mired in." He closed his eyes. "I keep thinking about all those poor kids. Brought into the world to be soldiers in a battle their parents didn't want any part of. Abandoned. Rejected." He sniffed. "I want to do something to help. I just don't know what."

Eve stroked his back. "You have money. Why not get a fund started? A charity that people could donate to or get help from."

He liked that idea. "I'd thought about setting up a trust for all the shifters who'd been part of the breeding program. You know, providing them with financial support to help them raise their kids."

Except there were shifters out there who wanted nothing to do with their kids.

As if she'd read his mind, Eve murmured, "But that still leaves a lot of children with nowhere to go. They need families. And a safe space until those families come along."

There *had* to be enough people with compassion, enough to take a kid—or two—under their wing and into their hearts.

"You know what?" Eve nuzzled his hair. "I can help."

He drew back, gazing into her liquid brown eyes. "How?"

She smiled. "You're looking at the owner of Gawthorpe Hall, Lancashire. An Elizabethan property with forty acres of land. I could do a lot with forty acres. But right now I have a house—and several outbuildings and former stables—that are big enough to provide space for a lot of children. The first Dellan Carson orphanage…."

Dellan sat up, his heart hammering. "You'd… you'd do that?"

She chuckled. "What's the alternative? Leave it to the nation so thousands of tourists can pass through its doors every year, paying to gawk at the architecture, the drapes, the furniture?" Eve locked gazes with him. "Or gift it to a man who I *know* will use it for good."

"Gift it? You can't simply hand it over."

"Of course I can."

"But… it could provide you with an income."

Eve smiled. "I already have that. How else could I afford its upkeep? Grandfather left me enough to maintain the place." Her eyes sparkled. "He probably never imagined what I'd do with it. And right now he's listening and throwing the biggest tantrum Heaven—or Hell—has ever seen."

"But—"

"And I discussed it with the boys last night. We promised to all look out for each other, so we're good on money." She grinned. "Besides, Hashtag has a few tech ideas that might prove pretty lucrative, so you really don't need to worry about us." She bit her lip. "I do have one proviso."

"Name it."

"Part of it will remain mine, for accommodation purposes. Because my mates and I will need a place to live—when I'm leading a Fridan team under Richard Deveraux."

He stilled. "The guy whose place we all stayed in?"

Eve nodded. "He's asked me to stay and work with him, and I said yes."

"Now *that* is sweet."

"What is?"

Dellan smiled. "The thought of Hashtag and Roadkill living in an Elizabethan stately home."

She laughed. "The way their eyes lit up when they saw the master bedroom? I think they'll take to it like a duck to water." Eve cocked her head. "Well? Is it a deal?"

Dellan held out his hand. "It is." They shook. "And thank you. The first orphanage of many. Except this one won't be named after me."

The Alec Carson Foundation had a better ring to it.

On the arm of the couch, Dellan's phone vibrated, and he glanced at the screen. He smiled. "Dad, Seth, and Brick have landed in Chicago. They'll be here soon." He typed *Great. We've missed you. Aric's been demanding rubbies from all of us.* Then he froze.

"What's wrong?"

"Dad says he has something to tell us. Something that is going to rock our world."

"A good something or a bad something?"

"No idea." Dellan's mind raced.

What did you discover in Rome?

In a very short time, they'd find out.

Gods, please let us get some good news for a change.

AELRYN CLIMBED down from the belly of the helicopter that had landed on the helipad inside the school grounds. All the way from New York, he'd been on the edge of his seat, unable to sit still, buzzing with anticipation at the thought of seeing Scott again—and meeting Kia. He'd seen her photo, and the sight of her had been enough to set his heart racing, but the idea of meeting her, holding her….

Christmas had arrived at the end of August.

He squinted in the afternoon sun, and it took him less than five seconds to locate Scott, who was standing at the edge of the pad, grinning.

Aelryn forgot about decorum and ran toward his mate.

The feel of Scott in his arms again brought him the peace he'd been seeking all the time he'd spent in the UK.

"I've missed you so much," he murmured into Scott's hair. Their lips met, and something inside Aelryn locked into place. It had been more than merely missing Scott.

Aelryn had felt as though a piece of his soul had been torn from him, and someone had put it back into its rightful place, mending it.

"She's nervous," Scott said in a low voice.

"Where is she?"

"In our room. She didn't want to come with me."

Aelryn drew back. "Well, we can't have that."

"Oh, it isn't only because she's scared of meeting her third mate. Part of it is because... well... because you're *you*." Scott's eyes sparkled. "Aelryn. The name they all know."

He huffed. "Then let's go find our mate and she can see I'm just like everyone else."

Scott walked at his side toward the school building. "What's happened with Theron?"

"I left him with our team in New York. He'll be transported to the upstate NY base." And if Aelryn never saw him again, that would be fine and dandy. "I have so much to tell you."

"I gathered that much from our call last night. Something about artifacts?" He pushed the door open for Aelryn, and they stepped into the cool interior. "Is Jake Carson still in Rome?"

"No, he left for Chicago this morning. He should be almost there by now." Aelryn's conversation with Orsini in the early hours had left him shocked to his core.

He could only imagine what its effect would be on Horvan, Dellan, and Rael.

They climbed the stairs, and Scott paused at the door. "This is ours until it's time to leave." He knocked gently, and it opened to reveal a tiny woman with dark, sparkling eyes and short, spiky black hair. She stared at him, her nostrils flared, and then she launched herself at him.

"You smell the same as Scott," she said breathlessly, clinging to him.

Aelryn laughed. "Well, that's a great opening line." He stroked her arms, breathing her in. "Hello there."

Kia jerked her head upward. "Oh my God, you're tall. I'm gonna get a crick in my neck every time I look at you."

"We can soon change that." He scooped her into his arms, and she wrapped her legs around him. "Better?"

She grinned. "Much." Kia bit her lip. "Hi there."

Aelryn closed the gap between them, and their mouths met in the sweetest kiss ever. Then Scott moved in behind her, one hand on her waist, the other over Aelryn's, and there they were, connected at last.

"We have a lot to talk about." Then Aelryn laughed.

That had to be the understatement of the century.

RAEL WAS overjoyed to have Jake, Seth, and Brick home again, but ever since they'd walked through the front door, Rael's stomach had been churning.

Something is coming. He could taste it on the breeze, feel it crawl over his skin, hear it in the way Jake spoke. Then Jake had asked for everyone to gather in the big living room, and that had been enough to send Rael's pulse racing.

"What's wrong?"

"There's something I need to share with you all, and I'd rather do it once, because it's going to wipe me out."

"I'm on it. Let me go find everyone." Dellan dashed out of the kitchen.

Horvan gave Jake a hug. "You doing okay?"

"Not really. You'll understand why later. And then I'll need some time with the three of you."

Rael blinked. "This is sounding pretty mysterious."

Jake snorted. "By the time I'm finished, you're going to need a new word, because *mysterious* simply won't cut it anymore."

That was all it took to have Rael's imagination going wild.

JAKE CLOSED the office door. "Okay, now you know everything."

"Hearing all that is one thing," Rael muttered. "I think you blew several minds out there." Once Jake had finished talking, there'd been nothing but stunned silence for a moment.

Then the questions started, and it soon became apparent to Rael that Jake didn't have all the answers.

Rael held out his hand. "Let me see that again." Jake handed him the phone, and Rael stared at the image on the screen. "This… this is a joke. *Tell* me it's a joke."

It had to be. Jake had told them what he'd discovered in the rest of the *Missal of Godwin*, and that had been earth-shattering enough, but this?

I know, right? Dellan sounded as numb as Rael felt. *Those lines at the end....*

"It's a lot to take in, I realize that, but—"

"A lot?" Horvan gaped at him. "You sit there and calmly tell us *we're* the reason all these mates are appearing left, right, and center? *We're* the catalyst? And someone predicted us *how* long ago? Almost a thousand years? That isn't *a lot to take in*—that's something *so* humongous that my brain keeps telling me *Does not compute. System overload.*"

"I think we're all in the same state," Rael remarked. Doc hadn't said a word the whole time Jake had been talking, and Eve, Hashtag, and Roadkill had stared at him openmouthed.

"And what are we supposed to do, now that we know this?" Dellan demanded.

"Nothing." Jake stared at the three of them. "All you need do is accept it. You've begun the process—now it will gather momentum." He paused. "But you need to be prepared. Because once word of this gets out—and it will—you've going to be the focus of a lot of attention. Not everyone will believe it, and I expect the Gerans will take the most convincing. And remember… you're not the only ones. *I'm* in there too, as Seth keeps reminding me. Remember the last line. Because of you three… *all things shall become possible.*"

"Now wait just one minute." Rael thought fast. "It isn't enough."

"What isn't?" Jake gave him an inquiring glance.

"How many billions of people are there on this planet? What are the odds that we're the *only* lion, tiger, and bear out there?"

Jake blinked. "Okay, but Dellan's probably the only tiger who was freed by a lion and a bear. I'd say that's pretty specific."

"Sure, it *seems* that way," Rael remonstrated. "But there's no guarantee it couldn't happen elsewhere. It needs something definitive."

"But do *you* believe it?" Dellan asked, his gaze locked on Rael.

"I… I don't know, okay? It seems so… fantastical."

Jake's phone buzzed, and he pulled it from his pocket. "It's Orsini. He says it's urgent." He clicked on Answer. "Hey, what's up?" He listened intently for a moment. "Where? … So what is it?" He froze, his eyes wide, and the hairs stood up on Rael's arms. "You've got to be kidding … Sure, send it." He hung up, his brow furrowed.

"Dad?" Dellan stared at him. "You're scaring me here. What's wrong?"

Jake met Dellan's gaze. "Nothing's wrong. Just absofuckinglutely *mind-blowing*, that's all. And until now, I thought I knew what mind-blowing meant. If what Orsini is telling me is correct, then it seems I was way off the mark."

"Dad…. Take a breath."

Jake took a moment to calm himself. "Okay. Orsini has been working on the artifacts—and he's found something else."

"What more could be left to find?" Horvan exclaimed.

"When we opened the caskets, all the sheets, documents, whatever, they were lying on layers of fabric. You know, to protect them from the stone. Then Orsini and his team started removing each document, putting them between sheets of glass so they could be studied." Jake paused. "Except then he thought to peek *under* the fabric. None of us had done that. Because who would do that, right?"

Dellan gaped. "There was another document hidden under there?"

He nodded. "Not in every casket, just the one that contained the *Chronicles*. And no text this time, but another painting."

Rael arched his eyebrows. "Let me guess. A gorilla and two humans? A polar bear, a tiger, and a kitty? Or maybe a Greenland shark with two humans riding on its back?" He stared at Jake. "I'm right, aren't I? We're not the only ones mentioned after all."

"I only have Orsini's description to go on, but it didn't sound like that. He's sending me a picture." Jake's phone beeped, and he clicked on the screen. "Holy fuck," he croaked.

"Dad? What is it? This is torture."

"Don't do this to us," Rael pleaded. "Show us what he sent you."

Jake swallowed and handed Rael his phone.

Rael gazed at the screen, and his first thought was that he was thankful to be sitting down. "Oh fuck."

The painting was in two halves. At the top were the lion, tiger, and bear from the previous painting, the one Jake had shown all of them, though this was obviously a different piece. But below it….

He was staring at portraits of three men—men who could only be himself, Horvan, and Dellan.

It was like looking in a mirror.

Chapter Twenty-Six

In silence, Rael passed the phone to Dellan, and Horvan inched in to take a closer look. Dellan made a choking sound, and Horvan dropped the phone onto the desk as if it had burned his fingers.

"This is getting too fucking weird," Horvan muttered as he handed the phone back to Jake.

"I'm with you on that one," Jake murmured. "But once you see this, there's no choice but to accept the rest of it. Seth was right. When you read that line, *When he who can see is freed from his shackles*, and then you see this? It *could* be me they're talking about."

Dellan gazed at Jake. "Please, tell me that's all of it. I don't think I can take any more shocks."

"You and me both. Of course, the Gerans might claim it's a forgery—well, they'd know all about *that*, wouldn't they?—but I think once it's undergone tests, they're going to have a hard time explaining *this* away." Jake stared at the image.

"Do you think Theron hid it under the fabric? Because if he'd seen it, he'd know straightaway it was us." Rael huffed.

"I have no idea." Jake sighed. "This makes my head ache just thinking about it. I have to believe if he knew of its existence, he would have destroyed it so it could never be used against him."

Dellan shook his head. "This is going to take some getting used to."

Horvan's eyebrows shot up. "What is? That we're all part of some mystical prophecy? That me and Rael saving Dellan has somehow started something? Because I gotta tell ya, I'm having a hard time getting my head around this. I ain't no legend."

Rael managed a smile. "Oh, I don't know. You've always been a legend in my mind. Now everyone knows it's true." He took a deep breath. "We need to get used to it—fast. Once word gets out, there's going to be a long line of people wanting to gawk at us, like we're in—"

"A zoo?" Horvan flung at him.

"I was thinking more along the lines of an exhibition, but yeah, something like that." He held out his hands to Dellan and Horvan. "And we're going to need each other, more than ever." Rael gazed at them, his heart full of love. "As long as I have you, that's all that matters to me."

Their arms around him had never felt better.

"So does this mean I'm holding a couple of legends?" Horvan murmured.

"I don't know, but I'm pretty sure a legend has his arms round me right now." Then Rael remembered they weren't alone. He broke the embrace.

Jake stood by the office window, gazing out at the lake.

Rael went over to him and touched him lightly on the arm. "You need to rest. And decompress. Go find Doc. He needs you right now."

Jake frowned. "Is he okay? He didn't mention anything in our calls."

"That business with Alec hit him pretty hard, and then Aelryn had a talk with him about stuff they'd discovered in the records from the Maine camp. His head must be as full as yours."

Jake squeezed Rael's hand. "Then I'll see you all at dinner." He hurried from the room, closing the door behind him.

That is one overloaded man.

Horvan and Dellan were at his sides in an instant.

I feel so useless.

Rael kissed Dellan's cheek. *Let them take care of each other. That's what mates do, right?* Then he gasped as Horvan hoisted him over one shoulder. *What are you doing?*

Taking care of my mates—in bed. He walked out of the office, Dellan behind them, shaking his head.

That's our mate. Trying to cure all of our ills with his dick.

Horvan snorted. *It works, doesn't it? If it ain't broke, don't fix it.*

He had a point.

"THIS FEELS wrong." Except that was a lie.

Nicholas was in Jake's arms, the bed was warm, and all was right with his world.

Well, for about thirty seconds before his tumultuous thoughts kicked in.

"What's wrong about it?" Nicholas murmured into the pillow. "Apart from the fact that we were in this bed about fifteen minutes after you came through the door. And five of those fifteen minutes, you spent in the shower." He chuckled. "Not that I'm complaining. Some afternoons were made for this."

"It feels so… lazy. Like we should be using our time for more—"

"Can't you switch your brain off for five minutes? And enjoy a little downtime?"

Jake sighed. "I'm sorry, I—"

Nicholas cut off his words with a kiss. "You have nothing to apologize for, okay? *Anyone* would be in a tailspin if they'd learned all the things you have. But now you need to rest."

"How can I do that? There's still so much to do."

"Yes, there is, but what I'm saying is… let others take the lead in this battle. *You* need to acclimate to your new life, and that requires time." He rolled over in Jake's arms and cupped his cheek. "I know you want to keep on fighting too, and you still can, but in a different way." Nicholas smiled. "I guess the concept of working from home is new to you, but it's one you could benefit from."

"I need to tell people what we discovered. They need to know shifters shouldn't be divided, that there were never meant to be Fridans and Gerans. They—"

"And you can tell them." Nicholas stared at him. "Only, you'll do it online."

Jake stilled. "That's what Orsini said too. He thinks I should talk about the artifacts, the prophecy…." The final parts of which had floored him.

No way can anyone argue with that.

Nicholas smiled. "Wise man. I agree with him. So I guess the first order of business is to determine where 'home' is going to be."

Jake had been thinking about that too. "I want to stay close to Dellan, but… I can't live here. They need their privacy, and so do we."

"I agree." Nicholas kissed him. "I'm glad you said it. I have a house, but that's all it is. I'd be willing to sell up and choose a place closer to here. A place that would be a real home."

"Big enough for three?"

He laughed. "Definitely. I must say, I'm intrigued to discover who our mate is."

"Are you hoping they're male?"

"Not really." Nicholas smiled. "You've already asked me that, remember? Whoever they are, we'll love them, because they're part of us, whether they're male or female, shifter or human." Another gentle kiss. "But right now, this is *our* time."

Jake hadn't asked the question he'd been dying to get out, but he couldn't wait a moment longer. "Are you okay?"

Nicholas blinked. "Why do you ask? Don't I seem okay?"

"It was something Rael said, about Alec…."

He sighed. "I thought I'd seen everything. And then the universe shifts on its axis and reveals a little more, and…." His face tightened. "I can't talk about this yet, all right? I need time too, to process it all. To make sense of it all, even though right now that feels like an impossible task."

Jake kissed him on the lips. "When you're ready, we can talk."

Nicholas's face glowed. "Thank you."

Jake held him close. "Do you think we might find time for a vacation?"

He blinked. "Of course. Did you have anywhere specific in mind?"

"Actually? Yes. Somewhere an elephant wouldn't be out of place." He smiled. "I've always wanted to ride an elephant." Nicholas chuckled, and Jake swatted him. "Get your mind out of the gutter. I'm not talking about *that* kind of riding." Then heat barreled through him when Nicholas's breathing hitched, and Jake caught a glimpse of what was in his head. "But *you're* thinking about it, aren't you?"

"Not riding, exactly. But ever since we spoke last night, there *has* been something on my mind."

"What?" The word came out as a whisper.

"I'll get to that in a minute."

Then Nicholas was kissing him, touching him, and Jake couldn't help but respond with equal passion. The feel of warm skin beneath his fingertips, the sight of Nicholas's chest, covered in a dense mat of graying hair, some black still showing, the scent of him, something that hadn't changed since they were both a lot younger.

"Now I know why we didn't recognize each other as mates all those years ago," Jake murmured between kisses.

"Hmm?" Nicholas chuckled. "You expect me to think when you're playing with my nipples?"

"Oh, so you like that, huh? Good to know." Jake closed the gap between them and flicked his tongue over the taut little nub, loving the shiver that rippled through his mate, the low moan that fell from his lips.

"You… you were saying?"

Jake stroked Nicholas's neck. "We couldn't have recognized each other because it wasn't time. We were waiting for the prophecy to click into place, and that didn't happen until Rael saw Dellan in that cage." And then Jake lost his train of thought as Nicholas kissed his neck, tracing a line with his tongue from earlobe to collarbones, dipping into the hollow at the base of his throat. "*Now* who's making it hard to think?"

"Is it?"

Jake blinked. "Huh?"

"Hard."

Heat rushed through him, along with most of the blood in his body that seemed to be making a beeline for his cock.

Nicholas's eyes focused on his. "Kneel, Jake, facing the headboard. In fact, you'd better hold on to it."

Oh gods.

Jake moved slowly, the mounds of pillows against his stomach as he leaned forward to rest his arms on the wooden headboard, his breathing quickening. "Aren't you going to tell me what's on your mind?" His voice sounded raw.

"No. I thought I'd let my fingers do the talking."

And suddenly, there were indeed warm fingers sliding under the hem of his shorts, teasing his asscheeks, the crease where ass met thigh, and then they were gone, replaced by fingernails raking up and down his sides. The mattress dipped, and Nicholas pressed his chest to Jake's back, pulling him upright, his hand on Jake's face as he tilted Jake's head back to kiss his neck, his chin, and finally his lips.

Nicholas's hand was on his chest, toying with Jake's nipple, tweaking it, and Jake swore he felt that all the way through his body to his balls.

"Nicholas," he whispered.

A gentle kiss on his ear sent a shiver through him. "Uh-uh. Right now, I'm Doc. Too many goddamn syllables in Nicholas. Save your breath."

"What am I saving it for?" Jake asked. Then Doc's hand was on his stomach, sliding down, until his fingers reached the elastic waistband of his shorts and slipped beneath them to mold around his thickening cock. Jake let out a low moan, and Doc's breath ghosted his neck.

"That. I want to hear you." Doc gave Jake's dick a gentle squeeze. "Oh, I think you like it when I do that."

"Then do it again?" Jake moaned softly when Doc stroked his shaft, still inside his shorts—until Doc lowered them, baring Jake's ass.

Jake's breathing caught, and his heart pounded, and then he was swept along on a tide of sweetness when Doc caressed his hips and ass with a reverence that took his breath away. Doc helped him out of his shorts, then leaned over him once more to plant a kiss between Jake's shoulder blades, followed by a trail of kisses down his spine until he reached Jake's crease.

When Doc pressed his nose between Jake's cheeks, Jake moaned again, the sound morphing into a startled gasp when a warm tongue flicked his hole.

"Oh dear gods."

Then Jake felt it, the joy that surged through Doc, the exquisite pleasure that washed over him when he licked a path over Jake's pucker.

Oh fuck. I can feel what you feel.

Doc repeated the action, and there it was again, a double layer of emotions as Jake heard the sounds of appreciation that escaped Doc's lips and felt that appreciation reverberate through him. When Doc stroked Jake's cock while he licked his hole, Jake had to fight the urge to come.

It's been decades since I felt like this. The last person to bring him such unadulterated pleasure had been Miranda.

Which is why I'm taking my time.

Jake forgot to breathe as Doc pressed his tongue against his pucker, his fingers wrapped around his shaft, pulling on it gently, slowly, while he worshipped Jake's hole.

Turn around, love.

Jake did as he was told and lay back against the pillows. Doc used his hands to gently spread Jake's legs as wide as they would go, Jake's cock jutting out, hard, precum already beading at the slit.

"What about you?"

Doc smiled and leaned in to kiss Jake on the lips. "I can wait. This time it's all about you." He flicked Jake's nipples with the tip of his tongue before kissing his chest, his stomach, moving lower, lower, until at last he reached Jake's rigid dick.

Doc bent down and rubbed his face along Jake's shaft, and Jake placed his hand on Doc's shoulder, stroking him, shuddering as he anticipated what he knew was coming, knew with every fiber of his being—

And then Doc knelt upright.

Jake wanted to growl, to yell, *anything* to feel that mouth on him.

Doc kissed Jake's inner thigh once again on a slow and steady path downward, heading for Jake's erect dick, and when he reached it, he traced the stony line of it with his tongue, flicking at the underside of the head, making Jake shiver, making him want—

At last, Doc's mouth closed around the head, and Jake's eyes rolled back.

Doc took more and more of it into his mouth, until his nose was in Jake's salt-and-pepper pubes and his lips were stretched around the root. Jake put one hand on Doc's head, stroking the graying hair, gazing into blue eyes that watched him as Doc gave his dick a hard suck.

Oh, Doc. Can't describe how good that feels.

You don't have to. I feel what you feel, remember? It works both ways.

Then Doc pulled free, and Jake groaned.

Doc chuckled. *Patience. You'll like this. Keep your legs like this. And touch yourself. Bring yourself to the edge.*

Jake curled his hand around his shaft and tugged on it, getting into a rhythm.

Doc stretched out on his front, his face inches from Jake's ass, and Jake pushed his head back into the pillows as Doc's tongue renewed its acquaintance with his hole, only this time with a great deal more enthusiasm. He pushed deeper, deeper, and Jake felt his body opening up for Doc, loving the moans Doc made as he ate Jake's ass.

When Doc slowly slid a finger into him, Jake groaned good and loud.

That's for another day, Doc told him. Then he licked a trail from Jake's hole and over his taint, reaching his balls. He took one of them into his mouth and sucked on it, and his thoughts left Jake under no illusions that Doc was loving every second.

Doc's gaze met his, the laugh lines around his eyes so prominent.

No one appreciates balls like a gay man.

Jake was inclined to agree. He pulled harder on his cock, chasing the sensations that trickled through him, lighting him up like electricity, zapping through his sac, along his dick....

Doc's mouth closed around both his balls, and Jake came, spurt after spurt that coated his stomach and thigh, each pulse as delicious as the one before it. The slow tongue that cleaned away every trace of come was the perfect ending.

No, scrap that. Doc's kiss as he shared the taste of Jake was the only way to end Jake's first consensual sexual experience in more than thirty years.

They lay together under the sheets, holding each other, Jake's heartbeat returning to its usual rhythm.

Then he became aware of the silence.

"Doc? You okay?"

Doc sighed. "I'm sorry, that was incredibly selfish of me."

"You've lost me. I got to be on the receiving end of a blowjob, I got to come, *you* did all the work... how is that selfish?"

He sat up. "You were a prisoner for thirty years. They forced you to breed. I said you needed to get yourself right before we moved on to sex. That taking it slow was okay. And then I go and—"

"And take my breath away with the sweetest, most unselfish act ever." Jake arched his eyebrows. "If I hadn't wanted you to do it, I would have said so. Have you ever thought that maybe I needed to *feel* again? To know the person worshipping my dick was doing it because he *loved* me?" Jake sighed. "And if we're telling the truth, I was so nervous. As soon as your lips touched the head of my cock, I was right back there." He took Doc's hand. "There was a difference, though. A *huge* fucking difference." Jake looked him in the eye. "*You* weren't drugged. *You* weren't a nameless, faceless person. *You* weren't doing it to get food." He smiled. "You were doing it out of love, and as your mate, I recognized that. I reveled in it. Am I ready to go further?" He shrugged. "Honestly, I don't know. I *do* know I'm going to talk to the therapist, like we said, but I think the love of my mate—of you—is helping to soothe the broken bits inside me. Or at the very least, helping to stitch them back together into a semblance of the man I used to be. The one I want to be again."

Doc cocked his head to one side. "I caught a fragment of a thought a moment ago," he confessed. "Maybe it's something you don't want to discuss, but—"

"I can't think of anything I would keep from you," Jake confessed. "Especially after what you just did. So... what did you want to know?"

"The Gerans captured you thirty-one years ago. Was… was there no one in all that time you could have formed a relationship with? Another prisoner?"

For a moment, Jake said nothing. At last he sighed.

"When they took me in Rome, I was a married man. As far as I was concerned, I was *still* a married man, right up to the point when Dellan told me Miranda had died. And every time they shoved me into a cage with another shifter, I fought to get free. My vows mattered, and they didn't give a fuck about them. So why would I take up with another woman? My wife was still out there with our son, not knowing what had happened to me." His throat seized.

"You'd been gone a long time when she finally remarried, hadn't you?"

Jake nodded. "I'm glad she got a second chance to find some happiness. The guy she married sounded as if he was all right. He took care of her and Dellan." He stroked Doc's chest. "So no, I haven't had sex like that since before I was taken. Every single fucking moment that took place after? Doesn't count." He cupped Doc's cheek. "Feeling your emotions when we make love? That is…." Tears pricked his eyes.

Doc rolled on top of him and kissed him on the forehead, nose, chin, cheeks, and finally his lips. "You deserve a second chance too. Don't forget that. It's time to live again."

Jake smiled. "And love again."

His mind went back to the prophecy.

Who's waiting out there for us? He no longer doubted there *was* someone perfect for them—he just wanted them to hurry up so the three of them could spend what time they had left together.

Tomorrow is never promised.

Chapter Twenty-Seven

"He's been gone for hours," Aric whined.

Seth laughed. "He's been gone thirty-eight minutes. I started the stopwatch the moment he left, because I knew you'd build it up in your head to be way longer. And let's face it, they have a lot to talk about."

Brick had asked for a meeting with Horvan, which had somehow grown into a Zoom meeting with Aelryn, all of which made Aric nervous.

This isn't just his future we're talking about. It's ours too.

Right then Aric didn't care where they ended up, as long as they were together. And he couldn't see Horvan or Aelryn sending Brick off to some far-flung country without his mates. They understood what torture that would be.

Except didn't Horvan leave Dellan and Rael at home once?

Then he recalled Rael telling him how they'd followed the team anyway.

So I'm not the only disobedient mate after all.

He glanced up when Brick strode into the bedroom, and beamed. "Hey, you. How'd it go?"

Yay. Go me, not showing how nervous I really am.

Brick flopped onto the bed, and in a heartbeat Seth and Aric snuggled against him. Brick kissed them both. "I've been looking forward to this for the last hour."

Seth laughed. "I swear, you two are as bad as each other. You need me around for balance." He returned Brick's kiss. "*Now* you can tell us how it went."

"Long. Tiring. Never let anyone tell you Zoom calls are less annoying than an actual physical meeting." He sighed. "I wouldn't want to be Aelryn right now."

"Why? Is something wrong?" Aric's heartbeat quickened as he imagined the worst. Except after the Fielding and Theron episodes, he couldn't for the life of him think what could be worse than that.

"He called us three times during my meeting with Horvan, and while he was online, two people I didn't recognize stopped by to discuss something. Once he was done with them, he started working on something else, until Horvan coughed to remind him we were still connected. You should've seen Aelryn's face. I get it, though. He's being pulled in a lot of different directions."

Jake's revelations might have provided a bombshell, but the Fridan leaders still had to get the word out about them.

And not everyone is gonna like what we have to tell them.

"How did Horvan and Aelryn react to the news that you're not quitting after all?" Seth asked.

"I guess it made things a little easier for them. It also gave them a little headache, because they'd been working on plans to move ahead without me."

"I'm sorry," Aric blurted. "I shouldn't have—"

"Hey." Brick kissed his hair. "This is *not* on you, okay? It's on me." He peered at Aric. "I *do* need to know, though. Are you *sure* this is what you want me to do? I mean, they're talking splitting us up and forming us into smaller strike teams. We'd have to move, for one thing."

Aric bounced upright. "Move? Where to? Please don't say the UK. The weather would depress the fuck out of me, and—"

"Will you let me finish?" Brick speared him with a steely gaze, and Aric mimed zipping his lips. "Okay, Aelryn said they have what is essentially a place where people go to chill out and recenter themselves. He says it wasn't meant for long-term use but could be modified. He also said if we want it, we'd be welcome to it. The place hasn't been used in a couple of years, so it would need a good cleaning and some patient tending to bring it up to home status."

"Okay, but where?" Seth demanded.

"It's near the Teton forest in Wyoming."

Aric had grabbed his phone before Brick could take another breath.

"Whoa, there." Brick placed his hand on Aric's arm. "The thing is, it's not really a place for a little kitty. Too many predators, for one thing. And it's remote, so you and Seth would run the risk of being lonely if I'm out on missions."

Aric smiled. "Keep us filled with your scent and no one will dare to bother us. I'd love to live anywhere you and Seth are."

"Anywhere?" Seth arched his eyebrows. "That covers a lot."

"Can I be honest with you? I don't like crowds or noises, and this place sounds like a slice of apple pie with ice cream."

Seth chuckled. "I might have known you'd make it about food."

"There's more to tell you. This new deal? It's not all about the fighting, according to Horvan. He said it requires diplomacy too." Brick snickered. "I told him that lets me out. But then he said you two might have a role to play."

"How?" Aric fought to keep calm, but his heart was racing. "I would *love* that. I can be diplomatic."

Seth let out a snort. "Excuse me? That *was* you who told Crank not to have another cookie because his shirts were looking a little tight around the middle?"

"Hey, he thanked me for that," Aric remonstrated. "He said it was a reminder to use the gym more." He turned toward Brick, batting his eyelashes. "And I can take part in missions too. I've done it twice now."

Brick coughed. "Can I remind you that first time was you disobeying me?"

Seth laughed. "Strolling into Thurland Castle has given you a taste for it, huh? Aric—spy kitty."

"Hey, I was good," Aric protested. "Aelryn said so."

"Horvan suggested you and Seth could talk to people. You were captives, so you have firsthand knowledge." Brick smirked.

Aric narrowed his gaze. "What *else* did Horvan say?"

Brick grinned. "He said I'd need to be okay with it, but it beat you stowing away in my gear. And Seth would be there to keep an eye on you."

Aric folded his arms. "And what did *you* say? Because you kept us out of that meeting."

Brick coughed. "I said a fly shifter wouldn't have enough eyes to keep on that little bastard."

He gave a mock gasp. "Little bastard? Were you referring to *me*?"

Brick's grin wouldn't quit. "Well, what would *you* call someone who stows away in your pack and barfs on your gear?"

Aric moved to sit astride him. "Take that back."

"Nope."

"Now."

"Nope." Brick's eyes twinkled. "Whatcha gonna do about it, kitty cat?"

A heartbeat later Aric shifted and stretched out his claws, holding them above Brick's chest. Brick flinched.

Seth laughed his ass off. "Now I've seen everything. The big bad polar bear is afraid of murder mitts."

Brick rolled his eyes. "Duh. I've seen what damage he can do with them."

Aric shifted back, buffing his nails on his chest. Then Brick flipped him onto his back and pinned him to the bed, his arms above his head on the pillow.

"You've been a *baaad* kitty. You need to be punished."

"What did you have in mind?" Aric replied breathlessly. "And does it involve your dick?"

Judging by the weighty cock rubbing against his own stiff shaft, Aric was about to be fucked through the mattress.

I need to be bad more often.

Horvan barged into the living room and flopped onto the couch. "Ignorant idiots." His Zoom meeting with one of the Italian leaders had not gone the way he'd hoped. He knew he shouldn't let himself get so riled up, but honestly, *some people….*

"I'm guessing it didn't go well?" Rael asked from the other end of the couch.

Horvan shrugged. "It could've been better, but then again it could've been a lot worse. Remember what Vic told us about his meetings with the Fridan leaders when he tried to gather support? He said most listened, and many joined the cause, but some flat out refused to hear him. Well, that's what I've experienced so far." He held out his arm. "Get your ass over here. I need to hold you for a while."

Rael moved closer and cuddled up to him. Horvan inhaled his scent, and as always it calmed his senses. Rael tilted his head and peered up. "What's really the problem?"

Horvan let out a chuckle. "I love how you can see right through me." He sighed. "I'm going to be honest with you. I don't know if what we're doing is going to help us or hurt us."

Rael frowned. "Explain."

"We've broken the back of the serpent, but the head and tail are still writhing. Since we shared what was in those caskets—and basically told shifters they'd been lied to for the last hundred years—a lot of people have called *us* liars. They said they were going to join the Gerans and prove the truth to us."

"Even if what you told them shows Fridans and Gerans only exist because of a lie? After you showed them the paintings?"

"Don't get me wrong. A lot of leaders have seen all the evidence *and* believed it, especially when we showed them that video of Jake, telling them all about the artifacts and about Ansfrid and Ansger. But not all of them." He expelled a long breath. "The battle is over, but I'm afraid the war may have just begun."

Rael was warm against his body. "No one said it would be easy. But we need to do this, to try and siphon off the disgruntled and keep them from reforming under new leadership."

"That's what worries me," Horvan murmured. "What if we can't? What if this war never ends?"

Rael shifted position to sit in Horvan's lap, facing him. "And what if it does? What if what they found in those caskets is right, and *we're* the ones who'll lead all shifters into a new era of peace?"

Horvan bit his lip. "You know I'm still having real trouble believing in that prophecy, don't you? Even *with* the painting of us. But it's a nice thought."

If only it could be true.

Horvan's phone buzzed, and he removed it from his pocket. When he saw it was Aelryn, he clicked on Answer. "Hey, what's up?"

"Someone got to Theron. He took poison."

What the— "Is he dead?"

Aelryn's voice was glum. "My guards got to him fast enough to save him. Is that the wrong play? Should we have let him die?"

Horvan thought hard. There was no doubt Theron deserved death after what he'd done, but…. He sighed. "No. He needs to pay for his crimes, and killing himself—or being helped to do it—isn't justice. If we kill him, we make a martyr out of him, and that gives the people who believe in him—in his cause—a reason to fight on. And if I'm honest, I think a lot of people on both sides will want to see him dead. So sticking him somewhere deep and dark? Bringing him out now and then to prove he's still alive and not some hologram? That's about the best we can hope for."

"Then we go ahead with plan A."

"I think so. Any idea who gave him the stuff?"

There was a slight pause before Aelryn responded. "An inkling of one, but if I'm right, their motives were totally understandable. I'm not going after them—put it that way."

"And if he'd succeeded in killing himself?"

Another pause. "I don't know what I would have done in that case." Noise in the background told Horvan their conversation had run aground. "I'll talk to you soon." Then Aelryn was gone.

Rael let out a low whistle. "I'm not sure whether Theron is lucky or not. But you know what? I don't want to talk about him. Did I hear right this morning? Saul saying Milo is going to join us? Well, the Fridans at any rate."

He nodded again. "Milo contacted Aelryn a while back and told him he wanted to be involved. Jana too. They're gonna be based in Texas."

Rael smiled. "I'm glad Milo's going to be on our side. We owe him a lot."

"Aelryn's paid part of that debt, apparently. He found them a place to live." He smirked. "One that'll be big enough for three."

"Oh, that's great."

"Aelryn also gave me the latest about Victor. He's recovering well, and he's going to be part of the team too." His chest tightened.

Rael kissed him. "I know," he said in a low voice. "It's good to know our forces are growing, but at the same time...."

Horvan held him close. "Yeah. Our family is about to go through some changes."

He smiled. "That's what families do. Kids grow up, they leave the nest.... But they won't be far away. And they won't be gone for good." He clambered off Horvan's lap and headed for the door.

"Hey! Where are you going?" Horvan called out after him.

"To see Mrs. Landon. I've got an idea."

EVE DID her best attempt at puppy-dog eyes. "Can I help it if I want rocky road and there's none in Dellan's freezer?"

"Fine, but right now?" Roadkill froze. "Hey... you're not...?"

She rolled her eyes. "No, I'm not, but when I am, you'll be the first to know. Can't a defenseless, helpless little girl ask her two big strong mates to go get her some ice cream?"

"Defenseless? Since when?" Hashtag narrowed his gaze. "You're up to something." He held up his hands. "But I'll play along, just to keep the peace. I'm sure we'll find out eventually." He grabbed Roadkill's arm. "Come on. You can drive."

"Gee, I don't get to do that too often," Roadkill quipped. "Although if I want to get back in one piece, it's probably better if I drive."

"Hey!" Hashtag squawked.

Roadkill raised his eyebrows. "Two words. Mexico City."

"And I'm shutting up now." They headed out the door.

Eve waited until the car had pulled onto the road before getting her phone out. She speed-dialed Aelryn. "Well? Any news?"

"We've found her."

Eve silently thanked whatever gods watched over shifters. "Where was she?"

"That's the bad news. She was in a camp in New Mexico. We'd gone there on a mission to dismantle a breeding program."

Hearing the words was enough to make her stomach turn. "Is she okay?"

"She's fine. But trust me, you don't want to know about the conditions in that place."

Eve's heart hammered. "They... they weren't trying to...." She'd heard the reports about Geran experimentation.

"No. As far as I can tell, she was being kept there until she was old enough. So now what?"

"My first suggestion would be to put her on a plane and send her here. Then once she's arrived safely, I'll send for her brother."

There was a pause. "How safe do you think she would be if she traveled with me?"

She blinked. "Aelryn, you don't have to do that. I know what's facing you right now. If you can't spare anyone, I'll come myself."

He chuckled. "I only said that because I'm coming to Illinois anyway."

"You are?"

"Yes, but you can't tell anyone. It's something Rael is planning, and it's supposed to be a surprise."

"So when do you arrive?"

"In three days. And I'll have a couple of guests with me."

She beamed. "Then I look forward to seeing you. And thank you again." She hung up, her heart light.

She was going to keep her promise.

Then she smiled to herself.

Seems I'm not the only one with secrets.

Chapter Twenty-Eight

Horvan was dreaming about a bell. Someone was ringing it repeatedly, and it was starting to piss him off.

Then it stopped, and he opened his eyes.

Rael leaned over him, his eyes twinkling. "So phones have these things called alarms. You're supposed to turn them off, not lie there and ignore them."

Horvan grabbed him and pulled Rael on top of him. "And good morning to you too." The feel of Rael's morning wood against his own gave him all kinds of delicious ideas.

Do I get to join in? Dellan snuggled against Horvan's side, joining them in a three-way kiss.

A phone ruptured the tranquil moment, and Horvan groaned. "Okay, which one of you didn't leave your phones on silent last night?"

Dellan snickered. "That would be you."

Rael peered at the phone. "And it's Aelryn calling." He clambered off Horvan and grabbed it, handing it to him. "Might be important."

"At this hour?" Horvan sat up and clicked on Answer. "Good morning. Well, it's morning here. I have no idea what time it is where you are." Aelryn had mentioned traveling at some point.

"Are you sitting down?"

Something in Aelryn's tone pierced the post-sleep fog that still enveloped Horvan's brain. "What's up?" He clicked on speaker.

"You know Orsini brought in scholars to document the artifacts?"

"Uh-huh. Jake mentioned it."

"Well, it seems word has gotten out about the contents of the caskets."

He frowned. "How can it have gotten out when I've already been talking to leaders for the past two days?"

"I'm not talking about leaders—I'm talking about your normal, everyday shifters. And it's growing."

"*What* is growing?"

"You'd better prepare yourselves." There was a pause. "You, Rael, Dellan, Jake…. People want to meet you."

"Excuse me?"

Rael and Dellan sat up, staring at him.

"I can't believe how fast this has spread. We're picking up talk in the US, Europe, Australia, everywhere…. The prophecy has gone viral."

Horvan rubbed his bald head. "I don't get it. Those leaders I spoke to, they didn't appear particularly bowled over by the prophecy."

"Only now those same leaders are facing questions from their own people. Questions such as why was this kept from them? How long have we known about it? Does everyone get two mates? And the most prevalent question seems to be… when can we meet the shifters from the prophecy?"

He frowned. "I don't like the sound of this. Don't get me wrong, I'm happy if they've heard about it and believe it, but wanting to *meet* us? The next thing you know, we're gonna have a cult following."

Another pause. "Horvan… we're already there. I'm getting requests to set up meetings with you."

He snorted. "I can tell you what my answer is gonna be right now." No way was he going to let his family become some kind of sideshow.

"And I agree with you, one hundred percent. But all this attention, it's having an effect. Those leaders who are facing a barrage of questions can't show themselves to be disbelievers. They have to be seen to support the prophecy." He paused again. "And there's something else."

"Seriously?" Horvan groaned. "Now what? They think Jake is the messiah? Or is he Ansfrid reincarnated? Because right now this whole business is getting weirder and weirder."

"Nothing like that. In fact I guarantee this will make you smile."

Horvan could hear the excitement in Aelryn's voice. "Then tell me. I could use a smile after that bombshell."

"Leaders are reporting the emergence of… mates. From all over the world, people are finding their mates. And a pattern is forming."

"What kind of pattern?"

"So far it seems mates are either all shifters or a mix of shifters and humans. But no triads that are completely human."

Dellan's breathing hitched. "That line from the prophecy about shifters finding the one who completes them—whether they're shifters or human—and all things becoming possible." His eyes widened. "Can't you see where this is heading? Humans are going to learn about shifters, but in a way that won't lead to distrust or animosity or prejudice. Because how can there be such things when people are joined in love?"

Horvan arched his eyebrows. "How can there…? Come on, you live in the real world."

Rael nodded, his eyes bright. "And *this* is how we change that world. Sure we need to tear down the old regime, and for a while, there'll be a backlash against Gerans, but it'll pass. It has to. What are you going to do if you're a Fridan, and you suddenly discover your mate is a Geran? You can't hate them."

"And the day will come when shifters realize they are not Fridan or Geran, but simply part of this changing universe," Aelryn concluded. "One world, one people, but some of them with special gifts that are accepted, supported… treasured."

Horvan had to admit that day couldn't come soon enough.

"It's not gonna happen overnight, you know." He had to be the voice of reason, of logic. "And it's gonna take a lot of work to get to that point."

"But we *will* get there," Aelryn insisted. "Don't you feel it?"

Dellan and Rael gazed at him, and the hope in their eyes couldn't be ignored.

Horvan sighed. "Yeah, I do. And now that you've *really* woken me up, I'm gonna spend some quiet time with my mates. You know, before there are hordes of people at the door, clamoring for autographs or selfies." He stilled. "Or worse—wanting to bear our children."

Dellan rolled his eyes.

Aelryn laughed. "I promise you, my friend, no one will learn of your location through me."

"Thank you. Have fun with your traveling. Going anywhere nice?"

Aelryn coughed. "Maybe. I'll leave you to your mates." Horvan caught voices in the background. "And it seems my mates are clamoring for *my* attention." He said goodbye and hung up.

Horvan replaced his phone on the nightstand. "Whoa. That was one helluva wake-up call."

"Do you think he's right?" Rael asked. "That the time is coming when we finally see an end to this division that should never have happened in the first place?"

"Part of me wants to believe that, but I think you nailed it too. There's gonna be a backlash. What the Gerans did is too huge, too horrific to sweep it under the table."

"But if I was right about that, then I'm probably also right about what will heal the rift." Rael kissed him. "You can't fight love. It's the strongest force in the universe."

"The prophecy nailed it too," Dellan reminded them. "'*Three hearts, beating as one. Three bodies, joined in love.*' Remember?"

Horvan let out a sigh. "I guess someone really knew what they were doing when they put us together. I'm a glass-half-empty kinda guy, but you two…."

They balanced him. Complemented him.

And suddenly he didn't want to talk anymore.

He peered at Rael and Dellan. "Now… where were we?"

Then he caught his breath when they moved farther down the bed, and two pairs of lips renewed their acquaintance with his shaft.

There was time enough to dwell on what was heading in their direction. Right then he needed to be with the men he loved.

The men who loved him.

JAKE GAPED at Dellan. "You've got to be kidding." He glanced at Doc. *Can you believe this?*

Doc chuckled. *I had no idea my mate was such a celebrity.*

"Want me to go so you can talk?" Dellan's eyes held amusement.

"It can wait." He aimed another glance in Doc's direction. *Can't it?*

Doc's innocent air was almost comical.

Jake folded his arms. "Nope. I'm not going to give rise to another Geran group."

Dellan frowned. "What are you talking about?"

"What you're describing has all the hallmarks of a cult. I may have been out of things for the last three decades, but I know what a cult is. Jim Jones? David Berg? Charles Manson? Do these names ring a bell?"

Dellan stared at him. "I don't think you're going to inspire the same kind of acts they did. You're benevolent, for one thing."

"So are most cults when they start out, but they quickly spiral down, and suddenly those who don't believe? They become the enemy." Jake stuck his chin out. "I'm not going down that route."

The light touch of Doc's hand on his arm was like an anchor.

"And no one is saying you should." Doc's voice was as gentle as his hand. "But you've been given a gift. Use it for good. Talk to people, even if it's in a Zoom meeting." He cocked his head to one side. "We discussed this, didn't we? Tell them what you know, what you've seen… what's coming. Remind them you're as human as they are." He smiled. "People are going to need to work together, and no one knows that more than you."

"You think it'll be that easy? We're talking exposing shifters to a world that thinks they're a myth. And sure, on an individual basis, knowledge of them will increase as more people find their mates, but we're not just talking individuals here. We're talking governments, and *they're* unlikely to be so benevolent."

Doc snickered. "Until they find *their* mates." He sighed. "But seriously… I believe once this starts, there will be no stopping it."

He could be right.

But the idea of achieving cult status disturbed him.

Jake frowned. "They're going to find us, you know that, right? Someone will leak the location. It won't be Aelryn, but there's bound to be someone who can't resist doing some digging."

"We'll deal with that when—if—it happens," Dellan assured him. He gave Jake a hug. "And now I'll leave you to have that conversation." He left the small living room.

Jake walked over to the window and stared out at the lake, nestled in green. "People *will* come, you know." When Doc chuckled, he twisted to peer at him. "What was funny about that?"

"It's a line from a famous movie, that's all." Doc joined him. "And they'll have to find us first. So I guess this is as good a time as any to show you what I've been up to the last day or so." He pulled his phone from his pocket, tapped the screen, then scrolled. He handed the phone to Jake. "Take a look at this."

Jake gazed at the image of a house. It was attractive, with cream siding and a reddish-brown veranda, a couple of trees out front. He peered closer. "Scotts Bluff County, Nebraska. What's there?"

"Us, if you like the house."

He stilled. "Really?" Jake scrolled, and when he reached the end of the images, the breath caught in his throat. "Ten and a half acres?" There was nothing to see for miles except hills in the distance and field after rolling field.

"Three beds, two baths, so plenty of room for all three of us. Thirteen hours' drive from here, but it has an airport in case you needed to get anywhere fast."

Jake studied the details. "Pinecone Drive, Gering." He glanced at Doc. "Population?"

"Eight and a half thousand." Doc smiled. "And ten point five acres is a whole lotta space for an elephant and a tiger to run around in. So what if we're spotted? We happen to have some exotic pets. But I'd say the likelihood of that happening is pretty small."

Jake scrolled some more. "I like the back porch. I can see myself sitting out there on summer evenings."

"Me too." Doc's hand was on his back. "And no neighbors. We can hide from the rest of the world if we want to—or need to."

"So this is it? You're retiring?"

Doc shrugged. "I was semiretired when I took that first call from Horvan to take a look at Dellan. It isn't such a big step to go the whole hog and call it a day. Besides"—he smiled—"I want to spend what days I have left with you. Making up for lost time."

Jake studied the image again. "Do *you* like it?" He was already in love with the place, and he'd only seen pictures of it.

"I wouldn't be showing it to you if I didn't. So what do you say? Fancy a trip to Scotts Bluff, Nebraska? Maybe after the weekend?"

Jake beamed. "I'd love one."

A little corner to call their own. A sign saying No Trespassers.

And privacy to shift.

"Of course, the first investment would be decent internet, so you can talk to people. No need to go traveling if you don't have to, right?"

Jake pulled Doc to him and kissed him, slow and sweet.

"Have I told you how happy I am to have you as my mate?"

Doc's eyes gleamed. "Not in the last two hours, so I might need to hear it again. For reassurance."

Jake rested his forehead against Doc's. "They're not going to let me disappear into the background. You *know* that, right?"

"Tough. This is your reward for thirty years plus of putting up with Geran hospitality. You get to kick back and relax. Like I said, let others take the lead in any battles to come."

Jake was hoping for an end to hostilities.

A new beginning.

Chapter Twenty-Nine

EVE KNEW the second she glanced at her phone for what had to be the third time in about ten minutes that it was one time too many.

Hashtag placed his tablet on the coffee table. "Okay, what's going on?"

She blinked. "I have no idea what you're talking about." She'd tried not to make it too obvious.

Duh. Hashtag noticed everything.

"Have you had news from the adoption agency? About Logan?"

"Not since the last time we talked about it. They said it shouldn't be long now." The waiting was driving her mad.

"And I don't suppose you know what's going on outside on the patio either."

Eve frowned. "What do you mean?" She'd been so preoccupied with the imminent arrival that someone could have driven a tank past the French doors and she wouldn't have noticed.

"Mrs. Landon has set up a whole load of tables. It looks great out there: tablecloths, glasses, silverware…. A bit too fancy for a cookout, so something's going on. Is it because Aelryn and his mates are here?"

They'd arrived the day before, along with their guest and much to Horvan and Dellan's surprise. The fact that Rael had a room ready for the mates should have let them know it wasn't exactly an unplanned visit.

Rael did a stellar job of blocking that *thought.*

Roadkill stuck his head around the door of the living room. "There's a car pulling up outside. Are we expecting visitors?"

Eve was on her feet in a heartbeat. "Yes." She hurried out of the room and through the hallway, arriving at the front door just in time to see—

Jamie and two humongous bearded men climbing out of a taxi. The car groaned and went up several inches after the last man stood.

Eve would hate to pay for that car repair.

They towered over him, one older, with a buzzcut shaped into a peak at the front, the sides of his head shaved, the other with dark brown hair swept up from his face, and both of them with broad shoulders and arms, their skintight tees stretched over acres of rippling muscle.

Almost as tight as the jeans they'd poured themselves into.

Oh my.

Down, girl, Roadkill admonished.

Don't tell me you don't find them hot.

Roadkill snickered. *Our mate does. I think his ass is puckering looking at them.*

Hey! I'm just... admiring. From a distance.

Jamie waved when he saw her. "Hey, I thought no one except Rael knew we were coming."

She chuckled. "He didn't say a word."

He grinned. "In that case—surprise!"

Eve glanced at Jamie's companions, then gave a sniff. She gaped. "Oh gods, you found your mates, didn't you?"

"There's no hiding anything from you, is there?" Jamie gestured to the older of the two men. "This is Shawn."

The younger guy gave a short bow. "And I'm Brandon. Based on what Jamie's told us, you have to be Eve."

"Got it in one." She gave Jamie a huge hug. "It's good to see you again." She stood aside to let them enter as Rael rushed to greet them.

"You made it." Yet more hugs were exchanged, and then Rael led them toward the living room, from which filtered the sound of music, soon replaced by shouts of delight the minute they entered.

Eve lingered by the front door.

He should be here by now.

Right on cue another taxi pulled onto the driveway. As it came to a stop in front of her, she spied a familiar face in the back seat. Eve dashed forward to open the door for him.

"Victor! Thank you for coming." Then she got a better view, and her stomach clenched.

The man looked awful. He'd lost some weight; his cheeks were sunken and his eyes listless.

Then she recalled he'd only recently arrived from the UK, and he'd probably gotten no sleep during the flight.

That's bound to make anyone feel worse.

Victor climbed carefully out of the taxi, and she watched yet another car return to its usual position.

Jamie's mates are big, but Victor....

He cocked his head toward the house. "Very impressive." He frowned. "Is that music I hear? It sounds like a party. I had no idea I would be interrupting," he murmured. "I'll come back another time."

"Uh-uh." Eve grabbed his large hand. "You're staying here. Trust me, you've arrived at the perfect time." The taxi driver opened the trunk, and Eve took Victor's bag before he got a chance. "And it's not a party, just a gathering of family and friends."

"But I am neither," he protested.

Eve knew she was tall, but even she had to crane her neck to look Victor in the eye. "Victor," she said in a low voice. "Please… trust me?"

He stared at her for a moment, then nodded.

She dragged him indoors. As soon as he stepped into the hallway, his head snapped up and his nostrils flared.

"What…. What is that odor?"

She wrinkled her nose. "What do you… oh. You *did* say you have a great sense of smell. Why don't you follow it to its source?" Anticipation bubbled up within her at the thought of Victor's surprise.

As though in a trance, Victor stumbled forward, and Eve opened the door to the smaller sitting room. Victor caught sight of its occupant, and his eyes widened. "Irena!"

His eight-year-old sister launched herself at him, and Victor held her against his massive frame. He kissed her hair, murmuring words Eve couldn't make out as he cradled Irena to him.

He met Eve's gaze, tears streaking his cheeks. "Where did you find her?"

"That doesn't matter. The important part is that you're together again." Irena was babbling in a language Eve didn't understand, but it was easy to see their joy at being reunited.

"But… how long has she been here?"

"She arrived yesterday," Eve told him. "With Aelryn and his mates."

Victor grimaced, rubbing his forehead. "Why would you do this? We fought. I hurt you."

She gazed into eyes filled with sadness and pain.

"Yes, we did fight. Now you tell *me* something. If it hadn't been for Theron, do you think we would have?"

His lower lip jutted out. For such a big man, he seemed so frail and innocent.

"I dislike fighting," he said at last. "I much prefer to wade in the water as my hippo. No one stares at me as if I'm filthy, disgusting." He gestured to his body. "I eat almost nothing, and yet look at me."

Eve put a hand on his arm. "Listen to me. Some shifters reflect their animal. You're one of those. And believe me when I say, you look very good." She smirked. "And if you want to talk about body problems, imagine how often a gorilla shifter has to shave her legs and armpits."

"And we wouldn't change a thing about you," Hashtag said from behind her. "We love the whole package." He held his hand out to Victor. "It's good to meet you again, Victor."

Tears slid down his cheeks. "I don't understand. I smell her on you. How can you not hate me?"

Roadkill joined them. "Because we've all done things we wished we hadn't been forced into. No one here blames you. What you did was for survival, and as former military, we can respect that." He grinned. "As long as you don't do it again, we're good."

Victor blinked, and then he smiled. "Never," he vowed. He patted Eve on the shoulder. "I would give my life for my savior."

She shook her head. "I didn't save you so you'd owe me. I did it because it was the good and right thing to do."

"I asked you to fight with us," Hashtag reminded him. "But if you'd rather have a peaceful life, we would totally get that."

Victor sneered, his lip curling up, showing his missing teeth. "The Gerans are murderers, and I will help bring them to justice." Then he jerked his head up, sniffing again. "But what *is* that smell?"

Eve frowned. "I don't understand. I thought you'd caught Irena's scent."

He shook his head. "No, this is different. It's...." His brows knitted. "I have never smelled anything like it before."

And then the penny dropped.

Eve's heartbeat quickened. "Kind of sweet and spicy, all at once?"

Victor stared at her. "Yes, exactly like that."

Eve met Hashtag's gaze, then Roadkill's.

There could only be one explanation.

"I think you need to come with me."

JAKE INCLINED his head toward the patio. "Do *you* know what's going on?" Mrs. Landon had been going back and forth all afternoon, preparing tables for some kind of meal.

And that was another thing. There seemed to be more place settings than people staying at the house.

Doc leaned back in the wide patio chair and gazed out at the lake. "No clue. Doubtless someone will fill us in at some point." He sniffed, and froze. "Do you smell that?"

Jake frowned and took a sniff. "Smell wha—" He gaped at Doc. "That smells like you."

"I thought it smelled like *you*."

Jake heard footsteps, and he turned to see who approached. Eve walked purposefully in their direction, accompanied by a mountain of a man who appeared to have been in battle recently, judging by his fading bruises and scars.

A man who was the source of that delicious scent.

Eve grinned as she came closer. "You're missing a third piece. I think I've found it." She gestured to the huge man at her side. "This is Victor Berzoner."

Jake blinked. "The guard Theron ordered you to fight?"

She nodded. "And apparently that was meant to be. Because otherwise he wouldn't be here now." She tilted her head. "I'm right, aren't I? He *is* your mate."

Doc's jaw was the first to drop.

"No. It can't be." He lurched to his feet, and Jake was maybe a second behind him.

That scent. It has to be.

Victor gaped at them. "You... you are my mates?"

Doc smiled. "It seems so."

Jake walked toward him, his hand outstretched. "I am so very happy to meet you."

Victor ignored his hand and pulled Jake into a bone-crushing hug. "Mate." Then he stilled. "But what are you?"

"A tiger," Jake told him, and Victor's face lit up.

"Always I have been a cat person." He peered at Doc. "And you? Are you also a sleek, fast cat?"

Doc chuckled. "No, I'm a huge, lumbering elephant. And what are you?"

Victor beamed. "I am hippo." He released Jake, and Doc got the chance to have his ribs crushed too. "I will protect my mates. Do you fight against the Gerans too?"

Doc shook his head. "I'm a doctor. My hands are made to heal, not harm." He glanced at Jake. *You realize what's the first thing we'll have to do when we get our home in Nebraska?*

Find the biggest bed ever made?

Doc laughed. *No—have a pond dug out. Or better still, a small lake. Something perfect for a hippo to wade in.*

Victor froze. "How can I hear you in my head?"

"Try it for yourself," Doc suggested.

Victor gave him an incredulous stare. *This is magic?*

Jake chuckled. *No, it's simply part of being mates.*

One of the mysteries he would never understand but would be forever grateful for.

He gestured to the chairs. "Please, join us. We have a lot to discuss."

Jake listened as Victor related what had happened since his encounter with Eve at Thurland Castle. Richard Deveraux had taken care of him, and once Victor was well enough to travel, he'd made arrangements to send Victor to Aelryn.

Something clicked into place. "The little girl who came with Aelryn? She's your sister?"

Victor nodded. Apparently, he'd had no idea Irena had been located, and the poor man couldn't stop his tears.

Thankfully, they were happy tears.

Jake had to admit they were a strange match, but he wasn't about to argue with whoever had decided they were a good fit.

What do I know?

One thing was certain—Victor needed some TLC, and Doc was the perfect person to provide it. Then it became obvious that two had become four, as Irena had no one to care for her except for her big brother. Jake had no qualms about that, except it might make life interesting in the future.

Soundproofing, Doc said with a grin. *Bedrooms spaced well apart from each other.*

Victor glanced from Doc to Jake, then back to Doc. *This is where I tell you that I have never....* He bit his lip.

For a moment Jake was confused. Then it hit him. *Oh. You've never been with a man?*

Oh. I see. Doc studied him. *And does this worry you?*

Victor laughed. *I think it should worry you. I am not small.*

Jake swallowed. *I hope he's talking about the size of his body.*

Doc grinned. *I have two words for you. Butt plugs.*

Chapter Thirty

"Try it again," Brick growled.

Seth jumped up on the beam again, but Aric was fussing. They'd been at it for several hours. At first, when Brick told them they were going to train together, Aric was the most excited. After his sojourn as a spy, he asked about being involved in more missions. Brick and Seth were both against it, but Aric, thanks to a fantastic blowjob and fuck session, had gotten them to see the error of their ways.

Aric fights dirty. I was too exhausted to say no.

The world was changing with each passing day. Where shifters had once been nothing more than a myth to humankind, the time was fast approaching when they'd be revealed, thanks to the emergence of more and more mates.

Brick wasn't sure how he felt about that. He'd inhabited a scary world for so long, and his instincts told him the danger was still out there. The fight wasn't over, he knew that much, and he needed Seth and Aric to be ready to defend their home and their lives by whatever means necessary. Seth was taking it in stride, doing his best.

True to his little kitty nature, Aric was hissy and annoyed.

Brick folded his arms. "You asked for this, Aric. Remember? 'I want you to train us'?"

In a few moments, the kitten became the man, still every bit as sleek and beautiful.

"I know, but why is it so hard?" he grumbled.

"Because you're not used to using these skills. You're in the mindset that things will work out, but after what happened with the two of you and more than a few of our friends, I think you need to put that thought out of your pretty little head. We're sitting on a powder keg here, and it's primed to blow."

"Wouldn't if you stayed with us," he said with a pout.

And then Brick understood.

"I'm still happy to quit, you know that, right?"

Aric's shoulders slumped. "I'm sorry. That was a cheap shot. No, I want you to get out there and save the world. Seth and I want to be part of it too. It's just...." He sighed. "This all comes so easily for the two of you. You're a powerhouse. Seth is limber and strong. But me? I'm a freaking *kitty*. In any chain, I'm the weakest link."

Brick grabbed his arm and dragged him into a fierce hug. Naked would be better, but this wasn't the time for that. His mate needed him to be calm and level-headed.

Horny Brick could come out to play later.

"I think you know that's not true."

Aric tried to push away, but Brick held him tight. "It is!" he cried. "I've always been this way. In high school, I could never do sports, no matter how hard I tried." He snorted. "That was hella fun. Kids would tease me about it all the time." His eyes gleamed. "But you know what? I was smart. *I* was the one they came to when they needed tutoring. Watching a six-six, two-hundred-fifty-pound football player practically *begging* me to help him so he wouldn't get kicked off the team was heady stuff. And once I did, he was so happy he became my protector. He wouldn't let anyone near me."

"What happened?"

Aric shrugged. "He went off to college on a football scholarship. I never heard from him again. Still, his name carried weight, and people left me alone. How messed up was it that I felt lonely all the time? It got so bad, I would have happily gone back to the teasing. At least then people were *talking* to me."

"I'm sorry that happened," Brick murmured in his ear.

Seth came over and took a spot on Brick's lap, wrapping his arms around Aric. "Why are you so hard on yourself? No one here thinks you're weak. How many others would have the balls to climb into Brick's duffel?"

"And throw up?" Aric countered.

"Think on something for me, would you?" Seth patted their mate's broad chest. "Brick is a wall. He defends people. And while I'm not exactly a fighter myself, I can learn." He gazed at Aric with affection. "It's not that you're soft. It's that you're...." He frowned. "I'm trying to say this and not make it sound patronizing. You're domesticated."

Aric rolled his eyes. "Duh."

"But think on this. How many domesticated cats lose their homes and are forced to survive on their own? The skills are there—we've both seen flashes of it—you just need to bring them to play. You know, *work* on them. With Brick. And if you want extra reasons to do it? Prove to him that a house cat can be every bit as sneaky and dangerous as any big cat. And remember, you have an amazing head on your shoulders."

Aric opened his mouth to answer, but Brick cut him off. "Stop defaulting to sex. He wasn't talking about that kind of head." Then he smiled at Seth. "You weren't, right?"

"You think we can't feel that thing pushing into us?"

"Well, I'm sorry," Brick whined. "Having you both near me affects my body. I can't help it." He kissed Aric's head. "And that's the thing. We're slaves to our bodies and minds. I know this is a serious conversation, and I keep trying to get my body to behave, but it knows what it wants. Or more accurately, where it wants to be. We're the masters of ourselves, though." He kissed them. "Yes, I want to be buried in you both again. Yes, I want to swallow your cocks to the root. But I'm more than a mindless beast who thinks with his dick. I'm a man with two mates who need him to be serious. What Seth is saying isn't necessarily wrong. Fighting might not be for you, but espionage? You can get into places few of us can. You're brilliant enough to figure out ways to protect yourself. Maybe think about that instead of rushing headlong into combat."

"So I wouldn't have to do these exercises?" he asked hopefully.

Brick chuckled. "Nice try, but I'm afraid you'd have to do more. You need both of your bodies to be limber and physically trained."

Aric rolled his eyes again. "You just want me to have my knees up to my ears. You won't be happy until I can suck my own dick while you fuck me."

Brick groaned. "You are *such* a brat. Now I've got that image in my head. But I'm not gonna give in." He pushed Seth and Aric from his lap gently, then swatted them both on their asses. "So get ready. We're going to do it again. And Aric, you're going to learn more. I have a friend who is the undisputed king when it comes to infiltration. I'll contact him and ask if he's willing to have a disciple."

Aric widened his eyes. "Seriously?"

"If you want."

"Yes! I want it. I promise I'll try harder. I want you both to be proud of me."

"We always will be," Seth said gently. "And that's a promise."

Thanks to their link, Brick could feel the warmth rushing through Aric, plus the new determination that infused him. He would never say he wasn't worried, but he hadn't lied. Aric was cut out for the spy life.

And Brick wanted to hurry with this training session to see if Aric could suck himself while Brick fucked him.

His boy had a lot of great ideas.

SAUL'S HEART pounded as he gazed into Vic's eyes. "Oh fuck." The words rolled out of him in a low moan of pleasure. Crank's tongue had never felt this good in his ass, but it was the thought of what was to come that sent trickles of electricity zapping through him from head to toe.

Vic cupped his chin. "I'm sorry you had to wait longer than you anticipated for this."

Saul growled. "Don't you dare apologize. I'm thankful you're here in one piece." He groaned as Crank pushed his tongue deeper. "Gods, that feels amazing." Then Crank was gone, and Saul growled once more. "Did I say you could stop?"

Crank laughed, and warm flesh pressed against Saul's back. He kissed Saul's ear. "Flip over, baby. I wanna see your face when I slide my cock deep inside you."

Saul shuddered, but he rolled over, his head in Vic's lap.

Vic stroked his cheek. "You still want this, right?"

He rolled his eyes. "Are you kidding? I've been dreaming about this ever since you watched Crank eat me out for the first time."

Crank covered Saul with his body and kissed him. "Me too. My dick is so hard, it aches." He locked lips once more, and Saul moaned into the kiss. "I'll take it slow, okay?" Crank promised.

Saul nodded. "You'd better." Thoughts of all the times Crank had teased him, sliding his slick shaft through Saul's crack, smacking Saul's pucker with the head of his thick cock, sent waves of desire and need surging through him.

Crank grabbed the lube and squeezed a generous amount on his dick before smearing it over his length. "Lube is your friend. I speak from experience."

He swallowed as Crank pressed the warm, wide head of his cock to Saul's hole.

"Breathe, baby." Vic's hand was gentle on Saul's face. "Next time, you'll be inside me while Crank fucks you."

Saul managed a chuckle. "You just wanted a ringside seat for the main event, didn't you?"

Vic grinned. "Watching you take a dick for the first time? You bet."

Crank pushed, the head popped through the ring of muscle, and Saul moaned. "Fuck, that feels huge."

"Which is why I won't move until you give me the go-ahead," Crank assured him. His hands were warm on Saul's thighs, his gaze focused on Saul's face, Vic's body equally warm beneath him.

I'm lying here, surrounded by love.

Fuck, he never wanted to lose this feeling.

And you won't, Crank said with a smile. *We've got you. You're ours.*

Saul breathed deeply. *I'm ready for more.*

Then Crank hooked his arms under Saul's knees, gave a gentle push, and slid into Saul's body with a soft sigh. "Aw fuck, you're so warm and tight."

Saul choked back a cry to find himself swamped with so much love, pouring from his mates, rolling off them, connecting them. Crank kissed him, then Vic, before three mouths met in a three-way kiss, his hole stretched around Crank's girthy shaft.

Crank pressed his forehead to Saul's. "Love you," he whispered as he began to move, slow, delicious strokes that lit up Saul's body like a goddamn Christmas tree. Saul groaned when Crank's dick nudged his prostate, and Crank smiled. "And *there* it is."

Saul arched his back, and Vic took Saul's hands in his, gripping them tightly. Crank picked up speed, and Saul's moans were in sync with Crank's thrusts, their combined noises filling the air.

"Can't last long," Crank gasped. "You feel too fucking good."

"Then come in me," Saul pleaded. He widened his eyes as Vic let go of his hand and curled it around Saul's shaft, tugging it, sending his pleasure into the stratosphere. It seemed as though mere seconds passed before he was creaming Vic's hand and Crank's dick throbbed inside him.

"Oh gods, that was worth waiting for," Saul moaned before Crank's lips met his in a lingering, tender kiss. Then Vic lay beside him, and Saul was enfolded in two pairs of arms, Crank's damp chest against his side.

"Love you both so much," Vic whispered.

Saul held Vic to him. "Get used to this, because we are never letting you out of our sight again."

Vic craned his neck to peer into Saul's eyes. "You do know that's not going to be possible, don't you?"

Crank snorted. "We're gonna give it a damn good try."

Saul knew what he was praying for—a time when there was no more fighting, when he could love his mates without fear of losing either of them.

Make it soon, please.

Chapter Thirty-One

Dellan pushed his plate away and patted his stomach with a contented sigh. "That was delicious."

Horvan had to agree. Rael's surprise meal in the open air had taken some organizing on Mrs. Landon's part, but she'd provided an amazing meal for—

How many people?

Rael grinned. *Twenty-two. You should have seen her face when I told her there'd be two more, but I had no idea about Victor and Irena.* He peered at the table. *And there are leftovers.*

Dellan snickered. *Not for long. Give it half an hour, and Saul and Crank will be raiding the fridge.*

A wave of satisfied groans moved around the tables, and Horvan gazed at the faces of his mates, his team—his friends. The lump in his throat threatened to choke him.

After all we've been through together, it's hard to believe we're about to go our separate ways.

Tell them how you feel, Dellan suggested.

He was right.

Horvan raised his glass of champagne.

"Firstly, thank you, all of you, for joining us. Even the ones we had no idea were coming." He gave Rael a mock glare. "This is what you get for having a sneaky mate who is *way* too good at hiding his thoughts."

Rael preened. "What can I say? I learned from the best." When Horvan pushed his chest out, Rael snorted. "I learned it from Dellan."

Laughter erupted around the table, and Horvan narrowed his gaze.

It was only then that it hit him. With the exception of Irena and Mrs. Landon, everyone gathered around the tables was part of a triad.

The thought staggered him.

Horvan took a deep breath. "When Rael turned up on my doorstep back in March, I learned that mates were real, and that I was a lucky man.

Then I learned about Dellan, and my good luck doubled." He gazed at the faces around him. "We thought we were the only ones."

"We were," Dellan interjected. "For about five minutes." That earned him more laughter.

"Then our world was turned upside down when Vic walked into it, and discovered he had two mates who were both human." Horvan raised his glass to them, and they did the same. "Jamie's entrance into our lives was… memorable."

Jamie chuckled. "I thought you were going to shoot me under the table." He glanced at Crank. "And *you* were going to put a bullet in me."

"That's my mate," Saul said with a touch of pride. "Shoot first, think later."

Crank dug him in the ribs with his elbow, amid laughter.

"And it took a DNA test to show us what was staring us in the face—he and Dellan were related."

Jamie sighed. "Not that I believed you right away."

"You got there eventually," Dellan said with a smile.

He glanced at Shawn and Brandon, who nodded. Jamie sighed again. "I have some news. Aelryn's people located my birth mom." His face tightened.

Aw fuck. Horvan wanted to hug the life out of Jamie, but he figured that was something for his mates. "Not good, I take it?"

"Nope. She wasn't interested. She really didn't want to be reminded of my conception, put it that way."

"Fuck her," Jake growled. "If that's her attitude, she's no great loss. You have family that loves you."

"Yeah, he does," Shawn said quietly before leaning in to kiss Jamie's cheek, and Brandon slipped his arm around Jamie's shoulders.

"Can I be the voice of reason here?" Doc said in a clear voice. "I don't think we should think unkindly of Jamie's mother. After all, she was essentially raped, correct? Can any of you blame her for not wanting to be reminded of such a heinous act, which she would be every time she looks at Jamie?"

Jake flushed. "You're right, of course. I'm sorry I said that."

Horvan glanced at the trio at the end of the table. "Then our favorite polar bear found one of his mates, Aric, and we learned the other, Seth, was Dellan's half brother, and that Dellan's dad, Jake, was still alive."

Dellan's eyes glistened. "In one fell swoop, I gained two half brothers and the prospect of seeing my dad for the first time in thirty-one years."

"And yet more mates kept coming." Horvan raised his glass to Eve, Hashtag, and Roadkill. "The highlight of all these meetings had to be when Hashtag and Roadkill found out that after a decade of fighting together, drinking, and—" Horvan coughed. "—other pursuits, they were mates."

Eve laughed. "You're not kidding."

"I beg to differ," Jake interrupted. "I think the most surprising meeting has to have taken place a few hours ago." He glanced at Victor and smiled.

"Can I take a moment to thank Rael for his invitation?" Aelryn stood. "It has been my pleasure to know Horvan and his mates, and to be included in their extended family."

Rael smiled. "We're honored to have you join us."

Brandon let out a raw chuckle. "Jamie sat us down and told us the whole story, but seeing you all here…. It's amazing." Shawn nodded.

"I too have news." Aelryn gazed at Scott and Kia, his eyes shining. "Our little family of three is about to grow into a somewhat larger family of eight." He beamed. "We have located all five of Kia's children, and very shortly, they will be with us."

Applause broke out, accompanied by a whoop from Crank.

"You're gonna have more, right?" he said with a grin. "I mean, baby red pandas… we're talking cute overload."

Scott laughed. "I think that could be a possibility. Unless they take after Kia or Aelryn. But I'll be happy with whatever we get."

"And on another note…." Aelryn smiled. "Yesterday, I learned that the archaeologist who discovered Berengar's tomb has been located. Sarah Delaney had been imprisoned in a Geran camp that we raided. She's well, and she'll be joining Orsini in Rome to catalog the artifacts." Aelryn glanced at Jake, Doc, and Victor. "And I would like to extend my thanks to Jake. Without him, we would not be in the fortunate position we now find ourselves. He gave us a glimpse into the lives of Ansfrid and Ansger, and in so doing revealed the truth." Aelryn's eyes sparkled. "A truth we are now sharing with all shifters." He raised his glass. "To Jake, the one who can see."

Jake swallowed as everyone toasted him.

Silence fell, but Horvan knew he wasn't finished.

"I want to say…." Tears pricked the corners of his eyes, and damn it, that wasn't like him. He fought to regain his self-control. "I want to say thank you to the best fucking teammates anyone has ever had the honor of working with. I cannot tell you how proud I am to have watched you all grow, find your own families, and prepare to embark on new adventures."

"Don't get all weepy, H," Hashtag called, "or else *I* might start bawling too."

Eve ran a hand over his back, but whatever she said to him was between them.

Horvan squared his shoulders. "I know we're splitting up and taking on new missions for Aelryn and his people. There are still a lot of smaller camps out there that we've yet to find and a lot more shifters to save." He raised his glass to Aelryn, who held up his own. "The fact you've seen the potential in each of them tells me that we did good, people. All of us." He sucked in a shaky breath. "I'm gonna miss the fuck out of you."

"It's not as if we won't see each other again," Dellan said. "Right?"

"Probably not like this, like a family. At least not until we get everyone out safe and bring them home."

"How many camps do they think are left?" Roadkill asked Aelryn.

"It's true a lot have been abandoned once the troops got to hear the truth, but conservative estimates are anywhere between seventy and a hundred still in operation. Die-hard Geran leaders who refuse to believe the fight is over. Of course that number might change if people start joining them."

"Pretty fucking stupid people, if you ask me," Crank grumbled. "Because how could anyone in their right mind see all that evidence and not believe it? I mean, if I was a shifter? Right now I'd be kissing the fucking ground you three walk on."

Horvan stuck his foot out. "Well, far be it from us to stop you. I prefer it right on the toes, please." That earned him another ripple of laughter. He gazed at their faces. "But yeah, the fight isn't over. That's why Aelryn needs help. It's also why he's taking the most experienced people to head up the squads." Horvan glanced at Hashtag, Roadkill, and Eve. "You guys are gonna be awesome in the UK." He grinned. "And at least we know we'll have a bed for the night if we visit."

Eve laughed. "Oh, I think we can find you some space."

"And then we'll get you babysitting Logan while we go out on the town," Hashtag added with a grin.

"And I'll be visiting regularly to see how the orphanage is doing," Dellan added.

"You're not getting rid of us *that* easily," Saul muttered. "Of course, we *will* be moving houses—all the way to the lake."

Vic laughed. "Yeah, that's going to be a tough commute, right?"

"And I'm gonna be up here every day." Crank chuckled. "You think I'm gonna miss out on Mrs. Landon's cookies? Think again."

Mrs. Landon laughed. "There will always be a box in the kitchen labeled Crank's Cookies." Her eyes twinkled. "Right next to the ones that say Saul's, Horvan's...."

"Do you deliver?" Brick asked. He glanced at his mates. "Wyoming might be fifteen hundred miles from here, but that's what planes are for, right? We'll be visiting you so often, you'll get sick of us."

"Never," Dellan declared. "Now that I've found my brothers, I don't intend losing track of them."

"And I'll only be in Boston," Jamie added. "I mean, *we*," he added hastily.

Horvan chuckled to see the stare Shawn gave him.

Looks as if they'll give Jamie a run for his money.

He beamed. "I think you'll make a great teacher. Those kids will be lucky to have you."

"I have an announcement to make."

All heads turned in Jake's direction.

"We've been searching for a place of our own, and we might have found one in Nebraska. Thankfully, it's big enough for three."

"It will need to be," Victor said with a grin, squeezing his mate's hands.

Of all the people Horvan had met so far, Victor seemed the most settled with the idea of having mates. He'd watched that afternoon as Victor grabbed drinks whenever Jake and Doc were thirsty. He'd listened as Victor checked to see if they were hungry. Doc had shivered once, and Victor offered to find him a blanket.

What was even more surprising was Irena.

She nestled in Victor's lap, but seemed to feel equally at home with Jake or Doc. It was as though they fitted perfectly into her world, making it calmer. Doc had promised to find a therapist for Victor and his sister.

They've both been through a lot of trauma.

Horvan had to admit it was a triad that shouldn't have worked, but somehow it did. In the wild, hippos were unpredictable and dangerous, yet in Victor, Horvan couldn't sense that at all. He was clearly a caring, nurturing individual. A man in charge, but one who needed to make sure those under that charge had everything they needed to be healthy and happy. With Jake's turbulent past, not to mention Irena's, maybe that settled something in Victor. It had given him someone to take care of. Horvan had little doubt Victor would be the top in their relationship, but he would be a gentle person outside of sex, he was certain.

Exactly what their new family needed.

Then Horvan felt Dellan's hand on his back, and he realized he'd zoned out.

"Nebraska isn't all that far away," Doc said. The three of them were still holding hands.

Dellan cleared his throat. "If you guys ever need us, call and we'll come running." His eyes glistened. "We owe you more than we can repay in a dozen lifetimes. Without all of you, we wouldn't have found our mates." He gave Horvan and Rael a warm glance. "Our families." He raised his glass. "To peace—and all things becoming possible."

Keep Reading for an Exclusive Excerpt from
Line of Sight
Book #4 in the Second Sight series
by K.C. Wells
Coming in Fall 2025

Prologue

Saturday, September 22, 2018
Fairmont Copley Plaza Hotel, Boston MA

I STOOD at the bar, sipping champagne, watching, waiting for the charity ball to stumble toward its end. About half the guests had already departed, but the remaining revelers were still on the dance floor, the DJ pumping out more music from the nineties, music that should have died with the decade, to be honest.

Not that I was listening. My mind was elsewhere.

This is ridiculous. I'm better *than this.*

I'd dispatched numerous people from this planet, four of whom had deserved their grisly fates—and one whose demise was purely a matter of self-preservation—and I'd kept my cool every single time. But from the moment Dan Porter and Detective Gary Mitchell strolled into the ballroom, I lost my focus. And with each passing minute my thoughts grew muddier.

Why don't they leave?

I wasn't worried about being caught. That was simply not a factor. I was more concerned they'd thrown a wrench into the well-oiled machinery of my plans. I'd known they were coming ever since I'd received the email with the guest list. Seeing Mitchell's name there had been the first surprise. There could only be one motive for his attendance—his brother's murder—but that didn't answer one all important question.

Why now? Brad's been gone for twenty-three years, so why is Mitchell coming to this *reunion? Something* has to have brought him here.

As I scanned farther down the list, I found my answer. Dan Porter would also be there. Anyone in Boston who didn't know that name by now must have been living under a rock for the last four months.

Now *I get it. The famous psychic is going to help Mitchell find Brad's murderer.* That could be the only reason for both of them attending the ball.

Porter could be a huge fake. There was always the possibility the news reports were nothing but hype. But what if he wasn't? And what if he was at the ball because he'd discovered something?

What if he'd somehow gotten on my trail?

I dismissed that thought. There was nothing that could have led them to me. Still…

The situation had been enough to set my mind working. I needed a test, something to help me decide whether Porter was a real threat. Sean Nichols's request for raffle prizes dating from our university days provided the answer. I knew *exactly* what I would be taking to the ball. To tell the truth, I was spoiled for choice, but I intended keeping something back for later.

A game needs clues, right? A mouse needs to see some cheese before he starts to make his way through the maze.

And if Porter truly possessed a psychic ability, my next game could prove to be extremely interesting.

Thinking back, the evening could have backfired spectacularly, and the blame for that failure could be laid nowhere but at the altar of my ego. It should have been a simple task of walking over to the raffle table and depositing my prize, but there was more to consider. For one thing, I took two DVDs, one of which I left with the other items when I was certain I wasn't in view of any of the guests, the other when I had an audience. I thought briefly about wiping my fingerprints from its plastic cover, until I realized there was no need: Countless fingers would come into contact with it that night.

Part one of the test complete.

Part two was a trickier prospect.

I watched Mitchell and Porter mingling with the other guests, and I instantly understood their intent.

They're checking out Brad's classmates. They're going to talk to everyone who knew him.

Including me.

I became adept at watching the proceedings in the mirrored doors rather than be caught paying too much outright attention. The temptation to turn and watch directly when Porter was introduced to the others was enormous. I knew *I* could keep a cool head, but them? A couple of them were already showing signs of cracking. I couldn't understand why. This was ancient history now. A string of unsolved murders. They'd gotten what they wanted, hadn't they?

More importantly, I'd gotten what *I* wanted.

I focused on Porter and Mitchell in the mirror, looking for a sign, a reaction.

Nothing.

Then I realized why. None of the four had shaken hands with him.

What did that newspaper article say? Something about his gift being related to touch?

They knew, then. They had more intelligence than I'd given them credit for. They'd avoided my gaze all evening, not that I was surprised. I'd issued strict instructions to that effect via email prior to the event. In some cases, that was the first contact I'd had with them in years.

I did my own mingling, joining in with the laughter, the reminiscences.... I always surprised myself with how easily I could fake interest, kindness, sympathy, even flattery. It still raised a smile that my nickname during those college years had been *Mr. Charm*. I'd perfected the art of appearing charming long ago. My grandfather used to say one could catch more flies with honey than with vinegar, and he'd been right.

The mask of charm was useful to help me achieve my goals and could be discarded when no longer required.

Porter and Mitchell were getting closer, and suddenly it was my turn.

I was ready for them.

Shaking hands was out of the question when mine were already filled with a glass of champagne and a plate of cake. I smiled, nodded, said all the right things, and waited to see if there was any reaction.

Nothing.

They continued on their way around all the tables, and I couldn't contain my smile.

So he is a fake after all.

I told myself it wouldn't have mattered if he'd been genuine. It wouldn't alter my plans. I wasn't troubled by some inner voice that said I should have made my excuses and pulled out of the event the second I saw their names. That was ridiculous.

All the more difficult to play cat and mouse when predator and prey aren't in the same room.

Then it was time for the raffle, and I stood at the periphery of the ballroom.

Let one of them win a prize.

The final play in the evening's game would be Porter's reaction to the DVD. And when he held up his ticket with a grin, I thanked whatever gods looked after killers and psychopaths for granting me the opportunity to know once and for all. Life had become boring of late, and I'd been on the lookout for something more exciting to capture my attention.

And in strolled Dan Porter.

Now we'll see.

I watched as the pair ambled over to the prize table. Porter was still smiling as he walked the length of the table, picking up items and peering at them before replacing them.

You don't see it, do you? You don't feel anything.

Then Porter froze, and my world narrowed as he became my sole focus.

Beside him, Mitchell rubbed his arms, shivering visibly, and I resisted the urge to do the same with the goose bumps that had erupted over my own, despite the warmth of the room. Not that I feared I was about to be revealed.

The game had just gotten more interesting. An unexpected thrill had been added.

Porter was talking to Karen Williams, his hand outstretched.

Why doesn't he pick it up?

I watched Porter's chest rise as if he'd taken a deep breath, and I turned my back once more, focusing on the reflections in the doors. He picked up a DVD—*my* DVD—and staggered, falling against the table.

Holy fuck. He knows.

There couldn't be any other explanation for his reaction.

I remained calm, forcing a smile at the photos of Dave Turner's kids, but inside I was ice. In the mirrored door, Dan scanned the room as if searching for something.

Or someone.

And then the light dawned.

He's looking for me.

I widened my smile. *But you can't see me, can you?*

Mitchell put his arm around Porter's waist, a gesture that shouted affection, even intimacy. That added a whole new dimension to the proceedings.

So, more like Brad than I'd realized. A significant detail that might prove useful.

I maintained my facade of calm, waiting until at last they left the ballroom.

He didn't find me.

Tonight. He hadn't found me *tonight*. But that didn't mean I'd evade Dan Porter's gift again.

So what do I do now? Wait for him to come knocking at my door?

It was more a case of what I *didn't* do. There would be no more killings for a while, even though I knew that could prove difficult. More often than not, doling out death was a safety valve, a way to cope with the stupidity of the people around me.

But why stop? I've been doing this for twenty-three years. Getting away with it *for twenty-three years.*

That still small voice in my head piped up.

Longer, surely. Have you forgotten? Who forgets their first kill?

I hadn't, of course.

Then I realized I'd been given a gift. Something else to occupy my time and thoughts. Something new.

I could keep tabs on Detective Mitchell and Dan Porter. I might even play with them.

And if Porter gets too close?

There were deeds he might see. Deeds that would have real-time consequences. *That* was what trickled through my mind.

But he won't. And making sure he doesn't is part of the thrill, the game.

Maybe this *new* game would bring about another death.

Or possibly two. After all, it would only be fitting if they left this world together, right?

Chapter One

Early November, 2018
Boston, MA

IN THE cold cases office, the whiteboard's pristine surface had been divided into four sections, and the crime-scene photos attached to them seemed to scream at Detective Gary Mitchell every time he glanced at them.

Wrongful death!

Avenge us.

Brad Mitchell wasn't screaming, however. He stared at Gary the same way he'd done from every photo of him Gary had ever seen in the twenty-three years since his murder. Photos that sat in his parents' dining room on the sideboard, the piano, showing Brad as a baby, a little boy, a teenager, at graduation. Brad staring at the camera. At Gary.

The quiet stare that said *Find who did this to me. Do it for me.*

For the first time in all those years, Gary was finally ready to do just that.

The aroma of freshly brewed coffee filled his nostrils, and he took the proffered cup. "You read my mind." Then he realized what he'd said, and he laughed.

"As if I needed to do that, even if I possessed the gift, which I don't." Dan Porter smiled. "You're a creature of habit. Let's face it, *anytime* I bring you coffee is the right time." He inclined his head toward the door. "Your coworkers, however? They clam up every time I pass by them, and it doesn't require mind-reading skills to know they're nervous around me." His eyes sparkled. "I can almost hear them. *Don't talk to the psychic.* What deep, dark secrets are they afraid I'll uncover? Although to be fair, since they found out we're a couple, some of them appear *less* nervous." Dan's lips twitched. "Because of course their straight asses are safe. I'm not about to jump on their bones now that I'm fully occupied jumping on yours."

Gary arched his eyebrows but said nothing.

He'd stood by his decision to come out as bi to his colleagues. It was early days, and while it was true there'd been no muttered comments, awkward silences, or inquiring glances so far, Gary knew his fellow detectives well enough to realize once the honeymoon period was over, they wouldn't pull their punches.

He dreaded the cartoons he knew would soon be pinned to his office door. Someone out there had a wicked sense of humor and a whole lot of talent.

Right then he had more important things to think about.

He gazed at the photos that were about to be the focus of his attention for a while.

Very similar photos.

"You work fast." Dan gestured to the whiteboard. "All I did was go out for coffee and you got all this done. This is all of them?"

He nodded. The department's tech whiz, Barry Davies, had scoured VICAP for all the cases that bore the same MO as Brad's—brutal, unusual murders that had so far gone unsolved.

What he'd uncovered had been shocking.

Some of the photos were in black and white, but the absence of color didn't rob them of their heart-stopping properties. Each section bore the name of the victim and the date of their murder.

Brad was the first, and Gary's heart had quaked as he'd attached the photos.

He looks so young.

The picture of his brother before his death was a study of a freckled, tousle-haired youth, his eyes bright with humor. Gary's mom had provided the police with the photo, and every time Gary glanced at it, he saw himself at that age.

I must have reminded them of him so much. Almost like a wound that was never allowed to heal.

He didn't have to look at the crime-scene photo. He knew it by heart. He'd visited the picnic table in Forest Park, Springfield, MA, countless times, and during one visit, he'd lost it when he spied a family sitting there, shaded by the trees, eating, laughing, joking....

A far cry from what had been discovered back on April 16, 1995. Brad's mutilated body lying there, blood soaking into the wooden slats of the picnic table, Brad's heart nestled in his hands, his chest open....

So much blood.

"Hey." Dan's hand was on his back, a comforting reminder of his presence. "I don't have to ask where your head is, do I?"

Gary tore himself away from his memories. "What surprises me? I remember one of these cases. I wasn't working on it, but I do recall how sickening it was at the time—and how frustrated detectives were that they hadn't been able to find the murderer."

"Which case?"

He pointed to the photo of a dark-haired woman, maybe in her mid-forties. "Heather Kelly." Below her name was written June 8, 2013. "I'd only just joined Homicide." He shivered. "Her murder was straight out of a horror movie."

The photo could have been a still from such a movie. Heather Kelly was seated at a desk, unrecognizable from the earlier headshot, her head a mass of crisped flesh, the result of high-pressure steam, the medical examiner had surmised.

The device employed to deliver said steam was on the desk in front of her.

What was noticeable was the lack of restraints. It was as though she'd sat there and let it happen.

Dan pointed to the photos next to Brad's. "This was before your time." He peered closer. "How old was he? Mid-twenties?"

Another nod. Mark Wilson's body had been discovered in Acadia National Park on August 17, 1997, another gruesome murder. He'd been found out in the open, his body suspended from his wrists, cuffs biting into them. The restraints were locked around metal loops hammered into what looked like a wall of rock, but that wasn't what made Gary's stomach churn. Wilson was dressed in shorts and a tee ripped at the neckline, hanging in two flaps, his innards tumbling from his torso, which had been cut open from the base of his sternum to the waistband of his shorts.

The final victim, Jeff Murphy, had been thirty-eight at the time of his death in January of 2018. His murder was uncomplicated compared to the others. He'd been found dressed in a shirt, bare from the waist down…

With the heel of a stiletto shoe lodged deep in his eye socket. Deep enough to penetrate his brain.

"So where do we start?"

Gary picked up a pen and wrote on the board. "We look at age. Social class. Schools. Locations. Any links, anything that connects them, any patterns."

The door opened, and Barry Davis poked his head around it. "Hey. You got a minute?"

Gary smiled. "For you? Several, especially after you did all this." He gestured to the board.

"How did you find these cases?" Dan asked. "I mean, apart from the fact that they're all unsolved and particularly gruesome."

"Once I'd found all the unsolved murders, I ran them through my computer to search for anything else that linked them."

"And what linked these?"

"The same names kept cropping up. Then I searched through tax records to locate those names and looked at any murders occurring in the same vicinity. What made me stick with these? They were all motiveless." Barry flung his arm out. "Et voila." Then he gave them an apologetic glance. "And as for why I'm here. Much as I hate to increase your workload… I've found another one."

Chapter Two

"Well, aren't you the little overachiever?" Gary quipped.

Barry shrugged. "I know you said to start with Brad's case, but something told me to double check, so I went back a little further." He handed Gary a manila folder. "And I found this. From January 1995."

Gary opened it, and his gorge rose at the sight. There was no doubt the subject matter was as gruesome as the others.

"Great. Now I have to redo my board," he declared with an eye roll. He wasn't serious, but anything was better than dealing with another grisly death.

And this one was every bit as grisly as Brad's.

Dan shook his head, picked up the eraser, and got to work. "So who was this guy?"

Gary peered at the sheet of notes in the folder. "Scott McCarthy, age twenty-two. Died January 13, 1995. Sure was unlucky for him. Must've been a Friday."

"It was," Barry announced.

"You sure there are no more before him? You're not going to waltz in here in an hour's time and tell me you've found three more cases?"

"I checked Massachusetts, Maine, New Hampshire, you name it. These are the only ones on VICAP that fit your MO."

Dan took the photo and attached it to the board next to Brad's. "These can't be the work of one killer. Okay, so they're all brutal, horrific even, but they're all different."

Gary stared at the image of a man seated in a bathtub, an ax planted in his face across his mouth, creating a bloody grotesque smile.

Scott McCarthy made it five.

"You said you had some names for us?" Gary murmured, unable to tear his gaze away from the photos.

"I went through the list of attendees at that charity ball." Barry tapped the folder in Gary's hand. "I've included some names I think you should be looking at."

"How did you arrive at them?" Dan asked.

"I ran all the reports through my software. These guys kept turning up. You'll see what I mean when you look into the cases. And now that I've given you more work to do, I'll get my ass out of here. You need anything else, you know where to find me."

And with that Barry left the office.

Gary located the list of names. "Okay, we've got Amy Walsh, Jason Kelly, Greg Collins, Jennifer Sullivan." He wrote them on the board. "One of those names is kinda familiar."

"It should be." Dan pointed to one of the victims. "Heather Kelly. If they're not related, that's one huge coincidence. And I've got the list of attendees here." He picked up a folder from his desk, removed the stapled list Sean Nichols had given them, and perused it. "Yup. They're all in here." He replaced the folder on his desk, then folded his arms. "Okay, we need to make a start. Want to look at Brad's case first?"

Gary shook his head. "No, we'll look at them in chronological order. But before we do, let's get our resident psychologist in to give her opinion."

He couldn't see a pattern either, but maybe Kathy Wainwright could.

KATHY STOOD in front of the board for several minutes, examining each photo. Dan leaned against Gary's desk, sipping his coffee, while Gary read through the notes they'd received for each case.

At last she shuddered. "Not something you see every day." She turned her head to gaze at them. "I can't see a pattern, except of course that they're all horrific cases." She frowned. "You think these are all committed by one person?"

"No," Dan replied.

"Yes." Gary stared at him.

Kathy chuckled. "O-*kay*." She returned her gaze to the photos. "What strikes me is how different they all are. A different MO for each one. That's fairly common. Some killers *like* to stick to one MO. It's a case of 'if it ain't broke, don't fix it.'"

Dan cocked his head to one side. "If they feel comfortable with it?"

She beamed. "Exactly. And if an MO doesn't work for them anymore? They change it. Serial killers are an adaptable breed, unfortunately. What you sometimes see is a progression."

He frowned. "Can you explain that?"

Kathy perched on the edge of Dan's desk. "Let's assume a serial killer is doing this for the high. They're always looking for the next rush, if you like. Well, that leads to more and more violent murders. The victims need to suffer more so that the killer gets what he needs." She pointed to the board. "But there's no progression here. They're all as violent as each other. It's as if he jumped feet first into the first murder and then just continued in the same vein." She stared at the photo of Heather Kelly. "When you *do* catch this guy, I'd be interested to know if there were any murders before these. Maybe not as violent, not as noticeable." She straightened and stood. "Let me know when you have more to go on." Kathy paused. "And by the way, Mr. Porter... are you related to Matthew Porter? The portrait painter?"

Dan blinked. "He's my brother."

She smiled. "There's a resemblance. A very impressive, talented man." She gave a nod in Gary's direction before heading for the door. "Good luck, gentlemen."

Gary glanced at Dan. "Your brother paints? Sounds as if he's famous."

Dan reached for his phone. "He must be in the news again." He flashed Gary a smile. "Matt's amazing. Let me just see what I've missed. He never tells me when he's going to do stuff like this." He scrolled and then grinned. "Ah—bingo. There's an article in the *Art Newspaper*." There was an image of an elderly man with a long straggly, wiry beard and wild hair, seated in a leather armchair in front of a bookcase, looking pensive. His hand rested on his knee, and Dan stared at the beautifully rendered fingers.

Oh wow, Matt. The detail....

Gary frowned. "Wait—isn't that Donald Hall? The poet?"

Dan nodded. "Matt started painting him in late spring this year, but Donald died in June. His son must have said it was okay for Matt to finish it." He gazed fondly at the image. "Matt said he and Donald used to discuss the Boston Red Sox for hours."

Gary scrolled. "Ah. *Now* I know why Kathy mentioned the resemblance." He handed Dan the phone.

Dan smiled when he saw the family portrait. "He did this for Dad's sixtieth birthday last year." He pointed. "That's Matt and his wife, Nicole, that's my sister Jessica and her husband, Ben, and that's my youngest sister, Mia, and her husband Leo." Dan laughed. "He left the kids out. I remember. Mom complained at the time, but Dad told her he loved it just as it was."

"You take after your dad," Gary murmured, staring at the photo.

Dan didn't need his gift to know what was going on inside Gary's head.

He put his arms around Gary, hoping for no unexpected visitors. His coworkers knowing he and Gary were in a relationship was one thing—being confronted by them embracing was something else, and it would bother Gary a lot more than it bothered him.

"They *will* meet you soon, I promise. And while we're on the subject of parents, I think it would be a good idea to visit yours again, to see if they can share any more information about Brad."

"How about Thanksgiving?"

Dan thought about it. "Here's an idea. We'll spend Thanksgiving with your parents and Christmas with mine." His parents would have a houseful on both occasions, and Thanksgiving wasn't that far off.

Dan wasn't sure what he expected to learn about Brad, but he never ignored his senses, and right then they were telling him this was important.

Sounds from the hallway filtered through the door, and Dan wasn't surprised when Gary broke the embrace.

"Sure, we can do that. I also think we should talk to Sean Nichols again. He might have more information too. You know, from when he and Brad dated." Gary took a deep breath. "Okay, enough talk of family. Let's do some work, okay?"

Dan nodded. He grabbed the folder Barry had brought and read aloud from it.

"Scott McCarthy, age twenty-two at time of death. Father—Owen McCarthy. Owen was a self-made man who formed his first company when he was twenty-four. Created an empire of businesses. Mother died when Scott was small. Owen remarried, a widow, Marie Collins, with a son, Gregory, the same age as Scott." He jerked his head up. "Greg Collins, who was at the ball. It has to be. Okay, that's interesting."

Gary walked over to the board and studied the crime-scene photo. "Where was he found?"

Dan scanned the report. "In the bathtub of a show condo. I pity the prospective buyers who walked in on this."

"What interests me are these." Gary pointed to the large tubs of lye that sat around the bath. "What are they doing there?"

"No idea. Scott was found dressed in running gear. Apparently, he went running every morning, following one of two circuits around Boston.

His father said he'd gone out that morning—Friday, January 13—at dawn, around seven, and didn't come back. His body was found later Friday morning, when someone showed up at the show condo of Reservoir Towers with—" He grimaced. "—a couple of prospective buyers. Autopsy stated he'd died in the early hours of that morning."

Gary frowned. "Anything in the report about who stood to gain from his death?"

Dan scanned the notes once more. "No one. Reports at the time of death suggest he was a good guy, philanthropic, helped out at shelters, worked at camps for deprived kids… There seems to be no reason why anyone should want him dead."

Gary snorted. "Well, someone did."

Dan found the autopsy report. "There were traces of ketamine in his system, enough to render him unconscious, the pathologist said."

"Maybe the killer didn't want Scott to feel any pain when they smashed his face in with an ax." Gary grimaced. "How thoughtful."

"What *I* want to know is why they used an ax in the first place. Or left vats of lye standing by the tub." Dan stared at the photo.

Gary chuckled. "You're sounding more like a detective every day, you know that?"

"I figure it has to mean something."

"Well, if it does, I can't think what. How about you? Any ideas?"

"Not yet. Except one." Dan shivered. "The killer left an ax where Scott's smile should be."

Scan the QR code below to pre-order now

K.C. WELLS lives on an island off the south coast of the UK, surrounded by natural beauty. She writes about men who love men and can't even contemplate a life that doesn't include writing.

The rainbow rose tattoo on her back with the words "Love is Love" and "Love Wins" is her way of hoisting a flag. She plans to be writing about men in love—be it sweet and slow, hot, or kinky—for a long while to come.

If you want to follow her exploits, you can sign up for her monthly newsletter: http://eepurl.com/cNKHIT

You can stalk—er, find—her in the following places:
Email: k.c.wells@btinternet.com
Facebook: www.facebook.com/KCWellsWorld
KC's men In Love (my readers group): http://bit.ly/2hXL6wJ
Amazon: https://www.amazon.com/K-C-Wells/e/B00AECQ1LQ
Twitter: @K_C_Wells
Website: www.kcwellswrites.com
Instagram: www.instagram.com/k.c.wells
BookBub: https://www.bookbub.com/authors/k-c-wells
BlueSky: @kcwwrites.bsky.social

A GROWL, A ROAR, AND A PURR

K.C. WELLS

Lions & Tigers & Bears: Book One

In the human world, shifters are a myth.

In the shifter world, mates are a myth too. So how can tiger shifter Dellan Carson have two of them?

Dellan has been trapped in his shifted form for so long, he's almost forgotten how it feels to walk on two legs. Then photojournalist Rael Parton comes to interview the big-pharma CEO who holds Dellan captive in a glass-fronted cage in his office, and Dellan's world is rocked to its core.

When lion shifter Rael finds his newfound mate locked in shifted form, he's shocked but determined to free him from his prison… and that means he needs help.

Enter ex-military consultant and bear shifter Horvan Kojik. Horvan is the perfect guy to rescue Dellan. But mates? He's never imagined settling down with one guy, let alone two.

Rescuing Dellan and helping him to regain his humanity is only the start. The three lovers have dark secrets to uncover and even darker forces to overcome….

Scan the QR code below to order

A SNARL, A SPLASH, AND A SHOCK

K.C. WELLS

Lions & Tigers & Bears: Book Two

As part of a military team, Crank needs to keep his head on straight. His unit depends on it. So the recurring sensual dreams he's having—the ones featuring a shark shifter with dark brown hair and eyes—really screw with his focus. Especially since the shifter is a guy.

Greenland shark shifter Vic can't stop thinking about Crank, a human military guy he met when Vic got called in for a consult. Crank seems handy with anything that flies, and Vic would be happy to have him at his back, in more ways than one. And that's a problem—firstly because Vic's in love with his boyfriend, Saul, but also because Crank is sarcastic, irreverent… and straight.

The problem comes to a head when Saul discovers Vic has been dreaming about a man who isn't him. Saul does not share. But when Crank starts invading Saul's dreams too, he has to reassess his feelings. His life may depend on it.

Exploring the growing connection between the three of them will have to wait, though. The upcoming mission demands the team's full attention. They're about to discover something huge, and they have badly underestimated the enemy….

Scan the QR code below to order

VISIONS, PAWS, AND CLAWS

K.C. WELLS

Lions & Tigers & Bears: Book Three

The lines between shifters and humans are blurring, and the journey of discovery that began when a lion, a tiger, and a bear found each other—and learned that mates exist—has taken a new direction. More mates are finding each other, and three seems to be the charm.

Brick, a powerful polar bear shifter, and his kitty shifter mate Aric are part of a shifter/human team searching for the camp where their third mate, Seth Miles, has been taken. Since Dellan's rescue from his stepbrother's clutches, the team has learned the horrifying truth behind the Geran faction's plan to capture and imprison shifters and ensure bloodline purity.

They also have another shifter to rescue from the same camp: Seth's father, Jake Carson. Except Jake is Dellan's father too, captured by the Gerans three decades ago and until recently, believed to be dead. The camp is like a fortress, and the rescue operation is looking like an impossible quest.

What no one anticipated was help from an unexpected source. Dellan is about to learn why the power-hungry Gerans took his father in the first place--and what they want next.

In this latest installment of Lions & Tigers & Bears, K.C. Wells doubles down on the intrigue... and the passion.

Scan the QR code below to order

IN HIS SIGHTS

K.C. WELLS

His psychic powers could help find the killer—unless the killer finds him first.

SECOND SIGHT　BOOK ONE

Second Sight: Book One

Random letters belong on Scrabble tiles, not dead bodies. But when a demented serial killer targets Boston's gay population, leaving cryptic messages carved into his victims, lead detective Gary Mitchell has no choice but to play along.

As the body count rises, Gary gets desperate enough to push aside his skepticism and accept the help of a psychic. Dan Porter says he can offer new clues, and Gary needs all the insight into the killer's mind he can get.

Dan has lived with his gift—sometimes his curse—his entire life. He feels compelled to help, but only if he can keep his involvement secret. Experience has taught him to be cautious of the police and the press, but his growing connection to Gary distracts him from the real danger. As they edge closer to solving the puzzle, Dan finds himself in the killer's sights….

Scan the QR code below to order